D0002747

THE
OUTBACK
SAGA

Since *Outback* was published in 1978, over 6 million readers have enjoyed the unforgettable books in this magnificent Australian saga.

Now Aaron Fletcher has written another towering novel that details the loves and adventures of the men and women who risked their lives in the outback—and created a brave new world:

Stephanie Brendell: Following a family tradition of treating the infirm, she battled the diseases that plagued the sprawling continent. Her skill and determination saved countless lives and inspired her son to continue the struggle.

Stephen Brendell: While helping settlers survive in the outback, he was captivated by the beauty of the land— and drew from it an indomitable strength that enabled him to win the woman of his dreams.

Alexandra Kerrick: Wresting Tibooburra Station from the primordial Australian wilderness had taken generations of her family's blood, sweat, and tears. But the golden legacy their toil had created was threatened when her great-grandson lay dying.

Deirdre Kerrick: Wealthy and beautiful, she could have led a life of idle luxury. But her fierce independence made her forge her own destiny—and plant the seeds of a shining future with the courageous doctor who risked all to save the heir to the Kerrick sheep station.

The Outback Saga by Aaron Fletcher:

WALLABY TRACK
WALKABOUT
OUTBACK STATION
OUTBACK

WALLABY TRACK

AARON FLETCHER

LEISURE BOOKS NEW YORK CITY

A LEISURE BOOK®

June 1994

Published by

Dorchester Publishing Co., Inc.
276 Fifth Avenue
New York, NY 10001

Printed in the United States of America.

PART
ONE

Chapter One

L   ike she usually did after attending to a childbirth
    through the night, Stephanie Thorpe had fallen
    asleep while returning home. Her horse, accustomed
to finding its own way to the house, drew her buggy down
the road at a slow walk. A wheel jolted through a deep rut,
waking her.

Stephanie sat up and yawned. Then, glancing around in
the thin light of dawn, she saw splatters of dried blood at
the edge of the road.

Jerking the reins to stop her horse, Stephanie scrambled
out of the buggy. The lilly pilly brush and kangaroo grass
beside the road were crushed down. Someone had fallen into
it, bleeding profusely, then crawled into the thick trees and
undergrowth back from the road.

Darkness lingered under the eucalypt trees, cockatoos and
other birds at roost in them just starting to stir, but Stephanie
could see well enough to follow the trail of broken foliage as
she stepped through the undergrowth. Glimpsing a man on
the ground ahead, she rushed toward him. He was sprawled

on his stomach, either dead or unconscious.

In the tradition of generations of women in her family, Stephanie was trained in medicine as well as midwifery. Kneeling beside the man, she felt his pulse. He was alive but only barely, his pulse weak and irregular. She carefully turned him onto his back. About forty, he was stocky and had craggy features that were ashen from blood loss. His coat and shirt were soaked with blood, two bullet holes in the right side of his coat.

Stephanie ran back to the buggy, grabbed cotton compresses and bandage rolls out of her bag on the seat, and returned to the man. One wound was in his right shoulder, the other high in his chest. She placed compresses over the wounds and hastily wrapped bandages around the man's chest and shoulder to hold them tightly in place. Then she began dragging the man toward the buggy to take him home to her father, who was a physician.

Twenty-three years old, Stephanie was tall and slender. The man weighed over fifty pounds more than she, but she had wiry strength and was accustomed to moving heavy patients about. She backed slowly through the underbrush, being as gentle as possible while pulling the man along the ground.

At her buggy, Stephanie hoisted the man across the floor of the small vehicle. Squeezing into the buggy with the man, she grabbed the whip out of its socket on the splashboard. She cracked the whip above the horse's back, and it leaped into a brisk trot down the road.

Stephanie and her father lived in Wallaby Track, a rural district with a village as its civic center. In a region once inhabited by large numbers of wallabies, the district was named for the ancient animal path that ran through it. The widespread community lay in a long, broad valley flanking the Hawkesbury River, with farms, sheep runs, and cattle pastures covering the fertile land back from the river to tree-crested hills overlooking the valley.

Dawn brightened into daylight, but the sun was behind

thick clouds on the cold winter day in June of 1845. Raw, gusty wind shredded smoke rising from chimneys at farmhouses, where people moved about at morning chores. Stephanie's house was on a side road that led up a slope to the village, with a forest farther up the road and the village at the top of the hill.

When she turned in at her house, a large, half-timbered structure that had been a farmhouse, Stephanie saw smoke rising from the kitchen chimney. She and her father shared household tasks, dispensing with a maid or cook, and he was preparing breakfast. Stephanie tethered her horse at the side door of the house and dashed into the surgery, formerly a parlor.

"Father!" she called down the hall. "I found a wounded man, and he's in my buggy! He's been shot!"

Her father rushed up the hall from the kitchen, following her outside to the buggy. Stephen Thorpe, a rangy man of fifty-two, was the origin for Stephanie's tall, slender form, blue eyes, and finely modeled features. Along with their close physical resemblance, they shared devoted love for each other and total, unstinting dedication to their profession.

Stephen leaned into the buggy, checking the man's pulse. "I believe I know how this man was shot," he mused. "He must have been the cause of the bother that took place hereabouts last night."

"What sort of bother?" Stephanie asked.

"A convict evidently escaped from the prison in the village last night," Stephen explained. "I heard gunshots and the constables shouting on the road, and this man is wearing convicts' clothing."

Having taken little notice of the man's clothing before, Stephanie saw that it was made of the coarse wool used for convicts' clothes. Transportation of felons to New South Wales had ended five years before, but some who had arrived prior to that were still serving sentences. Along with local residents jailed for misdemeanors, thirty convicts were kept at a prison in the village to maintain roads and bridges in the district.

"I'll have to notify the chief constable about him," Stephen added, "but he can't be returned to the prison in this condition. We'll keep him here for a time and attend to him, if he lives. But as I'm sure you know, that's very much in question. Let's get him inside, Stephanie."

Stephen lifted the man's shoulders, Stephanie gathering up his legs, and they carried him to a table in the surgery. She took off her coat and hat, then brought hot water from the kitchen while her father removed the man's coat and shirt. Stephen washed his hands and selected instruments from a cabinet, and Stephanie sponged the blood off the man's chest.

Blood still oozed from the wounds, the one on the man's shoulder bleeding more rapidly than the other, and Stephen began with it. He inserted a probe into the wound to locate the bullet, moving the thin steel rod deeper and searching with its porcelain tip. "Were there any complications with the lying-in that you attended to last night, Stephanie?" he asked.

"No, and the baby is a bonny girl," she replied. "The labor was perfectly normal, if such a word can be used for the miracle of birth."

Stephen smiled and nodded in agreement with her remark about childbirth. He stopped searching with the probe, holding it steady and reaching for an extractor. A slender instrument with toothed jaws at one end, it was grooved to match the diameter of the probe. After sliding it down the probe and into the wound, he released the lever that opened the jaws. He pushed the extractor a fraction of an inch deeper, then closed the jaws and lifted it and the probe out of the wound, the bullet clenched in the jaws.

Blood gushed out of the wound, and Stephanie stanched the flow with a cotton compress. Stephen inserted the probe into the other wound and searched with it for several minutes, then shrugged in resignation as he withdrew it.

"That's a very deep wound, and jabbing the probe around in it certainly isn't making it any better," he remarked wryly. "See if you can locate the bullet, Stephanie. You have a more delicate touch than I."

Stephanie took the probe and eased it into the wound. She felt for the least resistance, the path of the bullet. It was difficult to find, for the torn flesh had swollen together during the hours since the man had been shot. When the probe finally touched something solid, she knew from its position in the man's body that the tip was touching the bullet, not bone.

She slid the extractor down the probe and removed the bullet, Stephen placing a compress over the wound; then they bandaged the wounds. After years of attending to patients together, they worked in perfect coordination with each other while deftly wrapping and fastening the bandages.

When they finished, Stephen listened to the man's heartbeat with a stethoscope, a brass tube with flared ends. "The man seems no worse than before, a good sign," he said. "One of us will have to watch over him closely. How many calls on patients do you have today, Stephanie?"

"Several that can be deferred, and only four that I must make today," she replied. "I could finish up with them by midday and watch over this man during the afternoon, if you wish."

"Yes, that would be best," Stephen decided. "I'll look in my daybook presently to see what calls I have for today, but I'm sure that the afternoon will be sufficient for them. After we have breakfast, I'll go tell the chief constable about our patient. Rather than going to the trouble of hitching up my horse and buggy, I'll use yours, if you don't mind."

"I don't mind at all, of course, but I could do that," Stephanie offered. "I must go to the district clerk's office to record the birth last night, and I could stop at the prison and speak with the chief constable."

"Thank you, but I'll see to it, my dear," Stephen told her. "If you'll clean up in here, I'll finish preparing breakfast."

Stephanie gathered up the instruments, not pressing her offer; she disliked the prison and preferred to avoid it. After carefully washing the instruments, she replaced them in the cabinet and put the rest of the room back into order, then went down the hall to the kitchen.

The spacious farmhouse kitchen, with a brick floor and a large stone fireplace that reached up to the ceiling, also served as their parlor and dining room. Breakfast was simple and quickly prepared, like all of their meals, and consisted of porridge and toasted rounds of bread. After eating hurriedly, Stephen left to drive up to the village. Stephanie finished her breakfast and then set about washing the dishes. She was weary from having had little sleep the night before, which happened occasionally, and she paced herself to conserve her energy for the day that lay ahead.

Stephen returned just as Stephanie went back into the surgery. He parked the buggy at the door and came in, telling her that he had met a constable at the village and given him a message to relate to the chief constable. "He said that the man's name is Donald Grant," Stephen continued, pointing to the patient; then he grimaced wryly. "I saw the magistrate's horse at the prison, which is the main reason I sent a message instead of going in to speak with the chief constable. Life is burdensome enough without having to do with the likes of Thurlow Brendell when it isn't absolutely necessary."

Stephanie nodded in emphatic agreement. Brendell, an arrogant, overbearing man, had been the district magistrate for the past year. He had made that year a miserable one for many, imposing large fines and jail sentences on local residents for minor offenses, and sentencing convicts who had committed any infraction to savage lashings. "That man is a disgrace to the magistracy," she said, opening her medical bag to check its contents. "The officials in

Sydney must have taken total leave of their wits when they appointed him to the position of magistrate."

"They might have had little choice," Stephen suggested, examining the patient. "Magistrates are usually large land-owners who came here as free immigrants, and many of those who are eligible won't accept the position." He frowned worriedly, peering under the bandages on the patient. "There is still some bleeding from these wounds, Stephanie."

"Is it very much?" Stephanie asked in concern.

"No, very little, but any is too much." Stephen sighed, shaking his head in resignation. "When wounds are this serious, it sometimes takes a few hours for the bleeding to stop. We'll have to wait and see if it does."

Stephanie took her bag to a cabinet and began selecting the medications that she would need on her calls. Then, hearing horses turn off the road toward the house, she stepped to a window and looked out, her father following her. One of the riders was the chief constable, a large, bluffly friendly man in his mid-forties named Claude Durgin. The other one was the constable's superior, the magistrate. Stephen muttered in dissatisfaction, turning away from the window and walking toward the front door.

The two men reined up in front of the house and dismounted. Brendell, a short, overweight man of about fifty, led the way up the steps with a swaggering stride. A riding crop tucked under his arm, he affected the style of a country squire, wearing a cutaway coat, knee boots, and tight riding breeches that made his bulging stomach look like a large melon. Intemperate eating and drinking had broken capillaries in his face, creating the appearance of a thin red net over his coarse, petulant features.

Stephanie heard a brief exchange at the front door, then the men came down the hall. Brendell was first, strutting into the surgery. The mesh of red lines adding a grotesque cast to his ugly face, his habitual expression was a scowl. He darted a disdainful glance at Stephanie and then ignored her, looking at the patient. Exasperation had replaced the usual good humor on Claude Durgin's rugged, homely features, but he managed a smile as he touched his cap and nodded to Stephanie in greeting.

Brendell wheeled back around and stepped toward Stephen in a blustering manner meant to intimidate, his head and shoulders thrust forward. "You're guilty of harboring an escaped convict!" he barked, pointing to the patient with his riding crop. "That constitutes a felony, you know."

A flush of anger spread over Stephen's face. He took a step forward and closed the distance between himself and Brendell, glaring down at the shorter man. "I know that's one of the most foolish statements I've ever heard!" he retorted. "After attending to that man's wounds, I reported his presence to a constable, which certainly isn't harboring him."

"It is by the law!" Brendell shouted. "The law states that aiding an escaped convict amounts to harboring him, and you can't deny that you aided the swine lying there." He turned to Claude, stabbing a finger at Stephen: "I want him arrested for harboring an escaped convict!"

Claude gaped at Brendell, speechless with astonishment for a moment, then: "Arrest the doctor?" he exclaimed. "I can't do that. He attended to Grant, but he can't be charged with an offense for doing what he—"

"That's not for you to decide!" Brendell broke in furiously. "Your duty is to do as you're ordered, and I'm the one in authority here. And I'll see to it that the law isn't flouted where I'm in authority!"

Stephen shook his head in disgust. "What you're doing is making a fool of yourself, Brendell!" he snapped angrily. "You've become a petty tyrant and inflicted unreasonable sentences upon those who had no recourse, but you'll be brought up short if you persist in this foolishness!"

Brendell snarled a reply, Stephanie listening to the heated

argument with both anger and apprehension. Knowing her father well, she was keenly aware that his temper could be explosive. She was certain that a charge of harboring an escaped convict would never be upheld against him, but if he lost his temper and struck Brendell, that could cause serious trouble.

Stephanie crossed the room, ready to push herself between her father and Brendell if necessary. "I brought Mr. Grant here," she announced loudly, breaking in on the argument and fixing Brendell with a level stare. "I found him beside the road not far from Crossley Farm. If his presence here is athwart the law, I'm the one at fault."

"Well, that does it," Claude commented in poorly concealed glee. "The only jail for women hereabouts is in Parramatta, and the chief constable there would laugh me out of his office if I asked him to jail Mistress Thorpe on such a charge as this." He became impatient as Brendell turned to him in fury: "Magistrate Brendell, I'm telling you that this charge won't stand," he insisted testily. "A doctor can't be prosecuted for attending to anyone's wounds, whether escaped convict or not."

Brendell's thick features quivered and flushed with rage under the network of red lines as he glowered at Claude. "I don't forget it when I'm crossed," he growled warningly, then he pointed to the patient with his riding crop and raised his voice to a shout: "I want that swine returned to the prison where he belongs, and I want it done without delay!"

"It will be," Claude replied grumpily. "My men are fetching a wagon, and we'll take him to the prison as soon as they get here with it."

"No, you mustn't do that!" Stephen exclaimed in alarm. "Returning that man to prison in his present condition is a death sentence."

"Then so be it!" Brendell jeered, his gross features animated with cruel satisfaction as he seized upon that much of a victory. "If he dies, it'll be no more than his just deserts."

Stephen's hands clenched into fists, Stephanie poising herself to jump in front of him, but he kept his temper under control. "Then I'll go to the prison with him and attend to him there," he said angrily. "I'll not have the man deprived of the care that might enable him to survive."

"By all means, go to the prison with him," Brendell sneered, slapping his riding crop against his thigh as he stepped into the hall toward the front door. "You'll find an assortment of gleanings from gutters there, which appears to be the sort of company you prefer."

Brendell left, slamming the front door, and Stephanie was suddenly struck with deep misgivings. The fact that her father intended to go to the prison with Donald Grant made her intensely uneasy. She listened to him talking with Claude as she searched her feelings for an underlying reason, but she was unable to find a logical basis for her anxiety.

"Grant will have to be in his cell," Claude said, "but you can attend to him there. If it'll take several days, you can sup with the guards, and we'll fix up the best accommodations for you that we can."

"Whatever you can provide will do excellently well," Stephen assured him, then turned to Stephanie: "Will you be able to find time to make my calls for me for the next few days, my dear?"

"I'll make time, Father," she replied. "I'll look in your daybook each day to see what you have scheduled, and I'll take care of them."

Stephen thanked her, following Claude out of the surgery, and Stephanie went to the cabinet where they kept their daybooks. Thumbing through his, she opened it to the page for that day. She read the names he had written, making a mental note of them, then replaced the book in the cabinet.

In her anxiety about her father, Stephanie had a sense of being caught up in events with a life of their own, of being swept helplessly toward some unknown, menacing outcome. A wagon drew up in front of the house, Claude came in with two constables carrying a makeshift stretcher, and they carried the patient out. Stephen returned with his razor and other things from his room, and he put extra bandages and medications into his bag.

Stephanie had a strange impulse to shout at the top of her voice and make everything stop. Ignoring the urge, she helped Stephen on with his coat. "Father. . . ." Her voice faded as she groped for words to express the feelings that she was unable to define even to herself.

Stephen turned to her, and she realized that an explanation was unnecessary. Their deep love for each other and years of having worked together had created a rapport that produced communication without speech. She saw that he understood her feelings, at least to an extent.

"There's no cause for concern," he said, smiling affectionately and placing a hand on her shoulder. "I dislike the prison quite as much as you do, my dear, but we don't always have the circumstances that we would prefer. Let's save our worries for the patient, shall we?"

Stephanie forced a smile and nodded. They exchanged a hug and kiss, then left the surgery and went up the hall and out onto the porch. The wagon was in front of the steps, the constables waiting in it. Stephen went down the steps and climbed into the wagon, then it moved away from the house.

Stephanie wrapped her arms around herself against the chill, stepping to the end of the porch. The cold wind stirred her dress, and the wintry day seemed very bleak as she watched the wagon. It moved up the road toward the village, disappearing behind the trees flanking the road.

Perhaps several minutes or possibly a longer time passed—Stephanie was unsure. Until she began shivering in the icy wind, she was unaware of what she was doing. Then she realized that, irrationally, she was watching the road in an agonized yearning to see her father coming back down it toward the house. She crossed the porch and went back inside.

Her anxiety became more focused and took on the aspect of a premonition, but it remained nebulous, a threat of some unknown but dreadful result. Stephanie tried to shrug it off, but now more than ever, she was unable to dismiss it. In its form as a forewarning, it stirred painful memories. It reminded her of very similar feelings she had experienced some four years before about her mother, who had been a midwife.

Her mother had scratched a hand in some minor mishap. The scratch had been small and seemingly unimportant, but for some reason it had worried Stephanie. Her father had been concerned about it as well, warning her mother to wash it carefully and watch for any indication of infection.

On the same day she had scratched her hand, her mother had examined a woman in the primary stage of puerperal fever, or childbed fever, the disease not evident at the time. A fortnight later, Stephanie's mother and the woman had died within hours of each other.

Stephanie had been alone in the house numerous times, but it had never seemed empty to her before. Now it had a lifeless, deserted atmosphere. An oppressive silence reached through the rooms that was something more than a lack of sound. Instead of merely being by herself, she had a sense of utter solitude, of being all alone.

Chapter Two

"**G**ladys and Harold Crossley finally have a daughter," Stephanie said, filling in the blanks on a line in the birth registry. "After three boys, they're pleased beyond measure that the new baby is a girl."

Tipton Bellamy smiled and nodded, watching Stephanie write in the thick registry on his desk. "Are the mother and baby well?" he asked.

"Very well indeed," Stephanie told him, replacing the pen in its stand. "Even so, I'd look in on them tomorrow, but it'll have to wait for a day or two because of my having to make my father's calls. Having Brendell as the magistrate is a disadvantage to everyone in one way or another."

Tipton nodded somberly in agreement as he returned the birth registry to a shelf. A small, mild man in his forties, the district clerk wore a dark, neat suit and had the studious manner of a professional bureaucrat. Like the chief constable, he was subordinate to the magistrate, and he functioned as a district extension of the government ministries in Sydney.

Stephanie looked through the office doorway into the outer office, where the two apprentices were working hurriedly over stacks of files. "Your apprentices are very busy this morning, Tipton," she observed.

"They're researching information for the magistrate," he explained. "He wishes to know if any of the other convicts are from the same town as Donald Grant, or if any were on the vessel that transported him here. The magistrate didn't tell me why he wants the information."

Stephanie pondered for a moment, then: "I daresay I know why he wants it," she speculated, shaking her head in disgust. "Brendell will probably regard that as evidence of friendship with Donald Grant, and complicity in his escape. That illustrates the greatest shortcoming of a penal colony, Tipton. Some convicts are evil, but many others are made froward by having men like Brendell placed in authority over them."

"The position of magistrate was offered to others when Mr. Bloomfield went to his reward last year," Tipton told her. "For one reason or another, everyone but Mr. Brendell declined it."

Stephanie sighed and nodded, turning toward the door. "Perhaps we'll have someone else soon," she said hopefully. "Good day, Tipton."

The district clerk replied in farewell, and Stephanie exchanged a smile with the apprentices as she crossed the outer office to the front door. Outside, the clouds had thickened into a low ceiling of dark, swirling mist. Rain had started falling, but instead of a cleansing downpour, it was only icy drizzle that made the day colder and more dreary.

The district clerk's offices occupied a small wooden building at the edge of the village near the prison, a towering, bulky stone structure that had been built by convicts. Decades before, plans had been made to establish a convict compound at the village, and the prison had been built as a first step. The plans had been changed and the compound had been located at Parramatta, a town at a distance to the south.

From the first time she had seen it, the large, dark prison had seemed especially sinister to Stephanie. With its narrow entrance and tiny, barred windows set deep in its thick walls, it had a stark, somber atmosphere. It was a graphic symbol of the miserable existence of those who had strained at the heavy stone blocks, compelled by the threat of the lash to build their own dungeons. Now, with her father somewhere in the depths of the huge, bleak building, it seemed infinitely more forbidding to Stephanie.

She stepped into her buggy and drove out of the village, which consisted of some thirty freestone cottages and shops on lanes that joined at a cobblestone square. The main street turned into a road, which led down the hill to the main road in the valley. The view of the broad, lush valley from the brow of the hill was usually strikingly impressive, but today it was obscured by the gray veils of rain and by Stephanie's mood. She drove past her house and turned onto the main road, setting out on her father's calls.

They had come to Australia over three years before, making a new start after her mother had died. Several doctors in Sydney had been willing to sell their practice, the usual means of obtaining a clientele. Wallaby Track had urgently needed a doctor, however, and Stephanie and her father had been drawn by its scenic beauty and the way of life in the rural setting. The income from their practice was barely sufficient for their needs, but the intangible rewards were immense. Each day brought reassurance of their vital role and the warm regard of others in the closely knit community.

Early afternoon came while Stephanie drove up and down the muddy roads in the rain, attending to her father's calls. The people saw nothing unusual in her making the calls, for she and her father often worked together. Also, medical practitioners were largely unregulated by law, and the reputation of having skill and knowledge was more important than a university degree or a license from the examining board of the medical society.

All of her father's calls except one, which Stephanie left until last, were routine visits. She found that a young boy's broken arm was healing satisfactorily, and a woman with persistent headaches was obtaining relief from menthol salve applied to her forehead and the nape of her neck. An aged woman's rheumatic swellings had failed to respond to gaultheria, but they were diminishing from applications of betula in Seneca oil.

The last call was one that Stephanie dreaded, for it was a tragic situation. The patient was a boy of eight named Billy Digby, who had an abdominal condition known as perityphlitic abscess. An incurable disease that intermittently flared up and then subsided at unpredictable intervals, it always became acute and fatal during one of the onsets.

Billy was a handsome boy whose winsome nature made the situation even more trying for Stephanie. Examining him in his bedroom, she was relieved to find that the disease was becoming dormant. Her father had prescribed bed rest and easily digested foods, and the pain had diminished to a dull ache in the lower right quadrant of the abdomen. That was the location of the veriform appendix, which was the basis for the belief among some doctors that it was the point of origin for inflammation that spread throughout the abdomen during the acute and fatal stage of the disease.

"And you say that hurts only a bit now, Billy?" Stephanie asked as she gently palpitated the boy's stomach.

"Aye, I feel good, mo'm," he replied. "I'd like to get out of bed, because it's vexing to lie here. Also, I'd like to have some good tucker."

"Very well," Stephanie told him. "You can have both, but not too much of either, Billy. Do precisely what your mother tells you."

"Aye, I will, mo'm."

Stephanie returned to the front room and put on her

coat and hat as she talked with the boy's parents, Albert and Sarah Digby. From their attitude, she knew that her father had been characteristically candid with them about their son's prospects. In the eyes of the young couple, she saw what she had seen too many times before. It was contained grief, resentment toward fate, and a silent, agonized questioning of why nothing more could be done. Stephanie understood their feelings, having the same herself.

Leaving Digby Farm, Stephanie began on her own calls, most of which were pre- and postnatal visits. An exception was a middle-aged woman named Amanda Crawford, who had some unknown debility that made her pale, underweight, and listless. Over the years, Stephanie had become virtually as skilled as her father in diagnosing illnesses. Some were impossible to diagnose, however, and she had no idea of what was causing the woman's condition.

In such instances, her course of treatment was medication to alleviate the symptoms. Some doctors used large doses of purges and emetics when in doubt, but Stephanie followed what her father had taught her and administered the known minimum treatments that supplemented and avoided interfering with the body's natural ability to overcome disorders.

The treatment was working, Amanda's condition better. Lime water had ended her bouts of nausea, and gentian syrup had increased her appetite. She was more energetic and gaining weight, with a healthier color in her face from a blood tonic of iron chloride and arsenic trioxide. Stephanie handed over bottles of medicine she had brought to replace those the woman had used up, Amanda expressing gratitude and delight over her improvement.

It was late afternoon when Stephanie left Crawford Farm, and the light was beginning to fade into the long, slow twilight of a rainy winter day. She drove back to the main road, then down it toward the south end of the valley and

Mundy Farm, her last call of the day.

The owner, a man in his fifties named Gideon Mundy, owned properties scattered throughout the valley. One had been where Stephanie and her father lived, which had consisted of several hundred acres that included the forest on the hill below the village. Using the last of the money remaining from the sale of his practice in England, Stephen had bought the house, the outbuildings, and ten acres of the land around them from Gideon.

Stephanie's patient at Mundy Farm was Hannah Beasley, Gideon's only daughter, who was in the final stage of pregnancy. Gideon was inclined to be demanding and short-tempered with his two sons and son-in-law, Elmer Beasley, but the farmer was loving toward his wife. As for his daughter, she was the apple of his eye, and the only difficulty with Hannah's pregnancy had been her father's constant worrying about her.

Flora Mundy, a matronly, good-natured woman of fifty, met Stephanie at the farmhouse door. A moment later, Hannah came into the front room. Twenty years old, she was a buxom, large-boned woman in excellent health. She had her mother's pleasant, serene personality, and both of them were heartily amused by her father's anxiety about her.

Gideon had seen Stephanie arrive and came in from the barnyard, the kitchen door slamming, then his heavy footsteps came through the house to the front room. "I've waited hours for you to get here and see Hannah, Mistress Thorpe," he grumbled. "You're here very late in the day."

"Yes, and for a very good reason, Mr. Mundy," Stephanie retorted curtly. She briefly explained what her father was doing and why, then continued: "I had to make his calls, naturally. So while I've arrived here late in the day, I don't believe that I should apologize."

"No, but I should," Gideon muttered, his bearded, weathered face red with embarrassment. "I spoke too hastily, and I regret what I said. That magistrate has let his bit of authority make him as daft as a kookaburra, and sooner or later he'll be brought up short."

"Preventing such a sorry state of affairs would have been much better," Stephanie pointed out. "Unless I'm greatly mistaken, you could have been the magistrate in this district."

"Aye, that's true," Gideon admitted gruffly, "but I won't sit in judgment on others. It's against my nature."

"It's also the very best characteristic any magistrate could have," Stephanie observed. "It would ensure fair, sensible judgments." She dropped the subject, turning to the women: "Hannah, if you'll go to your room, I'll be there presently to examine you."

Hannah stepped into the hall toward her room. Gideon hung up his coat and sat down to wait, and Stephanie went to the kitchen with Flora. They collected up soap, a basin of water, and a towel, and took them to Hannah's room. Stephanie washed her hands, Flora returning to the front room.

After checking Hannah's heartbeat and that of the baby, Stephanie examined the woman. The baby had dropped down into perfect position, promising a relatively easy delivery within the next week. Stephanie washed her hands again, talking with Hannah and making certain the young woman knew each detail of what would happen, then she went back into the front room.

Gideon, sitting and talking with Flora, sprang to his feet. "How is she?" he demanded anxiously. "Did you find anything wrong?"

"No, everything is perfectly normal with Hannah," Stephanie told him. "I have my doubts about you, though. I hope that Hannah's baby can be born without causing you to have a seizure."

"I'm only concerned about my daughter, that's all," Gideon grumbled defensively, grabbing his coat and hat off the rack. "Hannah is inclined to be delicate, you know."

"Delicate?" Stephanie echoed in astonishment. "I wish

that all of my patients had Hannah's strong constitution and perfect health."

Gideon shook his head furiously, jerking on his coat and hat as he stamped toward the hall. "I know my own daughter, and she's a bit frail!" he barked. "And if anything untoward happens to her, I'll hang up that Elmer Beasley in the barn by what he used to get her with child!"

Flora laughed heartily, taking Stephanie's coat off the rack and helping her on with it. "He was the same when I had my children," she told Stephanie. "Each time I had one, he was like a wild boar that had backed into a thorn bush. He lived through the three that I had, so I daresay he'll be able to survive having a grandchild born in the house."

Stephanie laughed, making her farewells with Flora, and went out to her buggy. As she drove away into the gathering twilight and rain, her amusement faded. During the past hours, her work had distracted her to an extent from her anxiety about her father being at the prison. In the quiet of the muddy, deserted road at dusk, it returned with renewed force.

Upon reaching her house shortly before dark, she stopped in front of it and rushed up the steps. On the wall beside the door was a wooden box for messages, and even though it was unlikely, she hoped her father had sent a note by a constable about Donald Grant's condition or some other matter. Finding the box empty, she sagged with disappointment. Only hours had passed since she had seen him, but it seemed like ages to her.

As she drove around the house to the barn, Stephanie noticed that part of the prison roof was visible above the trees on the hill. She had never observed that before, and now the light had faded until she could only barely distinguish it. Even so, the section of slate roof that she was able to see through the rain and twilight looked grim and dismal.

Stephanie stabled her horse, then fed it and her father's

horse. By the time she finished and crossed the barnyard to the house, the light was so dim that she could hardly pick her way around the puddles. But while she was unable to see the prison, she was keenly aware of it now that she had noticed that she could see it from her house. In an eerie way, she could even feel it looming at the top of the hill above the house.

The house, built for a large, extended family, had five upstairs bedrooms and downstairs rooms for a maid and cook. Stephanie felt very lonely in it, the yellow glow of the lamp leaving the corners of the large kitchen in shadows. Her evenings were usually keenly enjoyable, a time of companionable conversation with her father about events of the day, but now the steely silence of the house surrounded her and pressed in upon her.

The pantry overflowed with vegetables, fruit, cheese, pickles, kegs of homemade beer, slabs of gammon, and other foodstuffs given in lieu of money for medical treatments. Stephanie had no appetite, however, and little skill in cookery. After making a quick meal on cheese, bread, and a glass of beer, she carried the lamp upstairs to her room and went to bed.

Even though she was weary from lack of sleep the night before, Stephanie was still wakeful for a time. Staring up into the darkness, she felt as if she could sense the baneful stone hulk on the hill, her father somewhere in its warren of cold, dark cells. It was like an inimical presence that reached out through the night with a hostile, chilling touch.

Dawn the next morning brought another dull, gloomy day, the rain continuing. While dressing, Stephanie heard someone put something in the box beside the front door and then leave. She hastily finished dressing, then rushed to the porch. Instead of a note from her father, the box contained two messages describing symptoms and asking her to call.

Stephanie cooked and ate a bowl of porridge, thinking

about going to the prison to see her father. Upon checking his daybook and her own, however, she saw that it was out of the question. The number of calls would make the day a long, arduous one, leaving her with no spare time at all.

When she set out from her house, Stephanie again attended to her father's calls first. Most were like those of the day before, follow-up calls to make certain patients were improving and to leave more medicine for some of them. Little could be done for one, even though the illness was less deadly than Billy Digby's perityphlitic abscess. The patient, a youth of sixteen named Roger Corbett, had consumption, or pulmonary tuberculosis.

With parents who were above average in stature, he was as tall as Stephanie but weighed little more than eighty pounds. He had the bright red cheeks common among those with the disease, along with the usual listlessness and racking cough. While the cough was being controlled with tincture of lobelia and camphor, no medicine could cure the disease.

After examining the youth and replenishing his medicine, Stephanie talked with his parents, Jacob and Mary Corbett, in the front room. Stephanie made certain that Mary was boiling the tableware that Roger used so as to prevent the disease from spreading in the family, then brought up a way in which the youth's disease might be cured. "Instead of the damp climate here in Wallaby Track," she explained, "he needs to be in the dry region to the west, in the outback. It wouldn't assure a cure, but it would make one possible. My father has mentioned this to you, hasn't he?"

"Aye, he has," Jacob replied. "Mary and I have talked it over. The only way we could send Roger to the outback would be to get him a job at a sheep station as an apprentice stockman, a jackaroo."

"But he mustn't do any hard work until his condition improves," Stephanie added. "All things considered, it would probably be impossible to get a sheep station to accept Roger on those terms."

"One might," Jacob told her. "A cousin of mine, Daniel Corbett, was the head stockman at a station until he was killed by a wild boar. In a letter I once had from him, he said that the owners were a most kind, generous sort. They're the Kerrick family, the owners of Tibooburra Station."

"Yes, I've heard that station mentioned numerous times," Stephanie recalled. "And the Kerrick family as well."

"Aye, they're known far and wide," Jacob observed. "One of the Kerrick sons is a businessman in Sydney. He was among those who devised a way for the colony to have its own money when we couldn't get British coin. I know you must have been as happy about that as the rest of us."

Stephanie assured him that she had been, the situation a hardship on her and her father for a time. Specie had become very scarce, making it difficult for them to buy medications, then a company had been formed in Sydney to provide the financial foundation for a local paper currency. "What do you think about sending Roger to a sheep station?" she asked Mary.

The woman sighed, shaking her head. "I'm loath to do it," she replied. "It would be different if we were sure of a cure, but we're not. The outback is a strange, dreadful place, as well as dangerous. Like you said, Jacob, your cousin Daniel was killed there by a wild boar."

Her husband agreed, then pointed out that it was Roger's only chance for a long, healthy life. Mary remained doubtful, an attitude that Stephanie could understand. With Roger's recovery less than assured, it could amount to sending him to a lonely death in a distant, isolated place among strangers, however kindhearted they might be. Jacob and Mary were still discussing it when Stephanie left, the issue remaining unresolved.

She finished her father's calls by early afternoon, then attended to the messages that had been sent to her house. At one farm she left a bottle of grindelia infusion to increase a woman's lactation for her baby, and at another she gave a woman a vial of wintergreen drops for an infant that constantly vomited its milk. Then she began on calls she had scheduled for the day, examining a child recovering from a severe scald with hot water, followed by a man whose leg was healing from a deep cut with an axe.

Her last call of the day was at the far northern end of the valley, where the river and the road curved away toward the coast at Broken Bay. A child in a large family had become infected with scabies, which had spread to two other children before the family finally had become convinced that the cleanliness procedures which Stephanie had told them to follow were necessary. Yarrow infusion and balm of Gilead were gradually curing the three who were infected, and Stephanie examined the other eight children in the family to make certain that no more of them were contracting the disease.

It was late afternoon and wisps of evening mist were rising when she set out for home. The rain stopped, and there was a sunset for the first time in days. Eerily strange and colorful, it was different from any Stephanie had ever seen. The feeble winter sun found a rent in the clouds on the horizon, its rays a rich, rosy hue. The ruddy glow flowed across the underside of the thick clouds, washing the landscape in shades of red.

The road was deserted, nothing moving on it except veils of mist. Along with the sky and the surrounding terrain, the mist swirling around the buggy and lying in filmy layers on the fields at each side was saturated with red luminescence. The peculiar sunset on the lonely road made Stephanie vaguely uneasy. It gave her a feeling of venturing all by herself into a strange and different world, with the ocean of color surrounding her deepening into crimson and then fading when darkness closed in.

Stephanie stopped to light the coachlamps on the buggy, and cold drizzle began falling again a short time later, making streaks on the night in front of the lamps. When she reached her house, she ran up the steps to check the box beside the door. It contained a folded sheet of paper, which she sheltered from the rain as she returned to her buggy. The indirect light of the coachlamps was too dim for her to read it, but she recognized her father's handwriting and rushed to the barn, driving inside it.

Standing beside the buggy, Stephanie held the paper up to a coachlamp and read it. The wound in Donald Grant's shoulder was still bleeding, and her father wanted her to bring him a set of surgical instruments the next day so he could operate to stop the flow of blood. In addition, he wanted some cheese, fruit, and other foodstuffs not available at the prison.

The message ended with an expression of affection, and Stephanie was deeply relieved as she folded it and put it in her coat pocket. Logic told her that her worries about her father were foolish, but she felt that emotions were in closer touch with fate than was rational thought, and she had urgently needed the reassurance that her father was well.

After attending to the horses, Stephanie went to the house. In its oppressive silence, with thick shadows pushing in on the edge of the lamplight, mixed feelings about what she had to do the next day dominated her mood. Being able to see her father answered to her loneliness and concern for him, but she also dreaded going to the prison, disliking it more than ever. Even now she seemed to detect its odious presence on the hill.

Shrugging off her depressed feelings, Stephanie busied herself with tasks. In the laundry room off the kitchen, she kindled a fire in the fireplace that heated a copper water tank and then collected up laundry that had accumulated. Contracting illness from a patient was a constant threat, and there were various theories on the nature of disease and how it was transmitted. As a practical matter, however, her father had taught her and Stephanie had seen for herself that cleanliness, including frequent changes of clothing and baths, at least inhibited the spread of disease.

While the water heated, she set about preparing herself a

proper dinner insofar as her limited cooking skills allowed. In the congested pantry, she filled a pot with vegetables and dried beef to make a stew. With the stew simmering on the hob, Stephanie returned to the laundry room, washed the clothes, hung them on a rack, and then took a bath.

The chores finished, Stephanie went to the surgery for the daybooks and annotated them with her calls of the past two days while she ate. The stew was just edible, with too much salt and too little pepper, but the daybooks revealed a favorable turn of events. Only a few calls were scheduled for the next day, leaving her with ample time to go to the prison.

That did nothing to ease her dread of going to the prison, however, and the somber quiet of the house closed in once again when she went to bed. The foreboding she had experienced over the past two days remained a chilling but unspecific warning. It was accompanied by her awareness of the prison looming over the house, reaching out its malign aura through the night.

The next morning, Stephanie woke to fading images of an appalling dream that left shrinking fear in its wake. She was unable to recall the substance of the dream, but its aftermath was a heavy weight of depression while she washed up, dressed, and prepared to drive to the prison. After putting on a dozen eggs to boil, she went into the surgery and gathered a set of surgical instruments and an assortment of swabs and bandages.

As always when she boiled eggs, a few cracked. Stephanie made her breakfast on the cracked eggs and toasted rounds of bread, then put the rest of the eggs into a bag, along with bread, a small cheese, apples, pickles, and other foodstuffs from the pantry. Carrying the bag and a box containing the surgical paraphernalia, she went out into the drab, rainy morning.

The lingering shadows of Stephanie's dream thickened as she drove up the hill. It was Friday, the end of the week approaching, and the village square teemed with people milling about the shops. However, the lane leading to the prison at the edge of the village was deserted. Quiet and isolated, it was never a place for laughter and cheerful conversation.

At the end of the lane, mist drifted around the dark, somber prison towering into the rain. Tipton Bellamy came out of his office, walking toward the prison, then waited for Stephanie when he saw her. She drew up her buggy in front of the huge building, exchanging greetings with Tipton, and explained her purpose for coming.

Tipton took the box off the buggy seat to carry it for her, telling her that her conjecture the day before as to why Brendell had wanted information about the convicts had been correct. "Two men by the name of Wilkins and Harkness were brought here on the same vessel as Grant," he went on. "The magistrate ordered that they have twenty strokes with the lash on the presumption that they are friends of Grant's and helped him escape."

"That's unconscionable!" Stephanie exclaimed in disgust, stepping out of her buggy and taking the bag of food off the seat. "When on earth will the authorities in Sydney awake to what that man is doing here?"

"It has come to their attention," Tipton replied, smiling. "The magistrate court records from this district are now being closely scrutinized. Only moments ago I received a letter from the superior court in Sydney, and it set aside virtually all of the sentences handed down by the magistrate during the past month. One was for confinement of a man, and I was just on my way to tell Claude Durgin to release him."

Stephanie nodded in keen satisfaction as she and Tipton stepped toward the prison entrance, then her mood became subdued again, the building looming over her like a dark cliff—massive and menacing. Tipton tugged a bell pull, and a cover inside a small hole in the door moved aside. A constable peered out, then steel locking bars clanked back and the hinges on the thick, heavy door groaned as it ponderously opened.

The interior was claustrophobic, with no entry vestibule, only a dim, narrow corridor leading away from the door. A few feet down the corridor, Tipton rapped on the door of the chief constable's office, and Stephanie was relieved that she would have to go no farther into the dismal, sinister building. Claude was talking with two constables, and he dismissed them when Stephanie and the district clerk stepped into the office.

"We've been expecting you, Mistress Thorpe," Claude told her. "I'll fetch the doctor. Did you want to see me about something, Tipton?"

"Yes, I do," the district clerk replied, placing the box on the desk. "You can also fetch John Whittacker from his cell, because the superior court has ordered him released." He took a letter from his coat pocket and handed it to Claude. "Here, read this, if you would."

Claude unfolded the letter and read it, his lips silently forming the words. A smile began forming on his face, then broadened into a delighted grin. "Well, fancy that!" he crowed, handing the letter back. "It's overdue, but better late than never. I've heard you tell Brendell many times that the sentences were too harsh. Mayhap he'll listen now."

Tipton nodded, returning the letter to his pocket. "One would hope so," he commented in satisfaction. "If not, he'll be heeding further rulings by the superior court. He should know about this as soon as possible, so I intend to ride down to Brendell Farm betimes and show him the letter."

"Let me go with you," Claude urged gleefully. "I want to see his face when he reads it. I have a few oddments that I must see to before I leave, but I can be ready to go with you shortly."

"Very well," Tipton agreed, turning toward the door. "I have things I can be doing at my office, so I'll wait for you there."

Claude grinned happily, following Tipton. "I'll let the

doctor know that you're here, Mistress Thorpe," he tossed over his shoulder.

Stephanie thanked him and placed the bag of food beside the box on Claude's desk as he and Tipton left. She sat down on a chair beside the desk, glancing around. The plain furniture and tidiness of the office reflected the chief constable's practical nature and sense of order, but the small, windowless room had a character separate from its appearance. It was a part of its milieu, distinctly a warder's office in a prison.

The many houses that Stephanie had visited while making calls had always been something more than inert stone, wood, and plaster to her. With one exception, people had either scoffed or failed to understand when she had tried to explain that, and she had mentioned it to no one else for years. The one who had agreed was her father, who experienced the same as she.

Human emotions were powerful, enduring forces, leaving an indelible impression on their surroundings that she could detect. Old houses that had sheltered generations were permeated with the imprint of the joys and sorrows of those who had long since crossed over into eternity. Homes that had been the scene of great tragedy were melancholy places, and hotel rooms had a feel of faint, fleeting vignettes from the lives of many.

The prison was saturated by lingering impressions of the most intense, primal, and violent emotions, the stone walls suffused with them. The murderously savage hatred harbored by evil criminals was mixed with the abject despair of more benevolent natures. All had been kept in submission through terror and agony—the lash. Hundreds had come and gone over the decades, leaving behind a residue of their emotions that blended together and formed the most oppressive atmosphere that Stephanie had ever experienced.

That much she had detected the first time she had seen the prison, making her dislike it, but now she knew there was more. And worse. Stephanie felt as though there were furtive movements just on the edge of her vision, but she knew she would see nothing if she turned. She was alone, yet not entirely by herself. More than convicts and constables inhabited the prison. Men had died here, but some had failed to cross over. In this dreadful place, some were still bound to the scene of their death. A vital part of their beings remained, roaming the dark corridors and cells.

Hearing well-known, beloved footsteps outside the door, Stephanie sprang to her feet. The door opened and Stephen stepped in, smiling happily. A rush of joy swelled within Stephanie, and she ran to him. "Father!" she cried. "It seems to have been forever since Wednesday morning."

"It does for me as well, my dear," he agreed emphatically, hugging her. "I've missed your company and conversation very much indeed."

Although he was physically present, Stephanie had to hold him tightly for a moment to satisfy some deep, inarticulate yearning within herself for assurance that he was safe and well, then she stepped back. "How can you endure being in this place, Father?" she asked. "Influences of the most vile and malignant sort are like a thick, smothering fog in here."

"It's far from pleasant," he acknowledged wryly. "I've found that our patient has a very strong constitution, and he'll probably recover. After I stop the bleeding in that shoulder wound, another day or two of close attendance might be sufficient." He put an arm around Stephanie, stepping to the desk with her, and looked in the box. "I see that you brought everything I might need," he mused, glancing over the things in the box.

"And the food you asked for," she pointed out. "I presume that the food in the mess for the constables isn't the best?"

"It's good enough," he replied. "I wanted the food for some of the convicts, because they never have such things as cheese and fruit. Some are little more than lads, misguided rather than criminals, and I've made friends with them. I believe an escape is being planned, and I intend to keep those young fellows from becoming involved in it."

"An escape?" Stephanie gasped in astonishment. "After what happened to Donald Grant? That's sheer madness, Father!"

"No, my dear," he disagreed soberly. "It's rage to the point of indifference for consequences. Brendell had two men lashed, accusing them of aiding Grant's escape, and the evidence was so flimsy as to be an insult."

"Yes, men named Wilkins and Harkness," Stephanie added. "Tipton told me about that, but Brendell is being taken in hand. The superior court has begun closely reviewing his sentences."

Stephen sighed, nodding. "Claude said as much, but it began too late to keep this place from turning into a hornets' nest. Wilkins and Harkness certainly didn't deserve that lashing, but they're hardened criminals, and no one can reason with them or the others like them. Those young fellows are different, and they'll listen to good advice."

"Father, please stand aside from this," Stephanie pleaded. "It has nothing to do with you. If you know of any plans for an escape, tell the constables and let them deal with—"

"No, I can't do that, my dear," he interrupted. "The little I know would be of no use. Also, I'm trusted little enough as it is, and I'd have no influence at all if those younger convicts thought I might do that. And I must do what I can to keep them from being caught up in something that might very well destroy them, because they're human beings, as I am."

Stephanie started to reply, then fell silent. A sense of responsibility toward others, regardless of who they were, was a fundamental attitude that she shared with him. Stephen smiled affectionately and placed a hand on her shoulder, telling her not to worry. Then he asked how their patients were faring. Still deeply disturbed, Stephanie collected her thoughts and told him about her calls during the past two days.

When she finished, Stephen turned to the box and bag on the desk. "Needless to say, I'd greatly prefer to enjoy your company," he commented, "but I must get back to our patient. Also, you have calls to make, and I don't want you to have to rush about at them or be out too late."

Stephanie was reluctant to part from him, tormented by her anxiety over his being in the prison. Once again she had a feeling of events taking control, sweeping her along with them. "I'll come here again tomorrow and bring more food," she suggested. "And a much larger quantity, because the amount there won't go very far among several men."

"No, that won't be necessary, my dear," he replied. "Seeing to both my calls and your own is more than enough for you to do. This food will be a treat for the men, and I know you don't like to come here."

"If you can stay here, Father, I can visit," she told him firmly. "I want to see you and talk with you again, and I'd like to know the results of the surgery. I'll be here tomorrow evening, after I finish the calls."

Stephen nodded in agreement, his warm smile revealing that he had wanted her to insist. They hugged and kissed each other, then he gathered up the box and bag and followed Stephanie out of the office. After exchanging a word of farewell, he walked down the dark, tunnel-like corridor into the interior of the building while Stephanie stepped toward the door.

With the unnerving, oppressive atmosphere very close around her, she looked over her shoulder and watched her father fading into the dim twilight of the corridor. He paused at a corner, and even though she was unable to see his face, Stephanie knew that he was smiling at her. She waved to him, then he disappeared around the corner.

The constable at the entrance pulled back the steel locking bars to open the door for Stephanie. As it groaned open on its hinges, she was suddenly seized by an urgent impulse to run after her father and warn him. She turned back, looking down the corridor, but she had no idea of what she would say to him, of what kind of danger might be threatening him.

The constable held the door open for Stephanie, puzzled by her hesitation. Feeling somewhat foolish, she nodded in thanks and stepped through the doorway, and the constable touched his cap. The foreboding she had felt during the past two days had never been more pronounced, but it had never been less specific and identifiable in nature.

Tipton and Claude were riding away from the district clerk's office, leaving for Brendell Farm. Looking forward to their meeting with the magistrate, they called out cheerful farewells to Stephanie, and she waved.

Chapter Three

Part of the lane leading to the house at Brendell Farm was in view from the scullery window, and Yulina saw the chief constable and district clerk riding up it. She and Mary Richards were scrubbing pots and pans, Yulina weighing whether or not it might be the right time to tell her the secret. She had to tell someone about it, and Mary was the closest friend she had ever had. They were both Aborigines, the only ones among the household staff, and they had known each other for several years.

Upon seeing the men, however, Yulina's only thoughts were of what their purpose might be. Mary also noticed them, pointing. "Look, it's Mr. Bellamy and Constable Durgin," she said. "They're here to see the master."

The woman's voice was anxious, and Yulina silently nodded, sharing the reaction. Until proven otherwise, anything out of the ordinary was presumed to be something that would anger Brendell, for he always vented his temper on those around him and created an atmosphere of terror.

Yulina rinsed a pot, stacked it with the clean ones, and reached for another one.

She began scrubbing the pot, knowing that it was now definitely the wrong time to tell Mary the secret. But as always when she thought about the secret, a glowing sense of satisfaction suffused her. Even if it had been the result of the most repulsive experience of her entire life, it was also the most wonderful thing that had ever happened to her.

It was also a severe problem, one that could be dangerous. But if it could be kept from others, she reflected, her life would be perfect. From the age of seven, when her mother had died, she had been at the school for orphans and Aborigine children at Parramatta. Friendships had been her closest relationships there and later, while working as a maid. Now the void in her life would be filled by love and inseparable ties with another.

A murmur of conversation carried into the scullery from the kitchen, the cook's helpers also seeing the men through a window, then the cook shouted: "Stop clapping your jaws and have a mind to your work!" she ordered.

Silence fell, and a moment later, the cook stepped into the scullery doorway. A stout, graying woman named Thelma Kershaw, she was always stern out of fear that Brendell would find fault with her work. "Yulina," she said, "when you finish with that pot, mix the dough to make bread."

"Yes, Mistress Kershaw," Yulina replied.

The cook turned back to the kitchen, leaving a tense, resentful atmosphere behind her. During the past months, Yulina had been progressing from scullery maid to cook's helper, and Mary was envious. Yulina knew that was a very strong reason not to tell her the secret and ask for her help, but there was no one else, and someone's help was essential.

Yulina rinsed the pot and turned toward the kitchen, reflecting that she had a better reason to envy Mary than the woman had to be jealous of her. Mary had been brought to the school in Parramatta as an infant, and according to the custom in such instances, she had been given a first and second name. Yulina longed to have a second name of her own, a symbol of family relationship with others even if none existed.

In the large, gleaming kitchen, the cook and her two helpers were washing and slicing fruit for tiffin. Yulina moved about the room, filling a bowl with flour from the bin and then taking it to the table to sift the lumps from it. The cook's helpers were hostile toward her, for she had worked hard and become skilled in cookery, and they regarded her as a threat.

In other households, the helpers would be preparing themselves for a cook's position at another home, but this one was too rife with suspicions. Whenever Brendell found fault with anything, his first thought always was to fire someone, and a domestic employee without good references could never get a position elsewhere. Everyone in the household was constantly on guard, ready to blame someone else if anything went wrong.

Any vulnerability or shortcoming that could be exploited by others had to be concealed, and Yulina exerted herself to be light on her feet as she stood and moved about. While sewing her last two dresses, she had made them bulky. The loose dresses, along with her relatively short, fleshy figure, had hidden her secret from the others.

She had also found a way to keep it hidden. No one ever went into the attic, where she had a nook beside a chimney that was far from all occupied rooms. She was due many afternoons off for when her time came; then she could slip away at intervals to feed the baby. At long last, she would belong to someone, and that one would belong to her. She earnestly wished she had a second name for her child, but it would still be hers. All she needed was a few hours' help from Mary, then everything would be perfect.

The housekeeper, a tall, angular woman named Alma Lowder, stepped into the kitchen. Bearing the brunt of Brendell's venom concerning the household, she was

nervous and frequently ill-tempered. "The district clerk
and head constable are here to see the magistrate, Mistress
Kershaw," she said. "He's been at the barns all morning,
and I sent them there."

"Aye, my helpers saw them coming up the lane," the
cook replied. "Did they give any indication of why
they're here?"

Alma shook her head worriedly as she and Thelma
stepped to a window that looked out toward the barns.
Yulina slowly sifted the flour, listening to the women
talk. They saw neither the visitors nor Brendell, the three
men out of view somewhere around the barns. The cook
speculated about the reasons the men had come to the
farm, suggesting that it might have something to do with
the arrival of Brendell's wife from England.

The housekeeper agreed that it might, her voice more
cheerful. The cook's helpers were working on the other
side of the table from Yulina, and they exchanged hopeful
smiles. The general opinion in the household was that
Brendell might be less malicious and conditions would
improve when his wife arrived, but Yulina knew that it
would be dangerous for her.

The last time he had come to her room at night had
been months before. Each time, she had been numb with
revulsion, but she remembered word for word his threats
of what he would do if she ever told anyone. She was
absolutely certain that he would resort to any means to
prevent his wife from finding out that a maid had borne
his child.

"There's Mr. Bellamy and Constable Durgin, riding
around the main barn," the housekeeper said. "They appear
to be leaving."

"Aye, they've finished their business with the master,"
Thelma mused, then her voice became more animated:
"They're laughing! Do you see? Whatever they came here
for, it couldn't have been contentious."

Alma agreed happily, the cook's helpers smiling in relief,

and Yulina also relaxed. A moment later, however, the general attitude abruptly changed to apprehension. The housekeeper and cook exchanged fearful comments, seeing Brendell shouting at the head groom about something. Then he began berating the grooms, furiously angry for some reason.

Her face drawn with anxiety, the housekeeper hurried out to check on the downstairs maids and make certain everything was in order. The cook rushed back to the table, snapping orders at her helpers. Yulina sifted the last of the flour in the bowl and gathered the salt, lard, yeast, and other ingredients, then began stirring them into the flour.

When the dough was mixed, Yulina placed it on the hearth to rise, then washed and put away the utensils she had used. The cook and her helpers finished preparing tiffin, but midday came and went, with Brendell still castigating the employees at the barns. It had become evident that something had happened which had made him exceptionally angry.

Her face tense and gray with fear, the cook became increasingly irritable, snapping at her helpers. They covered the tiffin with damp cloths to keep the cheese from drying and the fruit from discoloring, then set about preliminary preparations for dinner. During early afternoon, the staff normally came to the kitchen in twos and threes for their tiffin, but they continued working furiously, the house gripped with tension.

Yulina kneaded the dough and set it to rise again, becoming ravenously hungry. Food was scarce in the household—Brendell was frugal with provisions for everyone except himself—and Yulina was accustomed to some degree of hunger at all times. She drew her mind away from her hunger and the tension by thinking about her baby, directing her love to it.

The sound of Brendell's vicious roar at the front of the house was like the unleashing of a violent, raging storm that had been fearfully awaited. The household erupted into a frenzy of activity, and an ashen-faced downstairs maid raced into the kitchen to get his tiffin. She and the cook whipped the cloths off the plates and arranged them on a tray, their hands trembling, then the maid grabbed it up and ran out with it.

Moments later, the hall door almost flew off its hinges as Brendell kicked it open. He stamped into the kitchen with the tray, his face flushed with rage under its network of red lines. "Was this bloody tiffin made last week?" he bellowed at the cook. "It's so bloody stale a dog wouldn't eat it!" He hurled the tray at her, the woman ducking as the tray, dishes, and food flew through the air, then he turned back to the door. "For a change, send me a bit of what you pack into your own fat gullet!"

The cook's helpers scrambled about and began cleaning up the food and broken dishes, and the cook ran to the cabinet for more dishes to prepare another tiffin. Yulina assisted her, hurriedly collecting fruit from the bins and cheese from the food safe. In the hall, Brendell found something wrong with the way the floor had been polished, and his voice reverberated through the kitchen as he screamed in the housekeeper's face.

A terrified downstairs maid stepped into the kitchen and waited until the tiffin was ready, then ran out with it. When she returned with the dishes a short time later, the tiffin had hardly been touched, and it became more and more evident to Yulina that something extraordinary had happened. Brendell's rages usually lasted an hour or two, but instead of diminishing, this time his fury grew even worse while the afternoon wore on.

When the dough was ready, the cook was so distraught that she had forgotten about it. Yulina divided it into loaf pans, then put them into the oven. After the bread baked, she placed the loaves on the cooling rack and took the pans to the scullery. While she and Mary were scrubbing the pans, they saw two maids leave, Brendell having fired them. The women trudged down the lane, carrying their belongings and weeping.

The terror continued, Brendell prowling the house and his scathing roars coming from one part of it, then another. Yulina retreated from the upheaval into thoughts of her baby, pondering its destiny when it grew to adulthood. Her mother had told her about the Aborigine beliefs of how the world and all of the life-forms in it had been created, which had set a pattern that shaped the lives of people even before they were born.

Her mother had explained that at the beginning of time, the Creators had walked the earth and sung each life-form into being. That had established an invisible web of Songtrails covering Australia, and the knowledge of them had been given to tribal elders. The first time a baby moved in a woman's womb, it was a sign that the spirit of an animal had just invested the baby with life. An elder could examine where it had occurred and determine what animal had been sung into being at that spot on a Songtrail. That was the baby's totemic animal, and its characteristics would be reflected in the baby's personality when the child grew to adulthood.

Yulina assisted the cook and her helpers in the final preparations for dinner, recalling the first time her baby had moved. With no means of consulting a tribal elder, she had drawn conclusions about the implications of it herself. It had occurred when she stood on a stool in the laundry room and leaned over the mangle to get a pot of soap off a shelf.

At first, the circumstances had suggested that her baby would be a girl and eventually a laundry maid. Then she had thought again. The mangle, which had not been in use at the time, was a machine used to squeeze water from the laundry and to press wrinkles from linens. After thinking about it at length, Yulina had concluded that her baby would be a boy and would be a mechanic or involved with machinery in some way as an adult.

The scent of the beef roast and vegetables for dinner made
Yulina weak with hunger, pangs gnawing in her stomach,
but she ignored opportunities to grab tidbits when no one
else was looking. Like the others, she had no wish to eat
while Brendell was on his rampage. He fell silent, but he
continued prowling the house after he had eaten dinner.

Yulina helped Mary scrub the pots and pans from dinner,
then returned to the kitchen. It was the time when the house
normally settled for the night, but none of the staff had
come to the kitchen for dinner, and everyone continued
finding things to do and kept hard at work. Some of the
copper pans hanging on the wall had less than a brilliant
shine, and Yulina took them down and began polishing
them with whitestone and a cloth.

At the same time that Yulina heard his slow, menacing
footsteps in the hall, the cook and her helpers also heard
them. They began working harder at their tasks, and Yulina
ducked her head and polished a pan furiously. The hall door
squeaked open and he stepped into the kitchen.

Slapping a riding crop against his thigh, he stalked around
the kitchen. Yulina kept her head down, even when he
paused beside the table where she was working. Then, her
apprehension exploding into fear within her, she realized
that she was leaning against the edge of the table and
pressing her bulky dress against herself. She gradually
eased back from the table as she buffed the copper pan
rapidly with the cloth.

He reached out with his riding crop and pressed her
dress against her, outlining the bulge in her stomach.
Yulina stopped polishing the pan and slowly lifted her
head, looking at him.

The cook and her helpers were huddled over their tasks,
not watching. Yulina felt defenseless and isolated, all alone
in her terror. The eyes glaring out from the network of red
lines covering his coarse, ugly features were savage and
remorseless, those of a carnivore. He knew.

Brendell turned away and strode rapidly out of the

kitchen, slapping the riding crop against his thigh. The cook and her helpers exchanged quiet comments of relief over not having been fired or even castigated. Moments later, the household staff began flooding into the kitchen and gulping food the cook handed out, Brendell having gone to his room for the night. Yulina numbly replaced the pans on the wall and went to her room.

She wedged her stool against the door, but she knew it was futile. He would have many opportunities, a choice of when to strike. A quick stab with a knife, and it would be done. In the large fields of Brendell Farm, a hole dug and then covered over during the dark of night would never be noticed. Her secret would endure forever. His wife would never know.

Her own scream of terror woke Stephanie on Saturday morning. She lurched up to a sitting position in bed, the shadows of the dark night retreating grudgingly from the gloomy twilight of the rainy dawn that was creeping through the window. The somber quiet of the house hushed the echoes of the anguished wail that her dream had torn from deep within her.

Sweat made her face cold, but the images of the bizarre dream that were etched in her mind created a far more penetrating chill at the depths of her being. In the dream, she had been at the prison with her father. The stone wall had been drawing him into it, absorbing him. He had been struggling to pull himself free while she vainly tried to get to him and help, but she had been unable to reach his hand stretched out to her.

Stephanie rose and dressed, thinking of the previous morning, when she had awakened in the aftermath of a dream she had been unable to recall. She realized that it had been the same dream, and for no reason that she could define, its recurring nature made it much more frightening.

Trying to smother the haunting memory of the dream

with activity, she went downstairs and checked the box beside the front door, finding it empty. She stoked the fire in the kitchen, then cooked a small pot of porridge and toasted rounds of bread. While eating breakfast, she heard vehicles on the main road, some families setting out to spend their Saturday shopping and enjoying the entertainments in Parramatta or Sydney.

When she drove away from her house to begin the calls, Stephanie pulled back on the reins and stopped at the edge of the road. Evading her attempts to dismiss it, her dream deeply troubled her, making her depressed. She gazed up the road toward the village, longing to see her father for at least a few minutes instead of waiting until that evening.

Her personal wishes were always less important to her than the needs of patients, however, and she knew that her father would want her to attend to them first. She snapped the reins, turning toward the main road.

Although a large number of calls made the day a busy one, with much to occupy her mind, Stephanie was unable to forget the dream. The dreary, rainy day was also one for dwelling on morbid thoughts. While driving up and down the muddy roads between calls, the murky shadows of trees and other things through the rain reminded her of the strange images of the dream. She tried to tell herself that such an utterly irrational dream had been no more than a floundering attempt by her slumbering mind to give concrete form to her foreboding of the past days, but it still seemed more than that.

Dusk was gathering when she finished the last of the calls and drove back home. Just as she turned onto the side road leading to her house and past it to the village, a rider emerged from the rain and twilight. Coming down the main road at a gallop and shouting to Stephanie, he was Elmer Beasley, whose pregnant wife was Gideon Mundy's daughter.

A small, skinny man of twenty-two, his freckled face was transfixed by a mixture of joy and trepidation as he reined up. "Hannah's having the baby, Mistress Thorpe!" he shouted. "She started a while ago! We've been looking for you all over Wallaby Track!"

Stephanie bit back a cry of dismay, her eager anticipation of seeing her father withering into keen disappointment. Then she ruefully accepted the situation and resigned herself to waiting until the next day. "Very well, Elmer," she said. "I intended to visit my father, and he's expecting me. Please ride up to the prison and ask the constable at the door to tell him that I won't be able to come and see him until tomorrow."

Elmer touched his hat, turning his horse, and galloped up the road toward the village. Stephanie turned in at her house and parked her buggy at the side entrance. The prison roof was barely visible in the fading light, and it brought back the memory of her dream in chilling clarity. She sighed, pulling her gaze away from the prison, and went into the surgery.

Opening a cabinet, she took out her nitrous oxide flask. It was a large bottle with a rubber tube extending through a hole in the stopper, and a mask to fit over a patient's nose and mouth was at the end of the tube. She removed the stopper and took a metal cylinder filled with liquefied nitrous oxide from the cabinet. Upending the cylinder over the flask, she opened the valve. The chemical vaporized as it flowed into the flask, and she leaned back to keep from inhaling it. She closed the valve, then quickly replaced the stopper in the flask before any of the gas could escape.

Thick darkness was closing in when Stephanie carried the flask out to her buggy, and she lit the coachlamps. She drove away from the house, despondently glancing up toward the village through the darkness, and turned to the south on the main road, toward Mundy Farm. A few minutes later, hoofbeats approached from behind, then Elmer caught up with her.

The coachlamp shone on his freckled face as he leaned down to the buggy. "I waited until the constable had gone to talk to your father, Mistress Thorpe," he told her. "The doctor said he understood, and he'll look forward to seeing you tomorrow. I'll ride ahead to the farm and let everybody know that you'll be there shortly."

Stephanie replied in acknowledgment, and he rode away into the night. Then, summoning her will, she forced the memory of her dream and her longing to see her father to the far recesses of her mind. Having the full confidence of a woman in childbirth was crucial, and no patient would have complete faith in someone whose thoughts were elsewhere. She concentrated upon Hannah, and upon the new life that would enter the world within a few hours.

Lamps and lanterns at the scattered farmhouses back from the road glowed dimly through the darkness and rain, but the Mundy home was ablaze with light when it came into view. Typical of a birthing, neighboring women, relatives who lived nearby, and wives of hired men at the farm had gathered. The house teemed with activity on the quiet Saturday evening in the valley, and several of the women came out to carry in Stephanie's bag and the nitrous oxide flask when she drew up her buggy in front of the house.

In the parlor, Flora helped Stephanie off with her oilskins, coat, and hat, and the other women rushed to take basins of hot water, soap, and towels to Hannah's bedroom. The two strapping Mundy sons, Otis and Artis, were in the parlor. They looked very uncomfortable and out of place, and Stephanie suggested to Flora that they be sent to a friend's house.

"Gideon would throttle them if they left," Flora replied, amused. "He's still charging about in the valley and searching for you. You can well imagine the state he's been in ever since Hannah's labor began."

Stephanie smiled and agreed, going down the hall with Flora to Hannah's room. Several of the women were clustered around the bed, and the young woman's face was sweaty and pale from the pain of her initial contractions. Stephanie took charge, forestalling unwanted advice from

the women and any morbid conversation that could unnerve
Hannah. "Let's don't hover over her, please," she said
firmly. "Hannah, the happy event that we've awaited with
great anticipation has finally arrived, hasn't it?"

The young woman managed a smile and nod, the women
stepping to benches flanking the fireplace that had been
brought into the room for the occasion. Stephanie washed
her hands and examined Hannah, then washed her hands
again and checked the baby's heartbeat with her stethoscope. The cervix was dilated the width of two fingers
and the baby's heart was throbbing strongly at 140 beats
per minute, everything perfectly normal.

Stephanie sat down on a chair beside the bed, moving
the nitrous oxide flask closer, and took the tiny stopper out
of the tube inside the mask. "This will make you feel much
better," she said, placing the mask over Hannah's mouth
and nose. "Inhale slowly and deeply."

The woman took a whiff of the gas, then Stephanie lifted
the mask and replaced the stopper in the tube. Commonly
called laughing gas; it was used by some as a recreational
drug because of its intoxicating effects when taken in
sufficient quantity. In lesser amounts, it suppressed pain
and produced a general sense of well-being, and Hannah
relaxed, the strain on her face changing to a giddy, bemused
expression.

Just then, Gideon's arrival was announced by the front
door slamming and his heavy footsteps coming through
the parlor and into the hall. "Is Mistress Thorpe here?"
he bellowed. "How is Hannah? Is she all right? Somebody
tell me what's happening and if Hannah is all right!"

Flora and other women rushed out into the hall, trying
to reassure him in a chorus of voices, but he continued
shouting anxiously about his daughter. The commotion
disturbed Hannah, and Stephanie stood up from her chair,
smiling at the young woman and patting her hand. Turning
away from the bed, Stephanie marched toward the hall as
her smile disappeared.

The uproar ended, Stephanie shouldering her way through the women to face Gideon squarely. "This noise is upsetting my patient, Mr. Mundy," she said in a soft, steely voice. "It must cease immediately!"

Gideon blinked, his lips open after breaking off in the middle of a shouted question. Closing his mouth with a snap, he glared at Stephanie in wounded dignity and then stamped toward the kitchen. Flora and the other women quietly laughed and commented among themselves about how deftly Stephanie had dealt with the situation, following her back into the bedroom. She sat down on her chair again, waiting for a contraction.

When it came, she talked Hannah through it and encouraged her to scream. She analyzed Hannah's tolerance for pain, giving her a whiff of the gas to dull the peak of the pain and to conserve the young woman's strength for the hours of labor that lay ahead. After the contraction ended, Stephanie wiped Hannah's face with a damp cloth and sat back, waiting for the next one.

The women had brought knitting and clothes to mend, which they worked on while they talked and kept the fireplace stoked. Stephanie listened to them, ready to intervene if the topic turned to stillbirths or other gruesome matters, but most of their conversation was about her use of an anesthetic during birthings. It was a relatively unusual practice, and one of which the women approved in the strongest terms.

An hour later, with Hannah progressing in the first stage of labor, the women left to have dinner, then returned. After a contraction ended, Stephanie went to the kitchen. Gideon, distraught over Hannah's cries of pain, was sitting at the table with the food on his plate untouched. Elmer was worried about his wife, as well as intimidated by being blamed by his father-in-law for her travail, and he had eaten nothing either.

The two Mundy sons were also at the table, their plates cleaned off. They had asked if they could go and visit friends, and Gideon was castigating them for a lack of concern about their sister. "Mr. Mundy," Stephanie put in, "they cannot assist in any way. The most they could do here is worry, and you're doing that in lavish sufficiency."

Gideon glared at her, then at his sons. "Aye, very well," he growled. "If it means naught to you whether your sister lives or dies, go ahead and guzzle your fill of rum with your mates in Parramatta."

The two young men left, grinning gratefully at Stephanie. She filled a plate with vegetables and stewed beef from pans on the fireplace hob, then stood at the washstand to eat. Just as she finished and started to leave, Hannah began another contraction and cried out. Gideon groaned in anguish, glowering accusingly at Elmer. The young man averted his gaze, his freckled face remorseful, and Stephanie hurried back to Hannah.

The night became like many others for Stephanie, most of them similar but no two quite the same. As the hours wore on, some of the women on the benches began nodding off to sleep and waking again when Hannah cried out. Otis and Artis returned late in the night, their footsteps unsteady from rum as they went to their rooms. A short time later, Hannah started into the second stage of labor. Her cervix fully dilated to some four inches, the contractions began pushing the baby into the birth canal.

Checking the baby's heartbeat, Stephanie found that it was falling to 125 beats per minute during contractions. She knew it could be due to pressure on the umbilical cord, for the uterine muscles were as strong as a powerful man's biceps. However, it could also mean that the baby was being choked by the cord or in distress for some other reason, and she should hasten the delivery by tugging on it with forceps during the contractions.

The amniotic fluid membrane was bulging into the vagina in front of the baby's head, and if the baby was under any severe stress, its sphincter muscle would be relaxed, staining the amniotic fluid with fecal matter. Stephanie took a small, sharp scissor from her bag, washed it in a basin, then nicked the membrane with it and held a lamp close. In the yellow glow of the lamp, the trickle of amniotic fluid was perfectly clear.

At five o'clock, with the window dark but roosters crowing outside, Hannah began the final stage of labor. The baby's head crowned, starting to push through the vaginal opening. Stephanie took a small tin of powdered opium in menthol salve from her bag, ready to numb the perineum and cut it. She preferred not to, the incision and sutures presenting a danger of infection, and she watched to see if it threatened to tear.

It stretched, the baby's head pushing on out, and Stephanie supported the head with one hand as she put the salve back into her bag. After the head slid out in the usual facedown position, there was a pause. The baby's shoulders, in a sideward position, were too wide to pass through the pelvis. Stephanie gave Hannah a deep breath of the gas in preparation, then the baby began turning with the next contraction.

It was very painful, making Hannah scream in spite of the gas. Over the shrill cry, Stephanie heard Gideon pounding the kitchen table with his fist and berating the hapless Elmer. The baby finished turning, its face toward Hannah's thigh and its shoulders vertical, then the next contraction began pushing out a tiny shoulder hunched up against the neck.

When the other shoulder began emerging, Stephanie tugged the baby gently to assist Hannah. A moment later, it slid out onto the layers of cloth under Hannah in a rush of amniotic fluid. It was a perfectly formed boy, its color the normal blue under the white, cheeselike coating on newborns. Stephanie grabbed a swab and wiped away the mucus on its mouth and nose to keep the baby from aspirating the secretion when it began breathing.

The women gathered around the bed, gasping in delight and admiration over the baby. "Mistress Thorpe, aren't you going to smack it to make it cry and start breathing?" one of them asked.

"No, certainly not," Stephanie replied, quickly tying off the umbilical cord and cutting it. She slid a hand under the baby and stroked its back. "Life is more than enough of a battering, and there's no need to begin it with a clout. This lad will greet the world when he's ready."

The stimulus of her hand stroking the baby's back made it stir, its limbs twitching. Its tiny face puckered into a scowl as it uttered a thin, mewling sound. Then it drew in a deep breath, its blue color changing to a healthy pink glow, and a hearty, resounding wail burst from its lips. It was always a wondrous, ecstatically uplifting sound to Stephanie, that of a new human being setting out down the road of life. She blinked away tears of joy as she handed the baby to the women to wash and wrap in a blanket.

The cry triggered the usual pandemonium at the climax of a birthing. Hannah kept trying to sit up, wanting to see and hold her baby, and the women laughed and talked while they washed it. Elmer and Gideon ran down the hall from the kitchen, each trying to be first. They peered into the room, and Flora scolded them as she pushed them away from the door. Gideon roared at his sons and rooted them out of bed, and they stumbled about in the hall in their long nightshirts, miserable with hangovers.

When the afterbirth was ejected, Stephanie's work was finished. The baby had become the center of attention, and no one noticed when she left with her bag and the gas flask. She put them into her buggy, then stepped back inside to get her coat, hat, and oilskins.

The house remained in an uproar. The only ones not participating were the pale, haggard Mundy sons, who slumped against the hallway wall with their eyes closed. Gideon had an arm around Elmer's shoulders, the two of them talking and laughing in boisterous glee. In the bedroom, the baby howled lustily amid a bedlam of joyful conversation about it.

Another rainy day had begun when Stephanie drove away from the house, but it was anything but dreary to her. The birthing had been easier than many, ending with both the mother and the baby in good health, and Stephanie glowed with satisfaction.

Her mood changed abruptly two miles from the house. A middle-aged farmer named Jason Miles and his son, Tom, were repairing a fence that bordered the road. They called out in greeting, Jason adding that there had been either an escape or an attempt to do so at the prison the night before.

An icy uneasiness stabbing within her, Stephanie stopped her buggy. "Was anyone injured or killed?" she asked.

"That I can't say," Jason replied. "Our oxen broke down this fence just before dark last night, and it was late when me and Tom found them not far from the village. We heard gunfire and a ruction at the prison whilst we were driving the oxen toward home, and that's all I know about it."

"Yes, I see," Stephanie said, lifting her reins. "Good day to you."

The men tipped their hats as Stephanie drove away. Her disquiet was formless and without specific basis, simply there. She tried to tell herself that it arose from her wish for nothing unusual to happen at the prison so long as her father was there, but that failed to answer to her feelings. They were a sense of dread without a defined cause, impossible to quantify and equally difficult to explain away.

When her house came into view, she saw a rider in front of it. A moment later, he rode away from the house and up the road to the village. The rain and thin fog in the air obscured her view, but he appeared to be wearing a constable's uniform. Her disquiet swelled into fear. It was logical that he might have been putting a note into the box beside the door, but the explanation rang hollow to her.

At her house, she scrambled out of the buggy and ran up the steps to the box. It was empty. A panic-stricken need to go and see her father gripped her. As she raced back to her buggy and started to jump into it, she heard horses galloping down the road from the village. Claude Durgin and Tipton Bellamy came into view, turning off at her house.

Stephanie could see on their faces that something dreadful had happened. The two men reined up and dismounted, Claude taking off his cap and Tipton his hat. They gazed at her remorsefully, the rain pattering on their bare heads. "What's wrong?" she asked. "Why have you come here?"

The men exchanged an uncomfortable glance, reluctant to begin, then Claude spoke in a grave, diffident tone: "Stephanie, I had a man waiting here to come and tell us when you returned," he explained. "Three convicts tried to escape last night, thinking the constables wouldn't be as watchful on a Saturday night. They were wrong, because the constables—"

"Yes, I heard that there had been an escape or an attempt to do so," Stephanie broke in. "Does this concern my father?"

Claude had evidently decided upon what he would say, and he doggedly resumed, too perturbed to improvise: "The three that tried to escape were killed," he continued. "As best we can tell, they opined that the doctor knew what they planned and might tell a constable about it. He was the only gentlemen amongst felons, and they must have thought—"

"Claude!" Stephanie shouted frantically, "kindly tell me if something has happened to my father! Tell me!"

The chief constable fell silent, his lips moving as he tried to form an answer, then Tipton spoke: "The doctor was stabbed," he said sorrowfully. "Words cannot express my regret at having to tell you this, Stephanie."

"Stabbed?" she echoed in panic. "Do you mean that my father was injured? How serious is it, and who is attending to him? What sort of . . . ?" Her voice faded, their somber expressions giving a shattering answer to her questions. "Is my father dead?" she whispered.

The two men nodded mournfully. Stephanie turned and

stumbled aimlessly around the house toward the barnyard. Claude and Tipton followed, talking to her, but their voices were only meaningless sounds.

Her deep love for her father fueled a tormenting agony of grief, but there was more. The anchor of stability in her life was gone. The foundations of her life had turned to quicksand. She was all alone.

There was still more. And worse yet. Stephanie stopped in the barnyard, gazing at the prison roof through the rain and her tears of bitter anguish. Her close rapport with her father and her keen awareness of him prompted an inner voice that spoke, telling her a terrible truth. She realized that her dreams had been an omen, a forewarning.

She knew with absolute certainty that the bizarre, irrational images of the dreams had now become a dreadful reality. Another person had failed to cross over and had joined the ghostly presences of some who had died in the prison. The vital spiritual element that had been the life force of her father's body was now trapped within the thick, dismal stone walls, condemned to wander the dark corridors and cells through eternity.

Chapter Four

Immediately after the funeral, Stephanie returned home to change into workaday clothes. Cedric Calloway, a doctor from Parramatta, followed her in his buggy and tried to talk with her. He had visited occasionally, viewing her as a prospective wife, but she had no interest in him. She put him off, changed clothes, and set out to make her calls.

She kept her emotions contained, which had become a part of her personality over the years. Close rapport with terminal patients could create an unbearable mental burden, and she had developed an ability to maintain a measure of detachment from her feelings. While her grief over her father's murder was infinitely greater than that from the death of any patient, she was able to restrain it. Her work was also a means of isolating her emotions within herself, so absorbing that she could bury herself in it.

The season was one during which she could completely lose herself in her work, the cold, rainy weather continuing and winter illnesses increasing. She needed such a busy time to contain her flux of crushing sorrow mixed with burning hatred for Brendell. Her control over her emotions was threatened whenever people expressed condolences, and she turned the conversations to other subjects. Her composure was also strained when she learned during a discussion with Tipton that Donald Grant had died, which seemed to her an irony that made her father's death even more tragic.

The prison was a more prominent part of her surroundings than ever to her, drawing her gaze each time she left her house during early morning, then again when she returned at dusk. The scene of the calamity that had plunged her life into turmoil, it was also her father's tomb. Her attitude toward it was a mixture of abhorrence and reverence, creating a burden of anguish that she knew she would endure for the rest of her life.

As the days passed, Cedric Calloway began coming to see her more often. From when they had first met, she had made it clear that she had no interest in him, but he had persisted. At twenty-seven, he was a vapid, irritatingly pompous man who viewed the medical profession as a livelihood, and he was unable to understand that it was a mission in life to Stephanie.

When she returned home one evening and found him waiting for her again, Stephanie was annoyed. "I don't have time to talk with you, Cedric," she told him bluntly. "I have tasks awaiting me in my house."

In his usual way of adopting a rejection as his own intention, Calloway took out his watch and looked at it. "Well, I must be on my way," he said. "If you lived in Parramatta, you'd have a better class of patients than the old lags and their offspring here. And as a result, you would have far more money for much less work than you do at present."

"You should realize by now that I don't view my work in those terms," she shot back impatiently. "And certainly not the people here. Almost without exception, I'm extremely fond of them. I stay in Wallaby Track because I like it and I'm needed here, not for coin."

His condescending smile was a silent comment on her remarks as he spoke in farewell and stepped into his buggy, then drove away. Stephanie knew he would be back, his sense of superiority convincing him that she would eventually decide to marry him. In addition, they both realized that her choices for a husband were very limited.

It was an accepted fact that a professional midwife could marry only a doctor, no one else. Among other reasons, only a doctor could understand the inability of a midwife to be a housewife in any sense of the term. Marriages with others invariably developed into a misery of conflict. Men often displayed romantic interest in Stephanie, and she always firmly discouraged them. She wanted a loving marriage, a partner in life and her own children, but her prospects of having a family appeared poor.

Stephanie dismissed thoughts of Calloway, pondering a more important matter. During the past days, she had procrastinated over a duty associated with her father's death. She had aunts and uncles in Britain, all in the medical profession, and they had to be informed of what had happened. But she knew that writing about the events would be torturous for her.

However, she also knew that it would be no less onerous at a later time. After dinner, Stephanie cleared off the table and took out writing materials. While she wrote, she had to stop every few lines and control herself, wiping away her tears. She realized that she could never come to terms with her father's death until her sorrow was released, but it was an excruciating torment, much easier to bear when it was contained.

The next morning, Stephanie took the letters to the store in the village, which served as the district postal office. She set out on her calls for the day, the ordeal of writing the letters finished, but another confronted her a few hours later. A neighbor of the Digby family caught up with her on the road and told her that the family and neighbors were searching for her. Billy Digby had suddenly become ill, with intense stomach pains.

Stephanie rushed to Digby Farm and found what she had feared. At times, the deadly perityphlitic abscess reached the acute stage after days or even weeks of abdominal pain. In other instances, as now, it struck with sudden, devastating effect. The young boy was burning with fever, and he writhed and screamed in agony as he clutched his stomach.

With his shrill screams battering her ears, Stephanie sent the others out of the room. The boy was in such intense pain that she had to grip him tightly and force his mouth open to pour the first spoonful of undiluted laudanum down his throat. The powerful opiate began taking effect within seconds, then it was easier to give him enough to induce unconsciousness. When she finished, Stephanie went back into the front room.

It was crowded, Albert and Sarah Digby weeping and surrounded by neighbors who were distraught from the boy's screams. Someone suggested that Billy would be better now, and Sarah wailed as she shook her head. "No, it's the end," she sobbed. "The doctor told us what would happen."

The people turned to Stephanie for confirmation. She gave it by making no comment, silently walking back out into the cold drizzle and mist to her buggy. Albert followed her, wiping his tears. "The worst of it is Billy's suffering, Mistress Thorpe," he said. "You'll stop that, won't you? You'll keep him from suffering, won't you?"

"Yes, I'll return this afternoon and twice each day until. . . ."

She was unable to finish the sentence, but her meaning was clear, Albert nodding in understanding and turning back to the house. As she drove away, Stephanie struggled to detach herself emotionally and put her fondness for the young, handsome boy at a distance. She yearned to drive to the main road and then out of Wallaby Track, fleeing from being midwife for death. Instead, she grimly continued with her calls.

During late afternoon, she went back to the Digby house and administered more laudanum to the boy as soon as he was sufficiently conscious to swallow. The next morning, when she returned to give him another dose of laudanum, the virulent inflammation that was devouring his intestines was changing his face, making him appear prematurely aged. That afternoon, when she went to the house once again, his stomach had begun to swell.

The following morning, the end was only hours away. The boy's vital signs were weak, his stomach massively swollen, and his skin had the gray pallor of approaching death. He was in a coma, and Stephanie lifted his head and slowly dripped laudanum onto his tongue, waiting for the swallowing reflex to function. When she was absolutely certain that he would remain unconscious and feel no pain, she went into the kitchen.

The other two sons were at the table with Albert and Sarah, all of them weeping. "It's time to summon the relatives," she told Albert. "I must leave, but I'll return at midday."

Albert nodded sorrowfully, standing up to go and saddle a horse, and Sarah and the two boys sobbed bitterly. Stephanie went back through the house and outside to her buggy. She was thankful that three of her calls that day were essential, giving her other matters to concentrate upon, for it provided a respite during which to gather her strength.

While making the calls, Stephanie mentally composed herself as best she could. She knew that attending a patient until the end was a duty, but she had precious little emotional strength left, her reserves drained by keeping her sorrow over her father's death contained. When she finished the calls, she drove back toward Digby Farm and the ritual of the death watch.

The house was crowded with relatives and neighbors in the customary orgy of grief, the catharsis to exhaust sorrow so that life could continue in the absence of a loved one. Stephanie exchanged nods with those in the front room and went into the boy's bedroom. Striving to be clinical, she examined him and observed that his vital signs were weaker.

At a level where she was unable to be clinical, Stephanie noted that his young body was still fighting valiantly, even though the hopeless battle was lost. She moved a chair to the side of the bed and sat down, taking up her vigil. The wind moaned around the house, an undertone to the sounds of grief inside it. From time to time, a relative or friend looked in the bedroom door at the boy, then sadly turned away.

During late afternoon, when the boy's pulse became erratic, Stephanie returned to the front room. Sarah's father, a grizzled old former convict named Samuel Anley, was sitting beside the hall door. Stephanie spoke to him quietly: "The end is near," she said. "Please bring in the family and the others to make their farewells with Billy."

The old man nodded, pushing himself up from his chair, and Stephanie went back down the hall to the bedroom. Samuel led the people in a few minutes later, he and Albert supporting Sarah as she sobbed wildly. She kissed her son a last time, more people filing in and the room becoming congested. The people moved past the bed and touched the boy's hand as they wept. Then they found places to stand, the family at the foot of the bed.

While the seconds dragged past, Stephanie hoped that any convulsions would be brief and not violent, sparing the family further distress. Her prayers were answered. Billy departed with barely a sigh, scarcely a tremor in the small, swollen body. Stephanie completed the ritual, taking the small mirror out of her bag and holding it under the nostrils. Its surface remained unclouded. She closed the eyes and then pulled the coverlet over the face.

Amid the explosion of grief, Sarah collapsed screaming at the foot of the bed, others wailing and weeping. Stephanie closed her bag and then found her way out of the room and through the house, her eyes blurred with tears and her chin trembling. Her duty had been a vital support to her control over herself, and now it was finished, the support gone.

The raw, wintry day was drawing to an end, the gray light starting to fade into dusk as Stephanie drove toward home. After the ordeal, even her dark, lonely house seemed a refuge to her. A wagon moved up the road toward her, then the man driving it pulled back on his reins and asked if she was Mistress Thorpe. Stephanie collected her thoughts in her fog of depression, stopping her buggy. "Yes, I'm Stephanie Thorpe," she replied.

"I'm Fergus Grant, mo'm," the man said, then pointed to a long box covered with canvas in the wagon. "Donald Grant, the convict you and your father doctored, was my brother. I'm mightily sorry about what happened to your father, and also most grateful for what you did for Donald."

A laborer from his appearance, Fergus had an open face and direct manner that Stephanie liked. "I regret that my father and I were unable to do more for your brother, Mr. Grant," she told him. "You're removing his remains to the churchyard where you live, then?"

Fergus nodded and told her that he and his family lived at a village called Penrith, beside the Nepean River. "I'm glad I met you on the road so I could thank you," he continued. "I went to your house, and a man who said he was a doctor was waiting there for you. He told me that you wouldn't want to talk with me, and he sent me on my way."

Her temper flaring, Stephanie knew that the man at her house was Cedric Calloway. "My wishes were misrepresented," she assured Fergus. "I'm very pleased that we happened to meet so I could set the matter right."

"You can't be happier about it than I am, Mistress Thorpe," Fergus replied earnestly. "I'll always be grateful for what you did for Donald, and meeting you has been a pleasure that I'll never forget."

"It's been a pleasure for me as well, Mr. Grant. Godspeed on your journey, and please convey my best wishes to Mistress Grant."

Fergus lifted his hat and replied that he would, driving away, and Stephanie continued on down the road. She thought about what Calloway had done, becoming increasingly angry. Fuming with impatience to confront him, she grabbed the whip out of its socket on the splashboard and cracked it above her horse, and it surged into a fast trot.

When she turned in at her house, Calloway was waiting in front of the steps. She stopped her buggy, jumping out of it. "On what grounds did you assume the right to decide whom I'll speak with?" she demanded. "I've just talked with Fergus Grant, and he said you sent him on his way!"

Calloway shook his head in condescending patience. "The man is an old lag," he said, "and you shouldn't pass the time of day in—"

"How I choose to pass my time isn't your concern!" Stephanie broke in hotly. "I've endeavored to be courteous to you, but I won't tolerate your presuming to meddle in my affairs!"

"Endeavored to be courteous?" he echoed huffily, finally offended by something she had said. "You'll pass the time of day with an old lag, yet you must endeavor to be courteous to me? If my company means so little to you, then I certainly shan't come here again!"

"Fergus Grant is a good, honest man!" she shot back. "If I said the same about you, I'd be lying through my teeth! And if you choose not to come here again, I'll regard it as good riddance!"

Calloway glared at her indignantly, then leaped into his buggy and drove rapidly away. Stephanie led her horse to the barn, still seething with anger. Then, while unharnessing the horse and carrying fodder to it and the other horse, she shrugged off her resentment. She knew it was pointless, for Calloway was a pompous fool, and he would no longer trouble her.

Her anger passed, but not in isolation from other emotions. The turmoil of the death watch, combined with her harrowing grief over her father, had strained her control to the far edge of endurance. As her anger faded, it was dwarfed by a tidal wave of sorrow that rushed in to take its place. Her restraint over her emotions shattered, and a wail of anguish was torn from her as she collapsed in the straw on the barn floor.

The agony that gripped her was greater than any physical pain, her inner being writhing under the stinging lash of her pent-up grief. Tears flooded from her eyes as she wept, and convulsive sobs shook her in hard, driving spasms, as though her body was trying to disgorge some deadly toxin that was poisoning it. Hours passed while she lay on the straw, beating it with her fists and crying out in her excruciating torment.

When her tears were exhausted, Stephanie pulled herself to her feet and stumbled through the darkness to her house. Moments of dry sobs seizing her, she numbly attended to her nightly tasks and forced herself to eat a few bites of dinner. After she went to bed, tears came once again and she wept in the darkness of the large, quiet house until she fell asleep.

The next day, if anyone noticed that Stephanie's eyes were red and swollen, no one commented on it. Giving up all attempts to contain her emotions, she cried at times while driving down the roads. Her grief was tormenting, but its sharp edge was less agonizing than before.

Stephanie knew that through releasing her sorrow to run its course, she had begun a long, slow process of adjusting to her father's death. But she also realized that in a way, his death was a raw, gaping wound within her that would never heal. Her father's vital spiritual being would always be trapped inside the thick stone walls of the dark, somber prison, and that would remain a source of heartbreak for her as long as she lived.

As tragic as it had been, Billy Digby's death seemed to have been a low point, with favorable developments during the following days. A woman's incapacitating menstrual cramps that had been unaffected by other anodynes were completely relieved by syrup of viburnum, and a number of patients recovered from vernal catarrh. A woman's postpartum bleeding that was becoming worrisome was stopped virtually overnight by ergot extract.

Roger Corbett's consumption worsened during the wet weather, his cough becoming harder to suppress, and Stephanie became increasingly concerned about him. Then, when she started to set out on her calls one morning, she saw Jacob Corbett leading two other riders down the road toward her house. She stopped her buggy, waiting and studying the riders.

One of the others was Roger, the third a stranger who was clothed in unusual garb for the valley. Muscular and bearded, he wore a long sheepskin coat that reached his stirrups and a wide stockman's hat with the brim turned up on one side. His horse was also different, a very muscular animal that had longer, thicker hair than any Stephanie had ever seen.

They turned in at the house and reined up, and Jacob introduced the stranger as Ruel Blake, a stockman from Tibooburra Station. "I met him yesterday in Sydney," Jacob explained, "and he said the Kerrick family would take Roger as a jackaroo. Mary has given her consent, and we thought that Roger had best have plenty of medicine for his cough to take with him."

"Yes, he should," Stephanie agreed, looking at Roger and wondering about his condition for the long journey into the outback. The youth was happily excited about it, a grin on his thin, hollow features, and that meant much. But he was so frail and heartrendingly pitiful, bundled in oilskins over a coat that his mother had made for him from a blanket.

Stephanie turned to the stockman. "I'm certainly not questioning your commitment with Jacob," she said, "but I'd like to be sure you understand what is involved. For a time, Roger won't be able to do any strenuous work, and he'll need to have food that is especially rich."

"Aye, I can see that," Ruel replied. "Where he goes and what he does at the station will be up to Mistress Alexandra Kerrick, and I'll tell her what you said. But anyone who is kin to Dan Corbett is more than welcome and will be looked after properly at Tibooburra Station."

The man's attitude was as unequivocal as his words, satisfying Stephanie that Roger would have good care at the station. How well he would endure the journey remained in question, and as the conversation continued, her doubts on that point increased. The stockman explained that his party of stockmen and jackaroos had traveled to Sydney to buy sulfur and alum for sheep that were infected with a disease called scab. They had covered the vast distance in ten days, and expected to do the same on the return trip.

"I realize that you must return to the station as quickly as possible," Stephanie acknowledged, "but please do make the journey as easy as you can on Roger. Also, until he fully recovers, he must have his own eating utensils, and no one else should use them."

"Aye, I'll bear that in mind," Ruel told her. "There'll be some snow in the Blue Mountains, but once we're west of them, the journey should be easy enough. My party and the spare horses are waiting in Parramatta, and we set out from Sydney well before daybreak this morning so we could get across the mountains before dark tonight."

The last remark was a broad hint that the stockman was eager to be on his way, and Stephanie went inside to the surgery. Opening a cabinet, she had a sense of desperate finality as she selected a large bottle of camphor and tincture of lobelia. By the time the medicine was used up, Roger would be either much improved or he would be dead.

Stephanie went back outside and gave the medicine to Roger, making her farewells with him. He and the men turned their horses toward the road, and Stephanie stood on the porch and watched while they rode away.

When they disappeared from view, Stephanie stepped into her buggy and set out on her calls. The rainy day seemed even more bleak as she wondered about Roger's prospects. The youth, so weak and piteous, could be en route to a wasting death among strangers, and she was keenly aware that her own doubts were mild compared to those of Mary Corbett.

That concern remained very much on Stephanie's mind, and she stopped in at Corbett Farm during the afternoon to see Mary. Her assurances that Mary had done what was best for her son were useless, for Mary knew that. Logic was irrelevant to her feelings, those of a mother who was separated from her child in the uncertainty of whether he would even live or die.

During the following days, Stephanie stopped in and spent a few minutes with Mary whenever possible. Roger was never far from Stephanie's thoughts at other times, and she worried about how he was faring. She had a mental image of the frail, sickly youth struggling to find the strength to keep up with the party of stockmen and jackaroos on a narrow, remote track leading ever deeper into the wilderness of the outback.

On the tenth day after Roger's departure, Stephanie knew that he was either near or had arrived at the station. She hoped that Alexandra Kerrick would receive him with special understanding and sympathy.

The weak winter sun cast Alexandra Kerrick's shadow ahead of her as she rode up a gentle slope at one side of the home paddock and examined the grass. Recent rains had moistened the thirsty soil and produced green sprouts that would flourish in the warmth of spring and become rich graze for sheep. The condition of the grass here was excellent, but Alexandra wondered about its state elsewhere on the station.

Near the top of the slope, Alexandra reined up and gazed over the home paddock. It was as familiar to her as her own hand, yet the scene remained constantly fresh and new for her, a keen pleasure to contemplate. At most stations, the home paddock was a dusty plot set aside as a headquarters and an area for mustering sheep during shearing. At Tibooburra Station, it was a vast, grassy valley several miles in length and width.

Tibooburra Creek, a tree-lined stream that continued flowing during the most torrid, parched heat of summer, stretched the length of the valley. In the center of the valley was a low hill, the terrain forming a natural focus. At one side of it were the mustering pens and a large complex of station buildings that included the cookhouse, barracks, warehouses, and shearing shed. On the other side were orchards, vegetable gardens, and a row of neat, comfortable cottages for married stockmen. Farther down the creek was a village of wurlies, the residences of Aborigines living on the station.

The station house, surrounded by lawns and shade trees, stood on the hill. Three stories high, with wings reaching back on both sides, it was built of native granite. The entrance portico supported by columns was the only compromise to straight, unadorned lines that were at once severely plain and elegantly uncluttered. The effect was an aura of commanding authority, the huge stone mansion dominating the surrounding countryside.

The home paddock evoked something more than the scene in view. It conveyed a sense of its function as the heart and nerve center of the vast sheep station that reached across the distance in all directions, an area measured in square miles rather than acres. The immense expanse of the station often experienced several contrasting weather systems at the same time, and while the condition of the graze was excellent here, Alexandra was unsure if it was satisfactory elsewhere on the station.

Her horse perked its ears and gazed toward the track some two hundred yards away. Beginning at the foot of the hill where the house stood, the track led across the slope at the side of the valley. After crossing the rise, it stretched down through the southern paddocks of the station and then spanned hundreds of miles across the outback, joining other tracks and roads to eventually terminate at George Street in Sydney.

Riders, packhorses, and spare animals filed into view on the track, Ruel Blake and his party crossing the top of the rise. Alexandra turned her horse and cantered toward them, noticing the youth who was wearing a coat that was made from a blanket rather than sheepskins. Then she drew closer and saw that he was very ill, his face like skin stretched over a skull, with the telltale unhealthy flush of consumption on his cheeks.

The men and youths doffed their hats in a chorus of greetings as she rode up to them. Then Ruel explained the circumstances that had led him to bring the youth to the station. "Seeing as how he's Dan's cousin," Ruel concluded, "I opined that you and Mr. Kerrick would want him here."

"Yes, we certainly do," Alexandra confirmed, then turned to Roger: "Welcome to Tibooburra Station, Roger. What do you think of it thus far?"

A hacking cough shook the youth's frail body as he searched for words, then: "It's like a kingdom, mo'm," he responded, "with that great, grand house across the way as its castle."

"That suffices for a favorable impression," Alexandra remarked, amused. "Not everyone finds the outback agreeable, Roger, but your age is in your favor. Most of those who find it distressful are adults."

"I believe he'll abide," Ruel offered. "It didn't seem to vex him so far. Until he's better, he's to use only his own tucker tack, and he's supposed to have the most sustaining tucker that can be had."

"Yes, I'm familiar with practices for consumptives," Alexandra told him. "For now, find Roger a place in the barracks, and tell the cook that he's to have all the eggs, meat, cheese, and treacle he can eat. Instead of tea, he's to drink buttermilk." She turned to the youth: "You might know it better as sourdook, Roger. We use it mostly to fatten pigs, but it's very healthful. Be assured that having your own plate and such is no reflection upon you personally. It doesn't set you apart from everyone else any more than a bandage on a cut or something of the sort."

"Aye, I know, mo'm," he acknowledged. "Mistress Thorpe told me the same, and she also said I was to have sourdook with my tucker. We used it to fatten pigs too, but it goes down good with me."

Alexandra nodded in satisfaction and turned back to Ruel. "Did you have any difficulty in getting the alum and sulfur?" she asked.

"No, mo'm," he replied, smiling and shaking his head wryly. "But me and my mob here have spent the best part of a month and run thirty horses into the ground whilst getting it. Moreover, it cost many times more than that two score of sheep with scab are worth. All in all, it would have made better sense to knock them on the head and be done with them."

"Better sense only in terms of time, trouble, and guineas," Alexandra pointed out. "There are higher considerations that are the values here. We're not only graziers, Ruel. We're the guardians of our flocks here at Tibooburra Station, and there's a great difference between the two."

Ruel stroked his beard, listening, then shrugged. "Mistress Kerrick, I don't understand what you said any more than a kookaburra would," he admitted. "But I've got to say that saving those sheep gives me a kind of satisfaction in my heart. It's one not easy to come by, and one that no amount of good sense would give me. Are those scabby sheep still being kept up in the corner of Steeples Paddock away from the others?"

"Yes, send that sulfur and alum up there straightaway, along with a keg of whale oil to mix it into a paste," she told him.

Ruel and the others doffed their hats again and rode on up the track, Roger grinning over his shoulder at Alexandra. Already fond of the youth, she smiled warmly in response. She wanted to think that the time lying ahead would give her feelings for him the opportunity to grow into affection, rather than turning them into the fuel for sorrow.

The vast, illimitable expanse of the outback was different from other places, not only in what the senses could detect. Alexandra had both experienced in herself and observed in others that it exerted subtle, ineffable forces upon those who lived in it. Those influences were nourishing for some, but a virulent poison that affected the minds of others. She earnestly hoped that Roger possessed the characteristics which would enable him to feed upon that mystic source of energy, becoming healthy and strong. The only alternative was another tombstone in the station cemetery.

Chapter Five

Stephanie stopped her buggy several yards from the barn and peered at the wide double doors. Heavy rain was falling and the late afternoon light was dim, but she clearly saw that the latch on the doors was ajar. And she distinctly recalled that it had been closed that morning.

For a fortnight or longer, things in the kitchen had been moved slightly from how she had left them. It would have been unnoticeable but for the fact that she and her father had always kept everything in precise order to save time and effort in doing household tasks. Nothing had been taken except possibly from the pantry, which was so congested with foodstuffs that a large amount would have to be missing to make an evident difference. But someone had been in the kitchen, touching and moving things.

Now it appeared that someone had gone into the barn and pulled the doors shut, but the latch had failed to close completely. Housebreaking and thievery were virtually unknown in Wallaby Track, but children played pranks. Speculating that some child had been prowling about her property and was now in the barn, Stephanie walked through the rain to it.

After quietly raising the latch, Stephanie threw the barn doors open. The action startled someone, Stephanie hearing a movement in the dark hay loft above the stalls. She stepped into the barn, calling out: "Whoever is there, come down here and identify yourself!"

The hay stirred, but instead of a child, an adult moved to the ladder, then down it. A short, stout Aborigine woman emerged from the shadows, trembling with cold and fear. In her early twenties, she wore a coat and dress of cheap fabric and a maid's mobcap. Stephanie detected a meaningful fleshiness in the woman's face. Her full figure largely concealed it, but she was in an advanced stage of pregnancy.

"My name is Yulina, mo'm," she said, her voice quavering. "I've been taking some tucker from your house, but I beg you not to call the constables. I'll be on my way and cause you no further trouble."

Stephanie smiled warmly, stepping closer. "I'm Stephanie Thorpe, and you're more than welcome to the food," she told the woman. "I have no intention whatsoever of summoning the constables."

Peering at Stephanie in the dim light, Yulina seemed to be yearning for kindness so intensely that she had difficulty accepting it. "Aye, I've heard of you," she mused softly. "Everyone speaks well of you."

"I do my best to earn people's trust and regard," Stephanie acknowledged. "Why are you here in my barn, and where is your home?"

"For some years, I've worked at Brendell Farm," Yulina replied in the same soft tone. "I left there a fortnight ago, and I've been staying here because . . ." Her voice faded, her eyes filling with tears and her chin trembling, then: "Because I was afraid of what would happen to me!" she wailed, her tears overflowing. "Let me hide in your house, and I'll work my fingers to the bone for you. Please let me hide in your house."

Stricken with pity, Stephanie put her arms around Yulina. "Of course you can stay at my home," she assured the woman. She started to ask Yulina why and of whom she was afraid, then decided to let it wait until a more appropriate time. "You're welcome to stay at my home, and you'll be safe from any harm, because I'll protect you."

"I'm most grateful indeed," Yulina said earnestly, smiling happily and wiping away her tears. "I'll work ever so hard for you."

"No, you'll be staying as my friend," Stephanie told her firmly, making the point clear. "I don't want a maid, but I'll be pleased to have your company and friendship. Now go to the house while I attend to my horse. This barn is a very unsuitable place for a woman with child."

The happiness wreathing Yulina's features disappeared, replaced by misgivings. "It won't be an inconvenience for you," she promised. "But how did you know? Most people can't tell that I'm with child."

"If you've heard of me, you must know that I'm a midwife," Stephanie pointed out, laughing. "I'd be a poor midwife if I couldn't recognize pregnancy in a woman who is near to term. And childbirth is my life's work, anything but an inconvenience to me. Now go to the house."

Her round, pretty face radiant with joy, Yulina hurried out of the barn toward the house. Stephanie led her horse into the barn, and as she attended to it and the other one, she pondered what the small woman had said. It was common knowledge in the valley that Brendell mistreated his employees, but Yulina had fled from something more than that. She had spoken about a place to hide, in fear of her life. Moreover, her behavior and comments about her pregnancy had revealed that she had been hiding it from others.

Wondering who the father of the baby was, Stephanie started to leave the barn. Then she paused, recalling something that answered all the questions about Yulina. During the past few weeks, several people had mentioned having heard that Brendell's wife was en route to Australia.

In the light of that, Yulina's fear and the fact that she had concealed her pregnancy explained who had fathered her baby. "That swine!" Stephanie exclaimed. "That depraved, contemptible swine!"

Seething with rage, Stephanie stood in the barn doorway, the rainwater streaming off the eaves in the fading twilight. Even more than anger, she felt pity for Yulina, the victim of Brendell's lust, and she was intensely thankful that the woman had found her way to the house. She closed the barn doors, then walked through the rain toward the house.

Instead of being dark and uninviting, the kitchen seemed an entirely different place than before, but not only from the bright light of the lamps and roaring fire. Yulina's buoyant happiness suffused the atmosphere with jubilantly high spirits as she bustled about preparing dinner. "The pantry is more like a store," she commented. "I was spoiled for choice on what to cook, so I decided upon something quick for this evening."

"That's all I ever cook, so I'm sure it'll be more than satisfactory," Stephanie replied, taking off her oilskins. "There are bedrooms just up the hall, and I'll put bedding into one of them for you."

Yulina smiled her thanks, stirring a pan. After hanging up her oilskins, coat, and hat, Stephanie went to the linen closet in the hall for sheets and blankets. She carried them into one of the bedrooms, then kindled a fire in the fireplace to warm the room. By the time she returned to the kitchen, it was filled with appetizing aromas of food cooking.

More than preparing a meal quickly, Yulina had worked with astonishing speed, and she was highly skilled in cookery. Dried beef simmered in thick, savory gravy, smoked fish basted in butter sauce, and vegetables steamed in pans. A selection of pickles and relishes was on the table, and Yulina had made a confection of dried fruit and honey for dessert.

When the meal was ready, Stephanie set the table and helped dish up the food. The delicious dinner was an enjoyable change from her usual meals, and Yulina was ravenously hungry after weeks of inadequate food. The woman also had an even deeper hunger of the spirit, a need to reach out to others, and she kept up a lively conversation while they ate.

Her attractive features reflected a disarmingly open, guileless nature that was borne out in her conversation, and she had a cheerful, optimistic outlook on life. Replying to Stephanie's compliments on the food, Yulina explained how she had learned cookery by working with a cook, and she related amusing incidents that had occurred before Brendell had bought the farm where she had worked. Stephanie could see obvious gaps in Yulina's story as she skipped over unpleasant matters.

Intending to examine Yulina later, Stephanie guided the discussion toward the woman's pregnancy to find out her attitude toward it. An unwanted pregnancy usually resulted in a difficult delivery of a baby that became weak and sickly from lack of loving care, but Stephanie found that Yulina was looking forward with keen anticipation to having the baby.

She talked about it excitedly, smiling happily. "I don't have any relatives now, but I will have when it's born," she explained. "The only other thing I'd like is for it to have two names. But I have only one myself, so it'll have to make do with the same."

"Thurlow Brendell is the father, isn't he," Stephanie remarked.

Yulina sobered, then nodded. "Aye, and he said that he would throttle me if I told anyone that he came to my room at night," she replied. "He found out that I'm with child, and his wife will soon be here. I left the farm because I feared what he would do to keep her from finding out."

"I wouldn't credit him with any compunctions," Stephanie mused, "but taking a life entails risks that he would probably avoid. Most likely, he would have sent you to some remote place, but he can do nothing now. If you wish to take legal measures against him, I'll help you."

Yulina was appalled, shaking her head rapidly. "No, no, I don't want to do anything like that!" she exclaimed fearfully. "All I want is to hide from him until this passes and he won't do anything to me."

"He can do nothing now to harm you, Yulina," Stephanie told her firmly. "You're perfectly safe here, because I'll protect you."

Yulina forced a smile and expressed her thanks, but it was evident that she was unconvinced, in terror of Brendell. Stephanie dropped the subject, the conversation turning to other things. When the meal was finished, Stephanie filled a basin with hot water and found a towel, then took Yulina to the woman's bedroom up the hall to examine her.

The pregnancy was in the ninth month and perfectly normal, the baby's heartbeat strong. Yulina had only general ideas of how childbirth occurred, and Stephanie brought an anatomy text from the surgery and used the illustrations in it to show Yulina what would happen. Stephanie also promised that when the baby was at full term, she would arrange her calls so she could check on Yulina every few hours and watch for her labor to begin.

When they returned to the kitchen, Stephanie made notes on her calls in her daybook while Yulina washed the dishes and set about doing the laundry. For the first time in weeks, Stephanie was able to completely catch up on the entries in her daybook. In addition, instead of passing in a rush of household tasks, the evening was long and leisurely for her.

More than that, the ghosts of painful memories that had whispered to her in the lonely, hollow echoes of the house were smothered by warmly comforting companionship. The change was profound, making the evening keenly enjoyable instead of an ordeal. The somber aura of the prison on the hill still reached out to her through the night, as she knew it always would, but it was less oppressive than before, easier for her to endure.

The rain ended on the same night that Yulina became Stephanie's companion and a part of the household. The following days were bright after morning fog dispersed, the feeble winter sun beaming down from clear skies. The wind turned to the west, drying the muddy roads and fields.

For Stephanie, the days had a glow of contentment far brighter than the winter sunshine. Yulina was up before dawn every morning, preparing a hearty breakfast, and she had a delicious dinner waiting each evening when Stephanie returned home. The household chores were always done, and the house was never dark and lonely, its windows gleaming through the twilight.

Most gratifying of all, a firm bond of friendship formed between Stephanie and the small, winsome woman. Stephanie candidly acknowledged that she had a contained disposition, a serious outlook on life. Through both her profession and her nature, her milieu included a region that lay between life and death, which made her contemplative. Yulina was the perfect foil for her. The woman's outgoing, cheerful personality was always uplifting, making the evening hours richly enjoyable.

Winter illnesses diminished during the dry weather, and Stephanie's practice expanded. She delivered a baby for a new patient in Parramatta and acquired other new patients at a fishing village at Broken Bay, north of Wallaby Track. Few were able to pay in cash, and buying fresh supplies of several drugs took much of the money that Stephanie had on hand. She was even more short of time, but Gideon Mundy went to the chemist in Sydney for her and brought back the drugs when he made a trip to the city.

Stephanie looked at Yulina's stomach each day to see if the baby was descending toward the pelvis, and much of their conversation during the evenings was about the baby. Unlike most expectant mothers, who speculated endlessly about the gender of their babies, Yulina was convinced that her baby would be a boy, and as an adult he would be a mechanic or in a trade that involved machinery.

When she explained her belief, which was based on the fact that she had been leaning across a mangle when the baby had moved the first time, Stephanie was concerned that Yulina might be disappointed. "You won't be sad if the baby happens to be a girl, will you?" she asked.

"I wouldn't be, but it'll be a boy," Yulina replied positively. "It'll be a boy, and I intend to call him John." She sighed and shrugged wistfully. "I do wish he could have two names," she added. "I'd like to have two myself, but most of all, I'd like for him to have two."

The woman had mentioned that before, and Stephanie pondered for a moment, then: "You could give it my family name," she suggested. "If the baby is indeed a boy, John Thorpe is a name that has a pleasing ring."

Yulina was speechless for a moment, then her eyes flooded with tears of gratitude. "You would do that for my baby?" she asked softly. "You would give it your second name? Could you actually make it his name?"

"Yes, to each of your questions," Stephanie told her, gratified by her reaction. "I'll be more than happy to do it, and I can do it easily. I report births to the district clerk, and I'll enter the name on the registry. Once that is done, it will be the baby's name by law."

Yulina tried to stammer her appreciation until Stephanie shushed her, telling her that the issue was settled. It remained very much on Yulina's mind, however, the woman seething with such delight that Stephanie wished it had occurred to her earlier to make the offer.

As Stephanie and Yulina prepared to go to bed, a less pleasant subject came up. Yulina mentioned that the tea and sugar in the kitchen needed to be replenished, and she wanted Stephanie to get it from the village store. The woman was still terrified of leaving the house, fearing that Brendell would find out where she was.

Stephanie agreed to go to the store, then dropped the subject. Each time she had tried to assure Yulina that she was safe, the woman had avoided debating it, but she remained convinced that no one could protect her from Brendell. Stephanie yearned to confront him with what he had done and settle the issue, but she knew it would distress Yulina.

Before going to bed, Stephanie went into the surgery to get money from the cash box for the tea and sugar. The box was in a cabinet beside the account ledger for the year, reminding her that she was long overdue in posting the accounts up to date. It was a task that her father had always done, and ever since the day he had gone to the prison, she had been merely dropping money she collected from patients into the cash box.

It had been little of late, mostly because of the season. Many farmers had money at hand only during summer and early autumn, when the bulk of produce was sold. As she took the money out of the cash box, Stephanie resolved to post the accounts as soon as possible and make certain that she was collecting enough from patients to cover her expenses.

The next morning, she went to the store in the village and took the sugar and tea back to the house, then set out on her calls. It galled her for Yulina to be living in fear, as well as going without fresh air and exercise, all because of a man as despicable as Brendell. The temptation to confront him and end the situation, then tell Yulina later, was constrained by the fact that he would probably accuse her of having taken valuables from his house when she fled. That validated the woman's fears, and it also made the situation just that much more irritating for Stephanie.

The possibility of avoiding that danger presented itself during the afternoon, while Stephanie was at Bledcoe Farm. Having delivered a baby at the farm a few days before, she had stopped in briefly to check on it and Alma Bledcoe. During the conversation, the subject of Brendell somehow came up, and Alma continued going on about him.

"Bad cess on him," the woman grumbled. "He's done nothing but inflict misery ever since he became magistrate. And pity those who work for him. A maid at his farm up and left, and he's trying to find her."

Stephanie had been examining the baby and listening absently, and suddenly she was all ears. "Where did you hear about that?" she asked.

"There's a notice in the newspaper," Alma replied. She stood up from the kitchen table and stepped to a shelf beside the fireplace, then rummaged through newspapers and magazines stacked on it. "The weekly newspaper that's printed in Parramatta. I take it you don't read that one?"

"No, I get one published in Sydney when I buy a newspaper," Stephanie told her. "And that's been rare enough of late."

"This is it," Alma said, separating a newspaper from the others. "The notice is on the last page."

Stephanie handed the baby to Alma, then unfolded the newspaper. The notice was brief, only two sentences. The first described Yulina and stated that she was missing from Brendell Farm, and the second offered a reward of one guinea for information on her whereabouts.

The significant fact was what the notice failed to state, and Stephanie wondered if it placed Brendell at a sufficient disadvantage for her to confront him. Similar notices were in newspapers from time to time, virtually all charging the missing employee with stealing valuables or some other offense. Brendell had been very cautious, not wanting to reveal more than was absolutely necessary, but the lack of an accusation in the notice could cast strong doubts on any charges that he might make in the future.

If he did accuse Yulina, however, the extreme anxiety it would create for the woman made Stephanie hesitant. She pondered it when she left the farm and drove toward her next call, trying to keep her feelings from leading her into a rash decision. That was difficult, because her own hatred for Brendell was blended into smoldering resentment that the helpless, innocent Yulina was still being victimized by the man.

The firm, final decision came abruptly, like a thunderbolt, and she was burning with a raging need to face Brendell down, to vent her hatred and end Yulina's torment. She was on the west side of the river, and she cracked her whip over her horse's back, driving rapidly toward the bridge in the center of the valley to cross over to the main road.

Miles later, her horse still trotting swiftly, Stephanie passed Mundy Farm and then a side road between it and Brendell Farm. Then she turned in at the lane leading to the house. The original farmhouse had been demolished and replaced by one consistent with Brendell's image of himself. An attempt at an English country home in pseudo-Tudor style, it was brashly new, with weak, narrow bays and ornamental chimneys that were too fussy.

The housekeeper, a gaunt woman who looked long-suffering, at first refused to say where Brendell was at present. Stephanie seethed with impatience to face him, and she shouldered the door open and stepped inside. Surprised and flustered, the housekeeper backed away. She was tall, but Stephanie was inches taller, gazing down at her and moving in close.

"I have no wish to add to what must be your constant misery in this wretched house," Stephanie told her softly, their noses an inch apart. "But I must know where he is, and you must tell me."

The woman shook her head apprehensively, her back against the entry wall. "No, I'm not allowed to tell anyone who is unexpected, or—"

"Tell me!" Stephanie broke in insistently. "I have only sincere pity and goodwill for you personally, but you must tell me where he is!"

The housekeeper gave up, almost in tears. "Go around

the house and take the road past the barns," she whimpered forlornly. "He's back in the fields with some hired men. Please don't let him know I told you."

"Of course I won't," Stephanie assured her, turning away. "I'm sorry for distressing you, and I truly hope your lot in life improves."

The housekeeper stammered an incoherent response of good wishes and closed the door as Stephanie went back out. She jumped into her buggy, cracking the whip, and drove swiftly up the lane that curved around the house. It divided, one fork ending at stables and the other turning into a road that led past barns and then through the crop fields and pastures.

A mile from the house and barns, the road went up a low rise and joined a more narrow one that branched off to the left. It led down to the public road between the farm and Mundy Farm, where several men were repairing a gate that opened onto the public road. Brendell was watching the men work, his squire's garb and obesity identifying him from a distance.

Stephanie drove down the road toward the men, studying Brendell. He was in one of his usual poses, hands on hips, feet planted wide apart, and his riding crop under his arm. As she gazed at him, it was suddenly more than merely seeing him. It was an insight, a revelation that encompassed the man, his house, his position in the community, and the other accoutrements he had gathered around himself as a way of life in Wallaby Track.

All that was a facade, like a displaying peacock. Seen from behind, the bird was absurd, its rump perched on ungainly stilts for legs and sparsely covered with dull, ragged feathers. Stephanie realized that Brendell could be a threat, but he was too pathetic an empty shell to be her enemy. Her enemy in life was immense, formidable, invincible—a parasite that fed on her. A cancer of the spirit lying in an inaccessible region, it bound her own mind to a beloved being that was trapped for all eternity in the prison, in a purgatory of torment between life and death.

Brendell turned as she drove up, a dark scowl spreading over his thick, coarse features under the network of red lines. He came toward her in his usual belligerent charge, head and shoulders thrust forward. Stephanie stepped out of her buggy and met him halfway, confronting his glare with a gaze of disdain that stopped him in his tracks like an invisible wall.

In the battle of wills, control over the situation slipped away from him and he struggled to grasp it back: "Who told you I was here?" he blustered. "And what the bloody hell are you doing trespassing on my property?"

"Stop making a fool of yourself out of your own mouth," she shot back. "Any simpleton would know that my being here isn't a trespass. How I found you is irrelevant, and I came here to have a word with you."

A sound of suppressed mirth from her quick response rose among the men working on the gate a few yards away, and Brendell whirled toward them, his face crimson. The men bent over their task, busily hammering at the thick boards. Brendell ground his teeth in rage as he turned back to Stephanie. "Well, what did you come here to talk to me about then?" he demanded.

"A friend of mine," she replied evenly. "A woman named Yulina. Her whereabouts are none of your concern, but to answer the question posed in the notice you placed in the newspaper, she lives at my house."

Brendell's ugly face betrayed uneasiness, which he tried to cover with a show of confidence. "She's a fitting friend for the likes of you," he sneered. "She's a thief who fled with part of the silver service from my house, and now I know where to send the constables!"

"You'll be hoist with your own petard," Stephanie warned him. "I'll see to it that the matter is settled by a jury in open court, with the eyes of New South Wales looking on. You can explain why you failed to accuse her in your newspaper notice, and your household staff will be subpoenaed to testify whether any silver is missing. Moreover, Yulina will be there for all to see what she took with her, or rather within her, when she left your house."

Brendell tried to conceal his disquiet, and also tried to back away from his threat without retreating: "I wasn't going to send her to prison," he growled. "I only meant to send her to a farm near Newcastle, where she couldn't steal anything and run away again. But if she's settled in with you and makes no display of herself, mayhap I'll think again."

"No, that won't suffice," Stephanie told him. "I want this matter to be settled once and for all, here and now."

"By God, you can't lay demands on me," he snarled defensively. "I'll decide in due course, and you'll learn about it then."

"No, that will not do," Stephanie insisted, taking advantage of his uncertainty and forcing the issue. "You've accused my friend of thievery, and if you don't refer it to the authorities, then I shall in order to clear her good name. As an alternative, you can retract your accusation and assure me that you will never cause her further trouble."

The hired men at the gate had fallen silent, listening and waiting for Brendell's answer. As he spun around toward them again, they resumed hammering busily; then he turned back to Stephanie. The web of broken veins stood out in a brighter crimson on his choleric features, and he trembled in the throes of inner conflict, violently opposed to surrendering.

Prudence won out in his internal struggle, and he became sullenly subdued. "She stole naught," he grudgingly admitted in a choked voice. "So long as she does nothing to bother me, I'll cause her no trouble."

Nodding in satisfaction, Stephanie started to turn to her buggy, then looked at Brendell again. In defeat he was even more obviously an empty shell, without moral purpose or meaning in his life. At times she had disliked patients, but she had attended to them with dedicated care, her responsibilities toward others unaffected by her feelings. She knew that ignoring Brendell in his need would be a betrayal of her own humanity.

"You should try to see yourself as though from a distance," she advised him, speaking softly so the men at the gate were unable to hear her. "We are all mortal, treading a path to a tombstone. Our destination is set, but what we leave in our wake is our choice. I've seen with my own eyes that the suffering we create among others becomes ours at the great crossing over. As one human being to another, take care how you go on."

For a brief moment he listened and took it to heart, and his eyes were hollow with apprehension. Then he exploded in rage, rejecting the assault on the foundations of his life. "Who the bloody hell are you to lecture me?" he roared. "Look after your own paltry affairs, and I'll see to mine! Now get off my property, and don't set foot on it again!"

Satisfied that she had fulfilled any and all responsibilities, Stephanie met his anger with an unwavering gaze until he subsided into glowering silence. Then she stepped into her buggy, turning toward the road, and the hired men dragged the broken gate to one side for her. As she passed through the gate to the road, they grinned at her surreptitiously.

Stephanie drove toward the main road to continue with her calls, happily looking forward to at last convincing Yulina that she was safe and had no need to hide from Brendell. As for herself, Stephanie knew that she would have to be on guard against him. While she was too contemptuous of him to regard him as her enemy, it was certain that she was his.

Going to Brendell Farm made her late in completing her calls, and dusk faded into darkness while Stephanie was driving home from the last one. The night was dark, the moon and stars obscured by high clouds in an indication that the weather might change. The kitchen windows glowed invitingly in the frigidly cold darkness when Stephanie drove into the barnyard, and she hurriedly attended to the horses and then went to the house.

It took several minutes to overcome Yulina's shock and fear when Stephanie first began explaining what she had done, but the woman finally became convinced. Shrieking with delight, she raced to Stephanie and hugged her. Stephanie dismissed the small woman's profuse thanks, telling Yulina that she had done no more than what one friend should do for another.

Dinner was as delicious as usual, with tangy mint sauce to accompany the thick, flavorful slices of lamb roast, well-seasoned vegetables, and bread fresh from the oven. It was even more enjoyable than usual due to Yulina's exuberant happiness, but when it was finished, Stephanie recalled that she needed to post the account ledger. She resigned herself to the task, going into the surgery to get the ledger and the cash box.

In the still, dark front of the house, the wind outside became audible, and like the clouds that Stephanie had noticed, it portended a change in the weather. It was only a whisper, but it came in gusts and gathered strength. When she returned to the kitchen and began copying the names from her daybook into the account ledger, the wind gradually grew louder.

Some patients had paid for treatments, but far too few for her to have any difficulty in remembering who they were and the amounts. After writing in the amounts, Stephanie glanced through the pages for the previous months, and they highlighted a problem that she recently had begun realizing. Some men in the valley had always been reluctant to consult her regarding intimate personal complaints, and they evidently were going to doctors in Parramatta. As a result of that and the scarcity of money during winter, her income was far below what she and her father had earned.

Stephanie leafed through the ledger to the pages for expenses. On one for the household, she entered the amounts for staples and a few other things she had bought. Then she turned to the pages for professional expenses and wrote in the cost of the drugs that Gideon Mundy had brought from the chemist in Sydney. Then she thumbed through the previous pages.

Suddenly she froze, gazing at an entry with a sinking sensation in the pit of her stomach. On the first day of April, her father had paid the quarterly rates, a property tax levied on landowners. A payment had been due on the first of July, which had passed over a week before.

The amount was seven guineas, and Stephanie hastily opened the cash box. Even as she began counting the money, she knew that her house would now be on a list of properties in arrears that was kept at the district clerk's office. Anyone could pay the rates, then secure a lien on the house and begin legal action to evict her. Brendell had acquired several properties by that means, proving that he checked the list periodically.

The money totaled almost nine guineas, and Stephanie replaced it in the box. She was certain that Brendell was unaware that her rates were overdue, for his attitude had revealed no satisfaction over a way to strike back at her. If she went to the district clerk's office the first thing the next morning and paid the rates, her house would be safe.

Safe only for the present, however, with another payment due in less than three months. The threat was far more serious to Stephanie than merely having property at risk. The house was her home in every meaning of the word, fulfilling deep emotional needs. It gave her a sense of security, as well as a point of reference around which to organize her life, and there were also practical considerations. Her house was essential to her practice, and she now had a moral obligation to provide a home for Yulina.

Studying the ledger, Stephanie tried to think of some solution to the difficulty. She knew that Gideon Mundy and others would lend her money, but that was out of the question. Borrowing money would only lead to a quagmire of steadily increasing debt, because she was unsure of when or even if she could repay it. The problem was the difference between her income and expenses, and the only way to solve it was to close that gap.

Yulina went to her room for the night, and the wind seemed louder once she was alone. It moaned around the house and rustled the trees while she pondered, nothing coming to mind. When she went to bed, she listened to the wind and continued musing worriedly, then finally thought of one remotely possible solution before she fell asleep.

The next morning, the wind howling around the house appeared to herald more than a mere change in weather. The most powerful storms came from the sea, the direction of the wind. When she drove up to the village, Stephanie saw that the storm was indeed one that had gathered force in the far, open reaches of the ocean. The wind was still increasing, bludgeoning the trees and driving dark, low masses of clouds across the sky.

At the district clerk's office, Stephanie discovered that Tipton had kept her house off the list of properties whose rates were in arrears. "Thank you very much," she said gratefully, placing the money on his desk. "That was most kind of you, Tipton, and I'll pay the rates now."

Tipton began filling out a receipt for the money. Drafts from the wind stirred papers on his desk, the buffeting gusts rattling the windows. Stephanie looked out the window at the leaves and other debris flying through the air, waiting until he finished the receipt and gave it to her, then she asked him about the possible solution for her problem in paying the rates.

"My financial situation is very uncertain," she explained. "If I disposed of the acreage around my house, that would lower the overall value of the property and also the rates, wouldn't it?"

Tipton shook his head regretfully. "Only an assessor could be precise," he replied, "but it would amount to only a few pence. Your rates are based on the value of your house, which is a large one."

Stephanie forced a smile, trying to conceal her disappointment. "Well, perhaps I'll think of another way to deal with the problem."

"I sincerely hope so, but your property will never be on the list of those with rates in arrears," Tipton assured her. "However, if someone asks about your property, I'll have to reveal its status."

Stephanie nodded in understanding, the last comment an obvious warning about Brendell. She exchanged a word of farewell with Tipton, then stepped into the outer office and crossed it. As she opened the front door, she grabbed it against a blast of wind that tried to fling it wide open. She went outside, the wind whipping her coat, and tugged the door closed.

Pulling her coat closer, Stephanie trudged through the wind to her buggy. The thick, black clouds had turned the day dark, and the landscape writhed under the lashing of the shrieking wind. Trees thrashed wildly, leaves and branches flew through the air, and shingles on roofs stirred. Only the prison was unaffected. The towering, massive structure was impervious to the gale battering impotently against its dark stone walls.

While driving out of the village, Stephanie glimpsed flocks of birds riding the wind past the hill. They were storm petrels fleeing from the coast and taking shelter on the river. The full brunt of the storm was now making landfall, and it promised to be a savagely violent one.

Chapter Six

"It would be nigh onto impossible to find a place more different from Britain than this, wouldn't it, Mr. Brendell?"

Eric Brendell was studying the scenery as the ship *Leander* moved up the fjordlike harbor of Port Jackson toward Sydney Cove. The man who had spoken to him was Reuben Kelburn, an amiable, bright-faced sailor in his late teens whom Eric had talked with occasionally during the voyage. "Yes, that's true," Eric agreed. "It's also very impressive, isn't it?"

Reuben grinned, nodding emphatically. "Aye, it's mightily pleasing to the eye, even if it is passing strange. I suppose you have a home, as well as a situation and such as that awaiting you here."

"No, I'll be on my own," Eric told him. "I plan to establish some sort of business that has a good promise of being profitable."

The sailor hesitated, puzzled, then: "Well, you have your stepmother with you," he pointed out. "That led me to think that you would have a situation with your father awaiting you here."

"Her brother heard that I was coming to Australia and asked me to escort her," Eric explained. "It would have been difficult to refuse."

"Aye, that's true," Reuben agreed. He glanced over his shoulder as an officer called to him, then turned to go. "Well, I'd best keep busy, or I'll be on anchor watch all the time we're in port."

As the sailor hurried away, Eric turned back to the rail and gazed at the shoreline in fascination. As Reuben had said, it was entirely different from Britain. The wind helping the tide push the *Leander* up the harbor had the chill of winter, even though it was August. On the cold, cloudless afternoon, the sky was alive with colorful galahs, lyrebirds, and other birds that looked more appropriate to the tropics. The trees were in foliage in midwinter, eucalypts shedding bark and retaining leaves during all seasons.

The contrast with all he had ever known made the surrounding scene even more appealing to Eric, and he was confident of building himself a productive, enjoyable life in his new home. Twenty-five years old, with a range of skills learned during years of managing his maternal uncle's farms, he was over six feet tall and weighed two hundred pounds. His share of the increase in profits from the farms during his management, one hundred and eighty guineas in gold, was in a money belt under his shirt.

The ship teemed with activity, the crew preparing to anchor, and Eric decided to see if his stepmother was ready to disembark. Making his way past sailors running to and fro on the deck, he crossed it to the bulkhead below the quarterdeck and went into the cabin passageway. He stepped down it to his stepmother's cabin and knocked, and a moment later she opened the door. In her forties, Ursula Brendell was a plain, stolid woman with features that reflected a self-centered personality. However, Eric knew that she had been extremely attractive to his father through having been a moderately wealthy widow when they had married several years before.

Ursula nodded in reply to his question, pointing to her trunk beside the bunk. "Yes, I've packed everything back into my trunk, and it's ready for a sailor to carry out."

"There's no reason to trouble any of the crew with it," Eric told her, stepping into the cabin. "I'll carry it out."

The trunk was large and heavy, but Eric was muscular from years of having worked with as well as supervised hired men on his uncle's farms. He hoisted the trunk and then lugged it out of the cabin and up the passageway, sidling around other passengers stirring about in preparation to disembark. On the deck, with Sydney only a short distance ahead, sailors were swinging out boats on davits in readiness to lower them. Eric set the trunk beside the rail and went to get his own from his cabin.

After placing his trunk beside Ursula's, he went up to the quarterdeck to make his farewells with Captain Milo Chandler. The captain was fully occupied with shouting orders to the crew and helmsman, and Eric stood at one side and watched while Sydney and its port gradually came into view. Several ships were anchored in the harbor roads outside Sydney Cove, which was congested with vessels, and the captain kept the *Leander* moving straight ahead in the slackening tide to bring it alongside them.

Other passengers gathered on deck and the ship lost headway, sailors in the rigging furling the sails. Then a resounding cheer at the end of the long voyage rose among the passengers and crew when the anchors plunged into the water. As sailors began lowering the boats to start taking the passengers ashore, the captain crossed the quarterdeck to Eric.

Milo Chandler was a stocky man in his forties with a reserved, impatient disposition, but the warm smile on his tanned, bearded face reflected the close friendship that had developed between him and Eric. "For once, I have cause to regret the end of a voyage, Eric," he remarked. "Our many interesting conversations made it seem a short one."

"It seemed very short for me as well, and for the same reason, Milo," Eric replied. "I count myself fortunate in having been able to enjoy your company, and while that must end, I trust our friendship won't."

"It certainly won't for my part," Milo assured Eric. "I'll be unloading and then loading cargo for the next few days, and you're more than welcome to stay aboard whilst you're getting settled in here."

"I appreciate the offer, but the first thing I must do is see to it that my stepmother is rejoined with her husband. I'm unsure of how long that will take, but I may be gone from Sydney for a few days."

"Aye, you mentioned once that the place where you're taking her might be a considerable distance from Sydney, didn't you?" Milo recalled.

Eric nodded, explaining that he knew nothing about Wallaby Track except that it was a rural community. He and Milo continued talking while sailors on the main deck secured equipment and others rowed passengers to the docks in boats. When the boats returned for the last few passengers, Eric reluctantly drew the conversation to an end, commenting that it was time for him to take his stepmother ashore and find accommodations.

"Aye, it is," the captain agreed regretfully. "From what I've been told, the Sydney Arms is as good as any other lodgings in Sydney. Also, the scot and lot won't dip too deeply into your purse."

"That's where I'll go, then. I hope we'll meet again sometime, Milo."

"Aye, that's my fond wish as well, Eric. We probably will, because this is one of my ports of call from time to time."

They shook hands warmly, then Eric went down to the main deck and joined Ursula at the rail. He handed the trunks down to sailors in a boat, and she seated herself in a bosun's chair, a strip of canvas slung between ropes that were fastened to a rope through a pulley on a spar overhead. Sailors hauled on the rope, lifting her over the rail, then lowered her into the boat. When she seated herself, Eric jumped down into the boat.

As the sailors in the boat rowed away from the ship, Eric looked back and exchanged a final wave with Milo. Then the captain and the *Leander* were lost from view, the boat weaving around other vessels lying at anchor. At the docks, Eric summoned one of the carriages awaiting fares and helped the driver lift the trunks to the top of the carriage. The vehicle made its way through the congestion on the frontage street, then turned into a wide, busy street leading back from the docks.

Eric's impatience to look around in the city made the short drive to the Sydney Arms seem longer. It was a large, three-story hotel, filling a corner of an intersection in the business district. After registering at the desk in the lobby, Eric took Ursula to her room with her trunk, then put his trunk in his room and hurried back downstairs. As the sunset faded into dusk, he walked through the streets exploring the city.

Although there were familiar aspects, it was different from any city he had ever seen. The cobblestone streets and half-timbered buildings were the same as in Britain, but their character was completely changed by the tangy scent of eucalypt in the air and the distinctive Australian accent that he heard on every side. At the inland edge of the city, he passed a market where farmers sold livestock and produce, then he turned back.

In the streets at the center of the city, doors were boarded up on a few firms that had gone out of business, and Eric noted them as a warning to take care in how he invested his money. On up the frontage street from Sydney Cove, he passed several dry docks where ships were repaired and refitted. One of them also was in financial straits, a sign stating that its tools and other equipment were to be sold at auction.

Fog drifted in from the harbor at nightfall, making the

darkness thicker as Eric walked back toward the hotel. When he reached it, other guests were filing into the dining room adjacent to the lobby. Feeling that he should, Eric went upstairs to Ursula's room and asked her if she wished to join him at dinner, but she declined, telling him that she had made arrangements for a maid to bring her meals to her room.

After an ample dinner of roast beef and vegetables, Eric set about finding out the location of Wallaby Track. The desk clerk in the lobby had only heard of it, and Eric went back outside and down the street to a public house he had passed. It was at the end of the block from the hotel, the lantern that illuminated its sign glowing through the foggy darkness.

Inside the public house, fumes of beer and spirits blended with a haze of tobacco smoke from clay pipes, and a loud murmur of conversation rose from the patrons. Eric made his way to an open space at the bar and ordered a mug of beer. When the barkeep brought the beer, Eric paid for it and glanced around. "Does anyone here happen to know the whereabouts of a place called Wallaby Track?" he asked the men at large.

"Aye, I do," the man beside Eric spoke up. Stocky and broad-shouldered, he turned with a friendly smile. "I have a cousin who lives there. It's no more than thirty miles to the north, but onto half again that far by road. The street out in front is George Street, and it turns into Parramatta Road out beyond the brickyard and market. Follow it, then take the road north from Parramatta, and you'll end up in Wallaby Track."

"That would take three hours or thereabouts by horse and much of a day by wagon, wouldn't it?" Eric mused. "The easiest and least expensive way of getting there would probably be to ask around at the market for someone from there who happens to have either spare horses or a wagon."

"Aye, it would," the man agreed. "My name's Fred Gillie, by the way."

"I'm Eric Brendell, and I'm very pleased to have met you, Fred," Eric replied. "And I appreciate the information."

Gillie's cordial manner suddenly evaporated, and he frowned suspiciously. "Brendell, did you say?" he growled. "Are you any kin to Thurlow Brendell, the magistrate at Wallaby Track?"

"He's my father," Eric acknowledged.

"By God, I wish I'd bloody known that before!" Gillie declared angrily. "You'd have got no flaming advice from me. Last summer, my cousin merely got into a bit of a ruction, and the magistrate fined him three guineas for public disorder. I'd sooner give a helping hand to Lucifer himself than aid either Thurlow Brendell or any of his kith and kin!"

Eric understood the man's feelings, but deeply resented being blamed for his father's actions. "Any trouble that you have with my father," he said coldly, "is between the two of you. The only trouble I deal with is my own, but I also stand ready to do so anytime it comes my way."

Nearby conversation died away, others turning to look, and two men who appeared to be Gillie's companions glared at Eric. The barkeep, a burly man with stolid, beefy features, moved down the bar. "We'll have no trouble in here," he announced firmly, glancing between Eric and Gillie.

"I've no wish for trouble," Eric told the barkeep, then gazed steadily at Gillie: "But as I said, I'm always ready to deal with it."

Gillie seethed with anger, his face flushed and his broad shoulders rigid, but as he studied Eric, his eyes revealed a wary reluctance to force the issue. Muttering under his breath, he turned away. Eric stepped around the crowded tables toward the door, leaving the public house.

The fog had thickened, turning the night into impenetrable darkness, and Eric found his way back up the street by walking on the edge of the foot pavement. His anger faded, replaced by disappointment. He had liked Fred Gillie and wished that they could have been friends.

Friends were important to him. His best friends had

been his aunt and uncle, who had provided him a place
to live, guidance as a youth, and employment as a man. He
had never had a home and a family, and even the closest
friendships had fallen far short of filling that void in his
life. As a substitute, he had turned to ambition, planning on
success and wealth, and he was determined to fulfill those
plans in Australia.

The next morning, Eric dressed in work clothing, putting
on dungaree trousers and shirt, heavy boots, a canvas coat,
and a hat with a wide brim. He folded away his wool suit
and greatcoat in his trunk, then left the hotel and walked
up George Street toward the market.

Like markets Eric had frequented in Britain, the near
side was a clutter of carts and wagons, where townspeople
and farmers bartered over cheese, eggs, vegetables, and
other produce. On the far side, owners and buyers debated
the merits of sheep, pigs, cattle, and horses. He walked
through the crowd, asking the farmers if they could provide
transportation to Wallaby Track. The first few shook their
heads; then he asked a portly, white-haired farmer beside
a cart filled with tubs of butter.

"No, but there must be someone here from Wallaby
Track who has a wagon," the man mused, glancing around.
Then he pointed to the other side of the market. "Aye,
there's Gideon Mundy, and he always brings a wagon to
haul things he buys when he comes to Sydney." Cupping
his hands around his mouth, the aged farmer bellowed in
a stentorian voice: "Gideon! This young fellow here needs
transport to Wallaby Track!"

The shout carried across the noisy market to a large,
bearded man who turned and beckoned. Eric thanked the
farmer, then walked across the market toward Gideon. The
man was accompanied by two younger men who were
obviously his sons, with similar facial characteristics and
the same tall, muscular frame. A fourth man with them was
small and thin, with a freckled face.

Gideon had just sold two bullocks and was folding the money into his purse as a man led the cattle away. The four men nodded amiably to Eric as he stepped up to them, and Gideon pointed to the others, introducing them: "These are my sons, Otis and Artis," he said. "That's Elmer Beasley, my son-in-law. So you want to go to Wallaby Track, do you?"

"Yes, that's right," Eric replied. "I'm Eric Brendell, and I need transport for my stepmother, Mistress Ursula Brendell."

The men's attitude cooled markedly and silence fell, which Eric had expected. In situations short of an outright feud, however, farmers were traditionally reluctant to refuse any reasonable request to assist a neighbor. The silence stretched out, Eric waiting to see what happened, and the three younger men watched Gideon and awaited his response.

After a moment, Gideon spoke in a guarded tone: "Aye, I've heard that Thurlow Brendell's wife was on her way here. It strikes me that he'd want to see to her transport himself."

"He probably would, if he knew she had arrived," Eric agreed. "Rather than bothering with messages, I intend to escort her to him with as little ado as possible, then be about my own affairs."

"Your own affairs?" Gideon mused curiously. "You don't intend to settle at Brendell Farm and take a hand with it? Why not?"

"For private reasons," Eric told him bluntly. "I'd more than welcome the opportunity to talk with you about Australia and a host of other things, but I don't discuss my private affairs with anyone."

The younger men frowned at the outspoken reply, but Gideon was more judicious. Instead of taking offense, he studied Eric thoughtfully. "Aye, you're right," he acknowledged. "I acted the stickybeak about something that doesn't concern me. I might think twice about helping Thurlow

Brendell, but that has naught to do with you or his wife. Where is she?"

"At the Sydney Arms."

"Very well, I'll be there within the hour. I need to buy a few oddments in the city, then I'll come there with my wagon."

"We'll be ready to leave, and I'm grateful for your help."

Gideon accepted the thanks with a nod, still studying Eric. The three younger men followed Gideon's lead, their attitude thawing, and they exchanged a word of farewell with Eric as he turned away.

When he returned to the hotel, Eric told Ursula about the arrangements and then lugged the trunks down to the lobby. He settled with the desk clerk, then carried the trunks out to the foot pavement, where Ursula joined him. Gideon and his sons came into view a short time later, riding up the street among the traffic, and Elmer followed them in a wagon.

They drew up at the curb, Eric introducing them to Ursula, then Gideon dismounted and beckoned Elmer down from the wagon. "Take my horse and ride on back to the farm with Otis and Artis, Elmer," he said. "Boys, tell your mother that I'll be home about suppertime."

Elmer stepped down from the wagon and mounted the horse, and he and the Mundy sons rode away as Gideon gave Eric a hand in loading the trunks into the wagon. Eric assisted Ursula up into it and seated her on a trunk, then joined Gideon on the seat at the front of the wagon.

Gideon snapped the reins and drove away from the hotel, guiding the team of horses into the flow of traffic. "I'm struck by the fact that you've no likeness at all to your father, Eric," he commented. "In fact, you're unlike most in respect to your size. There aren't many of a size with me and my boys, but you're even a bit taller than we are."

"I take after my mother's family," Eric explained. "Her brother is a farmer in Yorkshire, and I lived with his family from when I was a boy. People often thought he and I were father and son. That was partly due to the fact that he and my aunt treated me like a son. They made me manager of their farms not long after I finished school."

"I daresay they also did it because you could handle the work," Gideon remarked. "Do you plan to buy a farm here?"

"No, I intend to go into business. I like the farming life, but the profits from business enterprises are better and more certain."

"And they don't depend on the weather," Gideon added wryly. "What sort of business do you have in mind?"

"I hope to have various ones eventually, but I'd like to begin with a manufactory of some sort. But before I do anything, of course, I'll have to get settled and learn all I can about commercial affairs here."

Gideon nodded, agreeing that was a necessity. They continued talking as the wagon moved up the street, and Eric looked ahead in keen interest for his first view of the countryside beyond the edge of the city. Presently, the wagon passed the market and a brickyard across the street from it, and then George Street turned into Parramatta Road.

After the city fell behind, small farms at one side were similar to those of Britain, but the setting was totally different. On the other side of the road, the Parramatta River was lined by large eucalypts with their drooping, gray-green foliage. Rosellas, lorikeets, crested pigeons, and other birds brought the cool, bright day alive, and Eric gazed around in fascination. Even the light here seemed different, having a penetrating quality that etched every detail of the surroundings in intense clarity.

The wagon rattled and bumped over ruts as it moved on up the road, Gideon talking about local farming methods and other facts about Australia. It had become obvious that the farmer had chosen to drive the wagon himself in order for them to become acquainted, and Eric was pleased that he had. He liked Gideon, the man's attitude revealing that the feeling was mutual, and their conversation became increasingly friendly as the hours passed.

Near midday, the river curved away from the road and scattered houses replaced the farms, then the road led into a cobblestone street through Parramatta. It was an attractive town, the main street busy with traffic and lined with shops in neat half-timbered buildings. Thick trees enveloped the town, church spires and large stone buildings rising above them.

The Blue Mountains came into view, miles away to the west. Eric had read about the mountains, but like everything else he had seen since arriving, the descriptions had only hinted at the visual impact of the scenes. Swathed in a blue haze, the immense, rugged range filled the horizon, with rocky precipices towering three thousand feet above deep gorges. Eric knew that in the folds of the mountains was a narrow road that led across the lofty peaks to the town of Bathurst, the gateway to the vast outback.

At the western end of the street, Gideon turned the wagon onto a road leading to the north. Houses were on each side for a distance, many of freestone or half-timbered construction, and some built entirely of wood. All were tidy and well-kept, but Eric noticed that the lumber used in most of them was of a poor quality, the boards varying in length and thickness.

Gideon agreed ruefully when Eric mentioned the quality of the lumber. The farmer explained that there was a sawmill in Sydney, but elsewhere the lumber came from saw pits, the workers in them usually convicts on tickets of leave from confinement. "None of them are skilled, as you can see," he added, "and they only do it when they can't find other work."

"I can understand that," Eric remarked. "I've stood in a saw pit and pulled on one end of a whipsaw while sawdust rained down, and it wasn't very agreeable. Why don't people here buy lumber from the sawmill?"

"It serves carpenters, cabinetmakers, and such in the city

first," Gideon replied. "Others must take what's left, and that's scanty pickings. It also costs a pretty penny, and then there's the bother and expense of transporting it. Lumber from saw pits is cheap and plentiful, because timber is as common as dirt here. You can see that by looking about."

Eric agreed, glancing around. With the town falling behind, on each side was grassy, open forest where cattle were pastured. Most of the trees had been girdled years before so the grass would flourish, and even though they were now excellent, well-seasoned wood, few had been felled and hauled away. Eric realized that he had identified a need for a product that was not being fulfilled, the basis for a successful business; then he put the thought aside and continued talking with Gideon about other things.

At farms set back from the road, few crop fields had been tilled all the way up to the fences. That was a contrast to Britain, where every inch of land was priceless, and Gideon explained that land was relatively inexpensive in the rural areas. The farmer described the various holdings he owned in Wallaby Track, then talked about two in particular.

Both properties were forested, but Gideon wanted to pasture cattle on one and grow crops on the other. He explained that he had hired a crew consisting of five men and a cook to clear the land, but the work had been proceeding at a snail's pace. "Like any oddment workers," he went on, "they need a firm hand. My boys and Elmer don't have enough sand in their craw to deal with that lot, and I don't have time to stand over them. As it is, they've spent a month on what could have been done in a fortnight."

"And collected a month's wages," Eric added, chuckling.

"Aye, they might be slothful, but they're not witless," Gideon agreed, laughing. "I'm not overly concerned about the money, but I do want that other plot cleared before time for spring planting. If you'd like a few weeks' work, I've no doubt that you could take that crew in hand. It would give you an opportunity to see how things are done here, and I'd be glad to pay you any fair amount for overseeing the work."

Eric thought about it for a moment, his initial reaction favorable. While it had nothing to do with establishing a business, the point of becoming familiar with the area and local procedures was a valid one. He knew that Gideon could make other arrangements, and the offer was at least partly one of friendship. "We could look at the land to be cleared and discuss it further," he suggested. "Tomorrow, if you like."

"That suits me," Gideon replied in satisfaction. "You can stop for the night at my farm, and I'll show you the land in the morning."

Eric accepted the invitation, thanking the farmer. The sky remained clear as the afternoon wore on, and Gideon began talking about the weather. He described storms the winter had brought, and speculated that there would be others before spring arrived. Eric kept up his side of the conversation, but he was increasingly captivated by his surroundings.

The lavish abundance of land was more and more evident, the farms far apart, and even small ones were of substantial size by the standards he had known. The crop fields were so fertile that scattered shoots of produce from the previous year were flourishing, and the enormous sheep and cattle runs were deep in lush grass. Most of all, the countryside had a gripping pastoral beauty, every small detail of it perfectly distinct in the peculiarly crystalline quality of the bright Australian light.

An even more surpassingly beautiful view unfolded when the wagon finally crossed a last hill and Wallaby Track lay ahead. The sun was low by then, shadows reaching from under the hills on the west side of the immense valley that cradled the broad river. Smoke from chimneys eddied up at the farmsteads and the clustered buildings of the village on a hill in the distance. The rural community nestled protectively in the valley was a scene so spellbinding that it seemed almost unreal to Eric. Instead of comparing with his memories of other places, it reminded him of a

Gainsborough landscape he had seen at an art gallery in York, a painting that had combined precision of detail with a hauntingly nostalgic, tranquil atmosphere.

Eric's reverie was abruptly ended by an unpleasant prospect coming to the fore when Gideon turned in at a lane, telling Eric that it was Brendell Farm. Back in the wagon, Ursula exclaimed in satisfaction over the large, elaborate house at the end of the lane. It seemed more of a display than a home to Eric, which was typical of his father.

At the front of the house, Eric jumped down from the wagon and helped Ursula down. A thin, nervous-looking housekeeper rushed out, introducing herself and greeting Ursula effusively. The woman apologetically said that Brendell was at present supervising work in the fields, and Ursula nodded indifferently as she studied the house, more interested in it.

Eric lifted Ursula's trunk down, then turned to Gideon. "I'll have to wait," he told the farmer. "My stepmother's brother asked me to escort her into her husband's company, and he isn't here."

"Aye, seeing is believing, isn't it?" Gideon commented. "I could wait with you until he gets home, Eric."

"No, I'd rather not detain you. I'll come to your farm when I finish here. You said it's the next one up the road, didn't you?"

The farmer nodded, willing but not wanting to wait. As the wagon moved away, the housekeeper summoned maids out of the house to carry in the trunk. The women struggled with it, Ursula and the housekeeper following them inside, then the door closed and Eric was alone in front of the house.

He watched the late afternoon shadows grow longer as the minutes passed, and he thought about his purpose for waiting. By any reasonable measure, he had accomplished what he had been asked to do. He still felt compelled to wait, but in contrast to his usual clear reasons for everything he did, in this instance his motivation seemed murky to him.

Exploring his feelings, he realized that while he detested his father, he wanted to see the man. Confronting him as an adult promised to be grimly satisfying after the man's cruelty on the few occasions they had been together years before. But then Eric wondered if he had a further motive at a deep, subconscious level—perhaps a need to search for a way in which to put the turmoil of his childhood into his past and forget it.

At the sound of hoofbeats beside the house, Eric turned. When his father rode around the house, Eric was struck by the fact that even though the man had changed greatly over the years, in a sense he remained remarkably the same. The man he was had emerged to the surface more clearly, his personality melding into his appearance and becoming evident at a glance.

Brendell reined up and stepped heavily down from his saddle, glaring at Eric. "Who the bloody hell are you?" he demanded brusquely.

"Your first wife's son," Eric shot back curtly. "I've escorted your present wife from England, which her brother asked me to do."

Brendell's thick, veined features reflected surprise, then he frowned. "I asked you for naught," he growled. "Any agreement you made with someone else doesn't obligate me to pay expenses or such—"

"I want nothing from you," Eric cut in. "I escorted your wife here because it was the right thing to do, not for any sort of payment."

Brendell nodded, grimacing sourly. "That's the sort of thing your mother's brother would say," he sneered. "As well as his manner of speech, you have a very close likeness to him."

"Thankfully, I do," Eric agreed. "I recognized you at once, even though those who know you less well than I might not."

"What do you mean by that?" Brendell snarled defensively.

"Your vile nature has molded your face to its form," Eric replied. "It's given you the look of a goblin conjured up from the netherworld."

Flushing with rage under the network of red lines on his face, Brendell lifted his riding crop and stamped toward Eric. "By God, you have the impudence of your mother's brother as well!" he barked. "But I can rid you of it in the same way that I put you in order years ago!"

The man charged belligerently, his head and shoulders thrust forward. Eric remembered it as a mannerism to intimidate others, and he also recalled when it had been terrifying for him in his childhood. He took long strides and met Brendell, glaring down at him. "I'd like for you to try it," he said quietly, seething with resentment. "I'd take that riding crop away from you and beat the skin from your back with it."

"I'll not listen to threats from you!" Brendell blustered, lowering the riding crop and backing away. "You'd best give thought to what you say to me, or I'll see that you regret it! You're naught here, but I'm a respected landowner and the magistrate of this district!"

"Respected?" Eric echoed, laughing humorlessly. "You're known far and wide here as the contemptible swine that you are."

"Have done with your insolent prattle!" Brendell stormed furiously. He wheeled and stamped toward the house, shaking his riding crop at Eric. "And get off my property, or I'll have you arrested for trespassing!"

Eric turned and walked down the lane toward the road through the long, dark shadows of the winter sunset. The scene around him was blurred by tears of rage and anguish that filled his eyes. He knew that if his purpose in seeing his father again had been to put his wretchedly unhappy childhood completely in his past and forget it, he had failed.

Chapter Seven

E ric turned from hitching a team to the wagon and watched Gideon, who had led a third horse out of the barn and was saddling it. "Why do you want a saddle horse as well as the wagon, Gideon?" he asked.

A grin spanned the farmer's bearded, weathered face as he cinched the saddle on the horse and tethered it to the tailgate of the wagon. "In one way or another, I intend to talk you into overseeing those workers," he replied, laughing. "You'll need the wagon whilst you're getting organized on the job. I don't want to walk home, so I'm taking a saddle horse."

Eric laughed, having more or less decided to accept the work. The warm welcome by the Mundys the night before had been a perfect antidote for his bitterness after seeing his father, and it had won him over. Moreover, in the dawn light of a new day, he was restlessly energetic, with a compelling need to set about some kind of constructive activity.

Gideon helped Eric finish hitching the horses to the wagon, then they climbed up on the seat and drove down the lane. From the road, Eric had a full view of Wallaby Track, and the strong attraction that he felt toward it was another reason inclining him to stay there for a time. With the mist from the river dispersing, the mellow chiming of bellbirds, bugle calls of butcher birds, and chatter of parrots greeted another bright, invigoratingly brisk day. The valley had a soul-arresting scenic beauty, and a closely knit, neighborly atmosphere in the community was reflected in the friendly greetings that Gideon exchanged with others as the wagon moved up the road.

When the village was a mile away, Eric noticed the roof of a large building that rose above surrounding trees at one side of the hill where the hamlet was located. The building looked out of place, and he asked Gideon about it. The farmer replied that it was a prison, built years before for a planned convict compound, but the plans had been changed.

"Upwards of a score of convicts are kept there to work on roads and such in the district," he added. "And it's also used as the district jail." He pointed to a large expanse of cultivated land that stretched from the road to the foot of the hill below the village. "That's a farm I bought a few years ago, and I plowed up the pastures and everything to make one big field. The property includes the forest all the way up to the village, and that's where I want the trees cleared so I can plant more crops."

"Much of it looks too steep to plow," Eric observed.

"Aye, much of it is," Gideon agreed. "But when we get closer, you'll see that the end of the hill on this side isn't steep. That's the part I want cleared, and it will give me several more acres."

Eric studied the hill as they moved on up the road, and he saw that the farmer was correct. A road branched off the main one and led up to the village, climbing the center and steepest part of the hill. Back from the near side of the village road, the forested hill sloped down to an angle suitable for plowing before it reached the edge of the cultivated land.

A few minutes later, Gideon turned onto the village road. A single large house was set a few yards back from the road, a barn behind it, and a rail fence enclosed several acres around the house. An Aborigine woman was hanging out laundry beside the house, much of it consisting of baby diapers. Gideon and Eric lifted their hats to her as they continued discussing the land to be cleared, and the woman smiled amiably in response.

Near the top of the hill, Gideon turned off the road and stopped the wagon at a place where the slope shelved and was less steep for a few feet. When he walked into the thick forest with the farmer, Eric saw that the shoulder on the hill fanned out into a flat expanse over a hundred feet wide. At the side of it below the village, large rocks surrounded a spring feeding a brook that trickled down the hill.

Isolated facts that Eric had learned since arriving on the ship suddenly came together into a highly promising idea, his spirits soaring. A large market for lumber existed in the region, and the equipment at a dry dock in the city was to be sold at auction. Pumps at a dry dock were driven by a steam engine, which would also serve for a sawmill. The level space was perfect for a sawmill, with water immediately at hand and ample room for lumber storage, several buildings, and other necessities.

Eric glanced around, exploring the value that Gideon placed on the property. "This is level enough just here," Eric pointed out.

"Aye, it would do for a house," Gideon replied dismissively, "if anyone would want a house here. But it's too small to grow any amount of crops, and the hill all around it is too steep to plow."

Eric nodded, the question answered satisfactorily. At the edge of the level area, they went down an incline that was thick with large trees and brush. Near the base of the hill, where the slope became gradual, Gideon led Eric through the forest and pointed out a line of trees he had blazed with an axe as a boundary for the land that he wanted cleared.

"We'll go to the other property now," Gideon said as they started back up the hill. "You can meet the workers and size them up, then we'll talk about wages and other terms for overseeing them."

Eric waited until they climbed up to the level area, then told Gideon that he would take the job. "Instead of wages, though," he went on, "I'd like to make a bargain with you for this land that you don't want cleared. If I can get the wherewithal, I'd like to set up a sawmill here."

"A sawmill?" Gideon exclaimed happily. "You may be certain that we'll agree on a bargain for this land, because I've often been driven to rage over trifling with poor lumber. I'll deed this land to you in return for overseeing the clearing of the land at the foot of the hill, and you can have all of the timber. How does that suit you?"

"It's too fair for me by far," Eric replied. "This land must be worth far more than you'd pay someone to oversee those workers."

"Not to me it isn't," Gideon insisted. "It's only a drain on my purse through paying the rates on it." He put out his hand. "Now do you want to make it a bargain, or do you want to keep on arguing?"

Eric shrugged, shaking hands with him. As they walked back toward the wagon, Gideon glowed with satisfaction and talked about the improvements he could make at his farmstead with a ready supply of good lumber. The farmer also assured Eric that he would have plenty of customers from Parramatta, Broken Bay, and other places, as well as in Wallaby Track.

Gideon turned the wagon back down the hill and drove toward the other property, still talking happily about the sawmill. Eric discussed it, but his thoughts had moved to a more general level. If he could set up a sawmill, he intended to work with it until its operation was routine, then place a reliable foreman in charge of it and go on to something else. The sawmill would be the first of numerous ventures that in combination would bring him wealth and success during the years to come.

The other property was on the east side and north end of the valley, and the sun was high by the time Gideon turned onto a side road leading to it. When the pasture came into view, Eric saw that the work had been completed, all of the trees felled and piled at the fencelines. The cook was busy over pots and pans at a fire in front of huts the men had made from large slabs of eucalypt bark. The other five men were halfheartedly milling about at final tasks, but mostly watching to see when tiffin would be ready.

"Well, they finally finished it," Gideon remarked, turning the wagon off the road into the pasture. "The chance of having steady jobs would perk them up. If you let them know that you're thinking about setting up a sawmill and you'll need some men, they'll work harder for you."

"Yes, but I won't bribe men to work," Eric told him. "They'll have to start working with a will, then I'll tell them about the sawmill."

"Aye, that's doubtless best," Gideon agreed. "After you move them and their swag to the other place, bring the wagon to the farm. You can pick up a supply of rations, along with your trunk."

Eric nodded, he and Gideon stepping down from the wagon near the huts and fire. The five men walked toward the wagon, the cook stepping over to it with a jaunty stride. A small, wizened man in his sixties with a snowy beard and hair, he had twinkling blue eyes and a joking manner.

"Jake Larkins is the name," he announced briskly, "but I've been called other things by men who were wroth over having ashes in their tea. I can cook up tea and tucker during dust storms, whilst a williwaw is blowing, and when it's raining so hard that fish are swimming through the air."

Eric laughed, immediately liking the aged man. The other five men gathered around, Gideon introducing them, and Eric saw at once who had controlled the pace of the work.

Four of the men were more or less typical day laborers and would be good average workers when treated fairly, but they had been intimidated by and followed the lead of the fifth man.

About forty, he was a muscular, grim-looking man named Ira Cade. His face was scarred from brawls, his nose squashed and his lips misshapen from being battered. A belligerently proud man, he stood with his head high and shoulders back. Having dealt with similar men before, Eric knew that the man would be either a far more valuable worker than any of the other men or worse than useless, but nothing in between.

All of the men looked askance at Eric's family name, which he expected, and he clarified the point when the introductions were finished: "Thurlow Brendell is my father," he told them, "but I have nothing to do with him or with Brendell Farm. I came to Australia entirely on my own."

The explanation satisfied all of the men except Ira Cade, who frowned skeptically. "What are we to make of that?" he muttered.

"Anything or nothing at all," Eric replied curtly. "I've told you how matters stand, and you can either take it or leave it."

"Beyond that, it's none of your concern," Gideon added brusquely, turning to the horse tethered to the tailgate of the wagon. He untied the reins and stepped into the saddle, speaking to Eric: "I'll see you when you bring the wagon to the farm for the rations."

Eric replied with a word of farewell as Gideon rode away, then turned to the cook. "How soon will tiffin be ready, Jake?" he asked.

"Anyone with strong enough teeth and gullet could eat it now," the cook responded jauntily. "But it'll go down easier and set better when it gets there if it boils for a middling short while longer."

"Very well, we'll use that time to start getting organized

to move to the other place," Eric said, turning to the workers. "Let's get all of the axes, saws, and other tools collected together."

No one moved. Ira gazed balefully at Eric, and the other four glanced uneasily between them, not wanting to defy either of them. Jake stepped toward the fire, watching over his shoulder to see what happened.

"We've done enough for now," Ira said truculently, his attitude a challenge. "That can wait until after tiffin."

Eric sighed in resignation, turning to the wagon, and took off his canvas coat. "Let's go ahead and get it over with, Ira," he suggested wearily.

"What do you mean?" the man growled.

"We're going to have trouble, so let's be done with it."

Ira laughed sardonically, shaking his head. "You mean that you want to fight me?" he jeered. "You've got me by a couple of inches and a few pounds, but I've got you by scores of fights. You'll regret it, jocko."

"No doubt," Eric agreed. "The last thing I need is practice in how to bleed and hurt, but this is something that has to be done." He tossed his coat and hat onto the wagon seat, then stepped toward Ira.

Ira took the initiative and rushed forward in an attempt to control the fight, and the other four men scrambled out of his path. A wily, experienced fighter, he swerved to the right and then to the left as he charged, trying to confuse Eric and throw him off balance. Having faster reactions than Ira, Eric adjusted his stance and was facing him squarely when they met.

Deflecting blows with his forearms, Eric planted a solid punch with his right fist into Ira's midriff. It felt like hitting a thick oak board covered with cloth, but the blow had enough force behind it to knock Ira backward. The man instantly charged forward again to stand and swap blows, and his appearance proved that he could endure brutal punishment. Eric backed away and kept a distance between them, using his longer reach to search for openings while staying away from the other man's fists.

Ira responded with an attempt to grapple and throw both of them to the ground, where he would have the advantage. When the man lowered his head and rushed in, Eric countered the move by pitching his weight forward as soon as Ira's arms locked around him. Eric began pounding his fists into the man's back, and Ira heaved his weight about and hammered a heel against the back of Eric's legs in a fierce struggle to make him fall.

They teetered to and fro, Eric almost losing and then regaining his balance several times. The blows thudding into Ira's back finally overcame his ability to tolerate punishment, and he started flinching and grunting in pain with each one. Then he gave up and leaped away, his fists flailing, but Eric was unable to dodge or deflect one heavy blow. The man's fist struck Eric's cheekbone with stinging force, bringing tears to his eyes.

Ira tried to follow up on the blow, charging and pumping his fists. He left his body unprotected for an instant, and Eric hit him in the chest, rocking him back on his heels. Ira recovered and sparred with Eric as they moved in a circle. Then Eric noticed that Ira always kept his chin tucked firmly against his neck, indicating it was a vulnerable spot.

Taking a pounding on his chest and stomach as he closed in, Eric drove a fist into Ira's forehead to tilt his head back, then hit the man on the chin. It was indeed a vulnerable spot, the blow only a glancing one, but Ira sagged on his feet. Shaking his head rapidly to clear it, the man backed away with his arms raised to protect his chin.

Eric followed him, slamming lefts and rights into the man's unprotected stomach. Ira summoned enough energy to fight back, but it was a feeble effort compared to before. Seeing an opening, Eric put his weight behind his fist and hit the man on the chin again. Ira reeled back and fell, sprawling on the ground. He twitched and groaned weakly, his eyes dazed.

The other four men gaped at Eric, astonished by the outcome of the fight. Eric drew in a deep breath, his bruised cheek stinging and his chest and stomach aching, then he beckoned the cook. "Bring some water over here and pour it on him, Jake," he said.

The cook trotted from the fire with a bucket and dashed water into Ira's face. The man jerked and spluttered, the cold water snapping him out of his stupor. He sat up shakily, looking around, then feebly climbed to his feet. "I'll collect my swag and bluie," he muttered.

"No, you won't," Eric told him. "We have work to do."

Ira blinked in surprise, then looked at Eric uncertainly. "You mean I'm not sacked?" he growled.

"That's exactly what I mean," Eric confirmed. "The fight is finished and done with, so let's get to work." He turned to the other men: "Let's all get to work and gather the tools into the wagon."

The men began bustling about energetically, collecting up tools and carrying them to the wagon. Ira joined them, unsteady on his feet, and his grim, scarred face pale with pain, but he made an effort to do his share. Eric inspected the tools as they were brought to the wagon, placing those that needed oiling and sharpening into a separate pile.

When the last of the tools were in the wagon, Eric went to the fire with the other men and took a tin plate, pannikin, and utensils from the rock where the cook had stacked them. The food revealed that Jake had worked on a sheep station at one time. It was mutton stew and damper, unleavened stockman's bread made with flour, salt, and water.

The stew was tasty, spicy and thick with chunks of vegetables and meat, and Eric ate with a hearty appetite. He chose that time to tell the men about his plans for a sawmill, explaining that it might result in their having permanent jobs. "But it isn't certain," he emphasized. "I believe I can get everything I'll need to set up a sawmill, but I'm not positive."

The lack of assurance failed to restrain the men's delight,

Jake and four of the other men talking among themselves in an excited hubbub of voices. Ira was silent for a moment and kept his head low over his plate as he ate, then he looked up at Eric. "Does that include me?" he asked.

"Of course it does," Eric told him.

Ira nodded and resumed eating, then joined in the conversation among the men. He showed less enthusiasm than the others about the prospect of a permanent job, but Eric knew that was only the man's nature. Eric also knew that the man would now be an excellent worker, and he hoped that in time he and Ira could become friends.

When the meal was finished, the men loaded their swag and the cook's paraphernalia into the wagon, then piled into it themselves. Eric drove the wagon down the valley and listened to the men laughing and talking merrily while they oiled and sharpened tools. Jake led the conversation, relating stories about when he had worked at a sheep station. The men hooted in disbelief at the more unlikely tales, including one about a dust storm so severe that there was mud in the eggs later laid by chickens.

At the shoulder on the hill below the village, Eric parked the wagon and helped the men unload it. With everyone carrying armfuls of swag and tools, he led the men through the forest to the level expanse and pointed out a place near the spring for huts and a campfire. He drove the wagon back down the hill, and before he reached the foot of it, he heard axes ringing against trees, all of the men working energetically.

While passing the edge of Mundy Farm alongside the road, Eric saw Gideon and one of his sons at a distance, moving cattle from one pasture to another. The farmer noticed Eric and waved as he reined his horse around toward the house and barns. Eric turned in at the lane leading into the farm and drove past the house to the barnyard, where Gideon was waiting.

The farmer took a closer look, then chuckled and shook

his head sympathetically as he pointed to the bruise on Eric's cheek. "I see that you had a ruction," he commented. "But I daresay you won it handily."

"No, no one ever wins a fight," Eric replied. "But he quit before I did, which is the best that anyone can do. It was with Ira Cade."

"Aye, I thought so. Did you sack him?"

"No, no need for that, Gideon. He'll be a good worker now."

Gideon nodded in approval as he and Eric went into the house. After bringing Eric's trunk out to the wagon, they began loading foodstuffs into it. They carried bags of potatoes and vegetables from the root cellar, cheese and butter from the springhouse, gammon and strings of sausages from the smokehouse, and flour, tea, and salt from the storeroom.

After they finished loading the footstuffs into the wagon, Gideon suggested that Eric return it and the team the next day. "It'll be late by the time you get these rations unloaded," he added, "and I won't need the wagon until tomorrow afternoon. When you bring it back, you can take a horse and saddle to use until you get your own, whenever that might be."

Eric thanked him, explaining that he needed to ride to Sydney within the next day or two and place a bid on a steam engine for the sawmill. He and the farmer talked for a few minutes longer, discussing the prospects for when the land below the village would be cleared and ready for plowing, then Eric climbed into the wagon and drove back down the lane.

Late afternoon came while Eric was driving up the road toward the village, and sunset brought a gloriously beautiful end to the day. The westering sun had a softer glow, its rays taking on rich, warm tones, and the first wisps of evening mist from the river drifted in the air. Eric's mood matched the scene, his plans now starting to be answered with results.

A buggy came down a lane from a farmhouse and turned onto the road in front of Eric, going in the same direction. It turned onto the village road, and after he turned onto the road himself, he saw that the buggy had drawn up at the large house beside the road. A woman stepped out of it, went up to the porch, and peered into a box beside the front door. She turned back toward the buggy as he started to pass the house; then she paused at the edge of the porch and turned, her gaze meeting his.

She was unlike any woman Eric had ever seen, incomparably more captivating. Taller than average, she was slender and surpassingly beautiful. The way she held her head and the set of her strikingly attractive features revealed a self-assured, contained disposition. In addition, there was a quality about her that he was unable to define, but it drew him to her with a compelling, beguiling force.

Eric lifted his hat and smiled. An instant passed, then her answering smile was just as different as she herself. It was restrained, even sparing, but he was certain that exceedingly few strange men would draw a smile from her. That made it a glowing radiance, like a luxuriously warm, gloriously beautiful sunrise after bitterly cold darkness.

The wagon passed the house, Eric turning and watching the woman as she went to the buggy, stepped into it, and disappeared behind the side curtain. He stretched and craned his neck, and then finally stood up in front of the wagon seat, trying to catch another glimpse of her. But she was lost from view, the buggy moving around the house toward the barn.

Driving on up the hill, he was in a flux of emotions, joy mixed with an urgently suspenseful need to know all about her. She was bewitching, her smile hinting at an alluring promise of interest in him, and his plans for the sawmill and future ventures were suddenly of secondary importance. He anxiously hoped the men would know her name and other essential facts.

At the shoulder on the hill, the men had cleared a path

for the wagon through the brush and trees, and Eric turned onto it. A fire was blazing up at the camp, Jake sorting out his pots and pans beside it, and the other men were building bark huts. They all left what they were doing and gathered around the wagon as Eric stopped it near the fire.

The men cheered, seeing the cheese, gammon, and other choice foodstuffs, and Eric raised his voice over theirs as he jumped down from the wagon: "Do any of you know who the woman is who lives at the foot of the hill?"

Silence fell, the men exchanging uncomfortable glances, then Ira Cade spoke up: "That's Mistress Stephanie Thorpe, the midwife and doctor hereabouts. She's uncommonly pleasing to the eye, but if you set your sights on her, I opine that you'll be brought up short."

"Why do you say that?" Eric asked.

"Plenty of others have tried and got the cold shoulder," Ira replied. "She appears to be already married to what she does, and I daresay you'd have even less luck than others." He explained that Eric's father had ordered a wounded convict returned to the prison, and Dr. Stephen Thorpe had accompanied the man and then had been killed by convicts plotting an escape. "So many here blame your pa for her pa's death," he went on, "and I've no doubt that Mistress Thorpe does as well."

Eric nodded numbly and turned away, his excitement of moments before turning into abject depression. Needing to busy himself, he stepped to the horses and started unhitching them from the wagon to hobble them so they could graze. The men resumed talking happily among themselves as they unloaded the wagon and carried the foodstuffs to a hut.

The image of Stephanie Thorpe's lovely, smiling face was etched in Eric's memory. It had been a fascinating pleasure to contemplate, but now it was a torture. He knew that instead of smiling, she would glare at him in revulsion when she learned his family name.

* * *

Stephanie seethed with buoyant delight as she finished unharnessing her horse and put it in its stall. Trying to restrain her soaring spirits, she kept reminding herself that she had felt drawn to other young, handsome men. But an inner voice continued rejecting the thought, instantly replying that it had been entirely different this time.

She knew that to be absolutely true. On other occasions, the attraction had been too largely sexual desire, a raw and unwelcome feeling that had made her uncomfortable. It had dehumanized the man and given her a sense of being devalued, invading a privacy that she held inviolate.

A strong erotic tug had been present this time, and little wonder. He was a tall, muscular man with strikingly handsome features. But he was also much more than that, with something very special about him. This time the libidinous response had been smothered in other reactions which had changed its nature. Instead of being invaded, that privacy within her had eagerly opened, creating a warm, melting glow that still suffused her.

Carrying fodder to the horses, Stephanie summoned her logic, and it provided a warning which the inner voice was unable to reject: A professional midwife could marry only a doctor. Whenever that dictum was ignored, the inevitable result was a wretchedly unhappy marriage. Judging by his clothing, the man she had seen was an artisan or perhaps a farmer.

Contemplating her memory of him, Stephanie closed the barn doors and walked toward the house. Then, hearing someone chopping firewood on the hill, she turned and looked up at the forest.

In the fading sunset light, smoke rose from a campfire in the forest, and Stephanie wondered if the man she had seen was camped there. The smoke partially obscured her view of the prison roof, conforming to her feelings of how he could affect her life. Although it was fanciful, she wanted to believe that that proved the campfire was his.

The bright, warm kitchen seemed especially cheery and cozy, the pretty, amiable Yulina more lovable than ever. The rich, spicy scent of beef and vegetable pie keeping warm on the fireplace hob increased her robust appetite to ravenous hunger. "That smells delicious, and I'm famished!" she exclaimed happily, taking off her coat and hat.

"I took it out of the oven only a moment ago," Yulina told her cheerfully. "You got home just in time for the crust to be good and fresh."

Stephanie crossed the kitchen to the crib near the fireplace and looked at the baby sleeping in it. With a dark tan complexion and features reflecting a mixture of Aborigine and Anglo-Saxon bloodlines, the baby was a large, healthy boy. "Judging from Master John Thorpe's sound slumber, he must have recovered from his stomach upset," she remarked.

"That medicine you gave him cured it completely," Yulina replied happily, setting the table. "He's now as chipper as one could wish."

Stephanie went to the washstand and washed her hands, then sat down at the table. She started to ask about the men camped on the hill, but the food claimed her attention, Yulina bringing the pie to the table and taking her seat. Stephanie helped herself to a generous serving and began eating hungrily, savoring the light, crisp pastry, flavorful gravy, and the thick, succulent chunks of meat and vegetables in the pie.

As with most new mothers, Yulina's baby was an inexhaustible topic of conversation for her. She began talking about him, telling Stephanie about the baby's smiles during the day and noises he had made that sounded like words. Presently, when Yulina paused, Stephanie brought up the subject of the men camped on the hill. "You went to the village today, didn't you," she added. "Did you see them or hear who they are?"

"They're woodcutters," Yulina replied, her usual cheerful

manner fading. "But let's talk of other things, not unpleasant ones."

"Unpleasant?" Stephanie echoed. "What do you mean?"

Yulina sighed in resignation, then explained: "The one in charge of the woodcutters is the magistrate's son. When I went to the store in the village, I heard that he had arrived yesterday with his stepmother. I saw him on the road, but I didn't know who he was at the time. He's a tall, hefty man, fairish and midway of his twenties, and his name is Eric. And he strikes me as being far worse than his father."

Stephanie's heart sank under crushing remorse, the description that of the man she had seen. "How is he worse than his father?" she asked.

"Anyone with the wits of a kookaburra can look at Thurlow Brendell and see that he's evil," Yulina replied. "The son is a sly one. He's pleasing to the eye and smiles like butter wouldn't melt in his mouth. All in all, he's as artful as a painted whore on the pissmire in Sydney."

Stephanie was suddenly nauseated, the food making a burning sensation in her stomach, and the kitchen felt intolerably hot and stuffy. She left the table and stepped toward the door, Yulina sighing regretfully as she stood up and began gathering the dishes on the table. Stephanie went outside, closed the door, and drew in deep breaths of the cold night air.

The campfire was a distant, flickering glow through the darkness and the thick trees on the hill. Stephanie realized that when the trees were felled, the entire prison instead of only the roof would be in full view from her house. It seemed typical of what a Brendell would do.

Chapter Eight

"**W**hen did that take place, Tipton?" Stephanie asked. "Late yesterday afternoon," the district clerk replied. "Eric Brendell and Gideon Mundy were here to transfer ownership to Eric on the land where he has his sawmill. Magistrate Brendell came in to look at the list of properties in arrears on payment of rates. He asked about yours, so I was obliged to show him the records. Then before the magistrate could say anything, Eric took out his purse and handed the money to me."

Stephanie opened the birth registry on Tipton's desk and reached for his pen. "So Eric Brendell paid the rates on my house," she summed up.

"Yes, and in gold," Tipton added. "It's been ages since I've seen gold coins. As you may well imagine, a heated debate ensued. I must say that Eric more than matched the magistrate in acrimonious turns of phrase."

The small, dapper man continued talking, describing the fierce argument between father and son. Stephanie made an entry in the registry on a birth the previous night while she listened, her feelings about Eric Brendell as conflicting as usual. It was the same response she had experienced when she had occasionally passed him on the roads during the past weeks.

It had been troubling for her, stirring an emotional reaction that mocked her control over her feelings. But that reaction had always met with the stark reality of her situation in respect to him, a reef where her emotions foundered. Beyond not being a doctor, which made any feelings about him completely irrelevant, he was Thurlow Brendell's son.

Now this, she reflected. At least for the present, her worry about the overdue rates on her house was removed, but her relief was eclipsed by resentment toward Eric Brendell. Even though she was grateful for what he had done, she wanted nothing to do with him. But he had invaded her life and seized a measure of control over her, placing her in debt to him.

Stephanie ended the conversation and went back outside into the bright spring morning of early October, which had been robbed of its cheerful aspect for her by the necessity to go and talk with Eric Brendell. Tipton's attitude toward him had been favorable, a view that she had noted was shared by very few others in the valley. Most of the people were wary of him, regarding him simply as Thurlow Brendell's son.

She drove out of the village and over the brow of the hill, where the trees on the south side of the road were thinner than before. The prison was now in full view from her house, a metaphor of Eric Brendell's effect upon her life. She felt as though some of her most vital emotional defenses had been stripped away, leaving her exposed and vulnerable.

The road that led through the trees to the sawmill had been smoothed by large logs dragged from various parts of the valley by oxen. Stephanie turned onto it, studying the scene in the wide, level clearing ahead. A combination barracks and cookhouse built of fresh lumber was at the side below the village, smoke trickling from its stone chimney, and piles of logs were alongside sheds at the far end of the clearing.

The sawmill, in the center, was driven by a chuffing steam engine. A drive belt spun in a vibrating blur between it and the shaft of a circular saw, turning the blade into a gleaming disc. The saw was mounted in a long, narrow frame of heavy beams that supported a movable platform. Eric and his five workmen rolled a log onto levers at one side of the frame, then they raised the levers and dumped the log onto the platform.

The men pushed the platform, sliding it, and moved the log past the saw. A cloud of sawdust blossomed, the blade whining shrilly and peeling a slab from the log. As the men slid the platform back into position and rolled the log onto its flattened side, one of them noticed Stephanie driving into the clearing. He plucked at Eric's sleeve, pointing to her.

Eric walked toward her with long, quick strides and brushed sawdust off his dungaree shirt and trousers. Stephanie reined up her horse and stepped out of the buggy, composing herself. At close range and on foot, she was more conscious of the tall, muscular man's size. Few men were taller than she, but he towered over her by several inches.

His warm smile, a contrast between his brilliantly white teeth and the suntan on his handsome face, was a battering ram against her attempt at an impersonal attitude. He lifted his hat, taking a receipt for property rates from his pocket. "This belongs to you, Mistress Thorpe," he said.

"No, it doesn't," she replied. "It is yours, because it is a bill of accounts of my indebtedness to you for seven guineas."

"I don't view it that way," he disagreed amiably. "As the owner of a business in which my employees and I can be injured, having medical help available is important to me. In keeping that assistance from being threatened or hindered, I only served my own best interests."

"Notwithstanding that," Stephanie countered, "obligations are a personal matter to me. That isn't to say that

I'm not grateful for what you did, because I am. However, I intend to repay you as quickly as possible. It might not be until the harvest begins, but you'll be repaid."

The saw shrilled and sliced another slab from the log in a cloud of sawdust. Eric pondered for a moment, then suggested, "You have several acres behind your house and barn where I could pasture my oxen and horses. If you insist on repaying me, that would be ample repayment."

"No, it wouldn't," she told him. "Pasturage for a few head of horses and oxen isn't worth a tithe of seven guineas."

"That's true," he agreed, "but it overlooks convenience. It would be well worth the money to me to have my horses and oxen where they could be fetched within a few minutes." He lifted a hand as she started to object again. "But if you still think you're getting too much of the bargain," he added, "you could invite me to your home for dinner."

"To what end?" Stephanie asked, prepared to challenge and bluntly reject any implication of romantic intentions in his reply.

"To help my lumber sales get off to a good start," he explained. "I've been too busy to get about and meet most of the people here. Many of them associate me with the magistrate, and until they get to know me for myself, they might be loath to do business with me. Certainly no one has suffered more than you at that man's hands, and if you and I are known to be on good terms, that will go far in making people think again."

The explanation was logical, but Stephanie detected a twinkle of humor in his bright blue eyes, and his attitude revealed keen interest in her, not his business. However, she knew that while her choices in what she could do were limited, his offer was reasonable, one that she could fulfill and then not feel under any further obligation to him. "Very well," she said. "Would you like to come to my home for dinner this evening?"

His quick, beaming grin had an appealing aspect of boyish delight. "I'll be more than pleased to," he replied, handing over the receipt, "and I'm very grateful for the invitation. What time do you have dinner?"

Stephanie shrugged and shook her head, pocketing the receipt as she stepped into her buggy. "Whenever I get home. Unless something detains me, I should be home a bit before sunset this evening."

"I'll look forward to seeing you then," he said, lifting his hat.

Stephanie nodded in reply, tugging a rein to turn her buggy, then drove back to the road. In the aftermath of the conversation, her feelings about him were more troubling than ever. He was the opposite of what her opinion of him had been at a rational level, but precisely what the deep, inner voice of her emotions had told her he would be.

Turning in at her house, Stephanie parked her buggy at the kitchen door and went inside to tell Yulina that Eric would have dinner with them that evening. "Like people say about some," Yulina muttered glumly when Stephanie finished explaining, "he's as sly as a fox. I've never seen a fox, but I'll venture that he's a match for the most cunning of them. What he wants in return for paying the rates would be clear to the most gormless."

Stephanie was annoyed by the remarks, as well as surprised by her impulse to defend Eric, and she softened her response with a smile: "If you're concerned that I might be taken advantage of by some man," she said firmly, "do bear in mind that I'm not a witless ninny."

"Of course not," Yulina agreed quickly. "But it's never amiss to watch where sly dogs are sniffing, is it?" She began bustling about, taking pots and pans off their hooks on the wall. "I'll cook up a purler of a dinner, and he won't be able to say he hasn't had a good feed."

Stephanie went up the hall and into the surgery to put the receipt in the cabinet with the account ledger. Taking out the receipt, she hesitated and looked at it, the paper still creased from Eric's pocket. With her different perspective after having talked with him, she realized that her opinion of him based on his father had been uncharacteristic of her. She always formed judgments of former convicts and everyone else on the basis of their individual character traits, ignoring their past and origins.

She realized it had been an emotional defense, a self-deception to shield a painful truth that was now rawly, bitterly evident. Only the necessities of her profession stood between her and the only man she had ever met who was so very special and different from all others. But her profession was her life, and she could never compromise her commitment to it.

Sudden rage seizing her, Stephanie crushed the receipt into a wad and hurled it at the cabinet. She clenched her hands to her face for a moment, fighting back tears of anger and sorrow. Then she despondently picked up the receipt and straightened it out to put it into the cabinet, forcing her thoughts away from her plight and concentrating on her calls.

Her last call of the day was at Mundy Farm, where little Gideon Beasley had a mild colic. While examining the baby, Stephanie heard another description of the argument between Eric and Thurlow Brendell from the child's grand-father, the farmer laughing gleefully as he related what had happened. The entire family had gathered in the kitchen, and they were among those who had held a highly favorable opinion of Eric from the very first.

The family had obviously heard the story from Gideon before, but they thoroughly enjoyed it once again. During the conversation that followed, one of the Mundy sons expressed regret about Eric's intention to leave after his saw-mill was operating to his satisfaction, immediately drawing Stephanie's attention. "I had the impression that he intended to settle here," she put in. "Do you think he'll leave soon?"

"It's hard to say," Gideon mused, sobering. "He's close about personal matters, but I know he wants to have other businesses in Sydney."

Flora commented that Eric was an exceptionally energetic man, the others agreeing with her, then the conversation moved on to other things. After she finished examining the baby, Stephanie took a vial of simarube and angelica extract from her bag and gave it to Hannah, telling her to put drops of it on the baby's tongue after each feeding. Amid farewells with the family, Stephanie put on her coat and hat and went out to her buggy.

Driving away from the farm and toward her house, she thought about Eric's intention to leave the valley. It had come as a shock, and while she intensely regretted it, she also yearned for an end to the disruption he had created in her life. Even more than before, her feelings about him fueled a turmoil within her, and dinner promised to be an ordeal.

The ordeal began when she drove into the barnyard and Eric stepped out the kitchen door. Wearing a neat, dark suit, he was so handsome that her heart quickened with a poignant ache, and his smile drew one from her against her will. "I'll attend to your horse and buggy, if I may," he offered.

Her first impulse was to decline and keep a defensive distance between them, then she reconsidered. Knowing how Yulina felt about him, Stephanie speculated that he had met with glowering silence in the house, which violated her sense of hospitality. She thanked him, picking up her bag and stepping out of the buggy, and hurried to the house to speak with Yulina and tell her to be at least courteous to Eric.

Her concern was unfounded, Eric having won over Yulina. "Look!" the woman cried happily, pointing to an assemblage of wire and wood hanging from the fireplace mantel. "Look what Eric made for John Thorpe!"

Stephanie studied the device, intrigued. Its function was the same as that of common objects that were often placed over cribs to occupy babies' attention, but this one had been made specifically for that purpose. Brightly painted bits of wood in various shapes hung on wires from a steel hoop, which in turn was suspended from the mantel on a wire. The warm draft from the fireplace made it revolve slowly, the baby watching it in fascination.

"It's a machine of sorts, isn't it?" Yulina went on. "That's why John Thorpe likes it so much, because he's going to be a mechanic himself. Eric was very kind to go to so much trouble, wasn't he?"

"Yes, it was considerate of him," Stephanie replied, laughing. "But only this morning he was a sly dog, wasn't he?"

"Aye, well, he didn't choose his sire," Yulina observed dismissively, turning to her pots and pans on the hob. "Nor did John Thorpe, but both of them had the good fortune to take after their mothers."

Stephanie agreed, hanging up her coat and hat, then began setting the table. While carrying dishes from the cabinet, she heard Eric's footsteps outside. She suddenly became annoyed at herself for allowing her emotions to run wild like those of a schoolgirl, and she summoned her determination to keep her response to him under control.

When he stepped inside, her upswell of reaction to him and his smile was less troublesome, even pleasant. Her feelings were spiced with a heady tinge of sexual magnetism between them, and upon entering the kitchen, he revealed a characteristic that she found extremely appealing.

She had assumed that his making the device to amuse the baby had been at least in part a tactic to ingratiate himself, but she had to think again. He stepped to the crib and smiled down at the baby, touching its face with a finger, and Stephanie knew without question when affection for a child was a sham. His was real, a true fondness for children.

During the conversation about the device, he explained that it was much like one his uncle had made, modestly disclaiming credit for the idea. Stephanie finished setting the table, then she and Eric sat down. Yulina dished up the soup course, a thick, hearty pottage accompanied by crisp barley rusks that were hot and buttery, and took her place at the table.

With interest more intense than mere curiosity, Stephanie wondered why he was completely unlike his father, and what he had done in the past. Just as though he detected her unspoken questions, Eric told her about having lived at his uncle's farm after finishing school. He said nothing about his early childhood or his father's household, evidently sad subjects, and dwelt entirely upon his school years and his work at his uncle's farm.

"Like many farmers," he went on, "my uncle distrusts banks. That was fortunate for me, because he had gold at hand when he gave me my share of the profits from the farm while I managed it. I'm sure you've read about how scarce specie has been in Britain during the past years."

"Yes, and as you found, it's unavailable here," Stephanie added. "Do you think that will be corrected in the foreseeable future?"

Eric shook his head and told her that he believed it would be many years before specie was plentiful. Elaborating on his reply, he revealed that he was well read on the topic. He explained that the specie shortage was due to Britain's gold reserves having been exhausted by imports that exceeded exports, and replenishing the reserves would be a slow process.

Yulina served up the fish course, thick fillets of smoked morwong smothered in steaming butter sauce, and the discussion moved on to other things. It became clear to Stephanie that Eric was well informed on a broad range of matters, and he was also resourceful. She listened in absorbed interest while he explained how he had modified the steam engine, gear box, and levers from a dry dock in Sydney to construct his sawmill.

It reminded Stephanie of her talks with her father, their absence having left a vast, hungry vacancy in her life. The conversation was even more enjoyable in many ways, as well as much livelier. Eric was conversant with a wide variety of topics, and he had an open, outgoing disposition. With her own more contained nature, Stephanie never felt the need to search for things to say, because he kept the discussion going, and the mutual attraction between them was a constant, piquant undercurrent.

Just as Yulina had promised, the dinner was special. The main course was tender, succulent pork loin, together with potatoes seasoned with drippings, chunks of squash mixed with peas and carrots, and fresh, crusty bread. After it was dished up, however, the conversation took a turn that was disagreeable for Stephanie. Eric mentioned that he was training a man named Ira Cade to be the foreman at his sawmill, and the reminder of his intention to leave the valley cast a shadow over her cheerful mood.

When the meal was finished, Yulina cleared the table and stacked the dishes to wash the next morning. She made another pot of tea, then wished Stephanie and Eric a good night as she picked up her baby and went to her room. Stephanie continued talking with Eric over cups of tea, wondering how far advanced his plans were for leaving. She yearned to know, but she preferred to wait until he spoke about it of his own accord.

She brought up the subject of little John Thorpe's parentage, feeling certain that Eric should and would want to know about it. Another side of his character was revealed when she explained the circumstances, his face flushing and his eyes becoming cold in outrage. He angrily announced that the next day, he would go and confront his father and ensure that the man made provisions to support both Yulina and the baby.

It took several minutes, but Stephanie finally convinced him to leave matters as they stood. "I agree entirely with your intentions," she assured him. "But at the end of the day, the decision is up to Yulina, not you or me. And all she wants from him is for him to leave her entirely alone."

Eric reluctantly accepted the state of affairs, his anger

fading. "Well, no one could do anything for her that would improve upon her situation here with you," he remarked. "She's obviously very happy, and for good reason." He smiled, moving his chair back from the table. "It's late, and I must go. This has been the most pleasant evening of my life, Stephanie, and I'm extremely grateful that you invited me."

"I'm equally pleased that I did," Stephanie replied. "Your company and conversation made the evening very enjoyable for me."

They crossed the kitchen to the door, where Eric wished her a good night and then stepped outside, disappearing into the darkness. His departure was almost abrupt, and Stephanie knew why. He had avoided lingering and talking until she would be placed in a position of either inviting him again or making it obvious that she had no intention of doing so at present.

It had been, she reflected, an instance of the consideration that was so characteristic of him. He was perfect in every way except the one overriding, most vital fact of all that he was not a physician. The kitchen seemed very quiet and empty without him as she stepped back to the table, thinking about the changes that the day had brought.

Her circumstances were now what she had wanted most of all for months. With her property rates paid and her home secure from threat, she could go about her affairs in freedom from anxiety. But the evening had brought yet another change, the realization of a new and desperate need that now made her life incomplete. She was ardently, hopelessly in love with Eric.

Stephanie picked up Eric's cup from the table. She gazed at the tea in the bottom of it, then lifted the cup and took a sip. Drinking from his cup was the outward expression of a deep, inner compulsion, and she expected the dregs of the tea to be unpleasantly bitter. The urge was satisfied, but there was more. Strangely, the tea tasted delicious.

*   *   *

Three days passed before Stephanie saw Eric again, the last two busy ones. At two farms, high spirits during the last harvest had produced a natural result, and she had delivered a baby at each of them. After the second birthing, she was dozing in her buggy while her horse made its way home in the late afternoon, and she woke when the horse suddenly veered.

In her shallow sleep, images of Eric had been unfolding in her mind. She opened her eyes to see him reining up his horse beside her buggy, and the reality of the tall, handsome man matched his intensely compelling masculine appeal in her dreams. "I'm very sorry for disturbing you, Stephanie," he apologized. "I didn't realize you were asleep, and I passed too close and made your horse shy away. That was most thoughtless of me."

"I was merely resting rather than sleeping soundly," she explained, sitting up. "Are matters proceeding well at your sawmill?"

Eric nodded, replying that he had begun to receive numerous orders for lumber. "Ira can now oversee the work well enough for me to attend to other things," he added, "and I went to Sydney yesterday. From what I've heard, you've been busy delivering babies these past two days."

Stephanie told him about the birthings, anxiously wondering if his trip to Sydney involved his plans to leave. Asking him about it now seemed awkward, and she decided upon a better setting to bring it up: "Would you like to have dinner at my home this evening?" she asked.

His prompt, beaming smile was an emphatic answer, then he reconsidered: "Another time might be better," he suggested reluctantly. "I know that you're very weary, and you need to rest, Stephanie."

"No, I learned years ago to rest when I can, and I'm not particularly tired," she assured him. "But please don't make any special effort such as changing from your work clothes. It's late in the day, and I'd greatly prefer that dinner be an entirely spur-of-the-moment occasion."

"Very well," Eric agreed, his blue eyes shining in his
warm smile as he gathered his reins and turned his horse.
"I'll go and close down the sawmill for the day, and I'll
see you at your house presently."

He rode away, and Stephanie drove on down the road
and turned in at her house. While she was attending to the
horses, it occurred to her that her worry about his moving to
Sydney was pointless, for the city was a relatively short distance away. More importantly, there was a more impassable
barrier between them than any physical distance. However,
she remained worried.

Yulina had broadly hinted that she considered Eric an
eminently suitable match for Stephanie, and upon hearing
that he would join them at dinner, the small, stout woman
exclaimed in delight. "I'll make a bit of pottage to go with
dinner," she announced gleefully, grabbing a pan from a
hook. "He seemed to have a right fondness for it the last
time. There's a freshly ironed dress in your closet that you
can put on, because that one's getting wrinkled."

With more than enough pressure from within herself,
Stephanie wanted none from Yulina. "No, I've worn this
dress only one day," she pointed out firmly. "As you know,
I change clothes and bathe often, and it helps me avoid contracting diseases from patients. But I've no need to change
my dress now, and you've no need to start rushing about
to cook anything more. The rack of lamb and vegetables
you've prepared for dinner are ample."

Yulina nodded and said nothing more about the dress,
but she had a mind of her own. She dipped stock into the
pan from the stock pot on the back of the hob, setting about
preparing pottage to go with dinner. Stephanie went into
the laundry room and freshened up, then returned to the
kitchen and began setting the table. A few minutes later,
Eric arrived.

His smile kindled a glow of pleasure within Stephanie as
he stepped into the kitchen, moving with masculine, athletic

grace. The room seemed transformed, not only by her inner feelings. Eric and Yulina had become warm friends, and the atmosphere created by their fondness for each other was like a richly nourishing sustenance of the spirit for Stephanie.

During the conversation over dinner, Eric said something that made Stephanie's concern about his trip to Sydney seem baseless. Yulina had heard about his trip, and with the candid inquisitiveness of a friend, she asked him why he had gone to the city. Eric explained that he had gone there to order extra blades for his sawmill from the foundry, and to buy other things he needed.

Still, Stephanie could not shake her worry that Eric might be planning to leave the valley. The conversation was lively and entertaining, moving from one topic to another. Whenever it touched upon his activities in the valley, his comments implied that he had come to regard it as his home. That was so directly opposed to what the Mundy family had said that Stephanie wondered if she had misunderstood them.

When the meal was finished, Yulina wasted no time in vacating the kitchen so as to leave Stephanie and Eric by themselves. She stacked the dishes, then picked up her baby and went to her room with haste so obvious that it nettled Stephanie. However, Eric stood up to leave as soon as Yulina left. "I'm sure you're very tired, Stephanie," he said. "I wish the evening would never end, but you need to rest. By the way, I noticed that some timbers in your barn need replacing, and I'll see to that, if you don't mind."

Stephanie thanked him absently, pondering the conflicting evidence about his plans to leave the valley. She stepped to the door and out into the cool night with him, then her attention was suddenly drawn to the prison. A full moon was rising above the crest of the hill overlooking the house, and it silhouetted the prison through the screen of trees remaining on the slope. The huge structure was a towering black mass etched against the gleaming disc of the moon, more somber and sinister than ever.

Eric looked at her face in the moonlight, then at the prison. "How utterly stupid of me!" he exclaimed remorsefully. "When I had some of the trees on the hill felled, it didn't occur to me that the prison would be in full view from your house. Stephanie, I'm most earnestly sorry."

Stephanie turned away from the prison, regretting that her thoughts had been so evident. "That makes no difference, Eric," she told him.

"Of course it does," he insisted. "Each time you step out of your kitchen door now, you're confronted with the place where your father met his tragic end. That must be distressing for you."

Gazing at the prison again, Stephanie realized that her dismissive remark had been true enough. Having the prison in full view brought the bleak structure to mind more prominently, but it was never completely absent from her thoughts anyway. However, she had no wish to try to explain what she only vaguely understood herself, and talking about it at all stirred a torment of grief within her. "It distresses me," she acknowledged, "but not for the reason that you think. I can't go into it further, and I'd greatly prefer to not discuss it at all. But being able to see the prison makes no real difference to me."

Eric studied her face, then nodded and turned away. "I'm very relieved," he said thankfully. "I do hope you're being completely forthright, and not forgiving my stupidity out of kindness. Good night, Stephanie."

She replied as he walked away, then she suddenly had to know about his plans to leave the valley. The words spilled from her lips as though of their own accord: "Eric, when I was at Mundy Farm a few days ago, they said you intend to move to Sydney. Is that true?"

"That's what I told Gideon once, but I've changed my mind," he explained, stepping back to her. "This isn't the best time and place, but I'll tell you about it, if you wish."

Stephanie felt uneasy, suspecting the subject was one

she should avoid, but she had to pursue it. "Please do," she requested.

Eric hesitated a moment, collecting his thoughts, then began quietly: "I've never had a home or a family. My life as a small boy was sheer misery because of my father. I didn't have a home or family then, nor at boarding school. My aunt and uncle were very kind to me, but they weren't my family and their home wasn't mine. So I decided that wealth and success would do instead." He stepped closer, taking her hands in his. "Then when I met you, I realized that love is what makes a home and a family. I've been searching for you all of my life, Stephanie. I love you, and I'll be the happiest man on earth if you will marry me."

With his large, warm hands gently holding hers, Stephanie was torn by a violent inner conflict. A compelling force of emotion tugged fiercely, urging her to throw herself into his arms and answer his love with her own. But the cold, hard voice of logic spoke a stern warning in her mind, and it won out. Taking her hands away from his required a strength other than that in her arms, but she pulled them free and stepped back.

"Eric, you're an exceedingly admirable man in every respect," she said. "I should think that any woman would have the warmest affection and love for you. However, a professional midwife can marry no one but a doctor."

"Why do you say that?" he asked, perplexed. "I've known of midwives who married farmers and artisans in various trades."

"A *professional* midwife," she repeated, emphasizing the qualifying term. "For those who occasionally deliver babies, it makes little difference, but it would for me. In addition to birthings, I'm trained to attend to women's and children's illnesses. I'm busier than ever now, of course, but work has always taken up all of my time. You've seen how I pass my days."

"I've also seen that the people here virtually worship you," he added, "and for good reason. You've devoted your life to them, and I deeply admire you for that. Some men might find fault with the hours you keep, but I wouldn't. I'd never interfere with your work, or—"

"The hours I keep are only part of the reason, Eric," she broke in. "The broader, more general grounds is the fact that those in the medical profession share a way of life. There are a multitude of considerations, not just the fact that I would be absent from home most of the time. It certainly isn't a criticism, but you wouldn't understand what I must do."

"No, I wouldn't," he agreed. "At least not at first, but what I didn't understand, I would accept. I promise that I'd never do anything to hinder your work in any way. If we were married, the only difference it would make in your life is that you would be much happier. You would be married to a man who adores you and who would do anything in his power to make you as happy as himself." He started to say more, then broke off and turned away. "For now, it's best that you think the matter over, and we can discuss it again whenever you wish. Good night, my love."

He walked away into the darkness, his footsteps fading, and Stephanie went back into the house. She knew him to be an honest, straightforward man, and she was certain that he had been completely sincere. Moreover, she longed for the happiness that would be hers if they married.

Countering that, her judgment told her that he had been sincere but too certain that love could overcome any problem. A softer voice also spoke in the back of her mind, a menacing whisper. It was a sense of foreboding that she had felt at other times, including the day that her father had gone to the prison. Now it warned of difficulties, or much worse.

The battle lines had been drawn, but it was a gentle conflict, a loving strife. When she returned to her house during late afternoon the following day, Eric had just finished replacing the boards on her barn that he had mentioned the night before. He attended to her horse and buggy, then joined her and Yulina for dinner. It was another entertaining evening, the conversation lively but impersonal, and it remained that way even after Yulina went to her room. The next morning, Eric hitched her horse to her buggy before taking his horses and oxen from the pasture behind the barn, and it was waiting for Stephanie when she left the house to begin her calls.

The subsequent days followed the same pattern, with Eric at the house for dinner each evening and attending to her horse and buggy in early morning and at night. True to his word, he waited for her to broach the subject of marriage, never mentioning it himself. His only urging was nonverbal, the mild and considerate pressure of his presence, with the enjoyable evenings demonstrating how happy her life would be with him.

While driving up the road one day, Stephanie tried to think of what could cause conflicts between them if they were married. Nothing specific came to mind, but she knew that she was unable to predict all the possible circumstances that could arise. She also suspected that her love for Eric could be blinding her to potential problems, because the warning of trouble in the back of her mind was a steady drumbeat.

For the first time, she envied others. At the farmhouses, the only question the couples had faced while contemplating marriage had been the compatibility of their personalities. More than merely being compatible, she knew that Eric's disposition was a rare combination of characteristics that perfectly complemented hers.

She stopped by a farmhouse where a group of children were at play, singing:

> "Ring around the rosies,
> Pocket full of posies,
> Ashes, ashes, all fall down."

Through her studies, she knew the origin of the nursery
rhyme. Though its meaning was now entirely lost, the chant
had originated centuries before during the last epidemic of
the Black Death. The rosy skin eruptions of the disease had
been surrounded by rings, and the custom at the time had
been to put posies into the pockets of the dead. The countless victims had been burned, relatives prostrate around the
pyres in grief and terror.

Her way of life lay between the sweet innocence of the
children at play in the spring sunshine and the macabre
meaning of their chant. Her hands greeted newborns at
birthings and comforted the dying at death watches. For
her, Eric was a bridge between that region and the world of
work, play, and laughter where the mortal condition could
be forgotten for a time. With his cheery good nature and
love for her, he balanced her intense seriousness of purpose.

Well over a fortnight passed before Stephanie and Eric
discussed marriage again, the subject finally arising on All
Hallows Evening. During the previous few days, Eric and
Yulina had worked together in preparation for that night.
He had fashioned a large number of toys and trinkets out
of bits of wood, wire, and string, while she had filled trays
and bowls with sweetmeats she had made from fruit, honey,
and treacle.

At nightfall, the darkness was alive with lanterns bobbing
on the roads through the valley, bands of children running
from house to house. Sporting rags and painted faces, they
raced up to the porch in a bedlam of demands for gifts
and threats of pranks. Stephanie enjoyed the spectacle and
excitement, but her greatest pleasure came from watching
Eric and Yulina's delighted laughter as they handed out toys
and sweetmeats.

It was late when the valley became quiet, the Southern
Cross having moved through its nightly arc from eastern
to western orientation. Yulina went to her room with her
baby, and Stephanie sat on the porch with Eric and talked

for a time. She made a remark about his enjoyment of the night without considering its full implications, saying that he undoubtedly looked forward to having children of his own, and he emphatically agreed.

In the rare silence that fell between them, Stephanie realized that she had indirectly brought up marriage, and she had to say more: "I'm grateful that you haven't persisted in talking about your intentions. That has made our time together much more pleasant."

"It would have been unfair, and entirely without purpose," he replied. "I've said how I feel, and only you can make your decision. I have wondered if you could tell me about the sorts of things that you think would cause trouble between us because of your work."

"No, I can't see into the future and predict circumstances." Stephanie thought about her intuitive feelings, but she knew that he was a very practical man and would take into account only realistic explanations. "All of my life, I've heard that a professional midwife should marry only a doctor, and that's been the practice in my family and others. There must be sound reasons for it, as well as sad experience for any who did otherwise."

"Perhaps for others," he acknowledged, standing up from the bench, "but not for us." Leaning over her, he touched her face with the tips of his fingers. "I would never let anything come between us." He turned away, crossing the porch to the steps. "Good night, Stephanie."

Stephanie's face tingled where he had touched it. She went inside and upstairs to bed, aware of a subtle change within herself. Even though the conversation had been inconclusive, resolving nothing, it had produced a distinct result. Lingering in indecision at a crossroads of choices was unlike her, and while the warning at the back of her thoughts was as pronounced as ever, she was becoming impatient with it.

The situation was the same as before, yet it was different. While going about her calls the next day and those that followed, Stephanie realized that a shift in attitude had transformed her view of her circumstances. Her commitment to her work remained as strong as ever, but she questioned her inability to claim at least a part of her life as her own.

The subject of marriage was avoided again until a week later, on an evening when Eric had to work late. Yulina kept dinner warm on the hob, and Stephanie applied the time to the disagreeable task of posting her account ledger up to date. The sound of the sawmill was faintly audible from the kitchen, and when it fell silent, Stephanie returned the ledger to the surgery as Yulina bustled about and set the table.

Eric arrived a short time later, apologizing and explaining what had kept him. The school year had ended and the children were joining their parents in preparations for spring planting, and a community effort was under way to replace the ramshackle schoolhouse in the village. Carpenters, masons, and other artisans were contributing their labor, and Eric had agreed to donate the lumber. He and his men had worked late on it so they could resume filling orders for paying customers the next day.

The project was one a magistrate would normally oversee, but Thurlow Brendell had ignored the decrepit state of the schoolhouse. Gideon Mundy had become exasperated with hearing complaints about it, and had organized the means to replace it. Work would begin the next day on the new building, which would be ready when school resumed after the harvest.

When dinner was finished, Stephanie and Eric went to the bench on the front porch. The moon cast its pale light over the valley, and the chirping of insects was a background of sound as they continued talking about the school. The village teacher was a widow who had an adequate education and the necessary strength to thrash any boy in the valley, and the people paid her a few shillings in cash or produce for each child they sent to learn the rudiments of reading, writing, and arithmetic.

"That's certainly better than no school," Eric commented,

"and it's all that many people here can afford, but I would send my children to a school in Sydney. At some of them, children can board during the week and come home on weekends, which would be a good arrangement."

Stephanie started to merely agree, then a different answer that reached into an infinitely more vital issue suddenly sprang to her lips. The decision had come gradually and almost subconsciously, but now it was steadfast, and she was resolved to accept any adverse consequences. "Yes, that would be best, and that's what we'll do, Eric," she told him.

Eric turned to her, studying her face in the dim light. "That's what we'll do?" he echoed, his voice tense and hopeful. "You and I, Stephanie? Do you mean that you'll marry me?"

"Yes, I will, Eric."

Eric moved toward her, and Stephanie met him, lifting her lips to his. He held her and kissed her with carefully restrained strength, but she pulled him close and opened her lips to his demandingly. Having committed herself, she cast off all reservations and searched eagerly to satisfy the impulses that she had kept restrained when he had been near.

He responded, their kisses becoming more passionate. A warm, melting glow enfolded Stephanie and combined with their kisses to make her breathless. He whispered his love in kisses over her face and throat, creating pleasure that intensified into a more urgent, profound need. Stephanie stood up from the bench, taking his hand, and they went inside.

Moving up the dark stairs with him, Stephanie answered his kisses with the burning desire that his caresses stirred within her. They reached the landing and stepped into her room, the moonlight streaming through the window and dimly illuminating it. Their clothes fell to the floor, their caresses becoming more intimate and ardent, and they moved to the bed.

A fleeting instant of pain disappeared into her triumphant joy of knowing him. She lifted in response to the movements of his hard, muscular body, the physical sensations combining with her emotional possession of his love and the quality that made him special and different. Keen pleasure swelled into a tide of rapture that also gripped him in quickening movements, and they surged together in wrenching spasms of bliss.

His lips and hands turned moments of quiescence into renewed passion, and Stephanie reveled in his strength as he came to her again and again. Time fell out of proportion for her, collapsing together into a constant, enduring present of lovemaking. She strained to reach a final peak, feeling his struggle for the same goal. The muscles in his wide, smooth back tensed under her hands as he reached the peak and passed over. She joined him in the throes of a consuming ecstasy that brushed the threshold of pain, smothering the cry that was torn from her against his lips.

Eric held her close and kissed her, satisfying a need for continuing contact with her. "When can we be married?" he asked softly. "It'll be when you wish, but I'd like for it to be soon. I won't have a moment's peace until you're my wife and I know I won't lose you, my love."

"We can post the banns on Sunday," she told him sleepily, "and be married a fortnight later. And I'd like a small, private wedding."

Eric agreed joyfully, pressing his lips into her hair. He was silent for a few minutes, then spoke again, assuring her that she would be happy as his wife. "Nothing will come between us or cause any problems, my love," he said. "Nothing at all, including your work."

Stephanie made no reply, pretending that she had fallen asleep, but she knew he was wrong. While she loved him and was content that she had made the right decision, the warning at the back of her mind was a steady, ominous murmur. She hoped that whatever difficulties arose could be resolved without creating any lasting disagreement between herself and Eric.

Chapter Nine

A horse tethered at the edge of the road ahead drew Stephanie's attention away from her troubled thoughts. It was in the glare of the torrid, late summer sunshine, the air oppressively humid from rain a few days before, and there was shade nearby where the horse could have been tethered. Stephanie gazed in disapproval, driving down the road toward it.

Brush beside the horse stirred, a lanky youth fastening his trousers as he emerged from it, and Stephanie realized that he had hurriedly tethered his horse and fled into the foliage to relieve himself. He was Jake Ginders, fourteen years old and a member of a large, extended family. The family was evidently afflicted once again with a recurring illness that she had treated several times before, one that had always baffled her.

When he saw Stephanie, Jake hastily put his clothes in order, his face flushing. He was good-natured and painfully shy, and she was extremely fond of him. She stopped her buggy, greeting him, but he was tongue-tied with embarrassment and could only fumble his hat off in response.

"I presume you were sent to ask me to call at the farm, Jake," she said, providing both sides of the conversation. He silently nodded, and she continued: "And the ailment is the same as before? Chundering, watery bowels, and weakness? The whole family became ill within a day or so?"

At the mention of bodily functions, Jake's face flushed to deep crimson. He turned away, the back of his neck the same ruddy color, and nodded again. "Very well, I'll call at the farm with medicine," Stephanie told him. "I'll be there as soon as possible, perhaps by midday."

Jake rushed to his horse, managing to scramble up to the saddle without turning his face to Stephanie, and rode away. She drove on down the road and continued with her calls, puzzling over the illness at Ginders Farm.

For some two years, the family had been plagued by a gastrocolic which always struck after rain that followed a dry period, but she had never diagnosed a specific disease or its cause. Symptomatic treatment cured it, or possibly the family simply recovered from it. Her father had also treated it a few times, and it had perplexed him as well.

Late in the sweltering forenoon, Stephanie was within a mile of home, and she turned toward it to get the medicine for the Ginders family. She again agonized over the problem confronting her, as she had done ever since it became evident a week before. Her foreboding about marrying Eric had been proven correct, his optimism wrong. She was faced with a direct conflict between her marriage and work, one that Eric could do nothing about.

It was so obvious that she wondered how she had failed to foresee it from the very beginning. At the same time, however, it arose from a fact which was so much a part of her life that she had long since become accustomed to compensating for it without even thinking. Her pondering had been no more than worrying, for there was no solution for the problem.

Along with her regret over the situation, she dreaded telling Eric. Her love for him had deepened since their wedding, because he was the most perfect husband any woman could want. For his part, he adored her, and his yearning for his own home and family had been fulfilled. That was symbolized by her house, which he had turned into the showcase of the valley.

The beams and window frames in the large, half-timbered house gleamed with fresh, shiny black paint, while the plaster facings were snowy white from a new coating of lime. The roof was new, the overgrown area around the house had been turned into a lawn, and a whitewashed picket fence now bordered the edge of the property along the road.

The interior of the house was also different from before. The surgery at the front of the house had been no more than a storage room since her father's death, and Stephanie had decided to return it to its original use as a parlor. The day after mentioning it to Eric, she had returned home to find that he had moved all of the cabinets, tables, and equipment into a spare downstairs bedroom, turning it into her surgery. The following day, he had gone to Sydney and bought new furniture for the parlor.

Stephanie parked her buggy in front of the house and checked the box beside the door for messages. Finding it empty, she went inside and down the hall to the surgery. The house was also empty, Eric out at work and Yulina probably at the village, but Stephanie knew they would both be home shortly. She herself only ate two meals a day, but Eric and Yulina always had tiffin. She momentarily considered telling Eric about the problem and then leaving on her calls, then she dismissed the plan as cowardly.

After filling two large bottles with gentian, essence of pepsin, and ginseng, along with a dash of diluted hydrochloric acid as an activator for the medicine, Stephanie returned to her buggy. She drove toward the bridge to cross over to Ginders Farm, on the west side of the valley. Isaiah and

Maud Ginders, former convicts in their sixties, had two married sons and a married daughter. In all, there were nineteen people in the family at the farm, and every one of them became ill when the sickness struck.

The drive leading into the farm had a dogleg curve where a house had once stood. Two years before, the family had demolished it after building a huge new house on a hill farther back. Stephanie suddenly recalled that the illness had started at about the same time. That seemed coincidental, however, for the hill was a more healthful site than the former one.

Maud Ginders, withered with age but still spry, met Stephanie at the door. The woman's wrinkled face was pale from the illness that had struck the family, but she was as amiable as always. "Come in, Stephanie, come in," she said. "We were just sitting down to tiffin."

"I'm sorry if I arrived at an inconvenient time," Stephanie told her.

"It isn't," Maud replied. "It makes no difference, because everyone is too euchred to eat. Come along, my dear."

Stephanie followed the woman to the huge kitchen, its centerpiece an enormous table where the family was seated. There were adults and children of all ages. Isaiah was a stern old man and the personification of dignity, his face the color and texture of aged leather above his flowing white beard and mustache. As a symbol of his authority, he sat at the head of the table, and Jake was at a corner beside his grandfather.

The entire family was obviously ill, and as Maud had said, no one was interested in the food. Isaiah thanked Stephanie as she set the bottles of medicine on a cabinet. "We're grateful for the nostrum, Mistress Brendell," he intoned in his grave manner. "It always puts us on the improve. But we'd be as grateful again if you'd find a prevention. More than being cured, we'd greatly prefer to not be in holts with the sickness at all."

Stephanie agreed with him, earnestly wishing she had

some idea of what was causing the illness. She turned to Maud and began discussing the family's food and its preparation. The others nibbled at their food and listened as Maud answered questions, telling Stephanie the same as on other occasions when the family had become ill: They had eaten nothing unusual and the food had been prepared in the customary way. As always, the women and children had become ill during the morning, the men and youths later in the day.

Wondering if the way the sickness spread in the family was a clue to its origin, Stephanie stepped toward the washstand at one side of the kitchen. "Could there be more lye than usual in soap used to wash dishes?" she asked. "A bit of lye on plates and bowls can cause colic."

"No, we made the soap the same way that we always do," Maud replied. "Also, we've been using that same batch of soap for weeks now."

Stephanie sighed in perplexity, glancing idly out the window over the washstand. She started to turn away, then spun back and looked closely. The well was a few yards from the house. At a suitable distance, and also suitably downhill from the well, was the privy. As she looked at them, Stephanie recalled something she had read in a medical journal, then everything fell into place in her mind. "That's it!" she cried triumphantly. "Sewage from the dunny is leaking into the well!"

Stunned silence fell, except for one member of the family. Jake, who had just taken a large drink of water, made a muffled, choked sound as he kept from swallowing it. His cheeks were bulging with water, and his eyes were fixed on Stephanie, wide in consternation. Then the water spewed from his mouth, the thick stream going straight into his grandfather's face.

The kitchen exploded in pandemonium, Isaiah roaring in outraged dignity as he reeled back in his chair from the gushing water, and Jake's father bellowing angrily at the youth. People scrambled up from the table in a mad rush for towels so the patriarch could wipe his face.

Isaiah grabbed a towel and mopped his face and beard, glowering at the cringing, mortified Jake. Then the old man directed his displeasure toward Stephanie. "That's puredee borack!" he snorted. "Anyone can see that the well is a goodly measure uphill from the dunny!"

"Even so, I read an article in a medical journal that explained how sewage can leak uphill into a well," Stephanie told him. "Underground rock strata don't always follow the same contours as the surface of the ground. During rains, water flows into the dunny pit and liquefies the sewage, and it can find channels through the rock strata to—"

"Then why aren't we sick all winter?" Isaiah broke in. "We should be, if what you say is true, because it rains much of the winter."

"The family does become ill at the beginning of each winter," Stephanie pointed out. "With the help of the medicine, your bodies become accustomed to it and it no longer affects you. During a dry spell, your bodies lose that immunity, and you become ill again after the next rain."

"That's borack!" Isaiah repeated angrily. "Puredee borack!"

"No, that's the cause of the illness," Stephanie insisted. "Each and every fact supports it. At breakfast yesterday, the men and boys had tea, which was made with boiled water. The women and children drank water from the well during the morning and became ill first. Then when you and the others came in from work and drank water later, you became ill."

Several of the people stirred uneasily and eyed their water glasses, appearing even more pale and drawn from listening to the explanation. Isaiah's glare swept across them, then returned to Stephanie. "If you don't know the cause of the sickness, Mistress Brendell," he growled irately, "that's no disgrace. But it's also no excuse for devising borack that doesn't give me credit for having the brains of a kookaburra."

Her temper flaring, Stephanie bit back a heated retort and turned to Maud. "Do you have any dye at hand, Mistress Ginders?" she asked crisply.

Maud glanced between her husband and Stephanie, puzzled. "Aye, I do," she replied. "How much do you want, and what color, my dear?"

"Any dark color will do, and about a gallon or so."

Maud motioned to one of the daughters-in-law, who left the table and went into the adjoining laundry room. A moment later, the woman returned with a bucket containing something over a gallon of dark brown dye. Stephanie grabbed it from her and carried it out the back door.

The dye sloshed in the bucket as Stephanie marched down the path to the privy. She threw open the door and saw a bench with two round holes in it occupying most of the small structure. Stephanie dumped the dye into one of the holes, then slammed the door behind herself and went back up the path.

The kitchen was silent, Isaiah's eyes fixed on the door and his glare awaiting Stephanie. She glowered back at him, closing the door solidly and setting down the bucket with a firm thump. Keeping her eyes on his, she grabbed up her bag, then stamped out.

Maud accompanied Stephanie to the front door and chatted amiably to smooth over the ill feelings. Controlling her temper, Stephanie was cordial as she made her farewells with the aged woman, then she went out to her buggy and drove away. She dismissed the incident and her annoyance with Isaiah, her thoughts returning to the problem confronting her.

Pondering it, Stephanie decided to tell Eric about it that evening. She knew he would be delighted at first, then he would realize her predicament. It was a reason for happiness, as well as a severe problem. She was pregnant, and she was also constantly at risk of exposure to the diseases that she always warned pregnant women to strictly avoid.

*   *   *

When dinner was finished and Yulina was clearing the dishes off the table, Stephanie told them. It created the outburst of joy that she had anticipated; then the difficulty in the situation occurred to Yulina, whose happiness became more temperate. Eric realized it next and sobered, commenting that he had failed to think of it before.

"Neither did I," Stephanie admitted. "All things considered, that seems strange. But being exposed to diseases and taking measures against becoming ill myself are so much a part of my life that they're a normal routine, and I don't dwell on them."

"But you take measures against becoming ill," Eric pointed out, hopefully picking up on her phrase. "That lessens the danger."

"Yes, but I've still contracted illnesses from patients," she told him. "None has been serious, but minor ones can be dangerous for an unborn child. Measles in an expectant mother can cause the baby to be born blind or with mental deficiency. I've had measles, and it's accepted that no one can contract it twice, but other illnesses are a threat."

Silence fell as Eric pursed his lips and pondered. Yulina began washing the dishes, her manner uncharacteristically subdued. After a moment, Eric thought to ask what Stephanie's mother had done when she was pregnant. "But then your father was a doctor," he added on second thought.

"Yes, my mother would attend only to childbirths then," Stephanie explained.

"And there's no one else to attend to ill people here," Eric mused, thinking aloud.

"No, only a large fee would draw a doctor this far from Parramatta," Stephanie said, "and few of the people here could afford that. But under no circumstances could I decline to treat someone who is ill."

Eric quickly agreed with her, then he took an optimistic attitude and expressed confidence that the danger would be avoided and nothing untoward would occur. Stephanie had the same strong doubts as before, but she said nothing more about them as she and Eric went to the bench on the front porch to talk for a time, as they did on most evenings.

Their conversation was always lively, Eric never at a loss for an interesting topic to discuss, but to Stephanie it had a somewhat forced aspect this evening. When they went to bed, Eric's breathing seemed to be shallow for longer than usual, indicating that he was wakeful for a time. At breakfast the next morning, both he and Yulina took a cheerful, optimistic attitude toward the problem, creating an atmosphere Stephanie disliked.

When she set out on her calls, she was less troubled than the day before in one way, but deeply depressed in another. She was relieved that she had told Eric, who had a right to know. But with that accomplished, the danger to her unborn child was at the forefront of her thoughts. She already loved the tiny being within her, taking intense pleasure in the fact that her body was nourishing its growth, and knowing that what she had to do might injure or kill it created an icy fear that dominated her thoughts.

During early afternoon, she finished the second of two calls that she had on the west side of the river, then drove to Ginders Farm. Maud answered the knock at the door, and she was much improved, her eyes brighter and her wrinkled face a more healthy color. Stephanie followed her into the kitchen, as the aged woman laughed and related what had happened.

"By dark yesterday," Maud said, "the well water looked like weak tea from that brown dye you poured into the dunny pit. The youngsters have carried water down from a spring on the hill, and between that and the medicine you brought, we're all far more chipper."

Stephanie saw that for herself when she and Maud stepped into the kitchen, where the other women were watching over the small children and moving about at tasks. With the vitality of the very young, the children were recovering rapidly from the gastrocolic, and the

women would soon be back to normal. Stephanie
went out the door and across the barnyard toward
the men and youths, who were repairing the doors on
the main barn.

Isaiah stepped toward her, his bearded face chagrined.
"You were right, Mistress Brendell," he acknowledged.
"Moreover, I owe you my most humble apologies. When
that boy spit water on me, I let dudgeon rule me, and I'm
very sorry for how I spoke and acted toward you."

Stephanie dismissed it with a smile, happy to make peace
with him. "Your family will soon be well, which is the
important issue," she stressed. "I understand there's a spring
on the hill. If I were you, I'd consider buying clay pipe
from the brickyard in Sydney and piping that water to
your house. You would never need to worry again about
contaminated water."

Isaiah stroked his beard musingly and agreed that the
idea was well worth considering. Stephanie talked with
him a few minutes longer, then went back into the house.
Maud saw her to the front door, thanking her gratefully
for finding the cause of the illness that had plagued the
family.

Stephanie continued with her calls, gratified that she had
at last resolved the puzzle of the recurring illness. She
knew, however, that it had been the result of good fortune.
The circumstances had been precisely right to bring all
the facts together in her mind, including recollection of
the article in the medical journal. She fervently wished
that some similarly fortuitous solution to her predicament
would materialize, but she had no idea of what it could be,
and the possibility seemed very remote.

When she went home that evening, Stephanie met with
the same atmosphere as that morning. Having much in common in their personalities, Eric and Yulina were disinclined
to dwell on problems for which they saw no solution. Their
attitude remained cheerful and optimistic to the point of
turning hopes into expectations, Eric discussing the baby

in happy anticipation, and Yulina chatting about little John Thorpe having a playmate.

Stephanie knew that they were also trying to keep her spirits up, which made it even more uncomfortable for her. She felt that she should be grateful and respond to their efforts, but what she wanted most of all was a continuing discussion of the problem that was an open and factual examination of what might happen. In her life, as well as in her work, she was accustomed to pondering serious consequences for weeks at a time.

The nearest that she and Eric came to a meaningful discussion of the situation was three days after she had told him about it. While sitting on the porch that evening, he brought up the nature of disease in a casual, offhand way, but Stephanie immediately knew that he was exploring the degree of risk to the baby. He had a more than average knowledge about the subject, and he mentioned that there was more than one theory on how diseases were transmitted and made people ill.

"Yes, there are two main ones," Stephanie confirmed. "A relatively recent one proposes that disease is caused by germs. And I'm sure you're familiar with the other one, the miasmic theory, which contends that illness is caused by a miasma that rises from decaying organic matter. Most doctors favor that one, as do people at large."

"That's what I've always heard people say," Eric acknowledged. "Which of the theories do you think is true?"

"I've no idea," Stephanie replied candidly. "Diseases can be contracted from those who are ill, so germs could be involved. However, diseases rarely occur in the absence of foul odors. There might be some truth in both of the theories, but I'm concerned only with results. I practice and recommend cleanliness, because I've seen that it prevents many illnesses."

Eric agreed with her standpoint, commenting that results were the important issue, then he talked about other things.

A few minutes later, Stephanie mentioned the previous topic and explained what specific diseases could be harmful to an unborn child. Eric let her finish, but instead of responding, he set about an attempt to talk her out of her worries.

Stephanie met with the same result when she brought up the subject at other times, and she stopped trying. There was no change in her relationship with Eric, for she had always known that their personalities were different. The problem was minor in the overall context of their marriage, both of them remaining happy and deeply in love with each other. It was only like a flaw in an otherwise perfect diamond to Stephanie, but it was there.

It remained there through the weeks of late summer, a time that made the problem particularly regrettable to Stephanie. Her favorite season was autumn, the time of harvest, and not only for farmers. It was when a portion of life ended, when credits and debits were reckoned. While the events of the year included the milepost in her life of marriage, the season of summing up would arrive with a continuing threat to her unborn child.

A sweltering day in late February dawned much like those preceding it, yet for Stephanie it held the promise of being entirely different. Something other than the temperature, the sultry breeze, and scattered clouds had altered. At a level more fundamental than rational thought, Stephanie sensed an ebb in the cycle of the seasons. A tide in the immense forces of nature was turning, the earth ponderously shifting, and summer was starting to give way to autumn.

The day was also different in another way. It brought a solution to Stephanie's predicament, one that was sudden and unexpected. When she returned home during the afternoon, a horse was tethered in front of the house and Eric was talking with a man on the front porch. Wearing a dark suit, the stranger was a heavyset man in his forties, with ruddy features, red hair, and streaks of gray in his muttonchop whiskers.

They came down from the porch as Stephanie stepped out of her buggy, Eric introducing the man as Dr. Hamish Mcfee. Stephanie liked him immediately, the man's bright hair and complexion matched by a sunny good nature, and he had a congenial Scottish burr in his speech. He explained that he and his wife, Miriam, had arrived from Britain a week before.

"I must say that it's a great pleasure to meet you," he went on. "I visited several doctors in Sydney to introduce myself around, and your name came up frequently in my conversations. You have an enviable reputation that has spread far beyond your practice."

"That's very gratifying to hear," she replied. "I've had a few inquiries from Sydney, but it's too far away to make calls, of course."

Hamish agreed, commenting on the hours it had taken him to make the trip on horseback, and Stephanie wondered why he had come to the valley. It would be evident to any doctor that with her attending to women and childbirths, the remaining medical practice in the valley would provide only a modest income at best. When the conversation continued, however, it became clear to her that Hamish was different from most doctors.

The man explained that he had entered the profession late in life, after having worked his way up from accountant to manager in banking. His wife had contracted infantile paralysis, and doctors had told him that she was beyond hope. Refusing to accept that prognosis, he had gathered information on the disease and taken his wife to Epsom. There he had worked with her in the baths, first to save her life and then to limit her paralysis.

When his wife had recovered as much as she ever would, he had given up his career in banking and enrolled in London Medical College. After graduating, he had worked with other doctors for a time, then had decided to emigrate to Australia. "It was mostly for Miriam," he continued. "She loves the country, and I couldn't find work with a doctor outside of London. This valley would be the perfect place for her, and I'd like to join you here and buy a partnership in your practice. My finds are limited just now, but I'd be glad to pay over a period of time."

Stephanie had begun anticipating the offer, relief and intense satisfaction building within her. "You're more than welcome to simply join me here," she told him. "I'll attend to women's illnesses and lyings-in, and you can attend to the rest. I couldn't in good conscience take money for part of the practice, because the income will be barely a living. More families settle here each year, though, and it'll increase in time."

"Meanwhile," Eric put in, "you'll have an ample pantry. The farmers here are generous when paying with produce. Also, there's an empty cottage in the village that you could rent or buy at a fair price."

Hamish was speechless for a moment, his ruddy features even more florid with surprise and delight, then he found his tongue: "That's most generous of you, Stephanie!" he exclaimed. "And a cottage in the village would suit my needs perfectly, Eric. I assumed that the income from the practice here would be small, but all I want is for Miriam to be happy and for me to make a living. I can't wait to tell her about this, and I'll make arrangements to bring her and our belongings here just as soon as possible."

"I'll bring a wagon to Sydney tomorrow and transport your wife and belongings here," Eric offered. "Before I leave, I'll go up to the village and speak with the owners of the cottage for you."

Hamish thanked Eric gratefully, accepting the offer. Stephanie invited Hamish to stay for dinner, but he was eager to rush back to Sydney and tell his wife the good news. He thanked them again and made his farewells, going down the steps to his horse, and rode away. Eric put an arm around Stephanie and exchanged a joyful smile with her as they went into the house.

Dinner was a celebration, as well as an end to the strained atmosphere in the house. Eric and Yulina were exuberant, while Stephanie had still another reason to be elated. In addition to the elimination of the threat to her unborn child, she would be able to once again concentrate upon women's illnesses and childbirths.

Eric left at dawn the next morning, and when Stephanie finished her calls late in the day, she drove up to the village. Eric had just arrived with·the Mcfees at a neat, comfortable cottage, which teemed with neighbors helping the couple settle in. Miriam Mcfee was prematurely aged and deformed by the ravages of her disease, but she had a sweet disposition that obscured her appearance. Immediately upon meeting her, Stephanie knew that she had enriched her own life with another close, warm friendship.

The following morning, Stephanie began taking Hamish with her on her calls and introducing him at each farm they passed. The people were at first reluctant to place their trust in a different physician, but Hamish made a good impression and quickly won their confidence. After the third day, he began making calls on his own.

The feel in the air of approaching autumn grew more pronounced, ushering in a time of intense happiness for Stephanie. Her marriage was a constant joy, her work more satisfying than ever. At last she had time to make extra calls and check on pregnancies, small children, and women's illnesses. The only thing that marred her contentment was the prison casting its baneful shadow over her life.

On the first of March, Stephanie attended a childbirth that lasted into late afternoon. Leaving during the usual bedlam of joy over the newborn, she drove down through the valley and turned onto the village road. Then, as she started to turn in at her house, she hesitated and stopped.

Because of attending the birthing, she had deferred three calls, which would make the next day a busy one. Tipton

Bellamy occasionally worked late in his office, Stephanie reflected, and if she could register the birth now, she could make an early start on her calls the next day. She tugged a rein, driving on up the road toward the village.

At the top of the hill, cockatoos and other birds were circling through the trees and finding roosts for the night. The village was quiet in the rich, golden light of sunset, the people in their homes for the evening and smoke from dinner fires rising above the chimneys.

The lane leading to the district clerk's office and prison at the edge of the village was more than quiet. It was oppressively still, with deep, vaguely portentous shadows creeping from under trees. When the prison came into view, the bleak, towering building appeared as devoid of life as always. The wretched humanity within was contained so tightly by its thick stone walls that no outward indication of habitation was ever revealed.

Stephanie stopped in front of the district clerk's office and tried the door. It was locked; Tipton was gone for the day. She started to return to her buggy, then on an impulse she stepped toward the prison.

With the huge, sinister building looming over her, she thought about her father, recalling her troubled feelings the last time she had seen him. Deeply remorseful, she fervently wished that she had acted upon her feelings and done anything necessary to get him out of the prison.

Then a sudden impression of something near swept over her, yet nothing was there. A silent sound rang in the air, a stir without movement. She was alone but not by herself, detecting a distinctive, unmistakable presence that had been beloved and familiar from her earliest childhood memories.

She clutched her hands to her face, swaying on her feet. A scream rose within her, leaving her lips as a whisper: "Father . . . Father. . . ."

Greeting touched her mind, fond and warm, but there was also a sense of the most crushing grief. It was a weary sorrow from being bound between life and death, without the joys of one or the peace of the other. Stephanie groped with her mind, seeking to maintain contact.

"Father, I'm married," she whispered. "His name is Eric, and he is the most wonderful of men. He adores me, Father, and I love him just as much. Father, I'm pregnant. I'm going to have my very own child. . . ."

The touch in her mind conveyed pleasure, an overlay to the tidal wave of weary sorrow. Stephanie continued, whispering about her friend Yulina, little John Thorpe, the patients, the Mcfees, and others.

When she finished, a sense of farewell came to her. Then there was a withdrawing beyond the reach of her mind, and she was by herself again.

Stephanie realized that she was sobbing brokenly, almost overwhelmed by a seething flux of emotions. It seemed as though an hour or longer had passed since she walked toward the prison, but the sun was still in the same place, sliding behind the hills on the west side of the valley. She turned and stumbled toward her buggy, crying and wiping at her tears.

She struggled to comprehend what had happened, but it was too strange. It had been the most wondrous experience of her life, but also the most troubling. That torment of sorrow was dreadful, and it would endure through eternity. She sat in her buggy, unable to stop crying.

Chapter Ten

"**G** 'day, Mistress Thorpe. No, it's Mistress Brendell now, isn't it? I beg pardon, mo'm."

Stephanie stopped her buggy, pulling the coach blanket closer against the winter wind, and studied the young rider curiously. He seemed only vaguely familiar, and his clothing was unusual. He wore a bulky sheepskin coat that reached down to his heavy boots, and a wide stockman's hat with the brim turned up on one side. His horse, a hairy, muscular beast that had ill-tempered eyes, also looked different from those in the valley.

The youth's appearance reminded Stephanie of the stockman from the outback whom she had met the previous winter. Then she realized that the youth was Roger Corbett, who had been pathetically thin from tuberculosis. "Roger!" she cried happily. "My word, how you've improved!"

"Aye, I have, mo'm," he agreed, laughing. "Tibooburra Station put me right, and I haven't coughed for months."

"I can see that for myself," Stephanie assured him, gazing at his tanned, handsome features. In letters his parents had received from him, he had reported that his health was better, but the extent of his improvement amazed Stephanie. He was still somewhat spare, but he looked vibrantly healthy. "You're content with life in the outback, then?"

"Aye, it's not for everyone, but it suits me to a turn," he replied. "Tibooburra Station isn't just a place where we work, it's a way of life. And the owners are the finest of people. It takes the outback to hold a family like the Kerricks, especially Mistress Alexandra."

Stephanie smiled, intensely pleased that he was happy. "What sort of work do you do at the station, Roger?" she asked.

"I'm a jackaroo, and I work for Isaac Logan," he told her. "He's the stockman in charge of Dingo Paddock. It was called Bushranger Paddock before, because three bushrangers were buried there. But the name was changed after a big foofaraw last summer, when we rooted up the bones of those bushrangers and cooked them down to dust in a rendering kettle."

"The bones were cremated?" Stephanie verified, uncertain if she had understood the youth correctly.

Roger nodded, explaining that Alexandra Kerrick had ordered it done just after she had returned from a journey to Sydney. The bones had been piled into a kettle used for rendering mutton tallow, then the kettle had been placed in an earth oven. "When the bones were cooked down," he continued, "we mixed the dust with chopped mutton, then set it out for dingoes to eat. Ever since then, the paddock has been called Dingo Paddock."

"What was the purpose in all that?" Stephanie asked in amazement.

"I'm not sure, mo'm." Roger hesitated, appearing to be puzzled by his own answer, then: "You know, it didn't seem a whit peculiar at the time. But now that I'm here where the place is so little and everything is crowded together, I've noticed that what happens there can sound passing odd when I talk about it. I don't know why, but there it is."

"The outback must be very different," Stephanie observed.

"Aye, it's that, and more," Roger agreed emphatically. "It's bigger than big, then a goodly distance on from that. The nights can be deep, with the Southern Cross looking so far away that you wonder how you can see it. But it's different in ways that some can't abide. It gets on their pip and they go crank, and the Kerricks have had to send a few back here because they got to where they wouldn't talk to anybody but theirselves."

The conversation continued, Roger talking about other things. The winter cold penetrated Stephanie's coach blanket and thick coat. Heavily pregnant now, she grew uncomfortable after sitting in one position for too long. But together with her intense satisfaction over Roger's recovery from tuberculosis, the discussion intrigued her. The youth explained that his horse was different because it was a colt from a brumbie, a wild horse. Then he told Stephanie that he had come to Sydney among a party of station employees who had escorted Alexandra Kerrick to the city.

"But you said that Mistress Kerrick traveled to Sydney only last summer, didn't you?" Stephanie pointed out. "She must have had some important reason to make that difficult journey again such a short time later."

"Aye, no doubt," Roger agreed, "but I don't know what it is. The family isn't the sort that one would try to be the stickybeak with them. The Kerrick daughter, Deirdre, is in a boarding school in Sydney. I heard that Mistress Alexandra got a letter from her, and that might have something to do with it." He gathered his reins, sitting up on his saddle. "I was given leave to pass the time with my family today, and I'd best get on back to the others. I hope to see you again before we bluie, Mistress Brendell."

"I do as well, Roger," she replied. "Good-bye for now."

The youth waved, riding away at a gallop. Stephanie drove on down the road to continue her calls, the dull day seeming brighter than before. She was delighted over

Roger's recovery, and the conversation with him had been fascinating. The questions it had raised and what Roger had said would provide lively discussion for the evening, and she looked forward to getting home.

The conversation with Roger had lasted over an hour, and it made Stephanie late with the remainder of her calls. Icy cold winter nightfall had settled by the time she drove into the barnyard at her house. Eric stepped out of the kitchen door with a lantern to attend to her horse and buggy. She crossed the barnyard to the kitchen door and opened it cautiously, for little John Thorpe was able to crawl now and might be hurt by the opening door. The path clear, she stepped into the warm, cheery kitchen, greeting Yulina.

Eric came in a few minutes later, and Yulina dished up large servings of beef and vegetable pie. While they ate, Stephanie described her conversation with Roger, Eric and Yulina listening closely and commenting. On the question as to why Alexandra Kerrick had ordered the bushrangers' bones to be cremated and then the dust mixed with chopped mutton for dingoes to eat, Yulina was certain that she knew the answer.

"It was to be rid of them," she stated positively. "My ma used to say that if you want to be rid of something, get a dingo to eat it."

"I would say," Eric remarked dryly, "that the bushrangers had already been disposed of very effectively. They were dead and buried."

"But having dingoes eat their bones gets rid of them entirely," Yulina explained. "Then it's as though they had never been. I opine that Mistress Kerrick knows something about Aborigine ways."

Stephanie agreed with Yulina, then continued telling them about the conversation. The subject of Alexandra Kerrick's current journey led to a long discussion. Eric commented that the woman was evidently undeterred by extremes of weather when she wished to travel. The reason for the journey remained only a matter of speculation, but it provided a topic of interesting conversation for the winter evening.

The following day, a Sunday, Stephanie learned the reason for Alexandra Kerrick's journey. With no calls scheduled for the day, she had planned to go to church with Eric, Yulina, and little John Thorpe. She and Eric were in their room and preparing to leave when he looked out a window and exclaimed in surprise, calling Stephanie to the window.

A large, gleaming carriage was moving up the valley road from the south, which was unusual in itself, for such vehicles were rarely seen outside of Sydney. Moreover, this one was traveling at breakneck speed, drawn by six horses instead of the usual two or four. The driver was standing in the box and cracking his whip above the horses, while a rider in front shouted and cleared the road of people on their way to church.

The people dashed off to each side and watched in astonishment as the carriage thundered past in a cloud of dust. Stephanie saw that the driver and rider in front wore long sheepskin coats and stockmen's hats. The horses were the shaggy, powerful offspring of brumbies, their eyes wild and foam flying from their lips in their pounding, headlong run. More than unusual, the scene was an invasion of an alien atmosphere into Wallaby Track. It was an eerie wind wafting across vast reaches from the strange, distant outback, a land of no half measures, no restraint, where nothing was held in reserve.

When the peculiar spectacle drew closer, Stephanie recognized the rider. He was the stocky, bearded Ruel Blake, whom she had met the previous winter. "Eric, I think the carriage is coming here," she mused in wonder.

"But why would it come here, and who would—"

Eric broke off as Stephanie rushed out of the room, and he hurried after her. By the time she reached the foot of the staircase, Stephanie could hear the thundering hoofbeats turning onto the village road. She dashed up the hall and threw the front door open just as the carriage skidded to a stop in front of the house, dust billowing around it.

Ruel Blake leaped off his horse and bounded up the steps, doffing his hat. "G'day, Mistress Brendell," he greeted her. "I'm here at the bidding of Mistress Alexandra Kerrick, who is with a friend in Sydney. The friend began having a baby a short while ago, and her doctor is ailing. He said that you're the most skilled midwife hereabouts, and I was told to ask if you would be so kind as to come and see to the lady."

"No, now just a moment," Eric interrupted sternly when Stephanie started to speak. "I'm Eric Brendell, and my wife's condition is plain to see. Even if she wasn't with child, I wouldn't have her put into danger by riding in a carriage the way that one was being driven."

"Ruel Blake," the thickset, bearded stockman said, introducing himself to Eric. "I assure you that your wife will be in no danger, Mr. Brendell. The driver there, Eulie Bodenham, is the best teamster you'll ever see. I'd trust him with my life, and Mistress Brendell will be safe."

The driver, a tall, lanky half-Aborigine, was moving around the carriage and examining the wheels, springs, and axles. At the mention of his name, he lifted his hat and grinned amiably, then resumed his inspection. Ruel's assurances failed to satisfy Eric, and he continued objecting, insisting that Stephanie would be exposed to too much danger in the carriage.

"No, I don't think so, Eric," she put in. "The carriage arrived here safe and sound, didn't it? Mistress Kerrick accepted Roger Corbett as an employee, which restored his health, and I feel that attending to her friend is the least I can do in return." She lifted a hand as he started to disagree. "Please, Eric, I'll come to no harm, and this is something that I must do. And with labor having begun, I mustn't tarry. If you and Ruel will take my things to the carriage, I'll get ready to leave."

Eric still had misgivings, but he followed Stephanie and
Ruel down the hall to the surgery. They carried her bag and
the nitrous oxide flask to the carriage while she put on her
coat and hat, then she went outside. Eric kissed her, his
smile forced and tinged with worry, and helped her into
the carriage. Stephanie settled herself on the seat as Eulie
Bodenham scrambled up to the box and Ruel stepped into
his saddle.

Eulie manipulated the sheaf of reins expertly, turning the
first two horses. The others followed, the double line of
horses snaking around and the carriage swinging toward
the road behind them. The horses broke into a trot, moving
down the village road, and turned onto the road down the
valley. Then Eulie whistled shrilly and his whip began
cracking like gunshots. The horses leaped into a run, and
the carriage lurched forward.

Stephanie gripped the strap beside the door and braced
herself, finding the ride less uncomfortable than she had
expected. The springs on the large, luxurious carriage
absorbed the impact of the wheels jarring through ruts
and slamming over rocks. Over the drumming hoofbeats,
the jangle of harness chains, and the rumble of the wheels,
she heard Ruel shouting and clearing the road.

The miles passed swiftly, and Stephanie wondered how
the pace had been maintained. The distance they had just
come from her house would have exhausted many horses
at a run, and it was inconceivable that they had run all the
way from Sydney. Then, when Parramatta came into view,
she saw how it had been done. Near the outskirts of the
town, men and youths in sheepskin coats were waiting at
the edge of the road with fresh horses.

The carriage slid to a stop beside the waiting horses, Ruel
jumping down from his saddle and uncinching it to put it
on a fresh horse. What followed looked to Stephanie like a
disorganized melee of kicking, rearing horses, and stockmen
and jackaroos dashing about. Roger grinned in the window,
waving to her, then he was gone. Then, only moments after

stopping, the carriage moved on down the road with fresh
horses harnessed to it.

The street through the town was crowded, and the horses
varied between a trot and canter while Ruel roared at people
to move aside. At the eastern outskirts of the town, Eulie
began cracking his whip and the horses charged into a
run. Stephanie watched the scenery flash past, reflecting
that what had begun as a leisurely Sunday had suddenly
turned into an extraordinarily strange, but keenly interesting
experience.

Once the carriage reached Sydney and skirted around
the center of the city to a district of neat, modest homes,
Stephanie met with another peculiar sight. Large wagons
were parked in a row, horses munched fodder in a pen of
ropes and poles, and jackaroos sat around a campfire. The
encampment would have been unremarkable at the side of
a narrow track somewhere in the wilderness of the outback.
Instead of that, however, it was in the yard in front of a
house, drawing startled, curious gazes from passersby.

The jackaroos raced to take the horses when the carriage
drew up in front of the house, Eulie leaping down to open
the door for Stephanie. He and Ruel gathered up her bag
and the gas flask, then followed her up the path. The front
door opened and Alexandra Kerrick stepped out.

As the motivating force behind all the unusual goings-on,
the woman was remarkably but appropriately different from
others. She had strikingly beautiful features, and her other
characteristics were just as distinctive. Stephanie knew she
had to be in her forties, yet she looked a decade younger.
Her dress, in the latest high fashion, was an expensive pale
brown brocade trimmed with matching lace, but there was
nothing snobbish about Alexandra Kerrick.

Her bearing was regal, yet she had a warm, charmingly
gracious manner that immediately won Stephanie over.
"It's so kind of you to come here and attend my friend,"
Alexandra said. "I realize it was asking much of you, and
I'm most grateful that you're here."

"It's a pleasure to respond to your request," Stephanie assured her. "Your accepting Roger Corbett as an employee was a far greater kindness, and it saved him from the certainty of an untimely death."

"It was also to the benefit of the station," Alexandra pointed out, drawing Stephanie into the house. "He's done more than well as a jackaroo, and he'll be an excellent stockman. I won't deny that there's satisfaction in helping others, of course, and I must say that I envy you the immense gratification you deservedly have each day from your work."

Stephanie made a fitting reply, continuing the verbal exchanges of becoming acquainted, and she concealed her surprise at seeing several maids. Uniformed in dark dresses and crisp white aprons and mobcaps, they were as out of place in the modest home as the encampment was in the yard. Two maids took the gas flask and bag from the stockmen and carried them to a bedroom, others following with basins of water, soap, and towels.

Alexandra led Stephanie toward the bedroom, telling her about the patient. "My friend's name is Clara Tavish," she explained. "Her labor began some four hours ago, and her physician, Dr. Oliver Willis, is bedridden with vernal catarrh. He said that while he hasn't had the pleasure of meeting you, you're known to be the most skilled midwife in the region." .

"I'm pleased to have Dr. Willis's respect, and I trust he'll recover soon," Stephanie commented. "Is Clara's husband at home or nearabout?"

"No."

The reply, spoken with a smile, was anything but brusque. At the same time, Stephanie gained an understanding of what Roger had meant when he said that the Kerricks discouraged curiosity. A door on a subject had been closed gently, but just as effectively as if it had been slammed.

In the bedroom, Stephanie washed her hands while talking and establishing a rapport with Clara. The woman was in her thirties, pretty and with lovely gray eyes, and her face revealed no undue strain or fatigue. Stephanie examined her and found the childbirth proceeding normally through the first stage, and she noted the striae from previous birthings.

"I'd say you've had three children," she estimated, washing her hands again, "and the last was about seven years ago."

"You're absolutely correct!" Clara exclaimed in wonder. "I understand why you're said to be the best midwife hereabouts, Mistress Brendell."

"My name is Stephanie, and I'm experienced," she replied, moving a chair to the side of the bed. "You are as well, so we'll work together and you'll have another beautiful child before the day is out."

Alexandra moved a chair to the other side of the bed, and Stephanie placed her bag and the gas flask within convenient reach. When the next contraction came, Stephanie talked the woman through it and gauged her tolerance for pain. It was higher than average, Clara having an iron will. Stephanie had to give her only a whiff of the gas at the peak of the pain.

The birthing settled into the usual watchful routine for Stephanie, even if the setting was anything but usual. Instead of the typical crowd of relatives, friends, and neighboring women, there was only Alexandra. And for Stephanie, there was also the perplexing question as to why Alexandra had traveled hundreds of miles through the wilderness of the outback in the dead of winter to be at the bedside of a friend giving birth.

The question remained unanswered for a time, but the conversation with Alexandra was as fascinating as she herself. Reliable information about the outback was rare in the coastal area, and Stephanie's discussion with Roger had been too brief to be fully informative. For the first time, she had something of an understanding of the vast region.

It was no more than that, however, even though Alexandra was extremely articulate. Stephanie realized that the outback was something more than the sum of its landforms and other physical features, and that its indescribable character was its fundamental nature, making it different from other places. That same quality was what made it unendurable for some, driving them either to the more settled regions or into the escape of insanity.

The second stage of labor began in the late forenoon, and a short time later, a maid came to the door and announced that a repast had been laid out in the front room. More than hungry, Stephanie had pains in her back from sitting too long. Upon taking advantage of the opportunity to move about between contractions, she found that along with the maids, an expert cook was in the house. The repast consisted of assorted vol-au-vents, the spicy, delicious meat fillings surrounded by feathery light, crisp pastry.

During the afternoon, Stephanie heard a different feminine voice call a cheerful greeting to the maids. The other two women also heard it, Clara smiling wanly. "If I'm not greatly mistaken," she said to Alexandra, "Lady Deirdre Augusta Juliana Hanover is here."

Stephanie recognized Alexandra's daughter's name, as well as that of the royal family. She concluded that the rest was a private joke between Clara and Alexandra, who laughed as she left the room. Stephanie's back began hurting again, and after the next contraction ended, she stood up and went toward the front room to meet Deirdre Kerrick.

Stepping down the hall, Stephanie heard Alexandra and her daughter talking, evidently alone in the front room. The girl raised her voice in annoyance, her words becoming audible: "Morton is my brother and I love him, but he's been churlish, Mother. He should be here with Clara, and if need be, you should drag him here by the scruff of his neck. . . ."

The girl lowered her voice and continued talking. Stephanie quickly and softly moved back toward the bedroom, the entire situation suddenly clear to her: Alexandra had traveled to Sydney to be present at the birth of her grandchild, Morton Kerrick's child out of wedlock, and she had commandeered the carriage and maids from his household. Stephanie moved forward again, taking steps that could be heard in the front room.

Deirdre was a vivacious, charming girl in her teens, tall and slender like her mother, and she wore a Sydenham Academy uniform. Stephanie exchanged greetings with her when Alexandra introduced them, and reflected that the girl was as attractive as her mother. There was a difference in personality, however, one that had been pointed up by the remarks that Stephanie had overheard. Alexandra preferred to achieve her ends through subtle means, whereas Deirdre had a more aggressive, confrontational disposition.

Stephanie talked with Deirdre for a few minutes, then went back to the bedroom. Presently, the girl left and Alexandra returned. The baby's head crowned a short time later, Clara beginning the final stage of labor.

Near the end of the labor, maids came into the room. When it was born, the baby was a large boy that was immediately very active, squirming and crying. Maids started to take the baby, but Alexandra shook her head as she lifted it and carried the baby to the table to wash it.

When the afterbirth was ejected, Stephanie made certain it was complete, then the maids began cleaning up. Alexandra stepped back to the bed with the baby wrapped in a blanket, her eyes filled with tears. She obviously wanted to hold it herself forever, but she handed it over to Clara.

A glance between Stephanie and Alexandra turned into a lingering gaze. Stephanie smiled sympathetically, Alexandra in acknowledgment. It was a moment of perfect understanding, sealing friendship between them.

Stephanie made her farewells with Clara and left, Alexandra going out to the porch with her. Dusk had settled, the campfire bright in the winter twilight, and it cast its flickering glow across the porch. Stephanie talked with Alexandra while the stockmen harnessed horses to the carriage and lit the coachlamps. Stephanie made no mention of payment for the delivery, for it had become a service performed by and for a friend.

"I'd give years from my life to take the baby to Tibooburra Station with me," Alexandra mused wistfully. "But I've far too much respect for motherhood to even mention it to Clara. I shall have to content myself with visiting my grandson when I'm in Sydney." She shrugged off her mood, smiling. "This day has been more remarkable for me through meeting you, Stephanie."

"I certainly feel the same, Alexandra," Stephanie replied. "I hope we'll meet again. If not, we shall remain friends at a distance."

"Indeed we shall," Alexandra agreed emphatically. "Despite the miles and different ways of life that lie between us, I hope to have the pleasure of your company again. And I shall think of you often."

The carriage was ready, Eulie waiting beside it. Stephanie exchanged a hug and kiss with Alexandra, then went down the path toward the vehicle. Halfway down the path she turned back, the firelight dimly illuminating the tall, beautiful woman on the porch. "I didn't ask Clara if she had chosen a name for the baby," she said. "Do you know if she has?"

"Yes, I discussed that with her this morning," Alexandra replied. "The baby's name is Jeremy."

Stephanie nodded, walking on down the path. Eulie helped her into the carriage and climbed up to the box. As the vehicle moved away, Alexandra waved, then went back into the house. Stephanie settled herself comfortably and tried to put the day in perspective with others. It was difficult, for the people of the outback were a different breed. Most of all, meeting the fascinating Alexandra Kerrick had been a unique experience.

However, she had a strong premonition that while the day was ending, its events had yet to be concluded. Even though she might never see Alexandra again, Stephanie felt certain that their fates were somehow entwined. At some future time and in some fashion, their lives would touch once more.

For the past three years, a mated pair of ganggang cockatoos had roosted in the tree outside Stephanie's room for part of the year. Migratory birds, they spent spring and summer in the mountains, then came to the valley during autumn for the winter. The small, owl-like birds were more cute than beautiful, the male with a bright red head and the female having a patterned tint of pale red. After trying different kinds of food, Stephanie had found that they preferred barley most of all. She kept an ample amount of it at the foot of their tree during autumn and winter, regarding them as pets.

Unlike many other species of cockatoos, they were usually inconspicuous and silent. Stephanie heard their characteristic staccato warble only twice each year, once upon their arrival in autumn and then just prior to their leaving during the first balmy days of spring. This year, on the same morning that the gang gang cockatoos sang their song of farewell and then flew away to their other home in the mountains, Stephanie went into labor.

The pain was what she had expected, having observed it scores of times in others, yet it was different. She remained a midwife at a rational level, analyzing her condition while the hours passed and Hamish Mcfee expertly attended to her. In a more personal way as a human being, she cringed under agony that the nitrous oxide only partially suppressed. But as the moment of birth grew nearer, the pain became a payment for forthcoming joy.

Her son, a strong, healthy baby, was born during late afternoon, and she named him Stephen. Then the pain she had suffered became insignificant when measured against her joy, which was on an entirely different scale. With her own child, the pleasure and wonder that she had always experienced over new life entering the world were incomparably more intense.

Stephanie was up and about a few hours later, but she decided to remain at home for a few weeks, with Hamish Mcfee attending to her patients. She felt that the time away from her work was due her after her years of service to others, for a fresh, new aspect of life had just opened to her. She had known love in its varieties, for her mother, her father, and for Eric, but she had never before experienced the quality and magnitude of emotion that utterly possessed her while contemplating her son.

Nature had run its course and finished the physical process of childbirth, but Stephanie knew that one thing remained to be done before her son was completely incorporated into her life. It was vital, constantly on her mind and pressing upon her urgently, but it had to wait for the right circumstances. The baby had to be a few days old before he could be taken out into the brisk spring air, and she had to have total privacy.

Those circumstances developed on a Sunday afternoon, when the baby was just over a week old. Eric was at the sawmill, making repairs to the steam engine in preparation for the following week, and Yulina took little John Thorpe and went to visit a friend at a farm down the road. The restful quiet of a sunny Sunday afternoon had settled over Wallaby Track.

With her baby wrapped warmly in a blanket, Stephanie hitched a horse to her buggy and drove up to the village. A steely, hostile coldness of the spirit more intense than the chill of winter pressed down upon the lane leading to the district clerk's office and the prison. On the Sunday afternoon, the lane was even more still and lifeless than usual.

Stephanie parked her buggy near the prison, then stepped out and carried her baby close to the dark, thick stone wall. Standing there and gazing sightlessly over the valley, she cast her thoughts into the void an unimaginable distance away, yet within a single heartbeat of every human. "Father, I am here," she whispered. "I am here. . . ."

The familiar, beloved presence was suddenly all about

her as a subtle, ineffable difference in her surroundings. A sense of greeting touched her mind, along with immense, weary sorrow from entrapment in the dreary place of terror and misery. It brought tears to Stephanie's eyes, and she began crying as she unfolded the blanket from her baby's face.

"Father, this is my son," she whispered, holding up the baby to display it. "This is my son, and his name is Stephen. . . ."

The touch on her mind conveyed pleasure, but it was only an overtone to that listless, overwhelming melancholy. Stephanie wept and continued talking about her baby, searching for words to describe how much she loved it. She yearned for a way to lift that burden of grief from the beloved presence, but it was eternal and she was only human.

PART
TWO

Chapter Eleven

S itting in his wagon across the street from the grounds of Belhaven School, Eric saw John and Stephen among the boys flooding out of the main hall. He waved to them, and their reactions encapsulated their personalities. Stephen smiled happily and waved, while John leaped into the air and flapped an arm vigorously, his wide grin radiating delight.

The boys crossed the street, wearing oilskins over their coats against the chill June rain, and John bounded into the wagon. Almost nine, he was a chubby, muscular boy with an exuberantly friendly nature, his dusky skin and hints of Aborigine characteristics in his features reflecting his bloodlines. "You didn't repair that gearbox yet, did you?" he asked.

Eric smiled and shook his head, taking great pleasure in the boy's precocious mechanical ability. "No, it's waiting for you to get those bearings in it, and we ran the sawmill at full speed off the flywheel spindle this week," he replied. "We couldn't use the fine blade at full speed, of course, but all the orders for finished lumber will wait until next week."

Grinning happily, John settled himself on the seat as Stephen climbed up to it. Tall and slender at eight, he was an exceptionally handsome boy with a close resemblance to his mother. While he was congenial, it was in a manner consistent with his sober, studious disposition. From his early childhood, his consuming interest in life had been his mother's work, and it was evident that he would be a physician.

Eric tugged the reins and turned the wagon away from the curb, taking care to avoid other boys scampering about and going home for the weekend. The school was on a side street that led into upper George Street, which was congested with traffic. Ever since the gold rush had begun three years before, the main thoroughfares of the city had become teeming arteries. Eric guided the wagon into the flow of traffic, the foot pavements overflowing with newly arrived prospectors carrying packs with digging tools and gold pans strapped to them.

The outskirts of the city had spread up Parramatta Road, replacing the small farms, and more prospectors were on each side as Eric drove up the road and talked with the boys. Both were in a happy frame of mind, John looking forward to working on the sawmill machinery, and Stephen eagerly anticipating accompanying his mother on her calls. Eric's mood more than matched theirs; the weekends were a time of the keenest pleasure for him.

The weekend was when his extended family, including John and Yulina, was at home. He and Stephanie had two other children, Erica now six years old, and Ralph almost three. They were a constant source of pride and happiness for Eric, and his greatest joy came when the entire family was around him.

The weekends were also when his satisfaction in his family overcame a discontent that troubled him in quiet moments. At no time had he regretted abandoning his goal of wealth in favor of the more richly fulfilling purpose in life of his family, but a reason had arisen that made him wish he had devoted more time and effort to business affairs.

The verges of Parramatta Road were littered with spots of ashes where wave after wave of prospectors had camped. A few of the new arrivals stopped at campsites as the rainy afternoon grew darker, but the lure of gold that had brought them from distant lands kept most of them tramping up the road. Parramatta had grown and pushed its outskirts down the road, and presently the wagon began passing houses at the edge of the town.

Dusk settled as Eric drove through the town, its main street crowded with townspeople and still more prospectors hurrying toward the gold fields. Then he turned onto the road leading northward from Parramatta, and the farther up the road he drove, the more the bustle and changes from the gold rush were left behind. Miles to the north, Wallaby Track remained a peaceful, rural backwater, its pace of life the same as years before.

After lighting the lanterns at the sides of the wagon, Eric drove on up the road through the dark night. It was past the boys' bedtime, and they dozed off to sleep, slumped against each other and Eric. He was just as content as when he had been talking with them, their presence providing him with the pleasure of their companionship even when they slept.

The boys woke instantly when he drove into the barnyard, scrambling down from the wagon and running inside. Eric unharnessed and fed the horses, then crossed the barnyard and went into the kitchen. Its cheery warmth dispelled the damp chill of the winter night, and the roast beef dinner awaiting him smelled delicious. But everything else paled into insignificance compared to the smile on Stephanie's beautiful face, his all-consuming love for her remaining the most profound and joyful aspect of his life.

The boys were eating their dinner and talking with their mothers, Erica and Ralph having gone to bed hours before.

Eric hung up his oilskins, coat, and hat, then took the
newspaper he had bought in Sydney out of his coat pocket.
He regretted what Stephanie would find in it. He knew the
information would leave her depressed, but she had asked
him to bring a newspaper.

Yulina dished up Eric's dinner, and he placed the newspaper on the table as he sat down. The happy conversation
between the boys and their mothers continued for a few
minutes, then the boys finished their dinner and went to
their rooms. Yulina gathered up the boys' dishes and took
them to the washstand, and Stephanie picked up the newspaper, unfolding it.

The pleasure on her lovely face faded, her wide blue eyes
clouding with worry. "The notice is still in the newspaper,"
she observed sadly. "They haven't found him yet."

Eric nodded sympathetically as he continued eating.
Stephanie always took a close interest in children she
delivered, and she seemed particularly concerned about
the disappearance of Jeremy Kerrick the previous autumn.
The family had placed notices in the newspaper during
the past months, offering a reward for information on his
whereabouts. "Yes, I saw the notice, love," Eric told her.
"It's a very strange state of affairs, isn't it?"

"Strange indeed." Stephanie studied the notice, shaking
her head in bewilderment. "What could have happened, and
where could he be? Alexandra and the rest of the family
must be distraught."

Eric agreed with her, the discussion much like others
ever since the reward notice had first appeared in
the newspapers. Yulina took his dishes and washed
them when he finished dinner, then went to her
room. Stephanie leafed through the newspaper, the
conversation turning to other things, and she said
that she had heard that Thurlow Brendell's condition
was worse.

Eric shrugged indifferently. Some four years before, the
man had suffered a heart seizure and had been confined to

his house since then, under the care of a doctor from Parramatta. Gideon Mundy had reluctantly accepted appointment as district magistrate. "As far as I'm concerned," Eric commented somberly, "I never had a father. He means nothing to me."

"If your father dies, that attitude will change," Stephanie warned him. "It will change to one that will distress you unless you take measures to prevent it. You should go and see him."

The suggestion seemed pointless to Eric, and the rest of what she had said was meaningless to him. However, he had long since found out that he would never know her well enough to understand everything she said and did. Her blue eyes perceived things no one else could see. She had remote depths and complexities of personality that were unfathomable, giving her a mysterious quality that made her endlessly intriguing and alluring.

"Even if I went there, he would probably refuse to see me," Eric said. "Do you have calls tomorrow that will be interesting for Stephen?"

Stephanie took the abrupt change of subject in stride, shaking her head doubtfully. "No, they involve conditions unsuitable for discussion at his age," she replied, "so I'll have him spend the day with Hamish. I spoke with Hamish about it, and he's very much in favor of it. He's treating a number of common illnesses and conditions just now, and Stephen might well learn things that he will find useful in years to come."

The reference to their son's becoming a doctor resurrected the discontent that had been troubling Eric. More than ever, he earnestly wished he had devoted more energy to business affairs so that he could now make an announcement that would delight Stephanie. Making her happy was his great joy in life, but the opportunity had been missed.

The train of thought passed quickly this time, however, for the conversation ended a few minutes later and they went upstairs to their room. During their private moments together, nothing was sufficiently imperative to intrude upon his adoring love for and fascination with Stephanie.

His feelings for her possessed him completely. Making love with her was a venture into the most intense ecstasy of body and emotions. Then holding her as they fell asleep provided a quiet pleasure that was just as fulfilling in its own way. When she was in his arms, the rest of the world was set at a far distance.

The rain ended during the night, dawn bringing a bright, brisk winter day that promised Eric an even more enjoyable weekend. Breakfast was its usual pleasant bustle, Erica and Ralph very vocal, and their childish talk was always entertaining for Eric. Stephen's regrets about not accompanying his beloved mother were compensated by the fact that he was more interested in the greater variety of Hamish Mcfee's patients. John bolted down his breakfast, eager to get to the sawmill and finish repairing the gearbox.

After breakfast, Eric harnessed a horse to Stephanie's buggy. She drove away with Stephen, taking him to the village to leave him with Hamish, and Eric walked up to the sawmill with John. The men were moving about at tasks, and Ira Cade stepped over toward Eric and John.

The previous week, Ira had grumbled about not having the gearbox repaired as quickly as possible, but Eric had considered encouraging John's interest in machinery to be well worth a temporary loss of the full capability of the sawmill. "Have you had a good look at the drive belt?" Ira asked. "Running at full speed all last week has bollixed it for fair."

Eric stepped to the saw and examined the leather belt stretching between it and the steam engine. The belt was frayed in places, and some of the rivets holding the sections of leather together were loose. "Yes, we'll need a new one," he agreed. "But we had ample use out of this one."

Ira lifted an eyebrow in doubt at the last remark, but made no comment about it. "I could ride to Sydney and order one from a saddlery," he offered. "It would probably be ready by Monday. I've given the men work to do, and it'll keep them busy for the day."

"Very well, go ahead and do that, Ira," Eric told him.

Ira nodded, turning away, and Eric and John walked over to the building that was used for tool storage and repairing equipment. The gearbox that regulated the speed of the drive belt was disassembled on the workbench, as Eric and John had left it the previous weekend. The bearings on the shafts at the ends of the gearbox had become worn, and part of the work to replace them had been done. Eric and John had filed all of the soft bearing metal out of the semicircular steel shells that held the bearings, then they had made sand molds to pour new bearing metal into the shells.

John dragged a stool over to the workbench and stood on it to bring himself up to the height of the bench. "I went to the school library and found out what Babbitt bearing metal is made from. It's forty percent lead, thirty tin, twenty zinc, and ten of copper. Do we have all of those metals?"

"Yes, I bought them in Sydney last week, along with a crucible to melt them," Eric replied, taking a box from a shelf. "Years ago, I found out the ingredients. I haven't forgotten them, and you won't either now that you've found out for yourself. We'll need about a pound of Babbitt metal. What would be an easy way to get it in the right proportions?"

John pondered for a moment, then suggested, "Make twenty ounces, then all of the metals will be in an even number of ounces."

Eric nodded in approval, reaching on the shelf again for a scale. John took a hammer and chisel from a tool rack, stepping down from the stool, and carried the box containing the metals to an anvil. The boy cut small pieces of the metals and handed them to Eric, who weighed the proper amounts and put them into the crucible. Eric carried the crucible out to place it in the steam engine firebox, John following him with a long tongs.

When the metals flowed into a molten mass, Eric lifted the crucible out of the firebox with the tongs and carried it back into the building. The sand molds, with the steel bearing shells embedded in them, were in wooden boxes on the workbench. Eric poured metal into each one, John craning his neck and watching. "What else will we have to do to them?" the boy asked.

"We'll have to smooth down the Babbitt so the bearings are a close fit on the shafts," Eric replied. "And do you remember those grooves in the old bearings? Those were oil grooves, and we'll have to cut some in these. They'll have to cool first, and for now let's tighten the rivets on that drive belt so it won't fly apart before we get a new one."

John led the way outside, eager for any task that had to do with machinery. He and Eric removed the drive belt and brought it to the building, where they draped it over the anvil. After showing John how to tighten the loose rivets with a hammer, Eric turned it over to him and watched him. The boy had a winsomely earnest manner as he closely examined the rivets, then cautiously tapped on the loose ones with the hammer.

It was midday by the time the boy finished with the belt, and he and Eric went to the house for tiffin. When they returned to the building, Eric broke open the sand molds and took out the bearings. Fitting them to the shafts was a tedious process of removing small irregularities and slight bulges until the bearing surfaces precisely matched the shafts, and Eric and John set to work on them with knives and small files.

The winter sun was well to the west when the bearings were finally finished. After the gearbox was reassembled with the new bearings, John funneled fresh oil into it, and Eric summoned the workmen. The men lugged the heavy gearbox out to the engine and held it in place while Eric bolted it on, then he fastened the drive belt pulley onto the outside shaft.

The men helped put the drive belt back on, and one of

them offered to start the engine and test the gearbox. "No, John can see to that," Eric replied. "Go ahead and fire up the engine, John."

A wide grin wreathed the boy's cheerful features as he leaped to the boiler valve and closed it to build a head of steam. When the needle on the pressure gauge climbed into the operating range, he pulled the lever to let steam into the cylinder. The engine cycled rapidly for a moment with explosive hisses and puffs of smoke lofting from the stack, then it settled down to a steady chuffing.

Eric pulled the lever on the gearbox to engage the gears, and the drive belt began spinning the saw. As he moved the lever back and forth through the gears several times, the drive belt smoothly changed speed, the gears no longer binding from the shafts wobbling out of alignment. Eric nodded in satisfaction, telling John to stop the engine.

The boy pushed the lever to stop the piston from cycling, then opened the boiler valve. Steam plumed high into the air with a roar, and Eric and John walked down the hill toward the house in the fading light of late afternoon. Eric's satisfaction over having the sawmill in full operation once again was greatly surpassed by his pleasure over John's expansive mood. The boy radiated a proud sense of accomplishment.

Hamish Mcfee had brought Stephen back to the house a few minutes before, and Stephanie had just returned from her calls. Dinner and the conversation afterward made a convivial gathering, Stephen talking about what he and Hamish had done, and John explaining all about replacing the bearings. Erica and Ralph were quiet for once to avoid drawing attention, succeeding in having their bedtime escape notice until it was long past.

The fair weather continued into the next day, along with circumstances making it perfect for Eric, because Stephanie had no calls and the entire family could go to church together. They used both buggies from the barn, Yulina taking John and Stephen in one, and the smaller children accompanying Eric and Stephanie in the other. After the service, they returned to the house to have a lavishly large, delicious tiffin.

It was the high point of the weekend for Eric, the one meal of the week in the dining room rather than the kitchen. Yulina had left a large, fat goose roasting on the spit, with pans of stuffing and vegetables simmering on the hob. Everyone helped her carry the food to the dining room and then took their places around the table in a warm, happy atmosphere that fed a wistful hunger within Eric which reached back to his childhood.

The weekend began drawing to an end after the meal, however, for it was time to return the boys to their school. Stephen and John made their farewells with the family while Eric harnessed a team to the wagon, then they set out for Sydney. Eric talked with the boys as they drove down the road, savoring the fading moments of the weekend.

After watching the boys go back into the main hall at the school, Eric found that the lonely drive back through the night always seemed much longer. High clouds moved in from the coast as he drove up the road, the forewarning of another winter storm mirroring his mood. The discontent that had been troubling him dominated his thoughts, and he pondered it once more.

For over a year, he had thought about preparations for the children to have successful lives as adults. A medical education for Stephen would be the most expensive of all, and how it was to be financed had preyed on Eric's mind. The least expensive but also the least desirable way would be for Stephen to attend a local college for courses in the sciences after secondary school, then apprentice with an established doctor.

Another way was for Stephen to obtain a degree in sciences at a local college, then travel to Britain and attend one of the smaller medical colleges. This course would give him a doctorate in medicine and place him among the better-educated doctors in Australia. But it would be very expensive, and even if the money could be found, nothing would be left to finance a higher education for the other children.

The very best way was for the boy to enroll in a good boarding school in Britain within the next year to prepare for entry into Edinburgh University for his sciences degree and doctorate in medicine. As one of the select few doctors with degrees from the world-renowned medical college at Edinburgh, he would be assured of an enviable career in medicine.

Over the years, Stephanie had kept in close contact with her relatives, who would be more than willing to act as her child's guardian. Virtually all of them were in the medical profession and at least moderately wealthy, with the influence to assure Stephen's admission to a highly regarded boarding school for boys and then into Edinburgh University.

But the obstacle, insufficient money, was insurmountable. It would be extremely expensive, costing several times the entire income from the sawmill. Nevertheless, Eric was unable to dismiss it. The facts never changed, but he continued to ponder them and wish he had devoted more energy to his business affairs. If he had, the money might be available.

His obsessive search for a solution was driven by a vital purpose over and above providing his son with the best possible medical education. His first objective always and his greatest satisfaction in life was making Stephanie happy. She had never mentioned it, knowing it was out of the question, but for her son to attend Edinburgh University would give her joy that would endure for the rest of her life.

A possible means for Eric to increase his income developed the following week. Ira Cade returned from Sydney with the new drive belt during the rainy Monday afternoon, and he told Eric that the *Leander* had arrived that day. Eric had seen Milo Chandler a few times over the years, the visits always enjoyable, and he had another reason for going to the city. The roofs on the sawmill buildings were leaking, and he had decided to buy corrugated iron and eliminate the frequent repairs necessary on the shingle roofs.

Eric left at dawn the next morning, just after the full brunt of a storm that had been moving in from the sea made landfall. The day was dark in the heavy rain, with bitterly cold wind lashing the landscape. Parramatta was quiet, the main street almost deserted. Some people were climbing about on shingle roofs and repairing leaks, reminding Eric that his men would be doing the same at the sawmill until he bought sheets of corrugated iron.

Sydney was much the same as usual. Despite the driving rain and icy wind, the streets teemed with vehicles transporting goods for gold towns and bringing back the precious metal in return. Eric decided to wait until after he had visited Milo to see about the corrugated iron, and he made his way down George Street to the waterfront.

At the docks, Eric peered through the rain for several minutes before he finally identified Milo's ship among the mass of vessels. It was anchored on the far side of the harbor roads, near the shore opposite Sydney Cove. There were numerous watermen about, boat owners who transported passengers and cargo for a fee, and Eric beckoned to one of them.

Outside the protected waters of the cove, the keening wind whipped up churning waves, and the waterman labored at the oars. When the boat passed the harbor roads and drew closer to the *Leander,* Eric saw why the vessel was near the shoreline. The sailors were unloading hundreds of tons of rocks that had been used as ballast and piling them at the edge of the water.

Eric had seen other vessels doing the same; the shoreline was littered with piles of rocks. Some ships had transported mining equipment that had large bulk and relatively low weight, while others had arrived with virtually no cargo, bringing prospectors willing to pay large amounts to reach the gold fields of Australia. In each instance, it had been necessary for the ships to sail with hundreds of tons of ballast for stability.

The familiar stocky, bearded Milo Chandler was on the quarterdeck, supervising the work. He saw Eric in the boat and waved, turning toward the steps to the main deck. The boat drew alongside the ship, and Eric paid the waterman, then leaped up and grabbed the rail. He pulled himself up and over it and walked down the deck toward the quarterdeck steps.

Milo was still slowly making his way down the steps and limping heavily, and Eric knew why. The captain's decades on a quarterdeck in all seasons had inflicted him with rheumatism that had become worse during recent years and always flared up during cold, wet weather. The man's face was drawn with pain, but he smiled warmly as he greeted Eric.

"It's a pleasure to see you again, Milo," Eric replied. "But I certainly wish I had found you in better health."

Milo's smile faded and he nodded glumly. "Aye, this weather would give a penguin rheumatics, and it's made mine such a torment that I'd have to get better to be well enough to die," he growled. "Let's go to my cabin, where we can thaw out and talk." He turned toward the cabin passageway, shouting to the first officer: "Mr. Soames, I'm going below!"

The first officer nodded and touched his cap, Eric following Milo into the passageway. They stepped into the captain's neat, spartan cabin, which was cozy with warmth from a glowing charcoal brazier, and took off their oilskins and coats. Milo sighed in relief and gathered a bottle of port and glasses out of a cabinet as Eric sat down at the table.

Milo took a seat at the table and filled the glasses, then he and Eric began discussing events since they had last seen each other. The captain was dissatisfied with the circumstances of his voyages during recent years, beginning with the fact that he disliked sailing under ballast. "It just goes against the grain, Eric," he explained. "I like to use the full capacity of my vessel, and for transporting cargo, not ballast. I must have moved half a continent across the seas during these past years."

"Your voyages have been profitable," Eric pointed out. "If you're to pay your crew and maintain your ship, profit is the main concern."

"Aye, it is," Milo acknowledged. "The delays I've had in port gall me worse, but I've finally managed to end that. As you know, I've been sailing between here and San Francisco for several years, and through delays in port, I've ended up at both places during winter. But I have a good shipping agent in San Francisco now, and I contracted with one here yesterday. After one more voyage, I'll have an end to my delays in port."

"After one more voyage?" Eric repeated, puzzled. "Why must you have a delay in port for another voyage?"

"The agent I contracted with here has a cargo for the Sandwich Islands, and it takes weeks to get a cargo unloaded there," Milo replied. "But he's promised to have only cargoes going to San Francisco for me in the future. I'll get to San Francisco during winter again, but my agent there will have a manifest of passengers waiting for me. Even though I'll be sailing under ballast again, at least my next call here will be during summer."

The feeling suddenly struck Eric that what Milo had just said was important to himself in some way. It was only a feeling, however, without any specifics as to how or why it was important to him. Milo continued talking, explaining that as soon as the ballast was unloaded, he would warp his vessel to the docks. His shipping agent had porters waiting who would load the cargo during the afternoon and through the night, and the *Leander* would put to sea on the morning tide.

Eric was impressed, commenting that the agent was indeed providing excellent service, then the conversation moved on to other subjects. Milo related events that had occurred and described places he had seen during his recent voyages, which usually held Eric's interest. But this time he was distracted by the conviction that the forthcoming voyage of the *Leander* was somehow of crucial importance to him.

He occasionally felt that he was on the point of grasping the personal importance of the vessel's next voyage, but it always slipped away. Eric knew that his opportunity to discuss it with Milo was passing, for this visit with the captain would be shorter than others. Once the ballast was unloaded, Milo would be too busy to talk while warping his ship into the cove and then loading cargo, and after that he would be gone.

The opportunity began fading rapidly when the first officer knocked on the cabin door and looked in, rainwater streaming from his oilskins. "The vessel has been cleared of excess ballast, sir," he said to Milo. "We're ready to lay out kedges and begin warping her to the docks."

The captain nodded, wincing with pain from his rheumatism as he stood up. "I'm sorry, Eric," he apologized, "but I must get to work. As I mentioned, my shipping agent has porters and cargo waiting."

"I understand perfectly," Eric assured him. "I need to go and buy some corrugated iron, because the roofs at my sawmill are leaking."

"No need to ask why, in weather such as this," Milo commented wryly, then he turned to the first officer: "Mr. Soames, have a boat put over the side and choose a good oarsman to take Mr. Brendell ashore."

The first officer touched his cap, closing the door. Eric and Milo put on their coats and oilskins, then left the cabin and stepped out into the frigidly cold wind and rain. Milo groaned, and Eric sympathetically reminded him that he would arrive in Sydney during summer the next time.

"It'll certainly be warm," Eric added, "particularly if there's no sea breeze. That's the only time when business comes to a standstill here. It gets so hot that—" He broke off, suddenly recalling something he had heard about California. "Milo," he said excitedly, "I've heard that the rivers and lakes inland from San Francisco are covered with deep ice during winter. Is that true?"

"Aye, those in the mountains are," the captain replied, puzzled. "I've seen the ice, because it's hauled to San Francisco and stored in icehouses. Fishing boats use it during summer and autumn to keep their catch fresh when they fish well out at sea. Why do you ask, Eric?"

"You could load ice for ballast," Eric explained. "We rarely get more than a skim of ice on ponds here during winter, so we have no source of ice. The glaciers in New Zealand are inaccessible, and icebergs are contaminated with seawater. Ice might find a ready market here during summer."

Milo smiled in surprise and delight, his rheumatic pain forgotten for a moment. "That's a grand idea!" he exclaimed. "Aye, I'll do that. I loaded five hundred tons of ballast for this voyage, and I'll bring a like amount of ice packed in sawdust. You build an icehouse, Eric, and I'll put you in business selling ice. I'm sure people here will buy it."

"It would seem so," Eric mused. "I could explore the costs and see how much of a profit—"

"The costs won't be that much," Milo broke in, wincing with pain and leaning on the rail to ease his weight on his legs. "I have to pay drayage for ballast at a port, and I'll buy ice instead. I'm sure it's cheap enough. My underwriters require that I charge something for cargo, but I'll charge you only half my lowest haulage rate. You get the icehouse ready, and we'll settle what you owe me when I return next summer."

"That's very generous of you, Milo," Eric said, still unsure about the idea. "It's more than generous, in fact, but—"

"It's no more than what one friend should do for another," Milo interrupted again, putting out his hand. "I'll look forward to seeing you next summer, and convey my best regards to your wife and family."

The captain, in pain and shivering from the cold rain and wind sweeping the deck, leaned against the rail and held out his hand. The first officer stood impatiently at one side, with sailors around him who looked miserably uncomfortable in the raw weather. A sailor was in the boat bobbing wildly about in the waves beside the ship, fending off the boat to keep it from colliding with the hull as he darted glances up at Eric.

Eric abruptly decided to let the agreement stand, shaking hands with Milo and wishing him a safe voyage, then he stepped over the rail and jumped down into the boat. But when the sailor had barely begun to row away from the ship, Eric immediately regretted his hasty decision.

However, he saw that changing his mind, more than being embarrassingly awkward, would be difficult if not impossible. The ship had come alive, the sailors racing about in preparation to warp the vessel to the docks.

While crossing the harbor, Eric thought of drawbacks that had failed to occur to him during his brief discussion of the idea with Milo. Even at a small haulage rate, the cost would be significant for an amount of freight that was a large proportion of the cargo capacity of a ship. The icehouse would have to be located near the waterfront, where property was extremely expensive. Having a large, subterranean building constructed would be costly in wages, keeping a work crew busy for months.

When he reached the docks, Eric looked at the *Leander*. The laborious process of warping the vessel across the harbor had begun, with sailors in boats hauling anchors out in front, and others marching around the windlass and inching the ship forward on the anchor lines. Once again Eric decided to let the agreement stand, resigning himself to the situation, but with deep misgivings.

Eric rode away from the docks and up George Street, trying to determine the chances that the undertaking would succeed. It was impossible, because too many unknowns were involved. The greatest one was whether people would buy the ice, but he was firmly blocked from making inquiries and drawing conclusions from what people said. The undertaking had to be kept secret, for someone might have some means of exploiting the idea more quickly than he, capturing any market that might exist.

While the prospects of the undertaking were completely uncertain, Eric was absolutely sure of two facts. One was that the workmen at the sawmill would have to continue repairing the shingle roofs. Buying corrugated iron or anything else not utterly essential would be foolish now.

The other indisputable fact was that whether or not he could sell it, when the summer came he would be the owner of an immense quantity of ice. Five hundred tons of it.

Chapter Twelve

"Three hundred guineas?" Maurice Crowder exclaimed in dismay. "No, the owner would sue me if I sold it for that. This is a very valuable property, over half an acre in size, and it has very good drainage."

"Very good drainage," Eric echoed scoffingly. "If you mean to say that it has a slope as steep as a cow's face, I'll agree with you."

The land agent, a short, portly man, shook his head firmly. "This is perfectly level where we're standing, Mr. Brendell," he pointed out. "A level plot that is generous in size, with a good view of Walsh Bay."

"It's level enough just here," Eric acknowledged, "but this plot isn't large enough for a commercial building. The way this land lies is the reason it isn't already being used for something."

Crowder shook his head again and stated that until recently, the land had been in litigation between heirs, but Eric knew the man was lying. The property, set three streets back from Walsh Bay, was a patch of wasteland in the midst

of a district of warehouses and small manufactories. But for
its steep, awkward contour that would be expensive to alter
through excavation, it would have long since been covered
with buildings.

At the same time, Eric could see that it was perfect
for his purposes. The level expanse was more than large
enough for the entrance area to a subterranean building,
along with parking space for wagons, a stable for horses,
and other necessities. There was convenient access to streets
on all sides, the property was virtually on the waterfront,
and the main artery of George Street was only a short
distance away.

It was also perfect because of its price, which would have
been set in the thousands instead of hundreds if its contour
had been more suitable for buildings such as those around
it. After bargaining with the land agent for several minutes
more, Eric agreed on three hundred and fifty guineas, less
than he had expected to pay even if it was more than he
could afford. It also yielded a much smaller commission
than the land agent had anticipated, and the man sullenly
stamped away to his carriage. Eric stepped into his saddle
and rode toward the business district of the city, making
his way through the busy streets to the Bank of New
South Wales.

After withdrawing the money from his bank account, Eric
met Crowder at the city clerk's offices. The land agent used
a power of attorney to sign for the owner and register the
change of ownership, then he took the money and left. The
property was only a few streets away, but Eric had no wish
to look at it with a sense of ownership when he had the
deed in his pocket. He rode up George Street, heading back
toward Wallaby Track.

Instead of his usual feeling of accomplishment after
making a favorable bargain, he had only the same misgivings
as before. He had always discussed his business affairs with
Stephanie, but he had said nothing to her in this instance.
He did not want to raise false hopes about the possibility of

being able to send Stephen to a medical college in Britain; and if he had foolishly wasted the money meant for all of their children's education, he wanted to keep it to himself as long as he could.

Eric also felt guilty, believing that in a way he was betraying Stephanie's trust in him. Ever since they had been married, he had managed their financial affairs. Although the population of Wallaby Track had grown and she worked brutally long, hard hours, it was for a purpose higher than money. After she paid her expenses she was left only a pittance from what people could afford to pay her. The money in the bank account had come from the earnings of the sawmill, but Eric regarded it as family funds entrusted to his management.

When he reached the valley near sunset, he rode past the house and up to the sawmill, where work was ending for the day. Stepping away from the other men, Ira Cade told Eric that most of the lumber they had discussed had been sawn. "It's all such heavy timbers that it appears to be enough beams and joists to build a small town," Ira added. "Does it have anything to do with that job you want me to oversee in Sydney?"

"Yes, that's exactly what it's for," Eric replied. "I've finished up all the other arrangements, and I'd like for you to ride to Sydney with me tomorrow so I can show you what's to be done."

"Aye, very well," Ira agreed. "You mentioned that this job would keep me in Sydney for a time. How long do you think it'll be?"

"For several months," Eric told him. "It might even be permanent, if you wish. And as I said before, you'll know all about it in due time, but I'd like to keep the purpose of it to myself for now."

"It's all the same to me," Ira assured Eric affably. "All I need to know is what's to be done. Living in Sydney permanently might suit me, but I'll have to be there for a while before I know."

Eric agreed to the condition, wanting Ira to be content, then he ended the conversation and rode down toward his house. He trusted the foreman, and not telling him the purpose of the project had nothing to do with fears that Ira might reveal it to others. The reason was simply that so long as he kept the facts from Stephanie, Eric intended to tell no one else.

During dinner and while talking with Stephanie after the meal, Eric concentrated upon acting as though nothing was troubling him, as he had every evening since making the agreement with Milo. She had often made it clear that she was more than willing to afford him any privacy that he wished, but he greatly preferred that the point not arise. He disliked keeping anything from her, and he looked forward to turning the entire matter over to Ira and putting it out of mind for at least the next few months.

After breakfast the following morning, Eric saddled a horse and rode up to the sawmill. Ira had saddled a horse and was waiting, and they set out for Sydney at a canter. The horses were frisky in the cold, dry weather, the miles passing swiftly at the steady pace. They passed the outskirts of the city at midmorning and rode down George Street, then Eric led the way through the side streets to the property he had bought.

They dismounted on the level area, and Eric took out two drawings he had prepared. One was a scale drawing of the icehouse, the other a diagram of the smaller buildings to be constructed. He handed them to Ira, then explained where the buildings were to be situated.

Ira was experienced in carpentry, and he expressed confidence in being able to oversee the work. "A considerable amount of excavating will have to be done to place this big building where you want it," he said. "How do you want me to dispose of all the dirt?"

"Part of it can go on the slope below here," Eric replied. "That will level it off to a great extent. As for the rest, I want the building covered with soil, and the sides and rear flush with the excavation in the slope. Only the front wall of the building should be exposed."

"Aye, now I know why you wanted all those heavy timbers," Ira commented. "That dirt will be heavy." He studied the diagram for the other buildings, then said, "This doesn't show how big the barracks is to be."

"That depends on how many workers you have, which is up to you," Eric told him. "I want all of this finished by early summer, and you have a free hand as to the number of workers and how the work is to be done."

Ira pondered, then decided: "Four should be enough. I'll hire others by the day to help with the digging, but they won't stay in the barracks. The first thing I'll do is bring the lumber here and get these smaller buildings finished off, then start on the big one."

Eric agreed that was a logical way to proceed, then he and Ira discussed remaining details. Ira intended to stay in Sydney that day and begin looking for workers, and Eric turned to his horse. "It's all yours now, Ira," he said, stepping into his saddle. "Keep the costs down as much as you can, but don't try to make do without anything you need."

"Aye, very well," Ira replied, studying the drawing of the icehouse again. Then he laughed. "This will be a monstrously big cavern in a way, but in another way it'll be a huge, great warehouse that you've hidden under the ground. Whatever it is, I hope you know what you're doing."

Eric merely nodded in response to the remarks, turning his horse away. As he rode toward the street, he sighed. "I also hope I know what I'm doing," he muttered gloomily, "but I fear that I don't."

For the next few days, the work on the property in Sydney occupied much of Eric's attention. The costs multiplied, the tools, horses, wagons, and other necessities for the work costing more than he had expected. Along with the rates on the property, which were much higher than those in

Wallaby Track, he found that as soon as a road was made on the property and it joined a city street, he had to pay an assessment for street maintenance.

Ira was at the sawmill every day or two with men he had hired, loading lumber onto wagons and hauling it away. Questions arose concerning specifics about the buildings that were not made clear on the drawings, and Ira came up with other matters that had to be discussed. Eric also had to meet with him occasionally to give him money to pay day laborers helping with the digging, as well as wages for himself and his workers.

The steady flow of wages was an unending expense, troubling Eric more than the initial, substantial costs of starting up the project. On a trip to Sydney, he made arrangements at his bank for Ira to be given the money each week. At the same time, the work on the property reached a point at which Ira could make any decisions that were necessary, and Eric's personal contact with the work ended for the time being.

Once he was no longer involved with the work, Eric thought about it rarely. As well as out of sight, other matters put it out of mind for him.

His attention was soon occupied by his father's illness, which became critical. The man's actions as magistrate were still resented, and people occasionally talked about him. Then, on a dark, stormy Thursday, scarcely anything else was discussed in Wallaby Track. Employees from Brendell Farm fanned out through the valley carrying messages to those whom Thurlow Brendell had wronged, requesting them to visit him.

Eric heard talk about it during the day until he was weary of it, everyone who came to the sawmill going over the various details. The messages had been penned by Ursula, because her husband was unable to write, and they had been sent to those who had been fined heavily, jailed, evicted from farms, and harmed in other ways. Without exception, the people viewed the messages with contempt, having no intention of visiting Brendell.

When he went home that evening, Eric found that a message had been left there, and Stephanie would talk about nothing else. She considered what others were doing as wrong in addition to being unwise, but regarded it as their own concern. As for herself and Eric, she firmly insisted that they comply with the request. Her attitude about what others were doing puzzled Eric, as her point of view on many things did. He was adamantly against going to visit his father himself.

The disagreement remained unresolved at the end of the evening, and by the next morning, Eric was having second thoughts. With his father at the point of death, he grudgingly realized that visiting the man would be the only right thing to do.

Eric knew that Stephanie would bring up the subject again at breakfast, and when she did, he had his response ready. "Very well," he told her, "we'll go and see him, but he must agree to see Yulina and John as well."

"Of course he must," Stephanie replied, "and I've attended to that. I drove by Brendell Farm yesterday and spoke with the housekeeper, and had her go to his room and ask him about it. He agreed to it."

Yulina was moving about the kitchen, her expression indicating that she would much rather forgo any such distinction, but she said nothing. Eric and Stephanie discussed the details of the visit. She wanted to go the next day, on Saturday. When he objected strongly to having the entire weekend disrupted, she relented and agreed to go on Sunday.

It still ruined the weekend for Eric, having a much more depressing effect than the storm that lingered over the region with drenching rain and blustery, bitterly cold wind. After assigning tasks for the men at the sawmill, he set out during the late forenoon to fetch the boys from school, and when he returned, the mood in the house was far more sober than usual on a Friday evening. Yulina dreaded going to Brendell Farm, making John feel the same. Stephen's attitude was less apparent, but he had no wish to go.

Eric had deferred replacing a leaky steam fitting on the engine at the sawmill until John could work on it with him, and they installed the new fitting on Saturday. The gloomy prospect for the next day made working with the boy less satisfying for Eric, and John also enjoyed it less than usual. Even coincidence seemed to make the day worse: Hamish Mcfee had few calls that day and Stephen spent most of it at home.

The weekend, such as it was, ended for Eric the next morning. There was little conversation over breakfast, then he and the others dressed in their Sunday clothes. They set out in the rain for Brendell Farm the way they went to church, Eric and Stephanie taking the smaller children with them, and Yulina following with the boys in the other buggy. While they were driving down the road, Stephanie told Eric that he should take his father's hand and speak to him in forgiveness for past wrongs.

"How on earth could I do that?" Eric demanded. "You know full well that I can't forgive what he did."

"Then lie about it!" Stephanie shot back. She drew in a deep breath, controlling her impatience, and put her hand on his. "Please try, Eric," she urged him. "I beg you to try."

Eric nodded grimly, but only to put an end to the conversation. What she asked seemed impossible, and he wondered how she failed to understand that, knowing as she did how she felt about his father.

When he turned in at the lane leading into the farm, Eric saw that it had changed since the only time he had been there. The lane was rutted, the fields on each side overgrown with weeds. More than neglected or even decrepit, though, the farm had a wasted atmosphere, as though an inner rot of some essential nature had settled over it. The house, with its chimneys sagging and part of its facade fallen down, looked like a crumbling mausoleum in an abandoned graveyard.

A thin, angular housekeeper opened the door, her gray, lined features and doleful manner matching the gloomy house. Stephanie and Yulina greeted her by name and the family filed into the dim entry, taking off their oilskins. The rustle of oilskins and Stephanie's quiet conversation with the housekeeper stirred whispering echoes like those in deserted houses.

"How is he feeling today, Mistress Lowder?" Stephanie asked. "Is someone with him at present?"

"The mistress is with him, mo'm," the woman replied. "He remains very poorly, each breath threatening to be his last, and he hasn't slept. It's been days since he's slept for longer than a moment."

"I'm very sorry to hear that," Stephanie said sympathetically. "If he could rest, it would ease his pain somewhat. Have others called?"

"No, mo'm. The mistress must have sent out a score of messages, but you're the only ones who've responded."

"That's most regrettable. We'll go up and see him now, please."

The housekeeper turned toward the stairs, Stephanie and Yulina following her. Stephen and John held Erica's hands and walked behind the women, and Eric carried Ralph and followed the boys. There was no conversation, only footsteps and the answering, hollow echoes, along with a disturbance to something more subtle than the quiet. It was that same disintegration as outside, but it was more dense, emanating from within the house. Here it permeated the musty air like a feel of swamp growth nurtured by decay and never touched by sunlight. Feminine beauty and the youthful vitality of children clashed with it.

The light on the staircase was even more dim than in the dismal entry, and the upstairs hall was almost completely dark. It was lighted only by a window at the far end that silhouetted the gaunt housekeeper against the bleak, stormy day outside. The woman tapped on a door, opened it and announced the family in a solumn murmur, and then stood aside.

Ursula sat beside the fireplace at one side of the room. The flames shone only on the peaks of her face and shadowed its hollows, but the character of her features was illuminated more revealingly than by the most glaring light. The years had brought out her nature more clearly on her jowly face, thinning her nose to a beak like that of a bird of prey and sinking her small, beady eyes back into their sockets.

She greeted the family with a silent nod, and Eric set Ralph down and stepped toward the bed. The reason Brendell had been unable to sleep was clearly evident: the somber bedroom was filled with the man's sheer, cold terror. He was gripped with such horror of what awaited him when his faltering heart ceased laboring that he had been unable to rest. Fear of dying while asleep immediately woke him after fatigue overcame him.

He had shrunk to a grotesque, gnomelike caricature of a man. There was a gray pallor of death under the red veins on his skeletal mask of a face. He was worse than alone, his only companion while facing death being Ursula, whose attitude conveyed louder than words her eager anticipation of his death and possession of his property. Eric experienced a sudden, fundamental change in his feelings toward the man. He knew that withholding forgiveness from a creature in such a wretched state would be inhuman, an act of cruelty beyond the worst his father could ever do in his most towering rage.

Eric stepped to the side of the bed, taking the withered claw on the coverlet in his hand. "For whatever comfort you may find in it," he said, "I deeply regret what has happened to you."

The bloodshot, anguished eyes searched Eric's face, then the wrinkled lips moved, uttering a whisper: " . . . forgive me . . . all I did. . . ."

"Yes, I do forgive you," Eric told him. "I bear you no ill will, and it's as though no reason for rancor ever occurred between us." He placed the man's hand back on the coverlet, then beckoned Yulina and John. "Here is your other son, John Thorpe, and his mother, Yulina."

Yulina was attuned to surroundings of love and good cheer which matched her sweet nature, and she was distraught in the morbid atmosphere of terror and impending death. Her lips trembling and tears filling her eyes, she reluctantly forced herself to move forward. She pulled John with her, the boy gazing in consternation at the man on the bed and trying to hang back.

Brendell whispered hoarsely, begging her forgiveness. Yulina gave it quickly and sincerely, never wanting to dwell on unpleasantness. Her tears spilled over as Brendell reached out his emaciated hand to touch John and the boy shrank apprehensively away from it. Yulina and John moved back, and Stephanie led her children to the side of the bed.

"Here are your grandchildren," Stephanie said. "They are Stephen, Erica, and Ralph. Pay your respects to your grandfather, children."

Erica and Ralph were crying, and Stephen was the only one of them who could speak, his face pale as he murmured a greeting. Then the children came to Eric, Ralph and Erica rushing and clinging to his legs. Stephanie held Brendell's hand between hers as she leaned over him and talked softly. He apologized for what he had done to her, and she forgave him.

"But it is more important that you forgive yourself," she went on. "You must forgive yourself for any and all misdeeds to others."

"Can't," Brendell whispered, shaking his head. "They must come here and speak with me . . . forgive me. . . ."

"No, that isn't necessary," Stephanie told him. "When one of us is at the threshold of the great crossing over, we are all brothers and sisters in our mortal condition. Their lack of compassion is a burden they must bear at their own crossing over, but it isn't yours. All you must do is repent of wrongs to others, and then you can depart in peace."

Brendell whimpered in disagreement, and Stephanie softly, persuasively assured him she was correct. Eric listened, recalling two deaths he had seen years before. One had been a drowning, the man's face twisted by panic in a convulsive frenzy of coughing as the current swept him under the water for the last time. The other had been a man crushed by a tree that had toppled in an unexpected direction when felled, and he had screamed in the agony of shattered bones and mangled entrails as his life ebbed away.

Both had been violent, ghastly deaths, but Eric reflected that they had been merciful compared to the death that confronted Brendell. He was clinging to life through a force of will that was a more malevolent affliction than his illness, one that sprang from terror and guilt that stretched the limits of human endurance. All the torment and despair that he had imposed upon others was now his, multiplied manifold into wrenching fear of death.

His voice gradually grew louder, and he became more and more agitated. Stephanie cautioned him to remain calm, then continued persuading him to forgive himself. He lay back and was still, fervently longing to believe her and to do what she said. "I should have heeded you years ago," he croaked. "What you told me years ago was true . . . so true. . . ."

"Yes, it was," Stephanie replied, "and what I say now is equally true. All you need do is be repentant for all wrongful acts and resolve that you would always be generous and kindly to others if you had the opportunity. Therein is self-forgiveness, and it will set your mind at peace."

Brendell groaned and shook his head, his face twitching in pain, and complained that it was too difficult. Stephanie again warned him to keep calm, then urged him to find a way within himself to do what she said. Eric noticed that while holding his hand, she had moved a finger down over his pulse. On the other side of the room, Ursula was gazing at the old man with a grim half-smile, her beady eyes glittering.

Clutching his chest with his free hand, Brendell suddenly cried out in pain and tried to sit up. Stephanie eased him back against the pillows, talking to him softly, then she glanced over her shoulder at Eric in a silent, urgent command to get the children out of the room. Yulina and all of the children except Stephen were crying, and Eric picked up Ralph as he guided Yulina and Erica toward the door. Stephen put his arms around John, moving him toward the door and reaching to open it.

Brendell moaned and then cried out again in pain, and Stephanie talked more rapidly in a quiet, pacifying voice. Stephen opened the door and led John out, Yulina and Erica following the boys. Eric carried Ralph out, glancing back into the bedroom as he pulled the door closed. Stephanie was holding Brendell in her arms and trying to comfort him in his agony and frantic terror. Ursula watched them intently, her attitude that of a hungry buzzard gazing at a stricken dingo in its death throes.

The housekeeper was in the hall, and she stepped aside as Eric guided Yulina and the children toward the stairs. When he got them down to the entry, he put on his oilskins and helped the smaller children with theirs, then took them outside. Yulina had recovered her self-control sufficiently to be able to drive a buggy safely, and she and all of the children crowded into one of them and drove away down the lane.

Gazing out at the rain pouring down on the overgrown yard, Eric stood on the portico and waited for Stephanie. After some thirty minutes, he heard her talking with the housekeeper in the entry. When the door opened, he studied her worriedly. She was perfectly composed, however, appearing only somewhat tired and pale after her emotional ordeal with Brendell.

Eric helped her into the buggy, then stepped into it and

drove down the lane. "I've always known that you stay with people when they die, of course," he said, "but I've only just realized what you endure."

"It's trying," she acknowledged. "The greatest difficulty is striking a balance between being too involved and becoming callous, and most go to their great crossing over peacefully enough. For those at the end of a life of wickedness or one of self-indulgence, it's far better that they depart while in a coma or asleep." She was silent for a moment, then said, "The funeral is tomorrow morning. Ursula has had the arrangements made ever since the last seizure. I understand that she intends to leave the farm with a land agent to sell and return to Britain as soon as possible."

Eric nodded, feeling grateful that Stephanie had been so insistent that they visit his father. Having gone the extra measure and forgiven his father, he felt deeply satisfied within himself.

A somber mood lingered at the house, but it began fading in the conversation over tiffin. Eric set out with the boys to return them to school, and both of them were in their usual spirits by the time the wagon reached Sydney. He drove back through the dark, rainy night to his late dinner, finding the atmosphere at the house much the same as always on a Sunday evening.

The funeral the next morning was hasty and shabby, the driving rain making it more dismal, and it seemed to Eric an ultimate testimony to the bitterness toward his father in Wallaby Track. Any funeral usually drew a few people paying homage to their own mortality through respect for the dead, but he, Stephanie, and Ursula were the only ones in attendance. At the graveside, Ursula was smugly satisfied behind her veil, and the gravediggers leaned on their shovels nearby and impatiently waited to finish their work so they could go home to their fireplaces and hot drinks.

The rain slackened and the wind began dying away the next day, and then by the time the sky cleared in the wake of the winter storm, Ursula was gone. The land was subdivided and sold to newcomers in the valley, then Brendell Farm was no more. After the decaying mansion was demolished and replaced by a farmhouse, the only remaining vestige of Thurlow Brendell in Wallaby Track was a small, forgotten stone in a far corner of the graveyard.

Ursula left and the property was sold in August, when the grip of winter was losing its strength. The outlook for the forthcoming spring seemed particularly fresh and bright to Eric, but he only gradually realized what had changed to make this spring different for him. The change in itself was slight, yet its effects were profound. It was a subtle shift in attitude arising from a final conclusion to events that had actually ended long before.

Even though Thurlow Brendell had been replaced as magistrate years before, he had been a blight on the placid rhythm of life in the valley. Consequently, it was only after his death that his magistracy changed from the present to the past among the people of the valley. Similarly, Eric discovered that his unhappy childhood was no longer a force in his life, becoming merely a time in the distant past.

The work on the property in Sydney came to the fore of Eric's attention again in September, when he went to the foundry in Sydney to buy new blades for the sawmill. The foundry owner had ordered a scale from Britain for weighing metals, and by mistake had been sent a steelyard scale with a maximum capacity of only five hundred pounds. It was useless to him, but returning it to Britain would cost a substantial portion of its value.

Eric bought the scale and its set of weights at a bargain price, but he ruefully reflected that it was probably another waste of money. After tying them to his saddle, he led his horse through the streets to his property. It had been transformed and was blending into the surrounding commercial district, with all of the smaller buildings completed and its contour largely leveled with fill from the excavation for the icehouse.

The framing, floor, and roof of the icehouse had been completed, the huge structure fitted into a notch in the slope. Eric turned the scale over to Ira, and told him to have the sawdust hauled from the sawmill and piled in the building while it was being finished. As always, Ira asked no questions, but he jokingly commented that every sawmill owner needed an underground warehouse to store his sawdust and a scale for weighing it.

A small hill of sawdust had accumulated at the sawmill, requiring several trips with a dray to haul it away. Stephanie saw the large vehicle on the road while making her calls, and when she mentioned it, Eric told her that the sawdust had become a fire hazard. Although that was true to an extent, the reply itself was the opposite, and Eric was relieved when she showed no indication of having detected his guilt over deceiving her.

He knew that she may have observed it under other circumstances, but a time of year had arrived when her attention while at home was largely occupied by a pair of ganggang cockatoos that roosted in a tree outside the bedroom window during autumn and winter. She had become very fond of the migratory birds over the years, keeping barley at the foot of the tree for them. The singing of the birds upon their arrival in autumn and departure in spring had become a milepost of the seasons at the house, and the time was approaching when they would leave.

The gang gang cockatoos began singing during breakfast on a sunny morning in mid-September, and Stephanie jumped up from the kitchen table and raced outside. Yulina, Erica, and Ralph were right behind her, Eric following at a less hurried pace. Stephanie stood near the tree, and Eric joined Yulina and the children at one side to watch and listen.

It was easy to believe that the cockatoos returned Stephanie's fondness for them and were bidding her farewell until the autumn. The small, attractive birds gazed directly at her, swaying on the limb and their breasts swelling with effort as they sang their sweet, staccato notes. Then they took wing, soaring into the sky and circling once, then flying toward their other home in the mountains. Stephanie lifted a hand and waved.

Yulina and the children went back inside while Eric harnessed a horse to Stephanie's buggy. Leaving the horse and buggy in front of the barn, he returned to his breakfast. Presently, Stephanie came into the house through the side door to get her coat, hat, and bag, then she left on her calls. Local folklore had it that gang gang cockatoos were very long-lived, but Stephanie worried about them until they returned in autumn.

That evening, Stephanie was her usual self, concealing whatever sadness she felt about the departure of the cockatoos. Later that same week, an event occurred which Eric thought might have a more fundamental and far-reaching effect upon her. The first indication of it was when they were awakened during the dark, early hours of the morning by a workman from the sawmill knocking at the door and shouting for Eric.

Scrambling out of bed, Eric threw open a window and called out, asking what was wrong. "There's a fire in the village!" the man shouted. "The others at the sawmill have gone up there to help put it out, and I thought I'd better come down here and tell you about it."

"I'm pleased that you did!" Eric shouted back. "We'll be up there in a few minutes to give a hand with it."

Stephanie was out of bed and hastily dressing by the time Eric closed the window. He quickly dressed, then they hurried out of their room. Yulina and the children were in the hall, awakened by the shouting. Stephanie rapidly told them what had happened and sent the children back to bed, following Eric down the stairs. They grabbed their coats and hats off the rack in the entry and ran out the front door.

It was a cold, clear night, the moonlight illuminating a thick column of smoke rising from the village. The trees on the slope blocked the view, concealing the precise location of the fire, but Eric and Stephanie heard the uproar it created as they ran up the road. A bedlam of shouting voices rose in the night from the people fighting the fire.

Reaching the street through the village, they ran down it to the lane leading to the prison and district clerk's offices, then stopped. The fire was down the lane at the isolated edge of the village, in the prison.

A moment passed while they stood there, Stephanie gazing down the lane. The prison was a closed subject, for she always refused to discuss it, and any mention of it saddened her. Her face reflected shock, along with other profound but obscure emotions that Eric was unable to interpret. He only knew that it was an expression he would never forget.

Then she ran down the lane, Eric following her. Pandemonium raged at the end of it, a crowd of half-dressed convicts, constables, and villagers working frantically in the glare of roaring flames. Fire was roaring in the wooden bowels of the prison, and sparks from it had ignited the shingle roof of the district clerk's office building.

It was doomed, the fire spreading rapidly while Tipton Bellamy, his apprentices, and others lugged armfuls of records out of it. Stephanie ran to join them, and Eric pitched in with those fighting the fire in the prison. Some were bringing barrels of water in a pushcart while others dashed bucketfuls on the flames, and Eric grabbed a bucket.

The interior of the prison was filled with thick, choking smoke, the flames glowing through it. Eric ran in and out with the bucket, holding his breath as he bumped into others and was jostled himself in the narrow corridor leading away from the entrance. The first glow of dawn was on the horizon when the men from Mundy Farm arrived, joining Eric and the others.

The fire in the prison began dying out, the lack of oxygen from its tiny openings helping control the flames. The office building turned into an inferno, and the people moved the furniture and records to a safe distance. When dawn spread across the sky, the fire in the prison was finally extinguished, smoke trickling from its windows, and the office building collapsed in a shower of sparks shooting into the air.

Constables gathered the convicts together, villagers collected in groups and talked, and the district clerk conferred with the magistrate and chief constable. Eric found Stephanie among the crowd, her expression giving no hint whether her feelings about the prison had changed as a result of the fire. They started to go up the lane to return home, but Gideon Mundy called to Eric. He turned back, Stephanie going on up the lane.

The men were discussing what to do immediately, as well as making plans for the future. As magistrate, Gideon had to organize whatever was to be done, and he was concerned about the condition of the prison. "I believe it'll have to be gutted and completely rebuilt inside," Eric told him. "It looked to me like the floor near the rear and some of the walls had burned through, and they support the upper stories. It's in a very unsafe condition, because parts of it could collapse."

"That's what I opine," Claude Durgin agreed. "I think the fire started from a lamp or something near the back of the building, and it's heavily damaged there. It doesn't show on the outside, because the roof and walls are still sound, but the inside is a death trap now."

"Well, you'll have to take the convicts to Parramatta, then," Gideon said. "Tipton and I will go to Sydney to let the authorities know what has happened and to see what can be done."

The three men continued discussing their plans, and Eric turned away, joining the sawmill workmen. It was evident that a building would be constructed to replace the district clerk's offices, and while walking through the village and down the road with the workmen, Eric told them to make preparations to begin sawing foundation beams and joists.

The workmen turned off at the sawmill, Eric walking on down the road.

When he was near the house, Stephanie drove away to begin her calls for the day, exchanging a wave with him. She was too far away for him to judge her mood accurately, but she seemed much the same as usual. A moment later, Tipton and Gideon rode past, en route to Sydney.

While he was having breakfast, Eric heard constables marching the convicts down the road past the house, taking them to the convict compound in Parramatta. He went up to the sawmill and set to work, going through the pile of timber with the workmen and selecting several thick karri logs, a choice wood for foundation beams. They rolled the logs over to the saw and started the steam engine, then began sawing the beams.

Among the workmen, as well as farmers who came during the day to order lumber, there was universal satisfaction over what had happened to the prison. In addition to dislike of the convict system itself, the prison inflicted a legacy of cruelty and despair upon the peaceful valley. Eric shared that attitude, but his personal interest was far more vital. He fervently hoped that Stephanie's sorrow associated with the prison, whatever its specific basis, would be eliminated by the events of the morning.

Late in the day, Gideon and Tipton returned from Sydney and came to the sawmill. The day of conferences with bureaucrats had been business as usual for the district clerk, but exasperating for Gideon. He gave Eric a purchase order for lumber from the colonial treasurer, along with a drawing of a building. It would provide an office for constables and a small jail, making it substantially larger than the previous building.

"Instead of where the other one was," Gideon explained, "it'll be over on the northeast side of the village. How soon can you have some of the beams so the carpenters can get to work on the building?"

"I have them now," Eric replied. "I'll start on the joists

and the rest of the lumber tomorrow. What is to be done about the prison?"

"I've no idea," Gideon growled. "Making heads or tails of what that lot of boracking squibs in Sydney says is like trying to milk a bull. The convicts will be left in Parramatta, and that's all I know."

"Consequently," Tipton added, "the prison will be left as it is. The reduction in the number of convicts has left numerous facilities for them vacant, and funds won't be expended to repair one. It's crown property, however, and it can be used only for official public purposes. I daresay that twenty or any number of years hence, it'll be just as it is now."

Eric pondered the comments, unsure of what Stephanie's feelings might be, but at least he now had definite information on what would happen. The conversation turned to arrangements for having the lumber picked up, then the men left. Eric set about ending work for the day, eager to talk with Stephanie and judge her reaction to what he had learned.

His conversation with her was unrevealing, however, her expression reflecting no more than casual interest. Making no reference to the prison, Eric told her that the convicts were to remain in Parramatta, and he let her draw the logical conclusion. Her only remark was that the village was expanding to the northeast, making it the best place on the hill for the new building, then the discussion moved on to other things.

It occurred to Eric that Stephanie might be uncertain of her feelings herself, the prison being of such complex, profound significance to her that any change in it would take time for her attitude to adjust. Several days later, he went up to the building under construction to talk with the carpenters, and he noticed that the prison no longer seemed even a part of the village. It was largely hidden from the street behind trees, and the spring rains had started weeds sprouting on the lane leading back to it.

On a Sunday over a fortnight after the fire, Eric finally gained full insight into Stephanie's feelings. While they were driving back down the street from the church, passing the lane to the prison, Stephanie asked him to stop the buggy. "I'll walk home, and I'll be there directly," she told him.

Knowing where she wanted to go, Eric shook his head as he stopped the buggy. "With the weather warming, snakes are everywhere now," he warned her. "I killed several at the sawmill during the past week. A horse can detect them, so you'll need to keep a buggy here with you."

"But that would be inconvenient for everyone else," she objected. "I don't want to cause any fuss and bother, and I—"

"Then I'll stay with you," he interrupted firmly. "I don't intend to look over your shoulder if you want to walk about by yourself, love, but I do want to be nearby. Then we can walk home together."

Stephanie nodded in agreement, and Eric stepped out of the buggy. He helped her out, calling to Stephen to drive the buggy home. The boy jumped out of the one Yulina was driving, then stepped into the buggy with Erica and Ralph. As the buggies moved away, Eric and Stephanie went down the lane to ward the prison. A few yards down the lane, Stephanie walked ahead.

Eric stopped halfway down the lane, watching Stephanie as she continued on down and crossed the yard in front of the prison. He was bitterly disappointed a few minutes later, his question during the past days emphatically answered. It looked as though Stephanie was whispering to herself, but he was unsure of that. However, he was certain that she was crying, the prison for some reason still a source of crushing sorrow for her.

Chapter Thirteen

A distant patter of hoofbeats woke Eric from a shallow sleep. His sleep had become increasingly restless because of anxiety over the impending arrival of the ice, and the bedroom was uncomfortably warm. There had been no sea breeze for over a week, and without it, the daytime temperatures soared to humid, stifling levels that persisted into the night.

The windows were open to catch any hint of a breeze, and Eric listened to the rapid hoofbeats. It was unusual for a rider to be racing about at night in the peaceful valley, but more than that, Eric had an inner conviction as to the identity of the rider. When he got out of bed, Stephanie stirred. He quietly told her that he was expecting a message about business affairs, and she murmured an acknowledgment, settling herself again.

After quickly dressing, Eric went downstairs and stepped outside. The hoofbeats drew closer, the rider coming into view in the moonlight. The horse turned onto the village road, then swerved in at the house. Ira leaped down from the saddle, he and the horse breathless from the fast ride.

"The *Leander* came into port just at nightfall," he panted, mopping sweat off his face with his handkerchief. "She put a mob of fossickers ashore, and I went out and talked to the captain." He laughed, shaking his head. "That ship is carrying a cargo of ice! That's an icehouse I built!"

"That's what it is," Eric confirmed. "Where is the ship anchored?"

"I showed the captain where the icehouse is, and he said he would warp up into Walsh Bay," Ira replied. "He also said he would start unloading as soon as he got there. It's been so hot in Sydney that at night and during the morning is the only time that porters and lighter operators will work, and I told my men to do whatever he said."

"Very well." Eric sighed grimly as he turned to the steps, his misgivings about the venture greater than ever. "Go saddle a fresh horse for yourself and one for me, and I'll join you directly."

Ira started to lead his horse away, then turned back. "It's been as hot as the doorstep of the netherworld in Sydney," he commented, "but do you really think that people will pay out good money just for ice?"

"We'll know by the time the day's out, won't we?" Eric growled, going up the steps. "Just see to the horses, Ira."

Ira nodded, leading his horse toward the barn. Eric went into the house and jotted a quick note to Stephanie, informing her that he had gone to Sydney on business. Leaving the note on the kitchen table, he went out the back door. Ira was waiting for him in the barnyard with the horses, and they rode away from the house and down the road at a steady canter.

The road unwound ahead and fell behind in the moonlight as Eric pondered the question that Ira had raised—whether people would pay out their money for ice. The point was one he had considered exhaustively, and he was certain only that wealthy people would buy it. That would be a small market, however, and others might consider ice a frivolous luxury.

Another point that he had thought about at length was how much to charge for the ice. An initial price that left latitude to be lowered was a good business practice, and he had more or less arbitrarily decided to begin with ten shillings per hundredweight and see how people reacted.

The horses sweated heavily and panted during the last miles, but they maintained the cantering pace through the outskirts of the city. Riding down George Street in the quiet and darkness of several hours before dawn, Eric easily identified the *Leander* when he glimpsed the harbor between buildings. A number of ships were being unloaded in Sydney Cove during the cooler temperature of late night, but only one in Walsh Bay. Its deck was illuminated by lanterns hanging from the yardarms, and a bargelike cargo lighter with lanterns on its low rails was alongside the vessel.

When the piers at Walsh Bay came into view, one of them was also illuminated by lanterns, a second lighter drawn up to it. The wagons had been brought from the icehouse, and porters and sailors were pushing a huge block of ice up thick boards laid between the lighter and the tailgate of a wagon. Milo Chandler was supervising the work, motioning another wagon into position when the ice slid into the first one and it moved away.

For the moment, Eric completely forgot his worries about the venture in his keen pleasure over Milo's appearance. The previous winter, he had seemed prematurely aged, barely able to move about because of his rheumatism, but now the stocky, bearded man was just as vigorously active as years before. He turned with a beaming smile when Eric and Ira reined up, and Eric jumped down from his saddle, greeting his friend happily.

Milo laughed and nodded at Eric's comment about his appearance. "Aye, this warmth has me as lively as a sprantling," he agreed. "I'm glad you're here, because we're long on hands and short on gaffers. I've been seeing to the pier and to the unloading at the icehouse, and Mr. Soames is attending to both hauling out of the hold and loading the lighters. If you and your mate will take over here, I'll go out to the ship."

"Very well, and I'm most grateful for how you organized everything and began work," Eric told him. "How much has been unloaded so far?"

"Only a few tons," Milo replied. He called to the lighter operator to wait, then stepped toward the vessel to jump down into it. "We should get half of the ice unloaded before the porters and lighter operators quit during the forenoon tomorrow. We can unload the rest tomorrow night, then we'll have ample time for a chin wag over a bottle of port."

The captain jumped down into the lighter, and Eric turned to Ira, telling him to take charge at the pier, and he would go to the icehouse himself. Ira stepped toward the porters and sailors, introducing himself, and Eric gathered the reins on the horses. Then he suddenly remembered an urgent question he had forgotten in the pleasure of seeing his friend in good health.

The lighter was several yards away from the pier, moving toward the ship out in the bay as the man at the rear worked a long sweep. Eric ran down the pier, cupping his hands around his mouth and shouting, "Milo, it slipped my mind to ask the cost of the ice and the haulage! How much is it?"

"Some two hundred guineas, all told!" the captain shouted back nonchalantly. "We'll have ample time later to settle the details."

Feeling as if he had been belted in the stomach by a powerful fist, Eric returned to the horses. It was more than he had expected, virtually every remaining penny in his bank account. Leading Ira's horse, Eric rode through the sloping streets toward the icehouse. He passed the wagons, the horses hitched to them toiling up the streets with the heavy loads of ice.

Lanterns hung on the front wall of the icehouse set into the slope, but no one was about it. After stabling the horses, however, Eric found sailors and porters inside the icehouse, taking refuge from the heat. The cavernous interior of the building, dimly illuminated by lanterns, was almost uncomfortably cool compared to the warm night outside.

The wagons arrived, the sailors and porters throwing open the large door at one side of the icehouse to let them in. A line of the huge slabs of ice was against the rear wall, a thick layer of sawdust covering them, and the men slid the blocks from the wagons on top of the first ones. When the wagons left, the men shoveled sawdust onto the ice they had unloaded in readiness to place another line of slabs on top of them.

Eric helped the men and found other things to do, trying to smother his anxiety in work, but it became even worse. Ira's workmen were driving the wagons, and while talking to one of them, Eric learned that the man had heard Milo making arrangements with the lighter operators and porters. Each porter was to be paid eighteen shillings to work until the heat became too intense the next day, and the lighter operators five guineas each.

In addition, Eric felt obliged to pay the sailors for their work, and he further found out that he had spent more than necessary on the icehouse. When drawing up plans for it, he had been uncertain of how large the volume of ice would be, and he had deliberately overestimated. The added cost had been only a fraction of the total, but now every penny was important. When enough ice was brought to the warehouse to give him some idea of the total volume, he saw he had greatly overestimated it and was furious at himself.

Dawn spread across the sky and heralded another sweltering day in Sydney, not a breath of a sea breeze stirring. The city began waking, but with only a shadow of its usual teeming activity, many rising late or even staying at home during the torrid heat. When the sun began climbing into the sky, water dripped from the tailgates of the wagons loaded with ice.

A dozen boys who were truant from school followed the wagons, gleefully catching the cold water in their hands and dashing it on each other. When they tried to sneak into the icehouse, Eric ordered them to leave. Then the obvious fact occurred to him that he would have to broadcast word about the ice through the city if he ever hoped to sell any at all.

Eric opened his purse and selected twopenny coins from the money in it. "Here, make yourselves useful," he called, tossing the coins to the boys. "Run through the streets and shout that ice is for sale here."

The boys grabbed up the coins and ran away as they whooped and shouted about the icehouse, their shrill voices fading. Eric forgot about them presently, having found another reason to worry. The ice was arriving more slowly with the temperature rising along with the sun, and he wondered if he might have to hire porters and lighter operators for a third night.

While helping unload the wagons once more, Eric heard someone shouting outside. In a thoroughly miserable mood, he stepped out and saw a man and two youths in a wagon that had a foul odor about it, the three of them wearing grimy aprons. "Are there any big buildings on this street?" the man asked. "All I see is that cellar, a stable, and sheds and such."

"That's not a cellar, it's an icehouse under the slope," Eric growled. "What sort of big building are you looking for?"

"That's it, the big icehouse that the boys were shouting about in the streets," the man told him. "How much does the ice cost?"

Realizing that the vehicle was an offal wagon, and the aprons were those worn by butchers, Eric's attitude underwent a transformation. He smiled cordially. "Ten shillings the hundredweight," he replied.

The man hesitated and then nodded, indicating that he considered the price substantial, but acceptable. "I'll take five hundredweight," he said, then turned to the youths: "Get those tubs unloaded."

Eric turned back to the icehouse and shouted to the men to leave the last block of ice on the wagon, then he ran to the sheds and found the scale and an axe. He set up the scale at the foot door and cleaved slabs off the ice, weighing them and filling the tubs as he talked with the butcher.

"I usually have some meat spoil during summer," the man complained. "But with the weather so hot that chickens are laying boiled eggs, I haven't been able to butcher even the smallest poddy of a pig or beef without losing half of it. I'll be back tomorrow for a like amount."

"I'll be here," Eric assured him. "That'll be fifty shillings."

The man paid and left. A dairy vendor drove his wagon up to the door only moments later. Exuberantly happy that ice was available to keep his milk, butter, and eggs fresh, he talked about having been unable to make his rounds for a fortnight because of the heat. A tavern owner was right behind him, followed by the head cook from a hotel kitchen.

Eric had no further need to look for work to keep his mind off his worries, which faded rapidly in any event. The first customers were the headwaters of a wave of business owners that kept him increasingly busy, wagons and carts lining up at the door. With the coins and bills he collected rapidly overfilling his purse, he hastily found a wooden box in the stable and placed it inside the door to use as a cash box.

When the porters and lighter operators ended their work during the late forenoon, Eric was relieved rather than worried that he would have to hire them a third night. Townspeople had swelled the wave of customers into a tidal wave, and he urgently needed Ira and his men to help chop and weigh out the ice. He took money from the cash box to pay the porters and lighter operators, who promised to return at midnight.

Milo came to the icehouse at midday with a cheese and loaves of bread, and he handed out chunks to Eric and the other men. Although he had eaten nothing since dinner the night before, Eric had given no thought to food, but he was suddenly ravenous. He and the others ate while they worked, and Milo pitched in and helped with the customers.

The flow of customers finally ebbed to a trickle once the blistering heat of afternoon settled over the city. Ira and his men rested in the cool, dim icehouse, taking turns attending to customers, and Eric sat nearby with Milo. The warmth of their friendship had never been more evident, for the captain was just as delighted as Eric over the spectacular sales of ice.

"I knew something you didn't," Milo admitted. "While in San Francisco, I talked with a captain who told me that cargoes of ice have been sold in Bombay. From what he said about it, I knew what would happen."

"I certainly didn't have an inkling this would happen," Eric said. "My only concern now is that I might soon run out of ice."

"No, I know something else you don't," Milo told him, laughing. "I didn't say anything about it before, because you were acting like you were off a lee shore with reefs abeam. But after I found out what happened in Bombay, I made arrangements with a friend to load ice as ballast. He's Jason Kaley, master of the *Indore,* and he'll be here within the fortnight."

Eric searched for words to express his gratitude, finding none that were equal to his feelings, then shrugged. "I don't know what to say except that I'm very grateful to you, Milo."

"Nothing else is necessary," Milo assured him. "And I've done no more than what a friend should. Jason will charge the lowest haulage rate, but he'll have about seven hundred tons, so it'll amount to a few guineas. I daresay you won't be hard pressed to find it, though."

"No, thanks to you," Eric added. "Your crew will need more than thanks, and I'll pay them for the work they've done for me."

"Give them a couple of days' wages, and they'll be the ones thanking you," Milo told him. He stood up, yawning and stretching. "If we're to be up and about at midnight, I need to keep company with my bunk for a time. You should get some rest as well, Eric."

Eric replied that he would, but he was more excited than weary. The captain left, and Eric stepped over to Ira. "You can lock up here any time you wish," he said. "You and your men need to rest up for tonight."

"Aye, very well," Ira replied, then pointed to the cash box. "You'd best look after that until one of us takes it to the bank."

Eric scooped up the money, sorted and counted it, and found that it was almost forty guineas. Pocketing it, he went out to the sheds and rummaged about in them until he found a canvas water bag. He saddled his horse and filled the bag with chips of ice, then stepped into his saddle and tied the straps on the bag to it, and rode away.

At a vintner on George Street, Eric bought a bottle of the best white Rhenish the owner had in stock, then put it in the bag with the ice and rode out of the city. The road was almost deserted in the sweltering heat, and he let his horse pick its own pace, a slow, steady trot. Eric savored his anticipation of telling Stephanie, the miles passing.

It was late afternoon when he arrived home, and Stephanie was still making calls on patients. After stabling his horse, Eric went to the kitchen for two glasses and put them in the water bag with the wine and remaining ice, then carried it out to the front porch and waited. At sunset, Stephanie's buggy turned in from the main road. Eric drew the cork from the wine bottle and filled the glasses as she stopped in front of the house.

Although she was uncomfortable from the sultry heat, Stephanie gave him her usual loving smile as she stepped out of the buggy. "What took you off to Sydney in the middle of the night, dear?" she asked.

"It had to do with this," he replied, handing her a glass.

Stephanie gasped in astonishment and almost dropped the glass as she took it from him. "It's freezing cold!" she exclaimed. She sipped the wine, sighing in pleasure. "How did you cool it, Eric?"

"With ice that Milo Chandler brought from California," he told her. "I've been working on a business venture connected with it."

"Yes, for months," she added, laughing. "I've wondered when I would finally find out what you've been doing."

Eric laughed and nodded. "I should have known you would at least suspect something," he observed. "I had an icehouse built, and Milo brought a cargo of ice for it. Right up until this morning, I had no idea whether it would be a success or a miserable failure."

Stephanie sipped the wine again, savoring it, then commented, "Judging from your manner, it must have been successful."

"Yes, far beyond anything I thought possible," he said. "Love, we'll have the money to send Stephen to any of the best boarding schools in Britain, then to Edinburgh University for his doctorate in medicine."

Stephanie did drop the glass then, her fingers going numb as she gazed at him speechlessly. It shattered on the porch, and she threw her arms around him with a cry of delight. The joy on her lovely face made the moment one of the most priceless of Eric's life, and he knew that he would cherish the memory of it as long as he lived.

Stephanie's undiluted joy soon passed. Once she was over her initial surprise and excitement, she was tormented by the prospect of sending her young son out into an unknown abyss that lay beyond her ability to insure his safety and well-being. She realized that the time had come for her to pay, in the form of a mother's worry and heart-break, for the infinite enrichment that her son had brought to her life, and it promised to be costly.

At the same time, hopes that had been too unrealistic to even consider had been fulfilled, and she looked forward to Stephen's reaction. The following Friday, Eric charac-teristically said nothing, allowing her to tell Stephen about it when he and John arrived home from school. Her own joy was renewed when she did, because for once, the boy was so happy that his usual earnest manner dissolved into boyish exuberance.

Yulina and John's pleasure was mixed with sadness, while Hamish Mcfee was delighted when Stephanie took Stephen to go on the doctor's calls with him the next day. Nothing in the man's manner even hinted at misgivings about Stephen's being sent off to Britain by himself, a viewpoint that Stephanie could well understand. Hamish knew that Stephen was far more capable than most boys his age of dealing with whatever might lie ahead of him.

Stephanie knew that better than Hamish, but her son was the child of her body and of her heart, and still only a boy. The physical pain of his birth had been nothing compared to the emotional agony of the coming separation, but she knew that above all else, she had to endure it silently.

In all things, Eric's first thoughts were of her, and he could be unyieldingly stubborn. Stephanie knew that if she revealed the full extent of her feelings to Eric, her mother's love for her son could well deprive him of his great opportunity in life. When discussing it with Eric, she admitted only to sadness far overbalanced by pleasure.

The following weeks were an easy time for her to conceal her sorrow from Eric, for he was gone virtually every day. He was hiring workers and setting up a shop in Sydney to make a different kind of food safe, their interiors lined with cork and metal, with a separate compartment for a block of ice. Almost every morning, he went to the sawmill after

breakfast to assign work for the day, then went to Sydney
and returned after nightfall.

While she made arrangements to send her son to Britain,
Stephanie's hidden feelings came to the fore in the form
of delaying over details. Among her relatives, she had no
need to even ponder a best choice to act as Stephen's
guardians. Her favorite uncle and aunt were Magnus and
Adeline Thorpe, and their letters had always been extremely
affectionate over the years. Well known in the medical community, they would have no difficulty in enrolling Stephen
in a good boy's school and Edinburgh University.

Even so, Stephanie's first attempts to write to them about
Stephen were pages filled with his likes and dislikes, and
pleas for attention to his needs. Discarding them one by
one, she finally concentrated upon a letter that covered
all the essential points, then she made two copies of it to
mail a week apart to make certain at least one reached its
destination.

Upon choosing fabrics for his wardrobe to accompany
him, she pored over swatches for many evenings after
finishing her calls, and then she forced herself to decide.
Her longest delay and most difficult decision, however, was
over the final step of booking his passage. Eric brought
home the newspapers and went over the list of scheduled
ship departures with her, and for many days, she found
reasons to reject each one on the lists.

Then her reasons became exhausted when a steamship
appeared on a list. "Not having to rely on the wind," Eric
observed, "the *Theophane* will be faster and safer than other
vessels. She's at a pier in Sydney Cove, and I saw her today
and talked with the captain. His name is Vincent Reece, and
he's a very trustworthy, capable sort of man, as well as an
experienced seaman."

"Given all that, though," Stephanie mused doubtfully,
"the vessel leaves in ten days. That's hardly enough time
to have everything in order."

"Everything is in order," Eric pointed out. "Everything

is ready for Stephen to leave." He hesitated, then, gently:
"I know you don't want to see him leave, love, and neither
do I. But is it more than that?"

"No," Stephanie replied quickly, realizing that she had
come too close to revealing her hidden feelings. "I'm only
concerned that everything be in order. But upon reflection, I can think of nothing that has been overlooked, so
proceed with booking Stephen's passage on the steamship."

The last phrase came from her lips reluctantly, her voice
fading, and she fervently wished that she could recall it. The
final step had been taken, and Stephanie knew that she had
spoken the words only under the pressure of having to allay
Eric's suspicions about the extent of her feelings. Absent
that necessity, her eagerness for Stephen to take advantage
of his great opportunity in life and her equally compelling
dread of sending him far across the seas could have reached
an irreconcilable deadlock.

That night was a wakeful one for Stephanie, those following it the same. The calendar was a silent drumbeat
on a march toward grief, with her sorrow reinforced by
that around her. Erica and Ralph failed to understand why
their brother had to go away, while Yulina did so only to
a degree. Other people became doctors without having to
leave Australia, and Yulina began wondering why Stephen
was unable to do the same.

It was worst of all for John, for he and Stephen were
brothers in every respect except bloodlines. The ship left
on a Friday, and Eric brought the boys home from school on
Wednesday. The following day, Stephen and John whiled
away the hours together prowling about the forest below
the village and tossing a ball. For that day, the future engineer and future physician were boys doing boyish things.
Stephanie had yearned to spend that day with her son, but
she relinquished it to John.

The atmosphere was funereal in the house that evening,
everyone reluctant to end it and staying up late. The next

morning was even more depressing, for the same emotions were compacted into the rush of preparations to leave before dawn and the breakfast that no one ate. After the tearful farewells, Stephanie and Eric set out in a buggy with Stephen.

During most of the drive, Stephanie restrained her feelings by joining in with Eric and raising Stephen's spirits. Although mature for his age, he was still only a boy. The hard truth had hit home completely that he was leaving everything he knew behind, setting out for a foreign land to live among strangers. The courage that Stephanie so admired in him asserted itself, however, and Stephen dried his tears and composed himself.

The sails on the wide yards of the *Theophane* were tightly furled, and smoke was trickling from the tall stacks amidships in preparation to leave under steam. The sawmill, icehouse, and icebox shop were closed for the day, and the workmen from them swelled those on the pier into a crowd. The men gathered around to make their farewells with Stephen and wish him Godspeed, then Stephanie went up the gangplank with her son and Eric.

Captain Vincent Reece was about fifty, with a stern face but kindly eyes, and Stephanie found solace in her agreement with Eric's opinion that the man seemed to be conscientious and thoroughly capable. She handed over the paper on which she had written her aunt and uncle's names and address, explaining that she had asked them to keep in frequent contact with the port master's office in London for word of Stephen's arrival.

The captain carefully tucked the paper into an inside pocket, assuring her that her son would be safe. "I'll look after the lad as though he was my own," he promised. "I'll see the port master immediately we berth, and the lad will stay aboard until your relatives speak with me personally and identify themselves. Put your mind entirely at rest, mo'm."

That was impossible, but his assurances made Stephanie

more confident. She thanked him, then went with Stephen and Eric to the boy's cabin. It was small and neat, the baggage that Eric had brought aboard earlier in the week stowed under the bunk. Stephanie searched out small disorders to correct and did other motherly things, and Eric talked with Stephen in the words and manner between loving fathers and sons.

A bell clanged, and a ship's officer shouted for visitors to go ashore. Stephanie steeled herself to contain her tears, stepping out on deck with Eric and Stephen. She knew it would embarrass her son if he began crying on the crowded deck, and his tears would spill over if hers did.

Stephen's slender arms clamped around Stephanie as she hugged him tightly and covered his small, handsome face with kisses. When the ship's officer shouted a final call, she forced herself to release the boy. Eric made his farewells and then she went down the gangplank with him, taking an agony of sorrow with her because she was leaving her son behind.

Sailors drew in the gangplank and hauled in lines from the pier, the ship bustling with activity. Its horn blared in a fountain of steam, the water at its stern boiled, and it moved away from the pier. Stephanie waved as the vessel steamed out of the cove and down the harbor roads. Her last blurred view of her son through tears was heartbreaking, the boy looking so small and vulnerable among the people standing at the rail and waving.

During the drive home, Stephanie was able to release her tears, but she still had to contain the depths of her grief. Eric had given her a gift beyond her wildest dreams, the opportunity for her son to be educated at Edinburgh University, and she knew it would be cruel to reveal the pain his gift had caused her. It was late when they arrived home, making the wretchedly unhappy evening in the quiet, somber house a brief one.

The next day was mercifully busy for her, with additional calls she had deferred from the previous day. It held her sorrow in abeyance, and weariness brought the respite of sleep that night. Her slumber disposed of hours until she could go to surroundings where she need have no secrets.

On Sunday, Stephanie had two calls that took her to the north end of the valley. By the time she returned, Eric had left to take John to school, and Yulina was sitting under a tree beside the house and watching Erica and Ralph take turns on the swing. Stephanie drove up to the village, its streets deserted on the warm Sunday afternoon.

More than deserted, the lane leading back to the prison was desolate, hostile toward being disturbed. At the end of it, the yard in front of the huge, derelict building was choked with rank weeds and wiry brush. Soot left by the smoke that had billowed from the prison windows during the fire had been washed into streaks by rain, and now instead of menacing, the small, dark windows looked like grieving, weeping eyes.

Her anguish had reached down the lane ahead of her, bridging the void beyond existence. The warm, still air was alive with a teeming stir, as though filled with swarms of gnats, but there were no insects. Stephanie stepped out of her buggy and concentrated, groping into that subtle disturbance with her thoughts and summoning. "Father, I am here," she whispered. "I am here, and I need you, Father. . . ."

Then the familiar, beloved presence was all about, touching her mind with greeting and its crushing, weary melancholy. The grief that Stephanie had kept contained rushed forth, and she began crying bitterly. "Father, I had to send Stephen away," she sobbed. "It was for his education and had to be done, but he's only a little boy. . . ."

The sympathy and understanding that she had known since childhood enfolded her with comfort. Stephanie continued pouring out her feelings in words and tears, drawing consolation from the gentle response, and she also gained a sense of proportion that made her torment easier to bear.

Her grief, even if great to her, was scarcely a ripple

against that vast ocean of dreary sorrow in the touch on her mind. Although years would pass, her son would return and her heartache would end, but the immense burden of sorrow borne by the beloved presence would endure forever.

PART THREE

Chapter Fourteen

"There you are, Mistress Gunnell," Stephen said, placing the baby on the bed beside the woman. "Your new son is a fine, healthy baby."

"Aye, and I'm most grateful, Dr. Brendell," the woman replied. "I've no complaints at all, mind. But your mother delivered my other two, and I'd sooner have her for any others, if it's all the same to you."

The remark delighted and amused Stephen, but from the corner of his eye, he saw his mother turn in annoyance as she set the nitrous oxide flask on a table. "You'd be very wise to do so," he advised the woman, laughing. "My mother is far more skilled in delivering babies than I."

"You're being generous to the point of going athwart facts, Stephen," Stephanie told him firmly, then turned to the woman on the bed: "Amanda, if you'd had complications, you would have been fortunate indeed to be attended by a doctor educated at Edinburgh University."

The woman agreed quickly, taken aback by Stephanie's stern tone, and the conversation became quieter among the women who were moving about in the lamplight and cleaning up. Stephen washed his hands in a basin on the table, his mother stepping to the door to tell the husband he could see his wife and new son. The man came in, grinning happily. In the joyful hubbub over the new baby, Stephen put his stethoscope and other things into his bag, picked up the nitrous oxide flask, and followed his mother out.

After donning their coats and hats at the front door of the farmhouse, Stephen and his mother went out into the cold, clear, early spring night. He helped Stephanie into the buggy and lit the coachlamps, then stepped into it. She tugged the reins, turning the buggy away from the house, and tucked the coach blanket around both of them against the chill.

"I had hoped nothing would interfere with our family reunion," Stephanie commented, turning the buggy onto the road. "It's been over a year since the other children were at home, and of course many years since you were, dear. I regret that this happened, and so near the end of our reunion, but I do appreciate your going with me to attend to Amanda."

"You appreciate it?" Stephen exclaimed. "Mother, from the time when I was following about at your heels, I've looked forward to actually attending a patient with you. I'm the one who's grateful."

Stephanie slipped her hand into his, smiling warmly. "Regardless of Amanda's narrow opinion, you're more skilled than anyone I've ever seen," she said. "I'm so proud of you. So very, very proud."

"If you're a tithe as proud of me as I've always been of you," he told her earnestly, "you're bursting with pride, Mother."

Stephanie squeezed his hand in a silent reply, then sighed happily and remarked that she was proud of her entire family. Stephen agreed that she had every right to be, with all of the family established in careers. Erica lived in Melbourne, where she was a lecturer in history at Queen's

College, and Ralph and John were managers of icehouses at Brisbane and Adelaide. John, a graduate of the Mining and Engineering College in Sydney, was also an inventor and held several patents on various types of machinery.

While talking with Ralph, Stephen had learned that the Brisbane icehouse had been established some four years before, after a road had been opened across the rugged Great Divide that lay west of the city. The mountain range had long been thought to be impassable in that region, but a trail had been found by a man whose name was familiar to Stephen from his childhood. During the months before he had left for Britain, Stephen remembered that his mother had often mentioned the name worriedly, the man then a boy.

What had happened to the man intrigued Stephen, but he was unsure if he had heard all the details correctly. "Was the fact that Jeremy Kerrick found a trail across the Great Divide at Brisbane the first news of him after his disappearance?" he asked. "If so, that was several years later."

"Yes, almost twelve years," Stephanie replied. "From what I heard, he wandered into the far outback with an Aborigine man and grew up there. He's married now, to a woman named Fiona, who is said to be extremely attractive. They have two small children and are at Tibooburra Station."

"It seems strange that he disappeared at all," Stephen observed. "From what I recall hearing about the Kerrick family, they aren't the sort of people to allow their children to wander about and get lost."

"That's true," she agreed. "All I know is from word of mouth, and I've disregarded much of it. The Kerricks and the Garrity family at Wayamba Station are favorite subjects for swagmen's tales, most of which defy common sense. I've no idea why Jeremy disappeared, but his circumstances weren't typical. He is Sir Morton Kerrick's son, born out of wedlock."

"Well, whatever the reason for his disappearance,"

Stephen summed up, "I know how relieved you must have been when you heard that he was safe and sound. You've always taken such a close interest in the lives of babies you delivered."

Stephanie was silent for a moment, her expression thoughtful in the dim, indirect glow of the coachlamps, then she nodded. "Yes, there's that," she mused, "but something more in this instance. I knew what torment Alexandra Kerrick was suffering, longing to find her grandson. Any grandmother would be the same, of course, but I've always felt a particular closeness with her. Alexandra is a most exceptional woman in every respect. . . ."

Her voice faded, Stephen reflecting that with abundant justification the same could be said of her. Ever since his return home a week before, he had been struck by how little his understanding of her as an adult exceeded that of when he had been a child. While they were bound together by the special relationship between mother and child, as well as by the ties of their profession, at times he detected indications of vast depths in her personality that no one could fathom. She had a mysterious, mystical quality about her, one that set her entirely apart from other people.

The conversation continued as the buggy moved down the road, then the large house that was so warmly familiar to Stephen came into view ahead in the waning moonlight. When they reached the barnyard, Stephanie carried the nitrous oxide flask and their bags inside, and Stephen unharnessed the horse. He led the horse to its stall, then crossed the barnyard to the house.

Just over a week before, Stephen's first glimpse of Jackson Heads, the towering sandstone bluffs at the entrance to the harbor leading back to Sydney Cove, had given him a sense of homecoming. That same feeling had been more intense the next day, when he had looked out at Wallaby Track from the window of the mail coach. It had been at a rational level in both instances, however, and that reaction within the depths of his emotions had been evoked only when he had entered the kitchen. Its smells and atmosphere of comfort and security had brought back his childhood in a rush, along with an instinctive conviction of having returned to his origins.

Stephen experienced that same feeling once again upon stepping into the kitchen. Vague, fleeting images that remained from forgotten memories flashed past his inner eye as he glanced around, the thick shadows at the corners of the large room crowding in against the flickering firelight and the yellow glow of the lamp on the table. Most of all, the formless emotional impulses conveying a childhood milieu of being nurtured and loved emanated from his mother, who was kneeling at the fireplace hob making cocoa.

The kitchen was unchanged except for a large icebox, a fact that Stephen brought up while he and his mother talked at the table over their cups of cocoa. "A fireplace for cooking is long outdated," he pointed out. "Except in the most modest of homes, stoves have been used for years."

"Yes, of course," Stephanie acknowledged. "But the kitchen is Yulina's domain. She wants to keep the fireplace, so we do."

Stephen took a drink of cocoa, then smiled. "I'm pleased that you do," he told her. "I like the fireplace better."

"So do I," Stephanie agreed. "I offered to have a stove installed, but I made no effort to change Yulina's mind when she declined it."

They laughed and continued talking, drinking their cocoa. When it was finished, Stephen and his mother carried candlesticks upstairs, exchanged a hug and kiss, and then went to their rooms. Lying in bed, Stephen thought about his conversations with his mother that evening and during the past week. Their discussions had been wide-ranging, but from his childhood, he had known to avoid one subject. At no time had he mentioned to her the old, abandoned prison at the top of the hill overlooking the house.

*   *   *

A stir in the house woke Stephen only a few hours after he fell asleep, but he immediately got out of bed to wash and dress. Erica, John, and Ralph were leaving that afternoon, and he wanted to make the most of his time with them. The appetizing aroma of gammon met him as he went downstairs and into the kitchen. The rest of the family was at the table, and his mother moved her chair to make more room for him.

Stephen replied to the hubbub of morning greetings, filling a plate from serving dishes on the cabinet, then seated himself. His father, Erica, and Ralph sat together at one side of the table, which emphasized the close similiarity between the three of them. John's strong, handsome features had some characteristics in common with those of his mother, and his face was expressive, revealing a self-possessed, cheerful good nature.

The hearty breakfast of gammon and eggs was delicious, but Stephen enjoyed the conversation and warm atmosphere far more. During the past week, he had grown to truly know his sister and brother for the first time. Both small children when he had left, Erica had become a charming, attractive young woman, and Ralph was a muscular man with a congenial personality. Even though John had grown to adulthood, he seemed the same to Stephen, because the brotherly affinity between them had been unchanged by the years.

Yulina was also the same as before, firmly declining any help with the dishes after the meal. "No, I'll see to them," she told everyone at large. "I've work to do, and I want elbow room. Erica, John, and Ralph won't be here for dinner, so we'll have a special tiffin. Go to the parlor or wherever else you wish and get yourselves hungry for it."

Stephen went into the parlor with the others, who began talking about a subject that he had heard discussed frequently in Wallaby Track during the past week. Some ten years before, a landowner near Geelong, on the southern coast in Victoria, had imported over a score of wild rabbits from Britain and released them on his estate to hunt for sport. Since then, they had been multiplying and spreading, destroying crops and pastures.

"They're spreading slowly," John said, "because they've been seen near Adelaide only during the last year or so. But they wreak havoc when they do arrive. So far, the only defense is to hire rabbiters, who make a living by charging landowners for each pair of ears."

"You should be able to do something about it, John," Erica suggested. "Invent some sort of device that will deal with them."

"That's already been done," John replied, laughing, "and it's called a gun. I haven't been able to think of anything more effective, and trying to develop a refrigeration system to freeze water has been taking all of my spare time. It galls me to have ice brought across the Pacific when it's at least theoretically possible to make our own ice."

"Don't invent a machine that will be cheap enough for people to buy for their houses, John," Ralph advised him jokingly. "If you do, you'll put us out of business instead of increasing our profits."

Everyone laughed heartily, John more wryly than the others. He commented that considering how much he had spent in trying to create such a machine, he doubted that it would be cheap. The conversation turned to Erica's work at Queen's College, where she was a researcher as well as a lecturer. She was compiling documentation on the history of convict transportation in Australia, a highly sensitive and controversial undertaking.

"I don't intend to publish it," she explained, "but it's part of our history, and I want to preserve it. There are people who spend freely to manufacture genealogies and conceal convict origins, and they'll resort to any means, including having records destroyed. Others would rather ignore that it ever happened, and I've lost friends through what I'm doing."

"That's false pride," Stephanie stated firmly. "Some might say that it's easy for me or other free immigrants to call it that, but I would point out that the Kerricks have never tried to conceal that David Kerrick, the co-founder of the family, was a convict. And those who criticize others because of convict origins have thereby proven that their opinions are worthless."

"But I hope that the friends you've lost haven't been all your gentlemen friends, Erica," Ralph quipped, turning the conversation back to a lighter note. "I wouldn't want to think you're without admirers now."

"You've no need to worry," Erica told him, smiling. "Needless to say, though, none of my gentlemen friends is as handsome as our Stephen."

Stephen laughed along with the others, amused by the remark. As an undergraduate student, derisive comments about his good looks had motivated him to join the university boxing team, where he had done well. Then in time he came to realize that he had no need to prove his masculinity, and he found it deeply satisfying that he so closely resembled his mother.

"Any of the doctors in Sydney will be eager to have you join their practice," Erica added. "Is that what you intend to do, or would you prefer to buy your own practice, Stephen?"

The subject had been touched upon during Stephen's conversations with the family, but never as a direct question. While the options Erica had mentioned were the obvious ones, he had decided upon a third: "No, I intend to seek a position in the hospital in Sydney," he replied. "I'd like to work there for a time, then go to a hospital in another city."

The announcement was greeted by momentary silence, with astonishment on the part of Erica, John, and Ralph. Eric was puzzled, but Stephanie nodded in understanding. Hospitals in general were only for those too poor to pay for medical treatments at home. They were supported by government allocations and charitable donations, and the staff salaries were so low that the physicians who worked in them usually had minimum qualifications.

"But why, Stephen?" Erica exclaimed, speaking out above John and Ralph as they also voiced their surprise. "With your education, you could have one of the best medical practices in Australia."

"Hospitals are at the center of the medical profession in any city," Stephen told her. "The directors are always prominent doctors, even though their only usual connection with the hospitals is soliciting donations and occasional overseeing. That makes a hospital the best place to demonstrate and disseminate information about the latest techniques at Edinburgh, which is what I wish to do. Also, I'll be of more use at a hospital, because patients there are the ones in greatest need of additional care."

The explanation met with understanding from everyone, as well as strong approval. "You won't get rich there," John observed, "but interest in what you do is always more satisfying than how much you can earn from it."

"And I can always reserve my old age for getting rich," Stephen added jokingly, then turned to his mother. "I recall hearing you and Hamish agree years ago that the hospital in Sydney is better than most."

"Yes, it is," she confirmed. "Its standards of care were set long ago by a Dr. William Redfern, and they're still followed. I don't know who works there, but the present director is a Dr. Edward Coleman. As you said, it's largely an honorary position. He selects the staff, though, and he'll be more than delighted to learn that you wish to work there."

The others emphatically echoed her opinion, then John, Erica, and Ralph began discussing their travel plans. They intended to ride to Sydney in the mail coach, then return to their homes on coastal vessels that plied back and forth around the continent. With the forenoon wearing on after another hour of conversation, the three of them went to their

rooms to pack their baggage, Eric and Stephanie going to
help them.

Stephen put on his coat and went outside, walking about
in the brisk, fresh air of the early spring day. Presently,
Eric came out to hitch horses to a buggy and wagon in
readiness to take everyone up to the village to meet the
mail coach. Stephen helped him, then they left the vehicles
parked beside the house and went inside to join the others
for tiffin.

The meal was all that Yulina had promised and more, a
delicious, succulent beef roast with all the trimmings and
freshly baked bread. Stephen regretted that the gathering
was drawing to an end, but he was also eager to proceed with his work. His mood matched the general attitude
around the table, with much talk about plans for another
reunion when circumstances permitted. After the meal, the
three women went out and crowded into the buggy. The
men carried all of the baggage to the wagon and climbed
into it, then followed the buggy up the road to the village.

The atmosphere of leave-taking was more intense during
the wait in front of the store at one side of the cobblestone
square, Stephen and the others searching for things to say
and trying to be cheerful. The wait was brief, however,
for the mail coach drove up the street to the square a few
minutes later. Drawn by four horses, it was a tall vehicle
that swayed and bobbed on soft springs, the driver sitting
on a high box in front.

The storekeeper came out and exchanged one mail bag
for another with the driver while Stephen helped the other
men stack the baggage on the coach and lash it down. After
final farewells, Erica, John, and Ralph boarded the coach
and waved as it moved away. When it disappeared over
the brow of the hill, Stephanie and Yulina stepped into the
buggy. They drove back down the street, Stephen and Eric
following them in the wagon.

Down the street from the square, a harness chain on one
of the horses hitched to the wagon slipped loose from the

doubletree. Eric stopped the wagon, then climbed down to reconnect the chain. A short distance down the street from the wagon, the lane leading to the old, abandoned prison was a thinner line in weeds and trees, almost completely overgrown, and the prison was barely visible behind a thick screen of trees.

Stephen jumped down from the wagon and went down the lane several yards, picking his steps through the matted weeds. When the prison came into full view, he stopped and studied it. Like many times before, he wondered why it was the source of such deep, abiding sorrow for his mother.

The weeds rustled as Eric stepped down the lane toward Stephen. Upon arriving home, Stephen had been intensely pleased to see that the years had hardly changed his parents. Aside from gray at their temples and a few wrinkles, they looked the same and were fully as energetically active as before. But now his father suddenly appeared to be years older, his wide, muscular shoulders slumped and his face more deeply lined in a grim expression, and Stephen realized that his mother's sorrow was just as much of a torment for his father.

"I didn't mention the prison to Mother, of course," Stephen said. "Have you ever learned anything about her feelings concerning it, Father?"

"No, nothing specific, son," Eric replied, placing a hand on Stephen's shoulder. "She will never talk about it. Her sadness certainly has something to do with her father's death there, though."

"But after all these years, she would have adjusted to her father's death," Stephen pointed out. "It must be more than that."

"Yes, it must," Eric agreed. "She loved her father deeply, but he's been dead many years. But I don't know what else it could be." He smiled wistfully, shrugging. "I thought that perhaps as a man, you might have some inkling about it, considering that you and she are much alike."

"No, not in the way that you mean," Stephen told him.

"Mother is a mystic, whereas I'm a scientist. I know far more about medicine than she, but she understands patients far better than I." He gazed at the prison again, fervently wishing he could somehow relieve his mother's sorrow. It was tragic, but it was also strange. The focus of bereavement for a loved one was usually the grave, not the place of death. "I don't recall if she visits her father's grave often," he said. "Does she?"

Eric frowned reflectively, silent for a moment. "It couldn't be very often," he mused, perplexed. "I've never thought of it, but as far as I know, she's never visited his grave. Now that you mention it, that seems more than passing odd, doesn't it? What do you make of it, son?"

Stephen silently shook his head and looked at the prison, unsure of what it meant. But he knew that it was a clue to her feelings. It was a vague insight that he could think about at length, and in time he might attach to it sufficient meaning for it to suggest some course of action.

Chapter Fifteen

The ambience of Sydney was as Stephen remembered it, a teeming bustle that flowed back from the waterfront. The center of the city, where he rented a room in a boardinghouse on Grantham Avenue, was also much the same. It was the outskirts that had changed most of all, the brickyard replaced by a railroad station and telegraph office. Across the street, the mail coach station was where the market had been, and the new market was up the road to Parramatta, which was now virtually an adjunct to the city.

Dr. Edward Coleman, a genial, portly man in his fifties, had heard of Stephen through a friend of Hamish Mcfee's. Receiving Stephen cordially in his surgery, he was at first surprised, then delighted, when Stephen asked about a position at the hospital and gave his reasons for wanting to work there. Edward quickly agreed, explaining that the two doctors and two apprentices presently working at the hospital were sufficient, but Stephen's qualifications and reasons justified his addition to the staff.

Putting other matters aside, Edward summoned his carriage and took Stephen to the hospital to introduce him to the staff. It was a two-story slab of a building, dark with age. The cleanliness of the foyer and waiting room off to one side reflected its reputation for conditions that were better than average, but it was permeated with the usual sickroom stench.

When he saw the director, the almoner came out of his office across the foyer from the waiting room. In charge of administration and the hospital orderlies, he was a small, spare man named Jonah Hislop. At a word from Edward, Jonah went into the wards and summoned the medical staff.

The senior doctor was Fred Humphrey, a former navy surgeon and a stout, middle-aged man. When he exchanged greetings with Stephen, there was an edge of wariness in his manner, a readiness to meet a challenge to his authority. The other doctor, Oliver Willis, was in his sixties and had a reserved, taciturn manner. The apprentices, Jerome Arnold and Matthew Butler, were large, rawboned men in their twenties. Having attended college for the required courses in the sciences, they were preparing themselves to meet the examining board of the medical society for licensing as physicians.

Oliver was something of a puzzle to Stephen, seeming out of place. Former navy surgeons often worked in hospitals, but Oliver was the type of doctor who would usually have his own practice. He was courteous enough and knew of Stephen's mother, asking about her, but he had an independent attitude and impatience with social protocols. Instead of joining in the general conversation with the director after the introductions, Oliver turned away and disappeared down a corridor toward his ward.

After the director left, Jerome and Matthew went back to their work, and the almoner returned to his office. Fred was by nature a gruffly amiable man, but his concern over having his authority usurped strained the atmosphere between him and Stephen at first. "Our funds are limited," he explained defensively, "but I don't think we do badly here. During the eight years I've been in charge, I daresay we've saved more than a few lives."

"Yes, this hospital has a very good reputation," Stephen agreed. "Dr. Coleman didn't make my purpose here entirely clear. I believe what I learned at Edinburgh would be useful to the staff, and to other doctors in the city. I'd like to demonstrate the latest techniques here for a few months, then I intend to go to other hospitals and do the same there."

Fred stroked his chin, his attitude thawing. "That puts a different light on matters," he acknowledged. "It struck me as peculiar that a young fellow with a degree from Edinburgh would want to work in a hospital, but it makes sense now. It speaks well of you that you're forgoing the goodly amount of money you could be earning, and I'm certainly anything but loath to adopt new methods that will be of benefit to the patients."

"That speaks well of you, Fred, and I'm looking forward to working with you," Stephen told him. "One of the most far-reaching discoveries of recent years at Edinburgh has to do with the nature of disease. It's been definitely proven that disease is caused by germs."

"Aye, well, I've never concerned myself with the theories about disease," Fred commented dismissively. "I've always been more interested in getting rid of illnesses than in worrying about whether it was germs or a miasma from decaying organic substances that caused them."

"Even so, this discovery has important practical applications," Stephen assured him, "and phenol has been found to be a highly effective germicide. If the walls, floors, and bedding in a hospital are washed frequently in a diluted solution of phenol, the spread of diseases is greatly reduced. It also drives away flies and eliminates the hospital odor."

"Then those last two things are more than sufficient reason for me to use it," Fred said wryly. "I've become accustomed to the stink in a hospital over the years, but that doesn't mean I wouldn't like to get rid of it. I'll never get used to flies, though. They're bad enough in here now, and by summer they'll be driving everyone mad. Needless to say, I'd be more than happy if phenol stops the spread of disease as well."

Noting the strongly implied uncertainty of the last remark, Stephen continued, "Phenol is also effective in reducing sepsis. When the bandages used on injuries or amputations are soaked in a diluted solution, the suppuration is either reduced or eliminated."

"Well, that would be of great value," Fred replied noncommittally. "I'm not questioning what you say, Stephen, and I'm always willing to wait and see. But it seems that the better new remedies are supposed to be when they come down the road, the quicker they slide into the ditch."

"That's true," Stephen agreed, not pressing the issue, for he understood Fred's viewpoint. Over the years, innumerable miracle cures had been touted that turned out to be useless or worse. As a result, when new techniques or treatments were under discussion, the skepticism of responsible physicians was in direct proportion to the claims being made.

At the same time, Stephen knew that a patient in circumstances which could demonstrate the use of phenol to best advantage would convince Fred, along with others. Far more than simply proving a point, it would ease suffering and save lives. Stephen hoped such an opportunity developed quickly, for the sooner it was proven, the more patients would benefit.

Fred spoke to Jonah Hislop, instructing him to obtain phenol and have the orderlies wash down the walls and floors with a solution of the chemical. The almoner grabbed a piece of paper and jotted a note, then Fred led the way into a corridor, showing Stephen through the hospital.

Half of the lower floor was taken up by the kitchen,

supply room, and laboratory. The other half was the lying-in ward, Oliver Willis in charge. The general and surgical wards were upstairs, each with an examination and treatment room. Some fifteen patients and empty cots for another half dozen were in each ward, and typical of any hospital, relatives were beside the cots to assist orderlies in attending to the patients.

Fred explained that he spent most of his time in the general ward and supervised the apprentices in caring for patients in the surgical ward. He suggested that Stephen take over the latter one, with Jerome and then Matthew working with him during alternate weeks. Stephen quickly agreed, knowing that it was in the surgical ward where the full benefits of using phenol could be most readily and dramatically proven.

Stephen was favorably impressed by the hospital, its reputation for being better than most borne out by everything he saw. While it was spartan, it was well-organized and clean. The almoner, more capable and dedicated than many, supervised orderlies who were the same. Within an hour of having been told to do so, Jonah had procured demijohns of phenol from a chemist and orderlies were mixing it in buckets of water. By the time that Stephen began his first full day at the hospital the next morning, the flies and noxious stench had been replaced by the fresh, pungent smell of the carbolic.

All the patients in the ward had infections in their amputations and injuries, some with spots of gangrene. Stephen set to work, Jerome assisting him, and began training the apprentice in using phenol and monitoring the condition of patients. A microscope in the laboratory had been largely unused, and Stephen instructed Jerome in how to detect increasing infection by the level of white blood corpuscles in the bloodstream of patients.

After a few days, Stephen had excised all the gangrene and stopped the infections from spreading. However, he knew that he needed a case other than those in the ward

to convincingly demonstrate the benefits of phenol. While
the patients in the ward would recover more quickly now,
it would still be gradual, and some always healed more
rapidly than others.

Word of what he was doing circulated among doctors in
the city, and one or two were always present to watch him
work over patients in the treatment room. Ardent believers
in the miasmic theory of disease were skeptical, while others reserved judgment, but one doctor accepted Stephen's
claims as promptly as had his mother and Hamish Mcfee.
Oliver Willis was present on occasion, silently observing
and listening to the conversation, and Stephen noticed that
the man had begun using phenol with his patients.

The opportunity to fully demonstrate the antiseptic capability of phenol came during Stephen's second week at the
hospital, but it was a case in which the risk of total failure
was high. Hearing an uproar of distressed voices in the
foyer, Stephen rushed out of the ward to the staircase,
Matthew right behind him. In the midst of a milling, noisily
anxious crowd in the foyer, a man on a crutch and a woman
were standing over an unconscious boy on a crude stretcher
and plaintively arguing with Fred.

Picking out words from the bedlam as he went down the
stairs, Stephen gathered that a dray had run over the boy's
legs. The man and woman were his parents, the others
friends and bystanders at the accident scene. Jonah was
pushing about in the crowd, asking questions and getting
information from the people to fill out an admission record
for the boy.

Tears ran down the man's face as he leaned on his
crutch and pleaded with Fred not to amputate the boy's
legs. "Please don't do it," he begged. "It's hard enough
for me to work and support my family, and life wouldn't
be worth living for my son if he had both legs cut off."

"Saving the boy's life comes first!" Fred protested, tormented by the people chiming in and supporting the man.

"His legs are in such a state that they must be . . ." His voice faded as he saw Stephen. "This is Dr. Brendell, and he's in charge of surgery," he announced in relief.

The people turned on Stephen with their frantic yammering as he reached for the admission record from Jonah. Glancing at it, he saw that the parents were Orah and Myrtle Hawkins, and the boy, Daniel, was ten years old. "Be quiet!" he snapped impatiently, handing the record back to the almoner. "A hospital is not a place for such a commotion, and you're certainly doing nothing to help this boy. Now stand back and be quiet."

Silence fell, the people breaking off in the middle of shouts, and they shuffled back as Stephen bent over the stretcher to examine the unconscious boy. Rags had been tied around his knees to restrict the bleeding, but the crude bandages on his lower legs were still soaked with blood. Peering under them, Stephen saw that the wide, heavy wheel of the dray had crushed the bones, ends of which jutted through lacerations.

He knew that Fred was right, amputation at the knees was more than justified. The inaccessible recesses of the injuries had already been invaded by germs from the dirty bandages, perhaps too extensively for phenol to control. Any infection that developed in such massive wounds could explode into terminal septicemia before an amputation could be performed.

At the same time, Stephen believed there was a chance that the boy's legs could be saved. While pondering, he glanced at Orah and Myrtle, and their woeful expressions were more eloquent than the loudest appeals. Stephen decided that he had to take the risk, doing his utmost for the boy. "I'll try to save the boy's legs," he said, turning to Fred.

"Good on you!" Fred exclaimed, dropping a hand on Stephen's shoulder. "Amputating that child's legs would be a shame, and I hope you succeed." He turned, motioning and barking orders. "Everyone but the family, be on your

way. You know what's going to happen, so let Dr. Brendell
get to work. Jonah, have orderlies carry the boy up to the
treatment room."

The people smiled and commented in satisfaction, filing
out the door, and Stephen went back upstairs with Matthew.
In the treatment room, the apprentice filled basins and
an atomizer with phenol, while Stephen prepared sutures,
splints, and bandages. Presently, the orderlies brought the
boy in and placed him on the table, then went back out.

Two doctors who visited occasionally stepped into the
treatment room while Stephen was spraying the wounds
with the atomizer. One of them left to tell others what
was being done, and a short time later, doctors began
arriving in ones and twos. The room became crowded with
doctors watching in grave silence, professional protocol
preventing unsolicited opinions, but their strong misgivings
were evident without words.

Matthew worked the atomizer and kept a mist of phenol
drifting over the table while Stephen tied off severed blood
vessels, aligned the shattered bones, and sutured the gaping
wounds on the boy's slender, mangled legs. All of the
surface wounds were on the shins, and Stephen placed the
splints at the sides and calves of the legs so the bandages
could be changed periodically. Most of the morning had
passed when he finally finished, placing bandages that were
dripping with phenol over the sutured wounds.

The doctors made courteous remarks about the neat
suturing and surgical technique, then they left, murmuring
doubtfully among themselves. Stephen followed the orderlies who carried the boy out to a cot in the ward, where Orah
and Myrtle were waiting. They began thanking Stephen
effusively, and he interrupted them. "Your son's condition
is most uncertain," he stated candidly. "I may yet have to
amputate his legs, and if I do, his chances will be far less
than if I had done it immediately."

"When will we know, Dr. Brendell?" Myrtle asked
apprehensively.

"Two or three days at the very soonest," Stephen replied. "Until then, we can only wait and hope for the best."

"Regardless of what happens," Orah said earnestly, "we're mightily grateful. You've tried to save the lad's legs, which is more than any other doctor would even know how to do." He turned to Myrtle: "That photography studio has another cartage job for me, and we need the money. I'll go see to that, and I'll be back as soon as I finish."

Myrtle settled herself on a stool beside the cot, Orah stumping out of the ward on his crutch, and Matthew joined Stephen as he turned to other patients. A few had infections still needing attention, while the remainder had to be roused from their cots. Extended bed rest had long been considered therapeutic for any injury or illness, but research at Edinburgh had proven that it merely allowed muscle tone to deteriorate.

In addition to being difficult and painful for the patients, moving about while recovering was contrary to everything they had ever known. Getting them up from their cots consisted of cajoling, helping, and quieting their loud complaints. From time to time, Stephen glanced at Danny Hawkins, the boy's pale face and small fingers on the coverlet twitching from his unconscious body's responses to severe pain.

The boy recovered consciousness during the afternoon, confused, fearful, and crying in pain. His mother coaxed him into taking spoonfuls of broth and drinking a glass of water, then Stephen administered a doze of laudanum. The boy subsided into drugged slumber until late afternoon, when Myrtle gave him more broth and water. Before leaving the hospital for the day, Stephen sedated the boy so he would sleep through the night.

The next morning, the boy's small feet were a normal temperature and color, proving that adequate blood was finding its way around the severed veins that had been tied off. The hopeful sign was countered when Stephen took a drop of blood on a microscope slide, stained it, and examined it. The boy's blood was thick with leucocytes, white blood corpuscles.

During midmorning, Jonah happily told Stephen about an unexpected development. A few minutes before, an errand boy from the photography studio where Orah Hawkins did occasional jobs had delivered a check to pay for Danny's medical care, along with a note requesting that the donation be kept anonymous. In addition to modestly avoiding credit, the owner of the studio was generous, for the check was in the amount of ten guineas, which was several times the amount that the medical treatment would cost.

Near midday, an orderly came up to the ward and told Stephen that his mother was in the foyer. Hurrying downstairs, he found her talking with Fred and Oliver. Both men were pleased at meeting her for the first time, and it had brought out a different side of Oliver's character, making him much more affable and talkative. Stephen exchanged greetings with her, then she resumed talking with Oliver, discussing the Kerrick family with him.

"I'll always be grateful that you recommended me to Alexandra Kerrick years ago," Stephanie told the doctor. "Meeting her was a delight that will be one of my fondest memories for as long as I live. I understand that Jeremy is married to a young woman from Brisbane named Fiona."

"Yes, formerly Fiona Donley," Oliver added. "She is a most attractive and charming young woman, with intelligence and spirit to match. I attended her mother, who unfortunately had terminal cancer."

"So you were in Brisbane, Oliver," Fred remarked. "I didn't know that."

The comment about his affairs closed a door of sorts on Oliver's open manner, reverting him to his usual taciturn self. He spoke to Stephanie once again, expressing great satisfaction at having finally met her, then turned on his heel and went back to his ward. Stephen suggested tiffin at a tearoom up the street, including Fred in the invitation, but he declined regretfully and explained that he had work to do. Stephanie accepted with a happy smile, and Stephen hurried back upstairs to get his coat and hat.

Leaving her buggy in front of the hospital, Stephen and his mother walked up the street to the tearoom. When they were seated and a waiter had taken their orders, she explained why she was in the city. Instead of having Eric buy drugs she needed the next time he came to Sydney, as she usually did, she had decided to make the trip to the chemist herself.

"Mostly to see you, dear, and to find out how you're going on," Stephanie added. "Also, Hamish wanted me to ask your opinion about a patient of his. The patient is a middle-aged man with a stomach tumor, and Hamish wondered if surgical removal of the tumor would be possible."

"No, definitely not," Stephen replied. "Unless it's cancerous, people can live for years with an abdominal tumor. At Edinburgh the mortality rate from infections following abdominal surgery was one hundred percent."

"That certainly dictates against it," Stephanie agreed. "The reason Hamish believed you might consider it possible was because of a discussion you had with him about lithotomies and surgery for hernias."

"The procedures used for those are relatively shallow operations, not deep invasion of the abdomen," Stephen said. "There are limits to the effectiveness of phenol as a germicide."

Having broached the subject, Stephen explained that he might have exceeded those limits with Danny Hawkins. He told her about the treatment he had used for the boy's injuries. The conversation moved on to other subjects while they finished their tiffin, then they walked back down the street.

At her buggy, Stephanie started to kiss Stephen and leave, then she hesitated and studied him, her expression both thoughtful and hauntingly melancholy. "What are you thinking, Mother?" he asked.

"That you're so much like your grandfather," she replied

wistfully. "You are the very image of him when I was a small girl, just like the tall, handsome man who sat me on his knee and . . ." Her voice faded, almost breaking with a sob as her eyes filled with tears. Then she controlled herself, blinking away her tears and smiling brightly.

Stephen smiled, but his thoughts were somber. More than ever, he wanted to pursue the subject, asking about her father and the prison. He longed to ask why her father's death still remained with her as though it had happened only the day before, and perhaps find some way to help her.

He knew, however, that it was a forbidden subject, one he could never broach with her. He had to be satisfied with the clue he had discovered, the insight into her feelings that he had thought about and would ponder again. After exchanging a hug and kiss with her, he helped her into her buggy, then went into the hospital as she drove away.

Danny Hawkins became feverish during the afternoon, his temperature up over four degrees on the clinical thermometer. It was an indication that the infection in his legs was spreading rapidly, and Stephen began thinking about returning the boy to the treatment room for amputation before septicemia developed. He hesitated over that final recourse, for other indications were either inconclusive or more favorable.

Stephen had no means of making a precise count, but the number of leucocytes in the boy's blood seemed about the same as the previous day. While Danny was conscious during the afternoon, he was more lucid than before, and he needed no urging to gulp down several glassfuls of water. He was also conscious for over an hour before he began crying from pain, revealing a strong will that was as beneficial as any medical treatment.

The boy's condition was the same at the end of the day, and it remained unchanged the following morning. It was still as before during the afternoon, when Edward Coleman visited the hospital, having heard about the boy. The doctor examined Danny, then talked with Stephen in the treatment room. He explained that he had a dinner engagement the following week with a wealthy couple, whom he planned to ask for a donation for the hospital.

"It's most useful to be able to cite instances of excellent work being done here," he went on. "Now I can ask for a larger donation. This is an extraordinary case I can tell them about."

"I should think that will depend upon the outcome," Stephen suggested, "and we'll know what it is well before next week. If he doesn't improve soon, I'll have to amputate and then try to save his life."

"Then for the lad's sake first and foremost," Edward stated sincerely, "let's hope he does improve soon. But if I can also solicit a larger donation, it will benefit all of the patients. The couple I'm dining with are Benjamin and Beverly Tavish. You've probably heard of them."

Recalling that his mother had mentioned the names, Stephen nodded. "I believe they're connected with the Kerrick family, aren't they?" he asked.

"Yes, very closely," Edward replied. "More than friends, the Tavishes are like family with Sir Morton and Lady Julia Kerrick. I might add that those two families have been among the most generous contributors to the hospital. Regarding your young patient, he is a most extraordinary case. I would have amputated without a second thought. Please keep me informed as to his progress, Stephen."

Stephen replied that he would, then left the treatment room with Edward and took his leave of him. Matthew was examining Danny and changing his bandages, and Stephen went to the cot. The boy's temperature was still elevated four degrees, his other vital signs also the same. While the bandages were removed and Matthew was preparing fresh ones, Stephen noted slight variations in the skin temperature of the boy's lower legs.

Like other symptoms, that fact was inconclusive. It was possible that the infection was relatively small and was concentrating in a few very localized spots of sepsis near the surface of the skin, which would be easy to treat. But it could also be massive and deep in the legs, where the only possible treatment was amputation.

The one absolute certainty was that the time when Stephen would have to make a decision was drawing closer. The spoonfuls of broth that the boy's mother gave him when he was conscious were far less than the minimum amount of nutrition that he needed. His body was fighting to overcome shock, loss of blood, and the invading germs, and it was doing so with steadily diminishing reserves of energy.

By the next morning, it was evident that Danny's strength was waning, his vital signs starting to weaken. During the forenoon hours and on past midday, Stephen hesitated over summoning orderlies to take the boy into the treatment room for amputation. Then, during early afternoon, he examined another blood sample under the microscope, and it appeared to him that the number of leucocytes in the boy's bloodstream was stabilizing.

If true, it was an undeniably promising indication, evidence that the infection was being contained. Stephen was uncertain, however, feeling frustrated over the lack of a means to make a precise count of the white blood corpuscles. Near the end of the day, the boy's temperature began declining very gradually but steadily. It was also a hopeful sign, although less important than the leucocyte level.

When the rest of the medical staff left for the day, Stephen remained at the hospital and found things to do between examining blood samples from the boy at intervals of an hour. Orah arrived after working at the photography studio, and he joined Myrtle at the side of their son's cot. Stephen peered into the microscope until his eyes smarted, remaining uncertain, but the number of leucocytes appeared to be the same on each succeeding smear of blood that he sustained and then examined.

The evidence came at midnight, when Stephen compared a slide with the three previous ones. Over the last four hours, the number of white blood corpuscles had decreased slightly. He put the slides away and extinguished the lamp in the treatment room, then went out into the ward.

In the dim light of a lantern in the center of the ward, with a murmur of blended snores rising from patients, Orah and Myrtle were dozing on their stools beside their son's cot. Stephen touched Orah's shoulder to waken him. "Danny's legs won't have to be amputated," he said when the man woke and looked up. "The lad will recover in good order."

Orah surged up from his stool with a cry of delight, losing his balance on his single leg, and Stephen grabbed the man to keep him from falling. Stephen then found himself squeezed in a tight hug, Orah stammering his gratitude. Mrytle woke and leaped up from her stool, wailing happily, and Orah turned to her as she threw her arms around him.

The couple clutched each other, weeping in joy, and Stephen returned to the treatment room for his coat and hat. He left the hospital and walked through the dark streets toward his boardinghouse, relieved and keenly satisfied. He knew that when other doctors saw what had happened, some would immediately begin using phenol. More would when the evidence accumulated and became undeniable, and innumerable patients would benefit. In addition, Edward Coleman would have a dramatic development to describe to a wealthy couple and solicit more money for the hospital.

Those results were gratifying, but Stephen's greatest satisfaction came from knowing that Danny Hawkins could now enjoy his childhood years and grow to adulthood with strong, sound legs.

Chapter Sixteen

"You say this happened by accident, Mistress Naseby?" Stephen asked.

"Aye, Dr. Brendell," the woman replied in a soft, dull voice.

"What sort of accident?"

"The boy fell, Dr. Brendell."

The woman kept her eyes downcast, her manner as meek and dispirited as her voice. Stephen turned to the young boy lying on the treatment room table. "How did you fall and injure yourself, son?" he asked.

"I stumbled, sir," the boy whispered, his eyes averted.

Looking at the admission form, Stephen saw that the boy, Ernest Clark, was nine years old, and his parents were Adam and Mary Naseby. Stephen handed the paper to Jerome Arnold, who grabbed it with an anxious air of avoiding any cause for annoyance at himself. Both apprentices had learned to recognize when Stephen was angry, and now he was boiling with rage.

Fractures in children's arms were almost always lateral,

usually the result of falling on an arm that was inadequately braced or supported to bear their weight. The boy had a bruise on his wrist, a longitudinal fracture in his forearm, and a cut on his forehead. He had been seized by the wrist and hurled against something, and in the process, his arm had been twisted with sufficient violence to break the bone down its length.

Stephen finished examining the boy, finding no evidence of concussion from the impact on his forehead. Jerome was waiting with a bottle of chloroform and an anesthetic cone, and at Stephen's nod, the apprentice placed the wide end of the cone over the boy's nose and mouth, and dripped chloroform on the sponge at the tip of the cone. Moments later, the boy was sleeping soundly. Stephen disinfected and bandaged the cut on the boy's forehead, then aligned the bones in the broken arm and set it with splints.

When he finished, Stephen turned to Mary and took hold of her hands. At first she tried to twist away when he began pushing up her sleeves, then she stopped resisting and stood with her face downcast. Her arms were covered with bruises, fresh ones over others that had faded into splotches. "Don't you have a brother who will deal with this for you?" he asked. "Or how about your father or another relative?"

Mary shook her head and began crying. "My father is dead," she replied, sobbing. "He was drowned at the same time as my first husband, when their boat overturned. I have only a sister who lives in Melbourne."

"Very well. Is Naseby on the premises?"

"Aye, he's in the waiting room, but please don't say anything to him," the woman begged. "He'll think I told you what he did to Ernest, and he'll beat me so hard that I won't be able to—"

"No, he won't," Stephen growled between clenched teeth, lifting her face with a hand under her chin and looking into her eyes. "Today is the day that swine stops mistreating you and your son, and you have my word on it." He turned toward the door, speaking over his shoulder: "Jerome, seat

Mistress Naseby on that chair in the corner."

The apprentice led the woman toward the chair as Stephen rushed out of the room. Orah Hawkins was stumping through the front door into the foyer on his crutch just as Stephen ran down the staircase, and the man's face lit up in a beaming smile of warm regard. He called out a cheery greeting, and Stephen muttered a reply, charging into the waiting room.

At first glance, Stephen was certain that he had picked out Naseby among the people on the benches. He was a paunchy, muscular man, his beefy face set in a habitual, petulant scowl of a sour and brutally vindictive disposition. "Are you Adam Naseby?" Stephen demanded.

"Aye, what of it?" the man muttered, standing up from the bench.

"I wanted a look at a cowardly swine who beats a woman and a boy," Stephen retorted. "How would you like to try beating on a man?"

Naseby's face flushed with anger and embarrassment as the others in the room glared at him in outrage, and he stepped toward the door. "I'd have no trouble with a skinny poddy like you!" he barked. "But I've no time to listen to your lying scavvy, so I'll be on my way."

Stephen stepped in front of the man, blocking his path. "No one calls me a liar and walks away," he said quietly. "Now you're going to fight me, and you'll find it different from beating on a woman and a boy."

Naseby snorted in contempt, starting to push past, and Stephen shoved him back. The man's eyes narrowed, his face turning crimson with rage. He hesitated an instant, then swung his fist at Stephen. Grim joy exploded within Stephen, his fury at the man finding an outlet.

Stephen fell smoothly into a boxing stance from his undergraduate years, lightly balanced on his feet. He fended off the man's fist with his left forearm, his right fist lashing out in three quick punches that opened a cut in Naseby's right eyebrow, flattened the man's nose, and crushed his lips against his teeth. Naseby reeled on his feet and staggered backward, shaking his head and bellowing in surprise and pain.

Benches toppled over with loud crashes, the people leaping up from them and flooding out the door. Naseby flailed his fists at Stephen in powerful but slow and uncoordinated blows. Stephen ducked and weaved on his feet, dodging and fending off the blows, and punched rapidly with his right fist. Each time it struck flesh, he gave his fist a slight twist.

In boxing it had been judged a foul blow and drew a heavy penalty, for the twist used the impact of the blow to split skin. Stephen opened cuts across Naseby's forehead, then punched the man's nose into a bloody, shapeless mass. Naseby began squealing frantically, slinging his fists wildly and trying to get to the door. Stephen cut him off each time, stepping lightly around him, and drove him back into the room with swift punches.

Blinded by blood flowing into his eyes, Naseby stumbled over a bench and fell heavily to the floor. Stephen stood over him, fists cocked. "It's not the same as beating a woman and a boy, is it, Naseby?" he scoffed. "Get on your feet! Get on your feet and fight!"

The man shook his head, stuttering incoherently and cowering on the floor. "Then stay there!" Stephen shouted, driving a toe into Naseby's paunchy belly. "Stay there and be kicked like the coward you are!"

Wailing in pain, Naseby tried to crawl away, and Stephen followed him and continued kicking him. Then muscular arms suddenly clamped tightly around Stephen. "Bloody hell, Stephen!" Fred exclaimed, laughing and pulling him back. "You've got this hospital overflowing with patients now, and you've no need to get us another this way."

Stephen agreed, his anger changing to disgust with Naseby. He followed Fred into the foyer, where the people from the waiting room were agog over the fight. At that moment, Oliver came in the front door with a constable.

In the quiet, effective way in which he did everything, the doctor had gone out and found the constable to deal with Naseby.

The burly peace officer was more than willing to do so. His face became stony and his fingers tightened on his nightstick when Stephen explained the situation. Naseby stumbled out of the waiting room, wiping blood from his eyes with his handkerchief and loudly denying everything.

Ignoring the man's protests, the constable grabbed him by the collar. "I'll take him out to the alley and have a talk with him, Dr. Brendell," the constable said. "It appears that you did well in your chat with him, and I'll add in a word here and there. You let me know if he does it again, and I'll track him down and have another talk with him."

The constable dragged Naseby out, ending the interruption to the morning routine at the hospital. Oliver turned toward his ward with a nod of approval to Stephen, and the people laughed and talked about the incident as they filed back into the waiting room and set the benches upright. Stephen spoke to Fred about Ernest, explaining that he would like to keep the boy overnight for observation, but all the cots in his ward were filled.

"That's hardly anything new, is it?" Fred remarked, laughing. "You've had upwards of a dozen patients in my ward at times, haven't you? Aye, go ahead and send him to my ward."

Stephen thanked Fred and beckoned two orderlies, who followed him upstairs to the treatment room. While the orderlies were lifting the boy onto a stretcher, Stephen explained to Mary what had happened. She burst into tears, stammering her gratitude, and Stephen told her to let him know if Naseby abused her or her son again.

"It's highly unlikely," he added, "because he knows what it would bring him. My greatest hope now is that word of this will get about and serve as a warning to other men like Naseby."

Mary agreed emphatically and thanked Stephen again,

following the orderlies and her son out. Stephen washed his hands in phenol, disinfecting his bruised and skinned knuckles, then stepped out into the ward. More cots had been moved into it, bringing the total up to thirty, and Orah Hawkins was leaning on his crutch in the middle aisle and regaling the patients with a colorful description of the fight in the waiting room.

"Don't make it better than it was, Orah," Stephen told him, laughing.

"I couldn't, Dr. Brendell!" the man exclaimed. "I've seen more than a few ructions, but never one like that. Your right fist was like a swarm of hornets. Where did you learn to fight like that?"

"At Edinburgh," Stephen replied, turning to the patients, "where I also learned that it's best for patients to move about as soon as they're able. It's time to get up and walk around a bit."

The announcement was greeted with loud groans of protest from all of the patients except Danny Hawkins, who sat up and reached for his small crutches. The boy had become the mascot of the ward during his recovery, even the most crotchety patients responding to his winsome good nature. He scooted off his cot onto his splinted legs, and Stephen and Jerome helped other patients as they slowly and painfully lifted themselves from their cots.

During recent weeks, the patients had become more variegated as well as more numerous. On the same day a few weeks before, a dock porter with a strangulated hernia and a businessman who had collapsed at the Merchants Exchange in agony with bladder stones had been unable to get medical attention from a doctor with a practice, and they had been brought to the hospital. After both had been sent home a few days after surgery with no sign of infection, people from all walks of life had begun coming to the hospital for various surgical procedures, many of them referred by their doctors.

When all of the patients were moving about amid moans

and sighs, Stephen returned to the treatment room and found Oliver waiting there. "I've noticed that you occasionally go to the tearoom up the street for tiffin," Oliver remarked. "If you're going there today, I'll go with you."

Stephen had intended to have a bowl of soup from the hospital kitchen that day, but he immediately agreed. "Yes, I'll be ready to go when my patients are back in bed," he replied. "I'll stop in at your ward."

Oliver nodded and went out, leaving Stephen pondering the implicit offer of friendship. He and Oliver had become well acquainted, making it ever more obvious that the man was the type of doctor who would ordinarily have his own practice, but his reasons for working at the hospital remained an enigma to Stephen. He liked Oliver and had hoped that they would eventually be friends, and he was pleased that the man evidently felt the same.

The discussion over tiffin was interesting for Stephen but unrevealing about Oliver, most of it concerning patients. The next time their work permitted both of them to leave at midday, Eric stopped in at the hospital to see Stephen, and the three of them went to tiffin together. Shipments of ice were arriving at the icehouse, and Eric had received telegrams from Ralph and John, reporting that ice was arriving in Brisbane and Adelaide. Most of the conversation was about that, as well as John's continuing efforts to design a machine that would freeze water.

The tearoom featured homemade beer, which Stephen always had when he went there for tiffin. Oliver drank water instead, and at first, Stephen concluded that alcoholic drinks might make the older man sleepy during the warm, late spring afternoons. Then, when their friendship developed and Oliver gradually became less reticent, he told Stephen that he avoided all alcoholic beverages.

The reason for that and other facts about Oliver came out in a piecemeal fashion during other conversations over tiffin, he and Stephen going to the tearoom every day or two. Twenty years before, Oliver had sold a practice in Sydney and moved to Brisbane, buying another there. His beloved wife of many years had become ill four years before, and he had been unable to save her. In despair after her death, he had begun drinking heavily.

With his nights and days passing in an alcoholic stupor, his patients had sought other doctors and his practice had disappeared. Three years ago, penniless and forlorn, he had taken control of his life again and had overcome his craving for alcohol. Returning to Sydney, he had obtained a position at the hospital and settled into a quiet, solitary life of working long hours and avoiding all alcoholic beverages.

On the day that Oliver finished relating the past events of his life, he also commented about his future while he and Stephen were walking back down the street to the hospital. Greatly preferring to have his own practice, Oliver had been saving to buy one. "The practice I intend to buy is in Wilcannia, on the Darling River," he explained.

"So you're going into the outback," Stephen remarked.

"No, not precisely," Oliver replied. "Wilcannia is in the outback, but it's a fairly large town. I wouldn't go there if it wasn't. The practice belongs to a doctor named Henry Barrow, whom I met in Brisbane. He's getting on in years and suffers with dropsy, and he plans to retire and live on a farm that a brother left to him in Victoria." Oliver added that he had made an offer for the practice, and he expressed confidence that he and Dr. Barrow could reach an agreement.

The old doctor's optimism proved to be well-founded. When they went to the tearoom two days later, Oliver told Stephen that a letter had just arrived from Henry Barrow accepting Oliver's offer for the practice. While no definite date had been set, Oliver would leave within a few months.

Stephen regretted that he would soon be separated from his new friend, but he knew it would happen before long in any event. The use of phenol and other treatment techniques developed at Edinburgh were becoming routine at the hospital, as well as among at least some of the doctors in the city. In the not distant future, Stephen knew that he should go to a hospital in one of the other larger cities and begin the same process there.

With the onset of warmer weather, repairs and improvements were being made on streets and other public facilities. When Stephen left the hospital one evening, new cobblestones were being laid down on his usual route to his lodgings on Grantham Avenue. Crews had resumed work the next morning, and he chose a circuitous route to avoid the confusion. He decided to walk up Grantham as far as Grosvenor Street, then go down side streets to the hospital. It turned out to be a fateful decision.

In the midst of the morning congestion of traffic on Grosvenor Street, Stephen glimpsed a woman driving a buggy. Her face was in profile to him, her features perfectly modeled and strikingly beautiful. The way she held her head conveyed an impression of a strong, self-assured nature, promising a fascinating personality. Then, after that one brief view, her buggy disappeared into the traffic.

Even though he had seen her for little more than an instant, the image of the woman's lovely face was clearly etched in his mind. He was more than intrigued by her, thinking about her at quiet moments during the day and then when he went to his boardinghouse that evening. The next morning, he took the same route to work, looking for her.

He peered closely whenever a buggy came into view, but his uplift of anticipation subsided into regret each time. Keenly disappointed, he made his way to the hospital. His memory of the woman's beautiful face remained just as clear and fresh as if he had seen her only moments before, and it haunted him again all during the day and at his lodgings that evening.

The following two mornings, he varied the time when he reached Grosvenor Street, hoping that would make a difference. He went a few minutes earlier on the first and then later on the second day, but he still failed to see her. However, he finally saw her again at midday on the second day.

While he and Oliver were walking to the tearoom, Stephen glimpsed a buggy crossing an intersection ahead. Looking more closely, he saw that the radiantly beautiful woman was driving it. "Oliver, do you know the lady in that buggy?" he asked, pointing.

Oliver craned his neck and looked, then nodded. "Yes, that's Mistress Deirdre Kerrick," he replied. "She owns a photography studio." He looked up at Stephen, chuckling. "No need to ask why you wanted to know. She's one of the most comely ladies of the city and many have wanted to get her to the altar over the years, but they were all brought up short. She's considerably older than you, in her forties."

Stephen was surprised, having thought she was about his own age, then he dismissed the point as totally insignificant. "Her studio must be the one where Orah Hawkins does odd jobs now and then," he mused.

"Yes, it is," Oliver confirmed. "It's on Grosvenor Street. I understand that she lives in the Whitlam district, in a house owned by her brother, Sir Morton. The house belonged to their grandfather years ago."

Stephen watched the buggy until it disappeared, determined to meet her and satisfy the feeling within him that was far more than mere interest. Absorbed in thought, he almost walked past the tearoom. Oliver plucked at Stephen's sleeve, and he turned and followed the man inside.

While they were having tiffin, Oliver talked about his plans to go to Wilcannia, saying it could occur on short notice. He explained that Henry Barrow wanted to stay at the town for a few more months, but the man's health was uncertain and he might have to leave at any time. While Stephen made the appropriate responses, he also pondered his own plans on how to go about meeting Deirdre Kerrick.

The customary way would be through a mutual acquaintance, and Stephen immediately knew who that could be.

Edward Coleman, who was certain to know both Deirdre and her brother, would be more than pleased to fill that role. However, it could result in becoming involved in numerous and time-consuming social activities through Edward, which Stephen wanted to avoid.

An alternative way was to simply walk up to her and introduce himself, which entailed some risk of seeming brash. It eliminated delays, though, and Stephen was impatient to meet her. Moreover, he always preferred the most direct means of doing anything. Judging by her self-possessed bearing, he suspected that Deirdre was the same.

Stephen thought about it at length during the afternoon, finally deciding upon introducing himself to her. When he left the hospital that evening, he went to Grosvenor Street and found the studio. Closed for the day, it was an obviously thriving business in a large, two-story stone building. In the alley behind the studio was a shed with hay in it where Deirdre left her horse and buggy during the day. He stepped back out of the alley and then walked through the evening traffic toward his lodgings.

The next morning, wearing his best suit, Stephen left his lodgings early and hurried up Grantham Avenue to Grosvenor Street. Several doors from the studio, he glanced at window displays and watched for Deirdre. When her buggy turned onto the street and then into the alley behind the studio, he straightened his coat and walked up the street toward it.

Deirdre stepped around the corner from the alley, exquisitely beautiful in a pale blue muslin dress and a matching blue cape and wide hat. More than merely an exceptionally attractive woman, her bearing and graceful stride denoted her total self-assurance and poise. She had shaped her life and her world around herself, forming it to match her wishes.

Taking a key ring from her reticule, Deirdre unlocked the studio door. Stephen walked more rapidly, stepping around others on the foot pavement, and closed the distance between them. "Good day, Mistress Kerrick," he greeted her, lifting his hat. "I'm Stephen Brendell."

Deirdre turned, unsmiling and unreceptive to offhand approaches by strangers. The large blue eyes in her perfectly sculpted face had immense depths, along with a blinding impact. Moreover, a force of personality about her was so intense that its effect was almost physical. With her reserved gaze focused intently upon him, Stephen felt painfully self-conscious.

Then her attitude changed, as if a chilling gale had been replaced by a balmy, refreshing breeze. For an instant, her lovely features revealed a warmly favorable response to him on recognition of his name. Then her feelings were hidden behind a polite, self-possessed smile. "Yes, you're the new doctor at the hospital, aren't you," she remarked. "Dr. Coleman and others have spoken highly of you, and Orah Hawkins has praised you incessantly. By his lights, you're the most skilled doctor on earth."

Relieved over her change in attitude, Stephen was also keenly pleased that she had heard complimentary opinions of him. "Orah has a generous benefactor," he observed. "The amount of the check you sent to the hospital was far more than the cost of Danny's treatment."

Deirdre dismissed the check with a shrug. "Will Danny recover completely and have the full use of his legs again?" she asked.

Stephen nodded and began telling her about Danny's progress, explaining details to make the conversation longer. Five employees consisting of a woman, three men, and a youth arrived and went into the studio as Deirdre introduced them to Stephen. The woman, who had an air of brisk competence, was named Verna Allen, and she was the studio manager.

The conversation about the boy drew to an end, and Stephen searched for other subjects to discuss with Deirdre.

Being near her nourished an avid hunger within him and turned it into a source of pleasure, and listening to her melodious contralto voice was intensely enjoyable. He mentioned his mother, saying that she had always been interested in Jeremy Kerrick and his activities, and Deirdre replied that she vaguely remembered his mother from their brief meeting on the day that Jeremy had been born.

That led to a discussion of her nephew, her deep affection for him reflected in a musing smile that made her lovely features even more bewitching. Even as he hung on her every word, Stephen knew that he had detained her for as long as he should, and he broached what had become a vital issue to him: "I would consider it an honor if you would go with me to see a play at one of the theaters. Or, if you prefer, any of the other entertainments in the city would be equally agreeable to me."

A momentary silence fell that seemed endless to Stephen. Deirdre was perfectly composed now, making it difficult for him to judge her reaction, but she seemed to have conflicting feelings. "Thank you for the invitation," she finally replied. "I'll give it careful consideration."

Her response was appropriate to a first meeting, and Stephen was delighted that it had been other than a refusal. "I truly hope your decision is favorable," he said, turning away. "Talking with you has been most enjoyable, and I'll look forward to speaking with you again soon."

Deirdre replied cordially in farewell, going into her studio, and Stephen felt as though his feet were inches above the foot pavement as he walked to the hospital. His jaunty stride drew amused glances from passersby, but he cared not a whit what they thought.

The morning had brought a crossroads of events, and his life had taken a new course. His all-consuming commitment to his profession had been joined by a force that was equally compelling, one that promised unimaginable joy. He was exuberantly happy, passionately in love with Deirdre Kerrick.

* * *

Gazing absently out her office window and pondering, Deirdre scarcely noticed when Verna Allen brought in a cup of tea, the newspaper, and a stack of invoices for supplies. Verna placed them on the desk, explaining something about the invoices that drew only an absentminded nod from Deirdre. "A penny for your thoughts, Mistress Kerrick," she said.

Reflecting that her musings were either worth less than a farthing or more precious than bags of gold sovereigns, Deirdre turned the question aside. "The weather is becoming warmer now, isn't it?" she remarked.

Verna agreed and took the hint, going back out and leaving Deirdre alone with her deep contemplation. Another ordinary morning in what at times seemed to Deirdre an increasingly uneventful life had suddenly become an entirely new and different kind of day, suffused with excitement and vitality. The tall, slim Stephen Brendell was surpassingly handsome and had a charming, interesting personality. His dedication to his profession was evident, a purpose in life that provided a vigorous intensity to his character. In every respect, he was by far the most appealing, attractive man she had ever met.

He was also, she reminded herself, a very young man.

Deirdre tried to dismiss thoughts of him and concentrate on her work. She sipped her tea, reaching for the invoices, and put her pince-nez in place on her nose. Then she paused, thinking about Stephen again.

Though only in his mid-twenties, in many ways he was older than his years. His bearing and his outlook on life revealed by remarks he had made were those of a mature, sober man who possessed keen sensitivity and understanding of others. In addition, judging by his admiring attitude toward her, it was obvious that he saw no difference in their ages.

Her pince-nez slipped out of position, and she took it off and looked at it. Twenty years before, her vision had been perfect, and the pince-nez was now concrete evidence of the span between her age and Stephen's. Deep within herself, she knew that meeting him could be a turning point for her, one that could join her life with Stephen's. But though he saw no difference in their ages now, that could change in years to come.

Deirdre tossed her pince-nez onto the invoices and crossed her office to the window as she thought about the former men in her life. Over the years, none had been a missed opportunity, some fact or characteristic about them forewarning her of future irreconcilable conflict with each one. It had been fate that her path and that of the right man had never crossed.

She wondered if Stephen was the right man for her, or if fate was mocking her with a cruel joke. In the majority of married couples she had known whose ages had been substantially different, the man had been the older one. Without exception, the marriages had been unhappy, the women often cuckolding their husbands with younger men. In the two she had known with the woman the older one, both marriages had ended in tragedy.

Both had been years before, one when she had been a student at Sydenham Academy. A history teacher, Roberta Markham, had been in her forties when she married a man of twenty-five. The marriage had seemed happy for a year or two, then the teacher's eyes had often been red from crying. One day, morning prayers had been suddenly canceled: The night before, Roberta Markham had hanged herself in the chapel.

The other, a widow named Enid Lathrop, had inherited money from her husband. In her early fifties, she had married a man some fifteen years younger. After a time, he had become bored with her but not her money, gambling with it and drinking heavily. When most of the money had been squandered, it had been rumored that he intended to leave her. Neither of them had been seen for a few days, and neighbors had summoned constables, who discovered that Enid had killed her husband, then herself.

Deirdre reflected that ignoring the experiences of others was unwise, but using them as a sole criterion to guide her own actions would be equally foolish. A truer basis for judgment was the fact that from the first instant she saw him, Stephen had touched some depth in her being that had never before been reached. He had also stirred lusty sexual desire within her. Her lovers had been few, and none at all for years, because many men liked to boast and she had always been wary of acquiring a reputation that would disgrace her family. Stephen would never boast, but having him as a lover would be a mistake. A sexual relationship alone would be far too little for them, but too much in another way.

That left exploring the situation and finding out more about him, which would reveal whether their difference in age was truly a barrier between them. The customary course of action would be to wait until he offered another invitation, but Deirdre dismissed that. She had always been impatient with social niceties, and the feelings that Stephen had stirred within her made her anxious to proceed as rapidly as possible.

Deirdre stepped back to her desk and sat down, picking up the newspaper. She heard Lewis Birely, the youth who cleaned the building and ran errands, sweeping the hall outside her office. "Lewis, come here, please," she called, unfolding the newspaper. "I have an errand for you."

The youth stepped into the office as Deirdre put on her pince-nez and studied the advertisements for plays. Selecting a comedy that she had heard favorable comments about, she opened her reticule and counted out the thirty shillings that was the advertised price of two box seats, then reached for pen and paper. "I'd like you to go to the York Theater and get two box seat tickets for tonight's performance," she said, dipping her pen and writing a brief note on the paper.

"The tickets for tonight are probably long since sold out,"

Lewis commented doubtfully. "Even the costly ones up in the gods'."

"No, I'm acquainted with the manager, and he always keeps a few tickets in reserve," Deirdre told him, blotting the note and folding it. "Ask to see him personally and give him this message."

Lewis took the note and gathered up the money, then left. Deirdre pulled the invoices closer and began studying them. She tried to concentrate on them, but for once her disciplined mind was rebellious. Thoughts of Stephen intruded upon her concentration, creating fantasies incomparably more fascinating than the invoices.

Chapter Seventeen

When an orderly told Stephen that Deirdre Kerrick wished to speak with him in the foyer, he was at first stunned. Throughout the morning and into the afternoon, he had pondered how long he should wait before going to see her again, and the last thing he had expected was for her to come and see him. Overcoming his surprise, he hurried toward the stairs.

People in the waiting room were gawking at her, and with ample reason, for her radiant beauty transformed the foyer. Along with his happiness over seeing her, Stephen had a further cause for delight. Her attitude was warmer than before, her smile and greeting more than cordial.

"If you're ill," he commented, "it is a disorder so difficult to detect that it will confound medical science."

Deirdre laughed charmingly, turning toward the door and leading him outside. "No, this is a social call, Stephen." They stepped out to her buggy at the curb, and she continued: "This morning you mentioned going to the theater, and I've heard that the comedy at the York is very good."

"Excellent!" he exclaimed happily. "I'll get tickets for the first performance for which seats are available."

"You've no need to bother, because I've obtained tickets for this evening," she told him. "Where are your lodgings?"

Stephen hesitated, taken aback, then replied, "The boardinghouse at the corner of Grantham Avenue and Cameron Street."

"Very well, we can go in my buggy," she said. "The performance starts at half eight, and I'll meet you in front of your lodgings at seven. Good-bye for now, Stephen."

He made a move to help her into her buggy, but she was already stepping lithely into it. She settled in, tucking her long skirt and cape around herself. Stephen spoke a word of farewell and waved as she drove away, then went back into the hospital, bemused by their complete reversal of roles in making arrangements for the theater. However, he knew it was completely in character with the independent, self-assured nature that made her so fascinating.

He was overjoyed by her evident interest in him. Strongly suspecting that she was very punctual, he set about his work and finished it in time to leave the hospital earlier than usual. At his lodgings, he shaved again, put on a clean shirt, and carefully brushed his suit. Shortly before seven o'clock, while the gaslights on the street brightened in the gathering dusk, he was waiting on the corner.

Just when church bells began chiming seven, Deirdre turned the corner in her buggy. She seemed too perfect to be real, like a bewitching fantasy of beauty in the soft glow of the gaslights, and the compelling quality of her personality reached out to him through her warm smile of greeting. In grand Victorian fashion, she wore a cape over a pale brown brocade dress trimmed with fine lace, her wide hat made of the same fabrics.

At the theater, Deirdre introduced him to numerous people in the lobby. Stephen saw that she lived at the very center of a vast web of friendships and relationships that interwove the history of her family with that of the colony. Among her acquaintances was the Williamson family, whose connection with the Kerricks dated back many decades to a friendship involving the man's grandfather, the Garrity family, and Deirdre's father.

More than the play itself, Stephen keenly enjoyed the time it was in progress. Deirdre's shoulder and arm touched his on the armrest between their seats, and he breathed the alluring scent of her perfume and her hair. He kept himself from staring at her, but when they exchanged a glance and laughed at amusing lines, she was spellbinding in the dim light. There were other times when he sensed her gaze on him for a moment, studying him, her attention too seeming to be as much on him as on the stage.

When the play finished and they joined the crowd flowing out, Deirdre saw Benjamin and Beverly Tavish in the lobby and introduced them to Stephen. They were an amiable, attractive couple, Benjamin very handsome and Beverly strikingly pretty. After a few minutes' conversation in the lobby, the couple invited Stephen and Deirdre to their home for a late supper.

Their home was a large, old-fashioned Georgian house on Grace Street in the Wooloo district, and the Tavishes were gracious hosts. Supper was a lavish array of cold meats, cheeses, smoked fish, and pickles and relishes, together with a choice Camden Park wine. In addition to the delicious repast and the lively, interesting conversation, Stephen enjoyed the affectionate attitude between Benjamin and Beverly. With two children and after several years of marriage, they were still as much in love as any newlyweds, and Stephen knew that he and Deirdre could be the same.

It was late when Stephen and Deirdre left the Tavish home, the city quiet except for the constant activity around the waterfront. They discussed the play and other subjects while driving toward his lodgings, and Stephen pondered what entertainment to suggest for them to see each other again. Then, when they were near Grantham Avenue, Deirdre mentioned it herself, saying that she frequently visited her brother and his family.

"Usually on Sunday, for tiffin," she added, "and I plan to go there next Sunday. Would you like to go with me?"

"I certainly would," Stephen replied quickly. "Beyond the pleasure of your company, I'll enjoy meeting your brother and his family."

"I know that they'll enjoy meeting you just as much," Deirdre said. "We can go there early for conversation before tiffin, if you wish, and I'll meet you in front of your lodgings at eleven on Sunday."

Stephen agreed happily, and a moment later, she stopped the buggy at his boardinghouse. "To say that I enjoyed the evening is a vast understatement, Deirdre," he told her, stepping out of the buggy. "In every respect, it was a very great pleasure indeed."

"It was a very pleasant evening for me as well, Stephen," she assured him, smiling warmly in the dim light. "Good night."

Stephen replied and watched the buggy until it disappeared from view, then went into the boardinghouse. The evening had been an exciting, delightful departure from his usual pattern of life, filled with memorable impressions and events. Its most profound significance had been Deirdre's attitude toward him, which had indicated that she shared his feelings to at least some extent. When he was in bed, he pondered that thrilling possibility for hours until he finally fell asleep.

The next day was Friday, and Sunday seemed a very long time away to Stephen, but the waiting room was full when he reached the hospital, the day a busy one that made the hours pass quickly. The following day was slow, however, with only routine work that he finished during the late forenoon. At midday he went to the stable at the icehouse for a horse, then set out for Wallaby Track to visit his parents and Yulina.

When he reached the house in midafternoon, his mother had returned from making her calls, and his father was also at home. Stephen ate a repast that Yulina prepared for him, talking with them. His mother was more cheerful than the last time he had been home, because on that same day, the gang gang cockatoos that roosted beside the house during autumn and winter had just flown away to their summer home in the mountains.

As well as being in much better spirits, Stephanie was as perceptive as usual, immediately detecting that some important development had occurred in Stephen's life. He told them about having met Deirdre, explaining that he was very fond of her and believed that she had the same feelings for him. Yulina and his parents expressed satisfaction over his having met a woman whom he regarded with affection, but Stephanie added a warning.

"It appears to me," she told him, "that Deirdre Kerrick is very cautious in this respect. I offer that as an observation on what has gone before, not a criticism. But you would be wise to bear it in mind."

Stephen acknowledged the advice, earnestly hoping it would be irrelevant. The conversation moved on to other things, Stephanie telling him about a recent letter from Ralph in Brisbane. Its purpose had been to report the completion of repairs to the icehouse, but Ralph had also mentioned an outbreak of several cases of typhoid in the Darling Downs.

"The victims are recent immigrants who went there," she added. "If the disease had developed in Brisbane, it would have placed many people at risk. The weather is still fairly cool, so in all probability the disease will fade out in the rural area of the Darling Downs."

Stephen agreed, her analysis seeming correct. However, a remote but disturbing possibility occurred to him that continued to trouble him after he ended his visit and was riding back toward Sydney. The streams in the Darling Downs were the headwaters of the Darling River, which flowed past Bourke, Wilcannia, and other towns before it reached the sea at Adelaide. If the typhoid bacteria somehow contaminated the headwaters of the river and survived until it reached the concentrated population in the towns, a devastating epidemic of the deadly disease could explode and kill hundreds.

The next day, his mother's warning seemed entirely irrelevant to Stephen when Deirdre arrived in front of his boardinghouse. She was stunning in a dress and hat made of bright yellow muslin, her smile more radiant than the balmy sunshine, and the affection it conveyed made his spirits soar. They drove across the city to the Wooloo district, a newer section several streets from the Tavish home, and turned in at the drive leading back to an ornate, three-story Victorian mansion set in landscaped grounds.

Although his house was imposing and his eyes were a pale blue that gave them a cold, penetrating aspect, Morton Kerrick was anything but ostentatious or intimidating. A pudgy, balding man of about fifty with a jovial, friendly disposition, he shook his head and laughed when Stephen greeted him with his title. "No, no, simply Morton will do, Stephen," he said. "Titles are useful only in trying to impress someone, and the older I get, the more I realize that attempting to impress others foils its own purpose." He pointed to his wife: "This is my dear and beloved wife, Julia."

A few years younger than Morton, Julia was equally good-natured and a slender, attractive woman with well-formed features and gentle blue eyes. Stephen exchanged greetings with her, then went into the parlor with the couple and Deirdre. The large, luxuriously furnished room was comfortably cluttered, Morton's newspapers scattered around his chair, and a boy and a girl playing with toys that littered the floor. Morton introduced them to Stephen, the boy about seven and named David Alexander, and the girl, Margaret Alexandra, some two years younger.

After an hour of interesting conversation in the parlor, the housekeeper stepped into the doorway and announced tiffin. The meal, at a long, gleaming table in the elegant dining room, was served by maids supervised by the housekeeper. However, formality was dispelled by the children chattering and laughing at the table instead of having their meal in another room. In addition, Morton was constantly up and down to assist the maids in helping the children with their knives and forks.

When the meal was finished, a nurse took the children away, and Stephen and Deirdre went out into the gardens at the side of the house with Morton and Julia. The conversation over iced drinks in a shady arbor turned out to be more than lively, one topic after another coming up. Aside from being interested in anything involving Deirdre, Stephen was intrigued by the Kerricks and their activities. Morton had received a letter from his mother not long before, and he talked about events at Tibooburra Station.

One incident had been the illness of his grandson, Christopher. The letter from Alexandra had described the symptoms, speculating that it had been colic, and the boy had recovered after a few days. Morton related the symptoms and asked Stephen for an opinion, but he declined to offer one.

"I'd have to examine the boy to make a diagnosis," he explained. "Those symptoms are common to any number of abdominal conditions, including simple colic." Starting to leave it at that, he thought again. He realized that the symptoms could also be those of the deadly perityphlitic abscess, which would be brought to an acute stage by a purge. "I believe it would be advisable for you to write to your mother and recommend that she never give the boy a purge if those symptoms recur," he added. "There are some abdominal conditions that a purge will make much worse."

Morton nodded, saying he would write the next day. The hours passed rapidly in free-flowing talk, and Morton and Julia insisted that Stephen and Deirdre stay for dinner. After dinner, they resumed their conversation in the parlor, and it was late when Stephen and Deirdre left. One subject discussed had been an interesting performance by a mesmerist

that Morton and Julia had seen at a theater, and on the way
to his lodgings, Stephen and Deirdre agreed to see it on
Tuesday.

Monday began an eventful week for Stephen, starting
with the addition of another doctor to the hospital staff to
take over Oliver's ward when he left. Carl Phillips was in
his mid-twenties and was recently licensed through appren-
ticeship, and Stephen regarded him as an excellent choice
for the staff. On that same day, the newspapers announced
that the first sailing regatta of the season was scheduled for
the following Saturday, and there was an advertisement for
a new comedy opening at a theater that week.

On Tuesday, Stephen and Deirdre met the Tavishes at
the mesmerist performance and joined the couple at their
home again for supper. They saw the new play on Thursday,
mingled with the crowds on the bluffs overlooking the
harbor to watch the regatta on Saturday, and visited Morton
and Julia again on Sunday. The horse racing and cricket
seasons opened the following week, and a coal gas balloon
that took passengers aloft was at Hyde Park.

When the next week began, Stephen came to the uneasy
conclusion that his mother's warning had been very much
to the point. After its rapid beginning, his relationship with
Deirdre had come to a standstill as a close friendship. Each
time he tried to discuss the possibility of their having a
future together, she told him that they must know each
other better. It puzzled him, for he was almost certain that
he saw far more than friendship in her lovely eyes when
she occasionally studied him thoughtfully.

While a commitment from her to marry him would fulfill
his fondest hopes, he made up his mind to be satisfied
with only an understanding. He needed that much from
her, because circumstances were closing in around him
that would, in one way or another, take him away from
Sydney for several months. The outbreak of typhoid in the
Darling Downs was a lurking danger that might demand
his presence somewhere on the Darling River to assist in

an epidemic, and the time was drawing near when he should go to another hospital.

On the Sunday afternoon when they went to the open lawns at the center of Hyde Park where the coal gas balloon was located, a crowd had preceded them. It was taking several minutes each time for the attendants to help people into the gondola under the huge, colorful balloon, then turn the winch to raise and lower the balloon on its cable. The line of people waiting their turn stretched all around the lawns. It would take hours to get a chance to go up. Stephen and Deirdre chose instead to stroll along the paths through the park.

Stephen decided to try again to discuss their relationship, but with a different approach. Instead of broaching the subject in a way that she would quickly turn aside, he spoke about his work: "It won't be long until I must go to a hospital in another city."

"You needn't if you don't wish to, Stephen," she replied. "If you prefer to have a practice now and are unable to buy one, the funds aren't an obstacle. I have a few hundred at hand, and if more is required, we can obtain it very easily from either Morton or the Tavishes."

Stephen realized that he had failed to make his meaning clear, but the implication that any part of his interest in her might be because of her money aggravated him. "I'm grateful for your offer," he thanked her stiffly, "but I still don't wish to have a practice. I should have said that I must go to other hospitals in order to continue passing along what I learned at Edinburgh. As for the fact that you're wealthy, I'm obviously aware of it, but it means nothing to me."

"I can do without your gratitude," Deirdre retorted in annoyance, "but I won't have you make little of what I've achieved. What I have was earned in the course of years of hard work."

Stephen turned to her, placing his hands on her shoulders and looking into her eyes. "I would never make little of anything concerning you, Deirdre," he assured her. "I greatly admire what you've achieved, but most of all, I admire the qualities within you that led to those achievements. What I wanted to say when I began this conversation is that I can't leave the city with matters between us in their present unsettled state. I'd like very much for us to discuss them and come to an understanding."

"We can't yet, Stephen," she told him, her pique fading. "Over and above the sundry concerns that any man and woman must consider, there is the substantial difference in our ages. We must know each other and our own minds much better than now before we can hope for an understanding."

"But the difference in our ages isn't a concern, Deirdre," Stephen protested. "To the extent that I even think about it, which is so rare that it hardly bears mentioning, I regard you and myself as the same age."

"Now, perhaps, but what of five, ten, and twenty years hence?" Deirdre pointed out. "That is the concern, Stephen. We can't see into the future, but we can and must carefully consider what it might bring."

"I don't have to consider it," he said firmly. "I know how I feel about you, and it won't change regardless of how long—"

"Please don't prove the merit of my concern about the difference in our ages, Stephen," she interrupted. "Riding roughshod over cares about problems that might lie ahead is evidence of immaturity. If you must go away for a time, I'll certainly regret your absence more than words can express, but I know that you must do what you must do." She smiled, linking her arm through his. "Now let's put all this aside so we can enjoy each other's company and this very pleasant setting in the park."

Stephen was unable to deny her anything she asked of him, her smile irresistible. In her dress and wide hat of pink, summery dimity, she was so exquisitely beautiful that his ardent love for her was a bittersweet ache within him. He agreed, walking on down the path with her.

Ending the conversation on the basis that discussion itself proved her point seemed specious to him, but he knew that forcing the issue now would be a mistake. Her attitude had warned that they might never be more than good friends, creating shrinking fear within him. However, he took comfort in the fact that her attitude had been tempered by her sincere remark about how much she would miss him if he left the city for a time.

After a few minutes, the subject of their relationship faded from the forefront of his thoughts, for he found it easy to fall into a mood that set worries at a distance when he was with her. Being near her was ever more fascinating for him, her captivating personality and beauty always having a spellbinding effect. He laughed and talked with her, planning their entertainment for the upcoming week.

When he was in his lodgings that evening, though, his urgent necessity to reach some sort of understanding with Deirdre returned in full force. He was certain that the difference in their ages was irrelevant to their relationship, regardless of how many years passed, and he tried to think of ways to convince her of that. Recalling remarks he had overheard during his boyhood about problems his parents had overcome before marrying, he wondered if the solutions they had found would be useful to him.

That possibility remained very much on his mind when another week began, and he had been contemplating visiting his parents soon. Wednesday was a relatively slow day at the hospital, Stephen finishing up everything he had to do by midday. Then he went to the icehouse stable to get a horse.

Stephen talked with his father at the sawmill, finding out the details of obstacles that had been between his parents before they married, but he learned nothing that he could apply to his situation with Deirdre. Hoping for a different perspective or advice from his mother, he searched for her on the network of roads through Wallaby Track. When he found her, she expressed an opinion that was anything but encouraging for him.

"Yes, I thought the difference in your ages might be a problem," she mused when he finished explaining the situation. "If I were Deirdre Kerrick, that would be my main concern."

"But why?" Stephen asked. "Mother, it's less than nothing to me, and I fail to understand why it should matter to her."

"You are thinking with your heart, and she with her head," Stephanie explained. "Children often have frivolous ideas about what they will do in life, then they put those aside and settle into useful, productive lives as adults. That change is obvious, but less evident changes continue throughout life. No man or woman in their forties is precisely the same person they were in their twenties. Those changes can create difficulties even for married couples who are well suited, and any untoward circumstances should be studied carefully before marriage. A substantial difference in age is just such a circumstance."

"Perhaps so, but no couple is perfectly suited," Stephen pointed out. "But their differences can be overcome through love and understanding."

"No, not always," Stephanie replied. "For any couple, a good marriage is a constant process of adjusting to the differences that increasing age and maturity brings to each of them. I've seen loving couples grow apart over the years, because some differences cannot be overcome. That isn't to say that a substantial difference in age is a bar to marriage, because it isn't. But it is a reason for due caution, my dear."

Stephen sighed, then laughed wryly. "Perhaps I should grow a mustache and beard so I'll look older," he joked.

"I truly wish I could be more helpful," Stephanie told him, smiling sympathetically. "But I assure you that from when you first mentioned Deirdre Kerrick, I've been delighted that she might become my daughter-in-law. Because of that and the fact that I love you and want your happiness above all else, I truly hope that she decides in your favor."

Stephen exchanged a farewell hug and kiss with his mother, then stepped into his saddle. Riding back toward Sydney, he pondered his situation with Deirdre. His frustration was compounded by the fact that this most important problem of his entire life was one over which he had absolutely no control. He was accustomed to confronting difficulties directly and aggressively, but with this one he could only wait until Deirdre arrived at a decision.

Reluctantly, he concluded that he would remain at the hospital in Sydney until Deirdre made up her mind. In large measure, that amounted to shirking his responsibilities to his profession, making him feel guilty. But the suspense of not knowing whether his love for her would be fulfilled was difficult enough even when he was near her and could be with her frequently, and he knew that if he was separated from her, it would be unendurable.

The threat that typhoid would reach one of the towns on the Darling River was another consideration, a dire possibility of extreme danger to many lives that placed his most compelling personal concerns into a completely different perspective. However, he put it out of mind, refusing to contemplate the painful choice he would have to make if an epidemic developed.

Chapter Eighteen

"**A** picnic! What an excellent idea!" Stephen exclaimed. "The entertainments here in the city are enjoyable, but they're always crowded."

His delight brought an upswell of heady emotions to Deirdre, a blossoming of an inner glowing warmth. Talking with him at the curb in front of the hospital, she kept a firm control over herself to conceal her reactions. "We've also exhausted most of the entertainments," she added, smiling. "The idea came to me during a conversation with Verna Allen. She's a member of the Picnic Society, a club like the one of the same name in London. Her club is going on an outing on Sunday and taking tiffin with them, as they always do, and I thought that you and I might do the same."

"I'm certainly very much in favor of it," Stephen assured her enthusiastically. "Where shall we go for the picnic?"

"There's a forest near Penrith that would be suitable," she told him. "We could go on the train to Penrith on Sunday morning and return in the evening. Over the years, some curious things have happened to some of my family at that forest, and you might be interested in hearing about them."

"I'll be very interested indeed," he confirmed. "The weather has been pleasant of late, and it should be the same on Sunday."

Deirdre agreed, studying him as they continued discussing the picnic. Tall and slim in his white hospital smock, he answered to everything she had ever wanted in a man, and she was desperately in love with him. But the luster of youth that remained on his handsome features was both a temptation, adding a keen edge to her desire for him, and a warning of what the years ahead might bring.

"Very well, let's go on the eight o'clock train to Penrith," Deirdre said, summing up the plans for the picnic. "I'll bring tiffin in a basket and meet you at the train station."

"Let me bring the tiffin, Deirdre," Stephen suggested. "You always make all the arrangements for everything, and that isn't fair."

"I have an errand boy, whereas you would have to leave work if you saw to arrangements," she pointed out, turning to her buggy. "The shop where I buy Christmas presents for my employees has very good baskets of comestibles from Fortnum and Mason's, and we'll take along one of those. I'll see you at the train station a bit before eight on Sunday, then."

Stephen assisted her into the buggy. The warmth of his hand through her sleeve created a tingle of sensation that lingered as she drove away, his hands the focus of her desire. His life-giving surgeon's hands were as gentle as a woman's, yet they were a man's powerful hands. She yearned to feel the gentle power of his hands on her body and then take him, making him part of her body and of her soul.

Deirdre had chosen the forest near Penrith for the picnic for a specific reason, about which she had said nothing to Stephen. Some events there involving members of her family had been greatly important in their lives, and over the course of decades, the forest had acquired a profound significance among her family. She wondered if going there with Stephen might yield some insight to help her resolve her turmoil of indecision over whether or not to marry him.

Logically, that seemed unlikely and even fanciful, but she had been tormented by indecision until she was now at the point of clutching at straws. Her final and always reliable recourse was to write to her mother, asking for an opinion on the importance of the difference in age between herself and Stephen. Before doing that, she wanted to make at least a tentative decision, but even that much of a conclusion had evaded her.

It was Friday, and when she reached the studio, Deirdre set about putting her agony of indecision out of mind until Sunday. During her travels around Australia in past years, she had taken a large number of landscape photographs, and there was a steady market for the scenic views in people who wanted them for their homes. Making the enlargements, which took full concentration, was how she always put troubles out of mind and passed the time. She selected twenty glass negatives from the file boxes in the storage room, then took them to the darkroom and began on the enlargements.

Long after dark, the employees having left hours before, Deirdre finished for the day and went home. The next morning, she gave Lewis Birely the money and sent him for the tiffin basket, then went back upstairs to the darkroom. That evening, after the last of the enlargements was done, the basket was in her office. She took it home with her, and as she carried it into her house, a disturbing thought occurred to her.

She suddenly realized that she had always assumed that the forest near Penrith would remain just as it had been the first time she had seen it. It had indeed been the same the last time she saw it, but that had been several years before. A thriving lumber industry was located in Penrith, sending logs to Sydney by rail. Deirdre wondered if she would find that the forest which was so closely entwined with her family was now gone, a pasture or crop field in its place.

The next morning, that worry was pushed aside from her thoughts by the promise of the day being enjoyable in itself. It began favorably, the weather perfect, and the tall, handsome Stephen stood out among the crowd when Deirdre arrived at the train station. The anticipation that always quickened her pulse before meeting him was fulfilled by the rush of excitement and delight that his loving smile created within her.

Then the day became less pleasant after she and Stephen boarded the train. The coach was crowded and noisy, many of the seats filled by a party of hikers. Most of them were about Stephen's age, laughing and talking with the buoyant exuberance of youth, and Deirdre felt somewhat old and sedate among them. Trying to ignore the young men and women, she talked with Stephen as the train chuffed out of the station and clattered down the track toward Parramatta.

After a stop at the town, the train labored over Prospect Hill; then the broad valley of the Nepean River opened out ahead against the backdrop of the towering Blue Mountains. When the train moved on down into the valley, Deirdre was unable to get a clear view through the coach windows, but it appeared that at least some of the forest near Penrith remained.

The train drew up at the platform in Penrith with a hiss of steam and squeal of brakes, then the passengers filed out of the coaches in a milling crowd. Stephen carried the basket, and he and Deirdre followed the hikers through the station and down the main street of the town. When the street turned into a road flanking the river, the boisterous cluster of young men and women hurried on down it, their voices fading.

The road led into the wide road stretching from Parramatta to Bathurst, west of the mountains. At the main road, the hikers crossed the bridge over the river and disappeared down the road toward the foothills. No one else was about, the only sounds the chatter of birds and whisper of the breeze through the foliage. Reaching the intersection, Deirdre and Stephen crossed the main road to the thick forest on the other side.

Far from being cleared away, Deirdre saw to her delight that the forest was untouched. With farms all about, for some reason the forest had remained a primal wilderness, just as it had been for innumerable centuries. She stepped away from the edge of the road, leading Stephen into the forest.

When they were only a few yards inside the forest, civilization seemed at a far remove. The huge trees were like the columns of a lofty cathedral, their dense foliage subduing the sunlight to green twilight. A gripping quiet pervaded the forest; even the birds were silent. Deirdre found herself and Stephen whispering as they walked through the trees and she told him about events involving members of her family in the forest.

The first, fifty years before, was when her father had been a convict at the compound in Parramatta. Spending his Sundays camped in the forest, he had dreamed of establishing a sheep station in the outback, a goal that had been fulfilled by Tibooburra Station. Many years later, her brother and his wife, Jonathan and Catherine, had come here while courting.

"As I mentioned once," Deirdre went on, "they're both dead. Jonathan was killed by a wild boar, and Catherine died by her own hand."

"I didn't know that Catherine had killed herself," Stephen said.

Deirdre hesitated, the subject a painful one, then explained: "Catherine was a very disturbed woman after Jonathan was killed. Some people are unable to endure the outback, and she became one of them. Yet she was unhappy in Sydney, so the last years of her life were spent in almost constant travel between the city and the station. On her last trip to the station, she took her life." Finished with the morbid subject, Deirdre turned to a more cheerful one: "This is also where Jeremy met his friend of many years, Jarboe Charlie. That was almost twenty years ago."

Stephen commented that he had heard very little about Jarboe Charlie, and Deirdre explained that the man, an Aborigine, had been on a walkabout when Jeremy had met him. They had traveled together to the man's tribe in the far outback, where Jeremy had grown to manhood. After his friend and companion had died, Jeremy had returned to the more settled regions.

Deirdre remembered that her mother had once mentioned that something of vital importance had happened to her in the forest. She had said nothing specific about it, however, and it had evidently occurred many years in the past.

Near the center of the forest, Deirdre and Stephen came upon a circle of stones for a campfire. Undisturbed for years, it was almost covered with leaves, and from the deep layer of ashes, it clearly had been used many times over a period of decades. Speculating about who might have camped there, they walked on through the forest, then came out into bright sunshine and the chatter of birds on a grassy bank beside the river.

Sitting in the shade at the edge of the trees, they opened the basket. It contained a variety of small cheeses, pots of pâté, tins of chicken and ham, treacle bread, fruit and pickles, and a choice wine. Deirdre enjoyed the conversation and being with Stephen even more than the delicious tiffin, but she was also disappointed. Even though the expectation that coming to the forest with him could provide some insight had seemed fanciful, she had nevertheless hoped it would. However, she had experienced no revelation to guide her in making a decision about marrying him.

On the contrary, a battle between logic and emotions that was more intense than ever raged within her. While she remained certain that having him as a lover would be both too little and too much, the temptation to abandon reason and give rein to her impulses had never been greater. In the isolated place, where the deep grass beside the river would make a soft, fragrant couch for lovemaking, her desire for him was a fiery, consuming hunger.

Her torment ended in late afternoon, when they returned to Penrith. The coach was quiet during the trip back to Sydney, the hikers weary, sunburned, and scratching at insect bites and nettle rashes. The setting sun shone through the window beside Stephen, silhouetting his handsome features. His profile stirred a dim, fragmentary memory of someone who looked like him. After a moment, Deirdre realized that it was a distant memory of his mother, whom Stephen closely resembled.

Darkness had fallen when the train reached Sydney. Deirdre took Stephen to his lodgings, then drove home. Sunday was the day off for her cook, maid, and the aged man who was her gardener and groom, and the house was dark and quiet when she finished stabling her horse and went inside.

After making herself a quick supper out of the icebox, Deirdre went into the parlor to think about the events of the day. The room depressed her, for she happened to notice that it emphasized the reason for her indecision about marrying Stephen. The walls were hung with photographs she had taken. The daguerreotypes, calotypes, ambrotypes, autotypes, and prints on albumen paper represented the development of various photographic processes over a period of decades, and they also illustrated her age. She sighed despondently, carrying the lamp upstairs to go to bed.

The next morning, Deirdre woke slowly from dreaming of Stephen. She drowsily reflected about the way his face had been silhouetted by the sun in the coach window. Then she thought of his mother, recalling her more clearly, and remembered that the woman had been pregnant at the time.

Deirdre sat up in bed with a jerk, suddenly wide awake as she realized that the woman had been pregnant with Stephen.

The memory that so graphically illustrated their difference in age set the tone for the morning. At the studio, Lewis Birely brought the newspaper and a cup of tea into Deirdre's office. Glancing over the front page of the newspaper, she saw nothing of particular interest.

Then, on an inside page devoted to social events and obituaries, a name leaped out at Deirdre as she sipped the tea: Alfred Hargreaves. Steam from the tea fogged her pince-nez. She put the cup down and wiped her pince-nez with her handkerchief as she thought about Fred, her lover for a short time years before.

The handsome, engaging man had been a good lover, she recalled, but too temperamental for her to even consider marrying him. Replacing the pince-nez on her nose, she read that Alfred Hargreaves, formerly of Sydney, recently died in Melbourne of a liver ailment and was survived by his widow, a son, a daughter, and two grandchildren.

Deirdre gazed at the newspaper in shock: *Grandchildren?* Fred had been older than she, but only by two or three years.

It seemed inconceivable that he could have grandchildren. Then, when she counted the years since she had known him, she realized that indeed it had been long enough for him to have married and then have an adult child and grandchildren. Time had flown, years slipping away so rapidly.

Saddened by Fred's death and feeling wretchedly old, Deirdre flung the newspaper aside. More than ever, her indecision about Stephen was a furious battle within her. It was also extremely frustrating, for it was so uncharacteristic of her. When facing other decisions, she had made a choice and then dealt with the results. This one was different, because she was deeply, ardently in love with Stephen, and she had to consider his future happiness as well as her own.

If, in years to come, his love changed into boredom with an older woman, both their lives would be sheer misery.

Deirdre sighed, realizing that she had to turn to her final, always reliable recourse. While she had intended to make at least a preliminary decision before asking her mother for an opinion, she knew that any decision at all was impossible. Taking paper out of a desk drawer, she dipped her pen into the inkwell and began writing a letter.

The letter was among others that Zachary Cooper handed to Alexandra Kerrick, who resisted the impulse to throw the mail in the stockman's face. She was immediately ashamed of the urge, for Zachary was an exceptionally capable, reliable man who could have been the head stockman at another station. He had remained at Tibooburra Station out of loyalty, fulfilling many responsibilities over and above those of a stockman.

Alexandra also knew that Zachary was blameless, but in a very real way, the crushing disappointment was more painful than the most savage physical blow. She was frantic with worry, and the drumming of the corroboree at the Aborigine village seemed to be knifing into every nerve in her body. "Do you mean that he simply up and left, Zack?" she asked.

Zachary shook his head somberly, his drooping handlebar mustache making his craggy, weathered face look even more mournful. "No, the doctor was nigh onto doing a perisher and had to leave, mo'm," the stockman explained. "He's been poorly for a time, and he got into worser holts with it. I found his housekeeper at the store, and I picked up the mail while I was there. She said that another doctor will arrive in Wilcannia within the fortnight, and she mentioned that there's a doctor at Menindee."

"His being any sort of a doctor is in doubt," Alexandra observed. "Elizabeth Garrity remarked once that she wouldn't be so cruel as to let him doctor an ailing dingo, and Menindee is too far away in any event. The

housekeeper didn't know precisely when the other doctor
will arrive?"

"All she knew was that he would be coming to Wilcannia
on the mail coach, mo'm," Zachary replied, "and that it
would be within the fortnight. How does Master Christopher
seem to be faring now?"

"No worse, but certainly no better," Alexandra told him.
"I'm still keeping him asleep with laudanum to ease his
pain."

"Mayhap he'll be on the improve soon," Zachary speculated hopefully. "I don't suppose Mister Jeremy and Mistress Fiona are here yet."

"No, they won't be back to the home paddock before
tomorrow morning at the earliest," Alexandra said. "I sent
a rider for them at the same time that you left for Wilcannia.
But they're up in Steeples Paddock, which is a farther ride,
of course." She stepped back from the door, starting to
close it. "You did everything anyone could have, and I'm
grateful, Zack."

The stockman touched his hat, turning to his horse at
the steps. Alexandra closed the door, but it had no effect
on the sound of the corroboree. The deep, mournful throbbing of didgeridoos, tapping rhythm sticks, and voices har-
monizing in a chant still reverberated through the house.
While she was unsure of its purpose, the corroboree frightened Alexandra. It had begun when her great-grandson had
become ill, but he had been stricken with a similar illness
before, and there had been no corroboree then.

Alexandra stepped into the parlor and left the mail on the
desk, then climbed the stairs and went down the hall. In the
end room, the maid who had called her to the door sat on a
chair beside the bed where the sleeping boy lay. The maid
stepped to the door and went out as Alexandra sat down.

Five years old, the boy was tall for his age and slender, his tirelessly energetic disposition having long since
sloughed away the last vestiges of baby fat. A handsome

boy, he had his mother's red hair and his father's pale blue eyes. Alexandra's adoring love for him made her anxiety a nerve-racking torment. He was feverish, his small, flushed features twitching as he occasionally tossed his head from side to side and whimpered.

Taking a cloth from a basin of water on the nightstand, Alexandra wrung it and wiped beads of sweat from the boy's face. Several hours had passed since his last dose of laudanum, and its effects were wearing off. The cool, damp cloth on his face made him stir, his whimpering becoming louder as he moved his small, slender limbs restlessly in pain.

After a moment, his eyes opened. Decades before, eyes with the piercing quality inherent to that icy, pale blue shade had struck terror into Alexandra's heart. But they had since become a cherished color of eyes to her, having gazed at her for many years with love from the face of her son, grandson, and now her great-grandson. His eyes were confused for a moment, his mind still emerging from the effects of the laudanum.

Then his eyes cleared, recognition in them, and he reached out a small hand to Alexandra. "It hurts, Greatgran," he moaned. "It hurts."

Alexandra wanted to scream her anguish to the heavens, fervently wishing she could take the sickness from his beloved body into her own. She forced a smile and reached for the glass of water on the nightstand. "I know that it hurts, dearest," she said soothingly, "but you'll be better soon. Here, drink some water, then take your medicine."

Lifting his head, she gave him sips of water, then replaced the glass and picked up the bottle of laudanum and the spoon. Only a few drops were sufficient, and the boy subsided into drugged sleep again moments later. Alexandra studied him, tormented by something more than agonizing worry. The pattern of the boy's sickness created a stark, haunting fear within her. It brought back a harrowing memory from many years past, and her conclusion about the boy's illness was supported by other facts.

The doorknob rattled, someone fumbling with it, and Alexandra turned and watched as the door slowly eased halfway open. Down near the floor, the cherubic face of Sheila Kerrick, three years old, peeked around the edge of the door. Framed in bright red hair, her bonny features radiated her sweet nature, and no monarch's crown had ever been set with emeralds so priceless that they could compare with her sparkling green eyes.

"Why is Christopher abed, Greatgran?" the girl piped in her thin, lisping voice. "It's time to be up and about."

Despite her anxiety, Alexandra was able to smile as she stepped to the girl and took her tiny hand. "Your brother is ill, my dear," she explained. "Come along now and let him rest, and he'll soon be well."

The nurse, Beryl Richard, came running down the hall in search of the child just as Alexandra led the girl out into the hall. Like Beryl's mother and the nurse of years before, Amy Godwin, Beryl was short and stout, with inexhaustible patience and a natural affinity for children.

Beryl apologized for allowing Sheila to slip away, scooping up the girl in her arms. The woman walked down the hall toward the nursery, and Alexandra returned to her chair in the bedroom. With the distant sound of the corroboree an undertone to the boy's whimpers, her memory of decades before came to mind again. It dated back over fifty years, and ever since the boy's first illness, it had taken on a menacing significance to her.

As a young woman in Sydney, for a time she had helped a Dr. William Redfern with children and female patients at the hospital. Her father had considered it inappropriate and made her stop, but he was almost preempted by an incident so shattering that she nearly stopped on her own. A girl of ten had an incurable intestinal ailment, and when it became worse, her stomach ballooned grotesquely. The only laudanum available had been too weak to keep her unconscious, and the hospital rang with her shrill screams of agony during the three days it had taken for her to die.

Dr. Redfern had said that the worst possible treatment for the illness was a purge, which would bring on the crisis stage, and the girl had been given a cathartic before being brought to the hospital. Remembering that incident the first time Christopher became ill, Alexandra had cautioned Fiona not to give him a laxative. The same advice, in a letter from Morton, had been offered by Dr. Stephen Brendell, a friend of Deirdre's.

Other than the advice about the laxative, Alexandra had said nothing about Christopher's illness, keeping her fears to herself. Now that it had recurred, Alexandra knew that she had to tell Jeremy and Fiona about the dire possibility. She desperately hoped that the boy's illness was merely some digestive disorder, but that yearning was overshadowed by her terrifying fear that it was the morbid condition of the internal organs known as perityphlitic abscess.

When sunset faded into twilight, Alexandra lit the lamp on the nightstand. A few minutes later, the door opened and an aged, half-Aborigine woman named Emma Bodenham came in. A maid for many decades, now her status in the household was the same as that of several old stockmen at the barracks. They did whatever odd jobs they wished and spent most of their time sitting about in conversation, enjoying their autumn years.

"Dinner is almost ready, Mistress Kerrick," Emma announced.

Food was the last thing Alexandra wanted in her anxiety, but she knew that she had already missed too many meals while watching over the boy. "I'll have soup and bread here, Emma," she told the woman.

The stooped, feeble woman went back out with her slow steps, and Alexandra pondered the fact that she was years older than Emma, but far less aged. Even though she had spent most of her life in the harsh environment of the outback, somehow she had evaded many ravages of age.

Robustly healthy and still fully active at nearly seventy, she was often mistaken by strangers to be Morton and Deirdre's sister whenever she was in Sydney.

Moreover, aside from missing those who had gone to eternity before her, her life was as happy and productive as ever. Always, however, it was misfortunes like the boy's illness that were the reefs and quicksands in her life. She had fought grassfires, floods, droughts, bushrangers, and other dangers, but even the strongest were defenseless against fate.

Emma returned, accompanied by Astrid Corbett, the older woman's grandniece. Carrying a tray laid out with soup, bread, and tea, they set a place on the table under the window. It occurred to Alexandra that Emma's mother had been from the same tribe as the Aborigines at the station, and the woman probably could understand the corroboree chant. As she stepped to the table, Alexandra asked Emma the purpose of the corroboree.

The aged woman obviously knew but preferred not to say, her eyes avoiding Alexandra's. "Aye, they're having a shivoo, aren't they?" she remarked evasively. "They're making a great clatter and all."

"It isn't a shivoo or any sort of celebration," Alexandra said. "I know that much myself from the tone of the chant, and I'm sure you know far more about it than I. Now what is its purpose, Emma?"

Emma glanced uncomfortably between Alexandra and Astrid, then sighed in resignation. "They're trying to drive death back to his lair," she muttered softly. "He lives in a big, deep cave in the gibbers desert."

Astrid's eyes grew wide with apprehension at the answer, and Alexandra regretted that she had questioned Emma, the corroboree sounding even more somber now. Emma and Astrid left, and Alexandra sat down at the table. She watched the boy while she forced herself to eat the food and drink a cup of tea, then she returned to her chair beside the bed. Presently, Astrid came back in and carried out the dishes.

Weary from only short naps while watching over the boy, Alexandra tried to sleep, knowing she would wake instantly if he moved. She made herself as comfortable as possible on the chair, but her oppressive worry kept her awake. Long, dark hours passed, the corroboree throbbing and the boy whimpering occasionally. Finally, late in the night, she fell asleep.

An absence of sound rather than noise woke Alexandra. She opened her eyes to the first thin gleam of dawn on the window, in the profound stillness before birds stirred on their roosts. With her mind emerging from restless sleep and burdened with fatigue, deep depression from anxiety was a sinister stain that tinted her thoughts in bleak shades of foreboding.

For an instant, the gripping quiet seemed to her a somber pause in which a soul might leave its earthly cares and depart into eternity. She sat up with a jerk, panic-stricken terror like sharp claws piercing her heart.

Then she realized that the corroboree had stopped. In the dim light, with the yellow glow of the lamp retreating from dawn reaching through the window, the boy was no longer whimpering and his breathing was slow and deep. Alexandra gently touched his face. His fever had diminished, and his stupor from laudanum had changed into sound, natural sleep.

Relief was an overwhelming physical force, draining her of strength. Alexandra slid from the chair and collapsed on her knees beside the bed, her tears feeling like a tidal wave surging up and possessing her. She buried her face in the coverlet, her body shaking with sobs as she wept. Fumbling blindly, she found the boy's small hand and held it in hers, and offered up a fervent prayer of thanksgiving through her tears.

In the trees outside, a bellbird's chiming, melodious call

was answered by a swelling chorus of other birds greeting the new day. When she heard a stir in the house, Alexandra summoned her will and stopped crying. She sat beside the bed for a moment, drying her eyes and wiping her face with her handkerchief, then she climbed to her feet.

Extinguishing the lamp, Alexandra gazed down at the boy in adoring love. While she wanted to grab him up and clutch him tightly, she satisfied herself with a light kiss on his forehead, then turned to the door. Every muscle in her body ached with fatigue, and she shrugged it off and squared her shoulders, walking out of the room with a firm stride.

Alexandra sent a maid to sit with Christopher, then stepped down the hall to the rear of the house. The cook and her helpers were at work, the scent of coffee wafting out of the kitchen. After freshening up in the bathhouse, Alexandra went to the dining room. Presently, a maid brought in coffee, along with porridge, toasted rounds of bread, and a fruit dish.

When she finished breakfast, Alexandra started to return to the boy's room, but she heard horses approaching at a run when she was halfway up the stairs. She rushed back down the stairs to the front door, stepping outside just as Jeremy and Fiona rode up the hill to the house.

As always when gazing at them, Alexandra glowed with love, pride, and joy. The tall, muscular Jeremy with his handsome, tanned features and pale blue eyes was a male counterpart to the slender Fiona, her green eyes and bright red hair making her strikingly beautiful. They were also the archetypal man and woman of the outback, with an unrestrained, expansive vigor and determination about them in everything they did.

Their horses slid to a stop, and they leaped down from their saddles. "How is Christopher, Grandmother?" Fiona asked anxiously, Jeremy echoing the question. "Is it the same illness as before?"

"He's out of danger now," Alexandra assured them. "It

was the same illness that he had before, but a much worse onset. He's improved greatly during the last few hours, and he should be himself within a day or two. But what troubles me most is the possible nature of his sickness." She related what she knew about perityphlitic abscess, including its inevitable outcome. "Needless to say," she added, "I hope and pray that his illness is only colic. But it might very well be the more serious disease."

Jeremy and Fiona gazed at each other for a moment without speaking, as they often did when contemplating some matter or making a decision. It was an illustration of the extremely close bonds of love between them, a form of silent communication that Alexandra had observed between only two other people. They had been Elizabeth and Sheila Garrity, and their close relationship had been severed by tragedy years before.

That tragedy had robbed Elizabeth Garrity of some essential part of her humanity, turning her cold and hard. Alexandra feared that something similar could happen to either Fiona or Jeremy, and she wished there was some reserve of self-protection in their love for each other. Human beings were mortal, making obsessive love dangerous. Some limits had to be observed so that a meaningful life could go on in the absence of a loved one.

Turning to Alexandra, Fiona spoke for herself and Jeremy: "At least for now, we must consider it colic, Grandmother. To have the belief that our son is doomed would be intolerable."

Alexandra nodded in understanding, following them into the house. Fiona and Jeremy rushed up the stairs to the boy's room, and Alexandra stepped into the parlor, feeling at loose ends. While she was very weary, she was too restless to even consider going to her room for a nap.

Thumbing through the mail she had left on the desk the day before, she found a letter from Deirdre and opened it. She scanned it, both pleased and having reservations over the fact that Stephen was more than a friend to

Deirdre. While she had never mentioned it to her daughter, Alexandra had always hoped that Deirdre would marry and have a loving companion. At the same time, caution and forethought were required before marrying a man who was substantially younger. Alexandra stepped toward the front door to go out to the station cemetery, her place for thinking about problems.

The cemetery was at the far side of the landscaped gardens on the western flank of the house, a white picket fence enclosing some twenty graves. Several of the native granite headstones were mossy with age, bearing the names of Daniel Corbett, Kunmanara, Jimbob Roberts, Adolarious Bodenham, Creighton and Martha Hammond, and others. Buggie Dobkin had been buried more recently, as had Silas Doak, Corley Bodenham, and a swagman known only as Tolley, who had died at the station the previous year.

Alexandra sat down on a bench near the fence, glancing over the graves reflectively. That of her husband, David Kerrick, was the only one in the first row. It was offset from center, providing a space for her. In the next row were three graves, those of her younger son and his wife, Jonathan and Catherine, and their stillborn son, Infant Kerrick.

Catherine's headstone, one of the more recent ones, was a source of deep remorse for Alexandra. The gory chaos that Catherine had created in her room had long since been cleaned up, but she had left behind an enduring legacy of guilt among the living for not having foreseen and prevented her grisly suicide. She had also become a legend in the outback, the tales related by swagmen including many about her irrational traveling back and forth.

Alexandra read the letter from Deirdre more slowly. Taken as a whole, it asked for an opinion on the importance of a difference in age between a married couple when other facts were considered, and those facts were described in detail. Alexandra pondered them, her reservations fading. She knew that love could overcome many difficulties, and

Stephen Brendell's maturity for his age and other characteristics were highly favorable.

Upon first reading about him in a letter from Morton,
Alexandra reflected, she had immediately recalled Stephanie
Brendell, the midwife who had delivered Jeremy. Over the
years, she had thought of the charming, intriguing woman
many times. She was virtually certain that Stephanie was the
doctor's mother, although the letter from Deirdre mentioned
nothing about his family. Alexandra considered that another
strongly favorable factor, and if Deirdre married him, she
would have an admirable mother-in-law.

Alexandra's attention was drawn to the front of the house,
where Jeremy came out and then led his and Fiona's horses
toward the pens. A moment later, Fiona stepped around the
path at the side of the house, carrying Christopher wrapped
in a blanket. Beryl followed her, leading little Sheila, and
they filed down the path toward the children's play area
behind the house.

The women smiled and the children waved across the
gardens to Alexandra. She waved in response, then studied
Christopher more closely. The blanket wrapped around him
looked uncomfortably like grave clothes for a child. His
small features even seemed to have that inner illumination
of innocent tranquility that Alexandra had seen on the faces
of dead children.

Turning back to the cemetery, Alexandra tried to fight
off an incipient intuition. It was formed of vague, half-
observed impressions, or fragmentary memories of things
William Redfern and others had said—she was unsure of
its origins—and it could not be stopped. As it unfolded
irresistibly in her mind, she tried to dismiss it as having no
factual basis, which was true, but it needed none. Having
experienced intuition before, she had learned that it was as
reliable as the most concrete facts.

It brought with it a heavy burden of wrenching anguish.
In her heart of hearts, she was certain that Christopher had
perityphlitic abscess. Gazing at the second row in the cem-

etery, she knew that a small grave was soon destined to be beside those of Jonathan, Catherine, and Infant Kerrick.

Numb with sorrow, Alexandra stood up from the bench, and the letter slid off her lap. In her grief, she had forgotten it. She gathered up the letter and walked toward the house with slow, shuffling footsteps, fatigue and depression like a heavy weight on her. Answering the letter at present was an onerous chore, but she knew Deirdre was anxiously awaiting a reply before making a crucially important decision.

Alexandra went into the parlor and sat down at the desk. Taking paper out of a drawer, she collected her thoughts through a fog of weariness and sorrow. It was difficult, for she felt like a solitary ironbark among a forest of paperbarks in the flood of time. Some mere saplings and others at full growth, their shallow roots had ripped loose and they had been swept away. Her deeper ones continued to hold her fast to enjoy the times of calm flow and to suffer when the currents raged savagely.

Each of the swift, brutal currents had taken a toll, and while she knew she would survive this buffeting, it would be a punishing ordeal. She adored the boy, and with her strength sapped by past sorrows, losing him would test the limits of her endurance. Dipping her pen into the inkwell, she wearily composed the first sentence in her mind and then began writing.

Chapter Nineteen

There was a knock on the darkroom door, then Verna Allen spoke: "Mistress Kerrick, is it safe to open the door?"

Apprehension gripped Deirdre, fear that Stephen had come to the studio to talk with her. The previous day, the newspaper had published a report by travelers who had brought word of an outbreak of typhoid in Bourke, on the upper reaches of the Darling River. There were no telegraph lines to the isolated town, and the travelers had described a scene of widespread panic that had begun days before, all who could fleeing.

Upon reading the article, Deirdre had known that Stephen would feel that he should immediately leave for Bourke. She had fled to her own escape of the darkroom to occupy her hands and mind, but she had been unable to evade her turmoil. They were to attend a band concert that evening, and while she knew it would inflict torment upon both of them for her to send him away with the situation between them unsettled, she remained as undecided as ever.

At the same time, she had dreaded the possibility that Stephen would come to the studio, not waiting until the evening. Deirdre took off her rubber gloves and stepped into the curtained alcove separating the door from the darkroom. She made certain that the thick, black curtain closed behind her, then steeled herself to face Stephen and opened the door.

Verna was waiting in the hall with a letter. "Here's a letter from your mother, Mistress Kerrick," she said. "I wouldn't have disturbed you, but you mentioned that you expected to receive one from her."

Along with being relieved that Stephen had not come to the studio, Deirdre was delighted by the letter, which had arrived days earlier than she had anticipated. She eagerly grabbed it with a word of thanks, then opened it as she rushed downstairs to her office. Dropping into the chair behind her desk, she put on her pince-nez and began reading the letter.

Her mood plunged again, and at first she was frightened, wondering if her mother was ill or if some disaster had occurred. With word choices and phrasing that reflected deep melancholy, the letter was dismal in tone, completely unlike her mother's usual cheerful, eloquent letters.

Deirdre then thought again, that fear fading. Based on past experience, if her mother was ill or some calamity had occurred, it would be mentioned in the letter. She was certain that her mother would view it as unfair to do otherwise, not as sparing a daughter from worries.

Then, when she studied the letter and searched for other interpretations, fear of another nature gripped Deirdre, along with sorrow.

The point of the letter was that a marriage consisted of the sum total of the characteristics of the two partners, and any which appeared to be untoward should be analyzed in terms of the ability of other characteristics to overcome it. Deirdre had to study the letter closely to grasp the point, for the sentences were rambling and obscure in meaning, a sharp contrast to her mother's usual lucid, concise explanations.

Deirdre was well aware of the point, which was so basic that she searched for another meaning in the letter. She found it, the letter seeming saturated with it. Interpreted in an allusive fashion and as a whole, the letter with its murky sentences could be construed to mean that marriage was an uneasy, uncertain balancing of characteristics of the partners.

Knowing it would be unlike her mother to offer direct advice on whether or not she should marry Stephen, Deirdre had expected none. But she had thought that the reply might express an attitude toward it in an indirect way, and she saw a powerfully strong viewpoint reflected throughout the letter. Moreover, it was anything but a favorable one.

The letter seemed to be saturated with subtle significance, carefully constructed to communicate its indirect meaning in a profoundly grave tone of foreboding. That interpretation gave the somber word choices and phrasing a distinct purpose and meaning, one of stern warning.

Verna stepped into the office, starting to say something about a customer, then broke off and glanced between Deirdre and the letter. "Is anything wrong, Mistress Kerrick?" she asked in concern. "Or I should say, can I be of any assistance in any way?"

"Thank you, no," Deirdre told her quietly.

Verna went back out, and Deirdre took off her pincenez as she put the letter in a desk drawer. Sitting back, she thought about what her mother had written. For a moment, she wondered if she had read too much into it, then dismissed that possibility. It was completely unlike any letter she had ever received from her mother, giving it special significance.

The letter contained a warning, she reflected, that she could either heed or disregard. Her mother's advice was invariably reliable, however, and it was more than supported by her own misgivings. She had nothing in common with the unfortunate Roberta Markham and Enid Lathrop, and Stephen was totally unlike the men who had married those women. But the situation was the same, inviting a grievous even if less tragic outcome.

Tears filled Deirdre's eyes as she reluctantly but steadfastly decided against marrying Stephen. Then, knowing that she had to be unyieldingly strong for a time, she summoned her will and forced her heartbreak aside. She wiped away her tears, stepping to the rack for her hat, and put it on as she went up the hall to the front of the studio.

"Verna, I'll be gone for the rest of the day," she said, crossing the reception room to the front door. "Please lock up this evening."

Verna turned away from a customer, studying Deirdre worriedly, then she forced a smile. "Very well, Mistress Kerrick," she replied.

Deirdre went outside and into the alley to her buggy. Driving out of the alley toward the hospital, she kept her feelings tightly suppressed, determined to quickly be done with what she had to do. While she knew that she would set about reassembling her life during the coming days, at the moment that was in the distant future to her. She concentrated solely upon enduring the coming minutes with her self-control intact.

At the hospital, instead of his usual self-confident poise, Stephen was troubled when he came downstairs to the foyer, his handsome face lined with worry. "I've wanted to come and see you ever since yesterday morning," he said as they stepped outside to her buggy. "I decided to wait until we met this evening, and I intended to ask you if we could talk instead of going to the band concert. Have you heard about the typhoid in Bourke?"

"I read about it in the newspaper, and I immediately knew that you would be extremely concerned about it," she replied. "I also knew that you would want to go there, and I believe that you should indeed go—"

"Deirdre, I must go there!" he blurted despondently, interrupting her. "I must go, because many lives are at risk."

"Of course you must," she agreed. "This is a fitting time for me to tell you that I've given our situation lengthy thought, and I've decided that it would be a serious mistake for us to contemplate being more than friends. So there is nothing between us that is an obstacle to your going."

Stephen was speechless for a moment, gazing at her in shock, then he found his tongue. "You can't mean that, Deirdre!" he exclaimed, appalled. "I'm sure that your feelings for me are in some measure the same as mine for you, and what is between us can't be dealt with that lightly. Please, let's go somewhere more suitable to discuss this."

"It would be pointless," she told him. "I am resolved on the issue, Stephen, and I shan't change my mind. It isn't a matter I regard lightly, because I never deal with people lightly at any time. I'm deeply remorseful for having raised your expectations, and I hope we can remain friends."

"I beg you, Deirdre, don't do this," he pleaded. "My heartfelt hope was to reach an understanding with you before I left, but anything would be better than this. Please, let's allow matters to stand as they were, then we can keep company again when I return from Bourke."

The anguish in his eyes and voice increased Deirdre's turmoil to a searing torment, and she felt her self-control starting to crumble. His hand was on her arm, the warmth from his strong, gentle fingers reaching into every fiber of her body and creating furious strife at the most fundamental level of her womanhood. Somehow she found the strength to maintain her composure, moving away from the alluring torture of his hand.

"That would be futile," she replied, "and continue only what in the end must come to naught. You've mentioned going to other hospitals, and while what you do is your affair, I believe that would be best after you finish at Bourke. If you return to Sydney in time, I'd be very pleased to meet with you as a friend and hear about what you've done." She paused for a response, then turned to her buggy when he merely gazed at her in despair. "Good-bye, Stephen, and

Godspeed on your journey to Bourke."

His quiet as she stepped into her buggy and drove away was answered within her by the stilling of an inner voice that had been choked off, one that had whispered ecstatically of a new life of joy with him. An entity conceived of hope and desperate yearning, now it had been mortally wounded, murdered. It silently screamed in the wrenching agony of its death throes, fueling the most excruciating grief she had ever known.

Deirdre struggled and managed to keep a weak, trembling mental barrier between herself and the surging wave of sorrow that loomed over her as she drove to her house, then she went inside and upstairs. In the privacy of her room, she released her control in an explosion of grief. Throwing herself onto her bed, she burst into tears of abysmal despair. She was certain that what she had done was best for Stephen as well as herself, but in avoiding upheaval in her life she had rendered it empty and meaningless.

The most coherent impression in the midst of Stephen's misery of sorrow and disappointment was that an identical stranger had seemed to have taken the place of his beloved Deirdre. Even though he had long known that she had a powerful will, her behavior had exceeded the limits of inner strength as he knew it. A polite half-smile on her lovely features had given her an impersonal attitude, her eyes like discs of blue glass as she had spoken the crisp sentences that had pierced him like sharp knives.

Stephen kept his feelings contained and made his farewells at the hospital, which took only a few minutes. The previous day, when he had learned about the outbreak of typhoid in Bourke, he had talked with Edward Coleman and the hospital staff, explaining that he had to leave. The only one with whom farewells would have taken longer, Oliver Willis, had left for Wilcannia several days before. Less than an hour after Deirdre had driven away in front of the hospital, Stephen had saddled a horse at the icehouse stable and was riding out of the city toward Wallaby Track.

The warm January day ended with a colorful sunset, then the soft darkness of a moonlit summer night settled after Stephen passed through Parramatta. It was bedtime when he reached the house, and his parents and Yulina were talking over cups of cocoa before retiring. Along with his mood, a brief comment sufficed to explain what had happened between himself and Deirdre. Stephanie and Eric expressed sympathy, then the subject was dropped by everyone except Yulina. She prepared a repast for Stephen, fuming angrily and muttering about a woman who lacked a full set of shingles on her roof.

The repast of leftovers from a roast beef dinner was delicious, but Stephen ate without appetite to still an empty gnawing in his stomach. Deeply loving his parents and Yulina, he usually enjoyed their companionship, but now he yearned to be alone and had to force himself to concentrate on discussing his plans with them. Eric asked if other doctors would go to Bourke, and Stephen told him that it was unlikely.

"Some would leave their practice and go there if the people had no medical assistance," he added, "but Edward Coleman told me yesterday that a Dr. William Brodie lives in Bourke. He's undoubtedly using the traditional procedure for typhoid, which derives from the miasmic theory of disease. That is to eliminate sources of noxious odors insofar as possible, then attend to those who become ill while the epidemic runs its course."

"Whereas antiseptic procedures, derived from the fact that disease is caused by germs, will be more effective," Stephanie observed.

"Yes, antiseptic procedures will end an epidemic when used properly," Stephen confirmed. "It's been discovered that typhoid bacteria are present in the excreta of those with the disease, and it spreads to others by means of flies and contaminated food and water. Phenol and hygienic measures can stop the bacteria from spreading and thus end the epidemic."

Stephanie commented regretfully on the lack of telegraph lines to Bourke, making it impossible to obtain current information on the extent of the epidemic. The conversation turned to practical matters, and Eric said he would go with Stephen in a wagon the next day to collect his belongings from his lodgings and to buy a supply of medicines. After discussing other details, they went to their rooms, and Stephen was alone again with his thoughts of Deirdre.

They kept him awake, hours passing as he stared up into the darkness and wondered if he had said or done something that had made Deirdre decide against marrying him. When he heard a stir in the house well before dawn, he dressed and went out to the barn to help Eric hitch a team to the wagon. After a quick breakfast, they set out for Sydney.

Dawn spread across the sky and then the sun rose, the wagon moving down the road. It reminded Stephen of his boyhood, when he and John had traveled to and from school. During those trips, they had often discussed life's difficulties with Stephen's father. Now Stephen mentioned his memory to his father.

"Making little of a child's problems is a serious mistake," Eric observed, "because they're important to the child. Even so, they're usually large only in the child's mind. But the one you're facing now is truly a vexing one, son. Do you think she might change her mind?"

"Everything I know about Deirdre points to the opposite," Stephen replied. "Once she makes a decision, she never changes her mind."

"Well, I wish I knew of something useful to tell you, son," Eric said remorsefully. "I know how I would have felt if your mother had refused to marry me, so I have some grasp of how you feel."

"It's something that I'll simply have to deal with," Stephen commented grimly. "I don't know how, but somehow or other I must."

Eric nodded sadly, dropping a hand on Stephen's shoulder in sympathy. When they reached the city, it was tormenting for Stephen, reminders of happy moments with Deirdre on every side. While collecting his belongings and driving to a chemist for medical supplies, they were only a short distance from Grosvenor Street. Stephen knew it would be pointless to go near Deirdre's studio, but the bare possibility of catching even a glimpse of her was an alluring temptation.

At the booking office on Circular Quay, Stephen met with an obstacle to his travel plans. He had intended to go by coastal vessel to Adelaide, then up the Darling River to Bourke on a riverboat. However, the booking clerk told him that all riverboats had stopped going farther north on the river than Wilcannia because the crews feared the typhoid in Bourke.

Stephen and Eric left the booking office, discussing the problem. Mail coaches transported passengers to Wilcannia and other towns on more or less regular schedules, but not to the isolated Bourke. Aside from riverboats, the only means of reaching the town was a track that stretched across hundreds of miles of the outback between Bathurst and Bourke.

When Stephen had discussed the outback with Deirdre, she had described her trips into the region to take photographs as enjoyable, but few in the settled areas shared her opinion. Among most townspeople, the outback was regarded as a strange, arid land, a forbidding place where the bones of the unwise and the unlucky bleached in the torrid sun. Eric had that attitude while he and Stephen talked about the journey.

"Using packhorses and traveling up the track is my only choice," Stephen pointed out. "May I use some of your horses?"

"Of course," Eric replied, frowning in concern. "I know you can look after yourself, son, but I don't like this at all. The outback is a dangerous place, particularly for anyone unfamiliar with it and traveling alone. I've also heard that it's a different sort of place, very strange and. . . ." His voice faded as he searched for words, then he sighed in reluctant resignation to the unavoidable circumstances and glanced at Stephen's suit. "You'll need clothing that will stand up to plenty of wear and tear."

Stephen agreed, stepping toward the wagon with his father. They drove to an outfitter for prospectors, where Stephen bought heavy boots, a stockman's hat, and trousers and shirts made of thick, durable dungaree. Eric helped him carry the clothing out to the wagon, then they drove back out of the city and up the road toward Wallaby Track.

When they returned home, Stephanie and Yulina also had extremely deep misgivings about Stephen's overland trip to Bourke. In reply to his remark that people lived at stations along the track and swagmen traveled it, Stephanie said that those people were exceedingly few in number and completely familiar with the outback. However, like Eric, both Stephanie and Yulina reluctantly acknowledged that Stephen had no alternative.

After dinner, Stephen went to the barn with his parents and Yulina to sort out the medical supplies and other things into loads for two packhorses. Working by the light of lanterns, they cushioned the medicines and demijohns of phenol with straw inside canvas bags. Yulina filled bags with foodstuffs in the pantry and carried them to the barn, and Eric brought out a Webley revolver. It was more modern than the pistol that Stephen had learned to shoot as a boy, and Eric showed him how to load and fire it.

When the packs were finished, they returned to the kitchen and talked for a few minutes over cups of cocoa, then went to their rooms. Stephen slept restlessly, his thoughts of Deirdre during wakeful moments merging into dreams of her when he was asleep. At dawn, he rose and dressed in his dungaree clothes with mixed feelings. He had an urge to find new surroundings and to bury himself in work, but even though Deirdre would never be his, he was still reluctant to travel hundreds of miles from her.

After breakfast, Stephen and Eric went to the barn and saddled a horse, then loaded the packs onto two others. They led the horses to the front porch, where Stephanie and Yulina were waiting. Misgivings about Stephen's journey into the outback were unspoken but evident, making the farewells more poignant. Then he stepped into his saddle and rode away, exchanging waves with his parents and Yulina as he turned down the main road.

The large, heavy packs on the horses limited their pace to a walk, and by the time that Penrith was a short distance ahead of Stephen, the sun was dipping behind the mountains. He had contemplated stopping at the town for the night, but his memory of the joyful time with Deirdre in the forest beside the road was too hauntingly painful for him.

Stephen rode past the forest and the road to the town, then across the bridge over the river. The road led out through the Emu Plains and climbed into the foothills, the Blue Mountains towering ahead and becoming dark, massive shadows when sunset faded into dusk. A full moon illuminated the road after darkness fell, and Stephen rode on through the night.

The horses labored up steep inclines into the mountains, and in places the road was a narrow shelf overlooking valleys that were bottomless in the darkness. At some of the wider verges, campfire embers glowed where other travelers had camped for the night. The warmth of summer was left behind at the higher slopes, and Stephen pulled his coat closer against the chill. In the waning light of the moon as it set, he rode through a high pass at the crest of the range, sheer peaks soaring above on each side.

Visibility closed in to a few feet after the moon slipped below the horizon, the darkness relieved only by thin star-light. Stopping at a brook beside the road, Stephen unsaddled and hobbled the horses to let them rest and graze, then searched about in the dim light and found wood for a fire. While he cooked a pan of porridge and made tea, the stars faded ahead of dawn, which was followed by the first shafts of sunrise thrusting between the mountain peaks and scattering the shadows on the scene to the west.

The steep slopes fell away into foothills that leveled off at a vast, rolling plain. Bathurst, the gateway to the outback, was a blur on the horizon. Stephen saw the town for the first time, never having been west of the mountains before. But while he had changed his surroundings, his aching sorrow tinted any scene with identical shades of depression.

When he resumed his journey, other travelers were on the road at intervals. Some were prospectors making their way to new diggings on foot, tools tied to their packs. Riders passed, a few wagons rumbled up the road, and slow, powerful oxen pulled large drays filled with hides, tallow, and other produce en route to far destinations through the port at Sydney.

The rest had been too brief for the horses, the animals plodding more and more slowly as the hours passed. Weariness also overtook Stephen when he reached the warm breezes on the lower slopes, and his eyelids grew heavy. Increasing traffic kept him awake, the road lined with farms and pastures in the lower foothills and out into the rolling plain.

The sun was low in the west when Stephen arrived at Bathurst, a large, teeming town with church spires and slate roofs of taller buildings rising above trees lining the streets. He crossed the bridge over the Macquarie River and rode down a wide, congested street through the business district, looking for a hotel or an inn. All of those on the street were noisy and crowded, catering food and drink more than lodgings.

The buildings became smaller and more scattered as the street led into the western outskirts of the town. Riding around a curve, Stephen saw a large, rambling inn ahead, its sign reading Bellwether Inn. Set back on an expansive yard, it was a busy place, vehicles parked around it and people milling about its stables at one side. It looked inviting in the long shadows of sunset, and Stephen turned in off the street.

Once he identified himself and the purpose of his journey, his reception matched the hospitable appearance of the inn. The innkeeper, a portly, bearded man named Josiah Dunkel, welcomed Stephen effusively. "You'll have the best that the house has to offer!" he declared. "What's more, your money won't spend here." He beckoned three youths sitting on a bench in front of the inn. "You spoonbills, bring the doctor's swag to the room at the end of the hall, then see to his horses." Turning back, Josiah drew Stephen into the inn. "Come right on in, Dr. Brendell, and welcome."

Stephen followed Josiah inside and down the hall. The three youths pushed past and rushed ahead, carrying the packs and saddle into a room. The innkeeper showed Stephen into the room, making certain everything was in order, then he and the youths left.

The room and its homemade furniture were neat and spotlessly clean, and Stephen's heavy fatigue made the bed look very soft and comfortable. After only two meals in as many days, he was also ravenous, the scent of food from the dining room creating gnawing hunger pangs in his stomach. He settled his belongings, then stepped back up the hall to the dining room.

Dinner was a thick, tender slice of roast beef and large servings of potatoes and vegetables, with tea and damper. Josiah sat at the table with Stephen, and people at other tables gathered closer to talk with him. Most of them were farmers and graziers who had come to Bathurst with their families for an agricultural show and fair, and some lived as far as a week's travel up the tracks that radiated into the outback from the town.

Several of the people had more recent information from Bourke than the newspaper report that Stephen had read, for they had talked with swagmen and some who had fled the town. "Me and my wife have a station near Gundaroo," a man said, "on the track to Wilcannia. We know of two families who came from Bourke and moved in with relatives at stations not far from ours."

"Have most of the people left Bourke?" Stephen asked. "If fewer people are exposed to the disease, that will improve matters considerably."

"No, they're mostly still there," a woman replied. "A swagman told me that the ones who left were only a small portion of those in the town. Many people in towns like that don't own horses, and they had no way of leaving. And any who left now wouldn't find a welcome anywhere."

Others commented in agreement with the woman, saying that people at large now feared that those from Bourke would bring the dreaded disease with them. The conversation continued, emphasizing that the people were trapped in the town. The track to Bourke was more isolated than most, the stations along it widely separated. Relatively few travelers used it, and it had been virtually deserted ever since the outbreak of typhoid in the town.

When he finished dinner, Stephen thanked the people for the information and returned to his room. Everything he had heard had been alarmingly ominous, but there was a potential for an even greater calamity. If the epidemic in Bourke became sufficiently widespread in the town, at some point it would produce sufficient bacterial contamination in the river to spread downstream to Wilcannia and other towns. With that troubling thought in mind, he went to bed and fell asleep.

The farming and grazing families in the inn were early risers, stirring about and waking Stephen an hour before dawn. He ate breakfast in the soft glow of lanterns suspended from the dining room ceiling. Dawn was breaking when the innkeeper and Stephen went outside to where his horses were waiting, others following them out. Stephen stepped into his saddle, exchanging farewells with Josiah and the other people, and rode away.

When the last buildings at the outskirts of Bathurst were left behind, the street turned into a wide road leading to the west. Flanked by farms and stock runs, it teemed with prospectors, people leading and driving stock, and wagons hauling produce to the markets in the town. At a distance from Bathurst, the traffic thinned out to a trickle and the road took on the aspect of a track. Stephen passed intersections where other tracks branched off, all of them leading in westerly or southerly directions.

A flock of sheep swarmed down the track, a dog keeping them bunched and a man following the animals. "Can you tell me how far it is to the track that leads to Bourke?" Stephen called to the man as he passed the sheep.

"Aye, about a mile," the man called back. "It's the next one to the right, and you'll have to keep a sharp eye out for it. In event you haven't heard, many in Bourke are in holts with typhoid."

Stephen replied that he had heard of the disease and thanked the man, riding on up the track. Several minutes later, what the man had said about having to watch closely to find the track became evident, along with what Stephen had been told the night before about its being used by few travelers. The track was much more narrow than others, hardly more than a trail that branched off to the right through the foliage.

The track led to the northwest across rolling terrain forested by gnarled gums in an undergrowth of thick brush. For the first few miles, Stephen saw houses and farms set back from the track. Then there were sheep runs that gradually became larger and turned into stations, the tracks leading back to them branching off each side at increasingly long intervals.

At midday, Stephen decided against taking time to stop and prepare tiffin. He passed a track leading back to a station during midafternoon, then saw no more tracks for the remainder of the day, the stations at each side stretching for miles. The sun sank lower in the west, the shadows growing longer, and at dusk he stopped at a billabong to camp for the night.

When he dismounted and looked around, his surroundings seemed to have changed from a few hours before. The foliage, track, and other features appeared to be the same as earlier, but something was different. While that difference seemed to be vividly distinct, it was still so subtle that for a moment he was unable to identify it.

Gazing around, Stephen realized that the change had been atmospheric rather than a physical difference. The bustle and noise of the busy road, inn, and town were a few hours' ride behind him. But in another way, they were now at a distance too great to be measured in hours or miles.

During the past hours, he had crossed a threshold where the very nature of the land had changed. He had entered the outback.

Chapter Twenty

"Can you spare any tobacco for my dudeen?" the man called out to Stephen, holding up a clay pipe. "The head stockman at the last station where I stopped for rations has such short arms and deep pockets that he's loath to give anyone the time of day, much less a fig of tobacco."

The man had appeared suddenly around a curve in the track, surprising Stephen. Four days had passed since he had seen anyone. The man was a bearded, ragged swagman, a blanket roll slung across his back and a canvas dilly bag hanging from his shoulder.

"No, I'm sorry," Stephen replied. "I don't use tobacco."

The swagman clamped the pipe in his mouth and shook his head ruefully. "If it was raining soup, I wouldn't have anything but a fork," he grumbled, passing Stephen. "Mayhap the head stockman at the next station will come to light with some tobacco instead of snouting me. I hope you have a safe journey and the wind stays at your back, jocko."

The swagman was gone just as abruptly as he had

appeared, striding down a slope behind Stephen and then dropping out of view. Once again in the most total solitude he had ever known, Stephen continued riding up the track. While he regretted that the swagman had been so hurried, it was mostly because the man might have had recent information about conditions in Bourke.

Even though he would have enjoyed company, Stephen had adjusted to being completely alone on the track, but it had been difficult. All of his life, the nearby presence of others had been like the air he breathed, so much an integral part of the tapestry of life that it had disappeared into the visible pattern. Here it also could be as essential as air to breathe, the fabric of life threatening to unravel in its absence. In the strange, mysterious outback, the presence of others provided a kind of vital reassurance and support, nourishing the soul.

Without that nourishment, the soul turned inward. During the past days, Stephen had experienced a profound introspection in ways that reached far beyond impartial examination of himself. While he had possessed the inner resources to face that pitiless glare, he had learned why it could be unendurable for others.

The track led up a slightly taller hill in the rolling terrain, the landscape opening out around Stephen as the horses plodded up the rise at their steady walk. From the time he had attended primary school in Sydney, he had been familiar with the geography of Australia, but somehow that knowledge was irrelevant here. Facts learned from maps and books were now less meaningful than an understanding that came from experiencing the land, a perception that seemed much more fundamentally true.

That perception was a kind of spatial disorientation, as though he had entered a house that was larger on the inside than the outside. He knew the dimensions of the continent, but the view that reached out around him against the expanse of the outback sky gave him a feeling of being surrounded by land on a scale so vast that distance became abstract. The land was so immense that paradoxically it was confining. A prison with walls of space, escaping from it took many long days of grueling effort.

The terrain had become increasingly arid during the past days, turning into a landscape of gray and brown. The hills were patchworks of rock outcroppings and thickets of sun-parched brush and kangaroo grass, and in the valleys were copses of eucalypts, competing for moisture with their undergrowth of hardy spinifex grass. The scattered creeks and billabongs were islands of green where lush grass thrived on the water, along with large river gums, paperbarks, peppermint barks, and other trees.

From the crest of the hill, Stephen saw the bright green of a billabong that he could reach near sunset. On the other side of it, the narrow track stretched off across the wilderness and disappeared in the remote distance. That distance was still well short of the horizon, and Stephen knew that when he reached that horizon, another would lie just as far ahead.

Two mallee fowl burst from the brush at the side of the track as Stephen rode down the hill, then a goanna scuttled across the track. The arid land supported an abundance of wildlife, with kangaroos, wallabies, and emus often coming into view on the hills. Koalas clambered about and munched leaves in eucalypts, and the undergrowth stirred with possums, bandicoots, wombats, quokkas, and other animals. Swarms of birds in an immense variety abounded, while the nights were alive with the mournful wailing of dingoes.

The animals were familiar ones to Stephen, only in greater numbers than he had seen before. The land was unlike any he had known, or had expected to find. Some impressions of his surroundings were unnerving, for they came from the land itself. He knew that the earth was inanimate, but while the outback lacked sentience, it seemed not entirely lifeless. It had moods and rhythms—a kind of sensibility of its own.

A forbidding place, it lacked hostility because it conveyed a feeling of indifference. It was merely there, Stephen having a constant sensation of a watching and waiting about him that was almost dispassionate, but something more. While he had never considered land in terms of age— the concept of time irrelevant to the earth—somehow the outback seemed incredibly old. Instead of merely dispassionate, then, the impression of scrutiny all about had an aspect of an ancient and profoundly weary wisdom.

For all that the outback was eerily different, Stephen found it fascinating, partly because it was so peculiar. It also had an austere beauty of its own; it was a spectacular land, none of its characteristics in moderate proportions. Even natural phenomena in the outback seemed more intensely robust, those elsewhere tame by comparison. The sun touched the horizon when Stephen was near the billabong, and sunset flooded the landscape with a burst of colors in breathtaking richness.

The vivid tints washing the scattered clouds in the sky were reflected in the billabong, which was surrounded by huge old gum trees towering over an undergrowth of deep grass. A breeze stirred, easing the torrid heat as Stephen turned off the track. A peppermint bark was among the trees, and its spicy scent made the billabong even more pleasant and inviting after the long, oppressively hot day on the track.

Even at its most disarming and agreeable moments, however, the outback remained dangerous. Stephen's horse balked when he rode toward a tree, intending to camp under it, and the packhorses snorted and stamped nervously. He saw nothing unusual about the tree, but during his boyhood he had learned from his father to take warning when a horse sensed danger.

Then, in the pile of bark that the gum tree had shed over the years, Stephen saw what appeared to be a black worm that twitched occasionally. Knowing what it was, he quickly rode away from the tree. He dismounted and picked up a stone, and tossed it at the bark.

The bark exploded as a thick, four-foot snake leaped out

striking at the stone. It was a type of death adder known
as a rattail, which concealed itself and used its slender tail
to attract prey. Its venom could bring death within minutes.
Stephen took out his pistol in readiness to kill the snake
if he had to, then threw stones at it. The snake struck at
them, furiously angry, then finally slithered away through
the trees.

After unsaddling and hobbling the horses, Stephen kindled a fire and prepared a quick meal, putting on a pan of
dried beef, peas, and rice to cook into a stew. The last
glow of twilight faded, limiting his visibility to the pool
of light from the fire, but his sense of being surrounded
by enormous spaces remained. It was even intensified in a
way, for nighttime in the outback was a gigantic cavern of
darkness, its ceiling a vast ocean of stars that appeared far
more numerous and brighter than elsewhere.

The impression of primordial antiquity in his surroundings also remained, the stony hills of the landscape like
wrinkles on a face of incalculable age. His entire life was
but an instant in comparison with the outback's span of
eons, and on the scale of its illimitable expanse, he was
less than a tiny grain of sand.

Lying beside the fire in his blanket after dinner, Stephen
fell asleep listening to the calls of owls, the plaintive howling of dingoes, and other sounds in the nighttime chorus of
the wilderness. As on most nights, he had a recurring dream
about Deirdre. He was chasing after her, and even as she
raced away, she looked back and reached out to him yearn-
ingly. At times he came agonizingly close to grasping her
extended hands, but he could never run quite fast enough.
When he woke at the first glimmer of dawn, the dream subsided into haunting, melancholy shadows that lurked in the
tormenting vacancy which losing her had created in his life.

Dawn brought the usual morning clamor from parrots,
wagtails, pittas, frogmouths, and countless other species
of birds, and animals began stirring in their daily for-
aging. After breakfasting on porridge, Stephen resumed

his journey. Flies were his only discomfort at first, the insects swarming about him once he was away from the smoke of his campfire. Then the sun climbed higher, the temperature soaring under its scorching glare, and the arid hills shimmered in the stifling heat.

Wind rose from the east after midday, a flow of air reaching inland from the distant coast with traces of moisture. The collision of the wind with the sweltering heat spawned thunderstorms that prowled the landscape like carnivores searching for prey, deep growls of thunder rumbling. A mass of dark clouds swept down on the track with fury characteristic of natural forces in the outback, the earth shuddering from a barrage of blinding lightning and deafening thunder. The storm seemed viciously taunting, displaying how it could wreak devastation if it wished as it ignited grassfires with its crackling bolts of lightning and then extinguished them with sudden, drenching downpours of rain. Then the storm passed the track.

A creek where Stephen stopped at sunset was little different from one at which he had camped a few nights before, the scenery varying little. The lack of distinct change in his surroundings, combined with the intense heat and constant swarms of flies, made one day much like others. With the days following each other in monotonous succession, the endless reaches of terrain seemed like a giant treadmill in which he had become trapped.

The outback produced a numbness to the passage of time, which gave Stephen an insight into swagmen. The vast distances and unchanging landscape fostered a lethargic inertia of the spirit, smothering both worries and desires. He understood how those lacking the driving force of a vital purpose in life could be content to pass their lives in wandering the tracks.

The rain from the thunderstorms painted the foliage with verdant tints of fresh growth for a few days, then the colors faded into the background of gray and brown under the parching sunshine. When he set out up the track one morning, Stephen heard the clanking of a loose shoe on a packhorse, necessitating a stop at the next station to get it tightened.

He had passed a track leading into a station the previous morning, and he wondered if he would reach another one that day at his walking pace, the stations stretching for many miles. It seemed doubtful as the hours wore on, but then he came to a track in midafternoon, a faded sign beside it identifying the surrounding terrain as Burnett Station. The track led eastward, and Stephen glimpsed flocks of sheep among the hills back from it.

The home paddock came into view, an oasis of habitation that looked tired and bedraggled from holding the wilderness at bay. A rambling house built of weathered, unpainted wood and roofed with rusty tin was at one side, flanked by vegetable gardens, an orchard, and wooden water tanks on stilts. Across a dusty yard from the house were a barracks, cookhouse, storage buildings, and a shearing shed with a large expanse of stock pens.

Two men working at the pens shouted as they ran to the house, and a moment later, a stocky, bearded man charged out with a rifle. He faced Stephen in bristling readiness for trouble, the two stockmen watching from behind him, and a woman and children peered out the door at Stephen. "Stand fast where you are!" the man ordered. "I'm Harvey Burnett, the owner here. Have you come from Bourke or from the south?"

"From Sydney," Stephen replied. "I'm Dr. Stephen Brendell, and I'm on my way to assist the doctor at Bourke with the epidemic. One of my horses is near to throwing a shoe, and I'd like to get it fastened."

"We'll be glad to see to it, and I beg pardon for how I spoke to you," Harvey apologized, his attitude changing to hearty friendliness. "We're mightily afeared here of the sickness they have at Bourke."

"I understand perfectly," Stephen assured the man, riding

on up to the house. "You have a family and employees to protect."

"Aye, I do," Harvey agreed. "Even so, it's not to my liking to snout any who come here, because we rarely have the pleasure of visitors. That's twice true for you, a doctor on his way to aid the ill in Bourke."

The woman stepped out of the house as Stephen dismounted, and Harvey introduced her as his wife, Aileen. He and the stockmen inspected the shoes on all three of the horses, the thickset man shaking his head doubtfully when he finished. "That one is indeed near to being cast," he said, "and a few of the others could use a new nail or two. You'd best spend the night so those shoes can be seen to properly, Dr. Brendell."

Stephen started to decline, reasonably certain that he could reach Bourke without further problems, then he thought again. At most, he could travel only a few more miles up the track before sunset. Moreover, the men, Aileen, and even the smallest of the children had a rugged, hardy quality, but their loneliness on the remote station revealed itself as a restrained, inarticulate distress. Stephen nodded, agreeing to stay overnight.

The announcement met with exuberant happiness among the people, along with a flurry of activity. Aileen and the children hurried back inside to prepare a room for Stephen, and Harvey and the stockmen unsaddled the horses. The men carried the packs and saddle into the house, Stephen following them through a large central room that served as both kitchen and parlor, then into a bedroom that two of the children had hastily vacated.

In most ways, the evening was keenly enjoyable for Stephen. Dinner was a rack of lamb with fresh vegetables and salad from the gardens, a delicious change from his quick meals on the track. After dinner, he went out to the veranda with the family. The two stockmen, along with four others and several jackaroos who had been working about the home paddock, sat quietly at one side and listened to the conversation between Stephen and the Burnetts.

The heat of the day had faded into a pleasantly cool evening, moths fluttering around the lanterns hanging from the veranda rafters. The earnest, industrious Harvey and Aileen were the type of people whom Stephen liked best. While their hard work had altered the outback to some extent, its effects upon them had been far more profound. Life in the harsh, perilous land had given them rare qualities of courage, determination, and endurance.

In one way, however, the evening was depressing for Stephen. Some years before, Jeremy and Fiona Kerrick, along with a friend named Buggie, had spent a night at the station. Harvey and Aileen talked about it at length, proud of having hosted the Kerricks. They also related other things about the Kerrick family, some touching upon matters Deirdre had mentioned to Stephen. The conversation reminded him of his joyful times with her, his sorrow over losing her at the forefront of his thoughts.

When the evening ended and Stephen went to bed, he had the recurring dream about Deirdre once again, this time with a gripping aspect of absolute reality. The aftermath of the dream lingered when he returned to the track the next morning, leading him into an intriguing train of thought. He wondered if for some reason Deirdre had acted against her own wishes, and if his dreams arose from some deep level where he had realized that.

During late afternoon of the following day, while lost in thoughts about Deirdre, Stephen was forcibly reminded that a lack of attention to his surroundings while in the outback could be mortally dangerous. A billabong where he intended to camp for the night was less than a hundred yards ahead, and he was completely relaxed in his saddle, his reins hanging slack. His horse suddenly stopped, its ears cocked as it studied the brush beside the track ahead. Then everything happened with blinding speed.

Twigs and leaves exploded from a clump of brush a

hundred feet away as a huge wild boar burst out of it. The animal's ferocious snorts were almost drowned in the terrified shrieks of the horses, all three of them rearing up. Stephen was tossed from his saddle and fell to the ground, his horse's hoofs barely missing his head as it and the other two raced away.

Sprawled on his back, Stephen was partially stunned by the fall. The pounding of the horses' hoofs faded down the track, that of the boar's hoofs and its fierce grunts growing louder as it closed the distance. Stephen grabbed his pistol out of the holster and rolled over to face the boar.

At fifty feet and apporaching rapidly, the animal looked massive. Completely unlike domestic swine, it was muscular and agile, its powerful shoulders scarred from savage fights with other animals. Long, sharp tusks jutted up from its hairy snout, its tiny eyes glittering as it sped toward Stephen. He cocked the pistol, aimed, and fired.

His aim from his reclining position was poor, and the bullet ripped a gash down the boar's back. Its snorts changing to a squeal of rage, rocks flew up from its hoofs as it lowered its head to slash with its tusks and charged faster. Stephen heaved himself up to a kneeling position, thumbing back the hammer on the pistol. He took careful aim and fired.

The bullet slammed into the boar's shoulder at a distance of thirty feet, breaking bones and knocking it to the ground. It was back on its feet immediately, its left foreleg dangling limply. Foaming at the mouth in rage and uttering deafening squeals, it hobbled toward Stephen. He cocked the pistol, aimed at the animal's chest, and squeezed the trigger.

Shot through the lungs, the boar slumped to the ground fifteen feet away. The foam boiling from its mouth with its squeals turned pink, and blood spurted from its nostrils. In its mindless, vicious fury, the boar found the strength to struggle to its feet once again, and it lurched at Stephen. He sprang to his feet and moved back, cocking the pistol.

Foam and blood spattered Stephen's trousers, the keen tusks passing within inches of his legs as the boar swung its head and slashed at him. It continued stumbling toward him and jabbing with its tusks, and he backed away. He had no need to aim, the pistol barely more than three feet from the animal's head as he held it at arm's length and pulled the trigger.

A red hole appeared in the center of the boar's head, surrounded by smoking, singed bristles that had been scorched by burning gunpowder. The boar swayed on its feet, its squeals choking off. Stephen drew back the hammer and fired again. The animal toppled to the ground, its limbs jerking in convulsive jerks of death throes.

The echoes of the last gunshots faded, absorbed by a steely silence. Stephen realized that bird calls and the other usual noises had stilled when the boar had charged out of the brush, and now no sound or movement disturbed the gripping quiet. More than ever, he had an impression of a dispassionate scrutiny all about him. One more among innumerable struggles to the death that had occurred in the outback over its span of aeons had just happened, and it had been watched in some eerie fashion, with a wearily indifferent waiting for the outcome.

A flock of galahs flew overhead, their pink breasts and then gray backs showing as they banked and swerved. A whipbird's snapping call rang out, followed by the melodious trill of a bellbird. Other birds resumed their chattering and chirping, flying about in search of roosts for the night. Stephen started to put his pistol back into the holster as he set out down the track to find his horses. Then, thinking again, he opened the cylinder and reloaded the pistol before returning it to the holster.

The horses were huddled together a mile down the track, and when Stephen led them back up it, they balked and refused to pass the dead boar. He led them off the track and through the brush, circling around the animal. At the billabong, they moved to one side of the pond after they were hobbled, getting as far as possible from the boar to drink and graze.

Nightfall closed in around the yellow pool of light from Stephen's fire as he prepared his evening meal. The howling of dingoes drew much closer than on other nights, then he heard them snarling and scuffling around the dead boar. He knew that if one of his horse's hoofs had struck his head and stunned him when he had fallen from the saddle, or if any one of numerous other circumstances had turned out differently, the wild dogs would now be squabbling over his body instead of the boar's.

The dingoes fought and fed on the boar through the night, their growling and yelps occasionally waking Stephen. The next morning, when he set out on up the track, kites and other birds were taking their turn at what was left of the animal. Surviving the encounter with the boar only through good fortune had been a sobering experience, and he remained alert to his surroundings while riding up the track instead of lapsing into deep thought.

The incident had fallen short of making him regard the outback as fearsome and inimical, his attitude toward it unchanged. He still viewed it as a strangely different, fascinating region with a severe beauty and appeal of its own. The exuberant flood of color and light of sunrise was typical of its extravagant characteristics. Everything about the outback was in giant measure, its dangers a test that he was more than willing to meet, and he enjoyed the journey.

At the same time, he was impatient to reach Bourke and eliminate the perilous threat to lives posed by the epidemic. During the conversation at Burnett Station, Harvey had told him that he had covered most of the distance to the town. But the track continued unfolding across an enormous expanse of wilderness ahead, just as in the previous days, and Stephen saw no indication that his journey would soon draw to an end.

The indication came two days later, when he passed

a track leading back into a station during the morning,
then another that afternoon. With the interval between the
tracks and the stations becoming smaller, Stephen knew
that he would reach Bourke within the next few days. The
following morning, he rode over a hill and saw hobbled
horses and two wagons among the trees that lined a narrow
stream in the valley below.

No smoke rose from a campfire, however, and there
were no people about. Instead, flocks of scavenger birds
swarmed around the wagons and nearby trees, feeding on
carrion. Riding down the hill, Stephen saw that the horses
had been hobbled for many days, their forelegs raw from
being chafed by the leather thongs. The animals also lashed
their tails and stamped constantly to drive away flies that
were tormenting them.

The wagons were some two hundred feet down the creek
from the track, and the stench of rotting flesh in the valley
was so strong that it was like a thick, fetid vapor in the
hot, still air. Along with the croaking of the birds as they
scuffled, dense clouds of flies made a steady, droning noise.
Stephen glimpsed pieces of the carrion that the birds were
fighting over, and he saw shreds of clothing on it.

He reined up and dismounted where the creek crossed
the track, and opened a pack containing medicines and
demijohns of phenol. Flies from the wagons began joining
those that had hovered around him on the track, but all of
the insects were driven away by the smell of phenol when
he dipped water from the creek and mixed a diluted solution
of the disinfectant. He dampened his handkerchief in the
solution and tied it over his nose and mouth, then walked
down the creek toward the wagons and horses.

The birds scattered in a roar of wingbeats and a bedlam of
protesting squawks when he approached them. He removed
the hobbles from the horses so they could move about freely
and make their way to the nearest home paddock, then he
looked around. It was a scene of tragedy.

Either a large, extended family or two families—it was

impossible to determine now—had fled from the disease in Bourke. But at least one among them had been infected with the deadly bacteria, which had spread through the entire party. The first ones to die had been buried in shallow graves beside the creek, but dingoes had dug up the bodies.

The feeding by scavenger animals and birds evidently had begun before the last one had died. In an attempt to avoid that indignity to human remains, one of the people had dragged a large trunk from a wagon, then either had spent the final hours of life inside it, or had placed the body of a loved one in the trunk. The effort had been futile, for dingoes had chewed and torn at the trunk until they had ripped it open.

Using a mattock and shovel from one of the wagons, Stephen dug a deep hole and gathered the scattered remains into it with the shovel. He filled in the hole and covered it with heavy stones to prevent dingoes from digging it up, then stepped back up the creek to his horses.

Stephen took his Book of Common Prayer out of a pack, went back to the grave, and read the burial service aloud. Returning to his horses, he washed his hands in the phenol and poured it over his boots. He closed the packs, then stepped into his saddle and rode on up the track.

The stench of death had permeated his clothes, still wafting about him when he was well away from the creek, but he knew that his memory of the scene would linger long after the odor was gone. Typhoid had killed the people, but the outback had claimed their lives. Now that strange, apathetic scrutiny would watch over their grave through eternity.

Chapter Twenty-One

"Can you give me directions to Dr. William Brodie's surgery?" Stephen called. "I'm a doctor, and I've come to help him."

A moment passed, Stephen watching the house and waiting. A curtain appeared to move, as though someone had heard his horses and peered out the window. The house was partially obscured by smoke from a fire in the yard, however, and he wondered if he had been mistaken. Just as he started to ride on past the house, the front door opened an inch.

"Doctor Bill isn't in his surgery," a woman called through the narrow opening. "He's using a warehouse beside the river as a hospital for the sick, and you'll find him there."

Stephen thanked her, and the door closed with a firm thud. He rode up the street toward the river, the clopping of his horses' hoofs loud in the silence. Using a warehouse as a hospital indicated to him that the epidemic was widespread, which was borne out by the atmosphere of terror in Bourke. The streets were deserted, the people taking refuge in their houses and avoiding each other. The town was like one under siege by an invading foe, but this enemy was invisible and attacked stealthily from within, making it infinitely more dreadful than any human threat.

The residential street leading into the town was filled with thick smoke billowing up from green boughs smoldering on fires in front of dwellings. The smoke was a practice from ancient folklore to ward off disease, and it was also consistent with the miasmic theory of disease in the belief that illness could often be prevented by eliminating noxious odors.

The smoke was left behind when he reached the business district, which was also quiet and deserted, the shops and offices shuttered. The horses' slow hoofbeats echoed hollowly between the buildings as Stephen rode up the street through the center of the town. The street led into a frontage street that paralleled the river. Across the street, a long line of piers extending out into the water was as lifeless as the rest of the town.

Two riverboats were at the piers, the crews evidently having contracted typhoid before they could leave. One was small, little longer than a barge; the name on its bow was *Cobdogla*. The other one, the *Taroona,* was as large as many deep-sea vessels, with towering stacks and a wheelhouse atop the deckhouse that contained passenger accommodations.

The stock pens and warehouses lining the frontage street were also deserted except for two men and a woman on the porch of a warehouse. Stephen rode toward it, a sickroom stench wafting up the street and identifying it as the makeshift hospital, and one of the men on the porch wore a hospital smock. A half-Aborigine in his early twenties, he started to follow the other two inside, then turned back when Stephen rode up to the porch.

"I'm Dr. Stephen Brendell," Stephen said. "Is Dr. Brodie here?"

The man was speechless with surprise at first, then a

grin wreathed his open, amiable features. "Aye, and he'll be mightily glad to see you, Dr. Brendell," he replied. "I'm Carl Safford, one of Doctor Bill's apprentices. This epidemic is nigh onto having us stonkered, and we weren't expecting any help. We've heard of you, and most especially we weren't expecting help from someone like you. I'll tell Doctor Bill that you're here."

The apprentice disappeared through the wide door of the warehouse, and Stephen dismounted and tethered his horse to the porch. As he went up the steps to the porch, a spare, bearded man in his fifties rushed out of the warehouse. "Stephen Brendell!" the man exclaimed. "I'm Bill Brodie, and words can't express how pleased I am that you're here."

"I'm just as pleased to be of whatever help that I can," Stephen assured him. "The situation appears to be very serious."

Doctor Bill sighed and nodded in agreement. A dedicated man with intense concern for his patients, he choked up and his eyes filled with tears as he started to speak, then he controlled himself. "I'm on beams' ends, Stephen," he admitted grimly. "This epidemic keeps spreading like wildfire, and the cooler weather that will end it is months away. Worse still, I've used up almost all of the bromides and senna that the town chemist has in stock."

"I have an ample supply of medicines," Stephen told him, pointing to the packhorses. "Along with senna and bromides, I brought cinchona, taraxacum, and other preparations that are effective in treating typhoid."

"You're a godsend, Stephen," Doctor Bill said fervently. "Dr. Tom Landry in Sydney is a friend of mine. He wrote to me about what you did at the hospital there, and I'll warrant that you'll save even more lives here." He beckoned Carl Safford and two other apprentices who had stepped out onto the porch. "Lads, take the saddle and packs on those horses inside. Stephen, I'll show you what we're facing and help you get settled in."

Stephen followed Doctor Bill into the warehouse. Blankets hanging in the center of the vast, dim building separated it into a ward for women and children and one for men and older boys. It was a nightmarish scene of misery. Dozens of patients moaned and tossed on cots, the foul odor almost overpowering in the sweltering heat, and the air thick with flies. Relatives attending to the patients moved about numbly like sleepwalkers in their utter despair.

The apprentices carried the saddle and packs to storage rooms at one side of the warehouse, which were being used for staff accommodations and a pharmacy. The three men began working over the packs, taking Stephen's belongings into an empty room and placing the medicines on shelves in the pharmacy. Stephen glanced into the staff kitchen and other rooms and saw that good hygiene was being practiced, the rooms spotlessly clean.

After he had seen everything, Stephen explained to Doctor Bill how the epidemic could be halted, regardless of the hot weather. The apprentices stopped working and listened in contained excitement, while the older doctor reacted with a mixture of hope and polite doubt. "Are you quite certain of that, Stephen?" he asked. "In my experience, epidemics almost always end during cool weather, which is still some months away."

"I'm positive," Stephen assured him. "Typhoid is caused by a bacterium, and flies are a main vector for the disease. In addition to eliminating the bacteria, phenol drives flies away with its odor."

"That alone will make using it worth the effort," Doctor Bill observed. "The flies here are maddening for everyone, but mostly for the patients. The phenol should be put in the water and used to mop the floor, then?"

"Yes, and the walls should be dampened with it as well," Stephen replied. "It should also be used in the water in which patients' nightshirts and blankets are washed. Those who are assisting with relatives will still be at risk at their homes, and I must explain sanitary procedures for them to use there. Moreover, we'll need to talk with the magistrate and get him to inform the town at large on how to avoid contracting the disease."

"Very well, let's proceed then," Doctor Bill announced briskly. "I'm always willing to use new methods to the benefit of patients, and the magistrate, James Crawford, is a good, sensible man." He turned to the apprentices. "Leave that for now and fetch buckets of water," he told them. "Carl, take Dr. Brendell's horses to the livery stable, then find the magistrate and tell him that we need to talk with him."

The conversation ended in a bustle of activity, Carl hurrying toward the door and the other apprentices rushing to fetch cleaning equipment and water from barrels in a corner. Doctor Bill stepped among the cots and gathered the people attending to the patients, and Stephen drew the cork out of a phenol demijohn. When the apprentices returned with mops and buckets of water, Stephen helped them hoist the heavy jug by the handles on its wicker basket and showed them how much of the dark, pungent liquid to pour into each bucket.

Leaving the apprentices swabbing the floors and walls, Stephen stepped over to the people caring for relatives. Certain that their clothing had long since been contaminated with typhoid bacteria, he started by telling them that it would have to be laundered in boiling water. Then he went on to other preventive measures, which included boiling all drinking water, eating only boiled food, and scalding dishes before each meal.

While relating the precautions, Stephen wondered if they would be considered too numerous and troublesome, but the people reacted with willing cooperation. Before, to them the disease had been an unpredictable unknown against which they had been defenseless, and they eagerly accepted the safeguards that promised to give them some protection.

Their spirits raised, the people became more energetic and talkative when the gathering broke up. Carl returned presently, after speaking with the magistrate, who had agreed to come to the warehouse. Stephen stepped out onto the porch with Doctor Bill to wait for the man, discussing another aspect of the epidemic. Doctor Bill explained that in addition to its disastrous effects in the town, it could create economic devastation throughout the region. Bourke was a commercial center where riverboats gathered to transport cattle and produce that graziers and farmers brought to the town, a process that should begin within some two months. If the epidemic prevented it, everyone involved would suffer financial ruin.

The magistrate arrived on horseback a short time later. A tall, rangy man in his forties, James Crawford listened closely as Stephen repeated the instructions he had given to the people in the warehouse. James nodded, saying he would ensure that all the people in the town were informed of the precautions, then he too mentioned the possible economic consequences of the epidemic.

"Lives are far more important, of course," he added. "But the likelihood that hundreds of families will be without food and other necessities for lack of money is no small consideration, Dr. Brendell."

"Indeed it isn't," Stephen agreed. "However, I believe the fundamental problem reaches beyond this epidemic. I'm reasonably certain that it was caused by contamination carried down the river from those who had typhoid in the Darling Downs. If other epidemics are to be avoided, this town must have an adequate source of purified drinking water."

"Very well, I'll bring that up with the town council," James said. "We certainly don't want any more epidemics here, and we want an end to this one as soon as possible. I'll have constables inform every household of what you said to do." He gathered his reins and turned his horse. "If there is anything else I can do to help, you need only let me know."

The magistrate rode away, and Stephen and Doctor Bill went back into the warehouse. Several people were helping the apprentices mop it with phenol, and it was strikingly different from when Stephen had first stepped into it an hour before. The flies and stench were gone, replaced by the fresh, penetrating odor of phenol. More than that, the lethargic resignation to fate among the people had been transformed to a sense of hope.

Donning a hospital smock that an apprentice brought, Stephen began making the rounds of patients with Doctor Bill. Analyzing each patient's condition and determining medications was totally absorbing, the hours flying like minutes. Dinner was vegetable stew that the apprentices prepared in the staff kitchen, the bowls still steaming hot from being scalded. After dinner, Stephen and Doctor Bill finished the rounds by the light of lanterns.

When he lay down on his cot in his room, Stephen's thoughts were entirely about individual patients and the medications he had prescribed for them, but his lost love claimed his hours of sleep. Throughout the night, he once again dreamed of frantically chasing after Deirdre while she fled and entreatingly reached back to him, then he woke to the light of dawn and the feverish moaning of patients gasping for water.

That day began a length of time which Stephen knew was indefinite, but limited. The townspeople would closely follow the sanitary precautions at first, but human nature would soon come into play. Unless the safeguards produced some concrete result, the people would begin ignoring them. Therefore he hoped to see some prompt, visible progress against the disease.

The first progress, coming quickly enough at two days later, was a sharp decline in mortality among the patients. The ample quantity and wide choice in medications to suppress the patients' symptoms was partly responsible. The conditions in the warehouse were another important factor, with less discomfort to sap the patients' strength.

The most significant development, a decline in admissions, was gradual. The incubation period for typhoid was up to fourteen days before the initial fever, aching, and nosebleeds appeared, but the intense heat shortened it. For a time, the admission rate was constant at two or three patients each day by those who had ingested the bacteria before the preventive measures began, then it slowly tapered off to one every day or two.

Finally, three days passed with no admissions, and the epidemic was on the wane. The town began stirring with life, shops opening for business and traffic on the streets increasing daily. Stephen observed it only from a distance, for some sixty patients were in the warehouse who had to be examined daily and their medications changed when their condition improved. He continued to work from dawn until after dark each day, his brief hours of sleep occasionally restless because of his recurring dream about Deirdre.

When the number of patients began diminishing, Stephen prevented it from happening too rapidly. Some felt reasonably well and wanted to be about their affairs, but he insisted that they remain, for they were either too weak or still in an infectious stage. The crews of the steamboats were the most difficult to convince, the captain of the *Taroona* in particular.

A large, muscular man in his forties named Tom Babbitt, the captain had the aggressively determined disposition essential to facing the hazards of the river. He struggled up from his cot at times, sweat breaking out on his craggy, bearded face, and debated with Stephen about being able to leave. After several arguments with the man, Stephen finally hit upon a compelling reason when he said that in return for his medical care, Tom had a debt to the people of Bourke that he was obligated to repay.

"I'm ready and willing to pay," Tom grumbled. "I'll pay in gold."

"No, that won't do," Stephen retorted. "You're being attended in your illness, and the only way you can repay that is with a service. You must wait until you and your crew are well enough to leave, then go downriver and tell other riverboat captains that the epidemic here is over."

"Aye, I'll do that," Tom growled. "I'll leave tomorrow."

"In your condition?" Stephen shot back. "The captains would take one look at you and never come here again. If you'll do as I said, it will ensure against financial difficulties here, and that will be a more than adequate repayment for what was done for you and your crew."

The appeal to his sense of fairness succeeded where other arguments had failed, and Tom reluctantly agreed to wait. Settling the dispute with him also ended it with others who had wanted to leave, but who lacked the captain's aggressive disposition and had been less insistent. Stephen was pleased it had been done without animosity, for he liked the man, but he had no intention of releasing a patient who could start another epidemic.

The following morning, Stephen saw Aborigines gathering on the other side of the river and asked Carl Safford about them. The apprentice explained that they camped across the river each year, and when the shipping season began, they worked on the waterfront as porters. Concerned that the Aborigines might contract typhoid, Stephen told Carl to borrow a boat from the piers and go and warn them about the disease in the town.

A short time later, Stephen heard a corroboree on the other side of the river and stepped out onto the porch. Carl was rowing back to the piers, thick smoke billowing up from the Aborigine camp behind him, and the blended sounds of voices chanting in cadence with rhythm sticks and the rising and falling notes of didgeridoos carried across the river. Stephen waited on the porch until Carl returned and then asked him the purpose of the corroboree. The apprentice shrugged, replying that he was uncertain.

"It's connected with the typhoid, though," Carl added. "Mayhap it's to ward off sickness from themselves, or to help people here recover, or both. I don't know about that, but I'm sure it has to do with the disease."

Stephen made no comment, having mixed feelings. As a

physician, he was unable to believe that a corroboree could have any effect on a disease. As an Australian, however, he was less skeptical. From his boyhood, he had known people of sound judgment who considered at least some Aborigine beliefs and customs to transcend logic and the laws of nature.

Alexandra Kerrick also had mixed feelings about the corroboree resounding through her house as she paced to and fro in the parlor. The sound was comforting, a reason to hope that Christopher's young body was being aided in battling his illness. But the unremitting, throbbing sound plucked at her nerves as well, straining her self-control that held panic at bay.

The loud, melodious chiming of the station bell at the shearing shed suddenly joined the sound of the corroboree, announcing travelers on the track. Alexandra turned toward the door, hearing running footsteps in the upstairs hall and then coming down the stairs, taking two and three at a time. The slender, redheaded Fiona darted past the parlor doorway and flung the front door open, racing outside, and Alexandra followed her out.

Across the broad valley of the home paddock, two riders cantered up the track toward the house. One was the tall, wide-shouldered Jeremy, the other a much smaller man. "Jeremy has the new doctor from Wilcannia with him, Grandmother," Fiona cried in relief, then frowned impatiently. "But why aren't they hurrying? Why are they riding so slowly?"

Alexandra studied the smaller man, her keen eyes picking out his white, neatly trimmed beard. "The doctor is an older man, my dear," she said.

Fiona peered closely, a moment passing while the doctor and Jeremy rode on up the track, then she nodded in agreement. The bell stopped ringing, its echoes fading under the sound of the corroboree. Fiona fidgeted anxiously, and Alexandra continued studying the doctor as they waited.

Something about the man seemed familiar to her. Then, when he was close enough for her to make out his features, she recognized him from many years before. "My word, it's Oliver Willis," she remarked in surprise.

"Dr. Willis?" Fiona exclaimed. "He attended my mother in Brisbane, and he's a very good doctor, Grandmother. Also, when he was in Sydney years ago, he attended Jeremy's mother, didn't he?"

"Yes, he did, my dear," Alexandra replied.

The minutes dragged past, then Oliver and Jeremy finally reached the hill and rode up to the house. They dismounted, Fiona and Alexandra exchanging greetings with the doctor. "Brisbane was very drab without your beautiful red hair, Fiona," he commented, then turned to Alexandra: "I'm astonished and also extremely pleased to see how little you've aged, Mistress Kerrick. Even though it's been well over twenty years since we last saw each other, you don't appear to be a day older."

"You're too kind, and I'm delighted to see that you enjoy good health and spirits, Dr. Willis," she told him. "I assume that Jeremy told you about my great-grandson's symptoms."

"Yes, he did," Oliver replied, untying his bag from behind his saddle. "I'd like to examine the lad without delay."

They filed into the house, Fiona taking Oliver's coat and hat, and he said that he would like to wash his hands. Alexandra called down the hallway to the rear of the house for a maid to bring water and soap to Christopher's room. Astrid Corbett replied from the kitchen, then Alexandra led the way up the stairs and along the hall to the boy's room.

Her torment of worry took on a fresh, sharp intensity as she went into the room with the others, for the boy looked so very small and helpless in his stupor from laudanum. Oliver placed his bag on the table and put on spectacles. Astrid brought in a basin of water, soap, and a towel, and went back out. Oliver washed his hands, then took his stethoscope out of his bag and stepped to the side of the bed.

The doctor examined the boy, then turned away from the bed, his aged, wrinkled features somber. "I deeply regret it," he began, "but the lad's symptoms are those of perityphlitic abscess, which is a——"

He broke off, Fiona wailing in anguish and throwing herself into Jeremy's arms. Alexandra had been certain of what he would say, but hearing it still added a keen edge to her grief. "We're well aware of what perityphlitic abscess is," she explained, "as well as its prospects."

"I could make a further test," Oliver offered. "There is always a large number of white blood corpuscles with this condition, but I would need my microscope from my surgery to examine a blood sample."

"What I know of the disease agrees with your judgment," Alexandra told him. "Aren't there any new remedies that might be of benefit?"

Oliver started to shake his head, then hesitated. "There might be a chance to help the lad," he mused. "Just a chance."

"What do you mean, Dr. Willis?" Fiona demanded, her voice joining Alexandra's in prompting Oliver to continue. "Do you mean that you might be able to cure Christopher's disease?"

"No, but I know of a doctor who might," Oliver explained. "I have no right to speak for him, but I have a friend in Sydney who is the most skilled, knowledgeable physician I've ever met. I'm not sure if he would attempt to treat perityphlitic abscess, but if any doctor on earth could do it successfully, it would be this man. His name is Stephen Brendell."

Alexandra was surprised as well as momentarily distracted at hearing the name, having often wondered what decision Deirdre would make regarding the man, then she collected her thoughts. "I've heard of Dr. Brendell," she said. "What sort of treatment would he use?"

"A surgical treatment," Oliver replied. "It's generally accepted that before the acute stage, the inflammation in perityphlitic abscess is confined to a small appendage on the intestine known as the veriform appendix. The treatment would consist of removal of that appendage."

"What?" Fiona gasped in horror. "Do you mean that my son's stomach would be cut open? That would kill him!"

"Not inevitably, but it would be very dangerous," he acknowledged. "As far as I know, it's never been done. But if you're aware of what this disease is and its prospects, then you know it's as dangerous in itself."

Silence fell, Jeremy and Fiona exchanging a gaze of understanding, then Jeremy turned to Oliver. "Christopher can't be taken to Sydney," he pointed out. "Do you think Dr. Brendell would be willing to come here?"

"I have no right to speak for him," Oliver repeated. "I can't say if he would or not, and I must emphasize that I don't know if he would consider trying to treat this disease. On the other hand, he doesn't have a practice that would require him to stay in Sydney. He works at the hospital, and he's often made it clear that his position there isn't permanent."

The last words were scarcely out of the doctor's mouth before Jeremy was gone, leaving the room with long, fast strides. Fiona spoke over her shoulder as she followed him: "Grandmother, I'd be most grateful if you would fetch a bag of bread and cheese for Jeremy from the kitchen."

Alexandra excused herself to Oliver for not seeing him downstairs, and he nodded amiably in understanding. She stepped out of the room and toward the stairs just as Fiona disappeared into her and Jeremy's room at the end of the hall. Jeremy had barged out the front door and left it open, and he was riding down the hill to the stock pens. Alexandra closed the door and hurried down the hall to the kitchen.

The cook and her helpers scurried about, found a cloth bag, and took a cheese and loaves of bread out of the pantry. Alexandra carved chunks from the cheese and put them into the bag with the loaves, telling the cook to prepare a repast for Oliver in the dining room. She tied the top of the bag, then grabbed it up and stepped quickly back up the hallway.

Fiona ran down the stairs, lugging Jeremy's dilly bag, pistol belt, water flask, and a blanket wrapped in his oilskins. Alexandra went out the front door with her, meeting Jeremy as he rode up the hill to the house on a fresh horse. He jumped down from his saddle and buckled on his pistol belt while Fiona and Alexandra tied his swag behind his saddle.

Alexandra exchanged a hug and kiss with Jeremy. "Godspeed, my dear, dear grandson," she said. "Do be cautious during your journey."

"Yes, I will, Grandmother," he replied affectionately. "Please guard your health and don't plague yourself with worries."

Jeremy turned to Fiona and took her into his arms, and they embraced closely for a moment, gazing into each other's eyes. They kissed, then he stepped to his horse and leaped into the saddle.

The horse charged into a headlong run, racing away from the house and down the hill. On the track, Jeremy and the horse disappeared into a cloud of dust, the furious pace having a recklessness that troubled Alexandra. His journey would be long and arduous, and also dangerous.

When he reached the other side of the valley, the pounding hoofbeats faded under the sound of the corroboree. Alexandra and Fiona went back inside, where Oliver was waiting in the entry. Fiona restrained her tears with a visible effort as she spoke with Oliver briefly, making her farewells and thanking him for telling them about Stephen Brendell. Then she went up the stairs to resume her vigil beside her son's bed.

Alexandra seated Oliver in the parlor and went to the desk to write out a check for his fee. He tried to decline it, saying he had done nothing, and he considered the five guineas that Alexandra had always paid the other doctor as too much. She insisted that he take it, then led him to the dining room. The maids were laying out the repast for him, and she suggested that he rest and leave for Wilcannia the next day.

"That's very kind of you," he replied, "but I must return as soon as possible and see to a patient whose condition is uncertain."

"Very well, I'll have a fresh horse saddled for you," she told him, then, detecting an uneasiness in his attitude, added, "And I'll have a stockman accompany you to the town, if you wish."

"I would appreciate that," he confessed, shamefaced. "It seems foolish, but I'm very uncomfortable when alone out here in the wilderness."

"It isn't foolish at all," she assured him. "The outback is a strange place to those unaccustomed to it. I'll leave you with your repast, then, and have a stockman saddle horses in readiness to accompany you."

Oliver thanked her, seating himself at the table, and Alexandra stepped down the hall to the kitchen. She sent a cook's helper to tell Zachary Cooper that he was wanted at the house, then she went up the hall and out the front door to wait for the stockman. Presently, he walked up the hill. The lean, leathery man nodded in understanding as Alexandra told him to travel at a moderate pace and stay with the doctor at all times. Then he led Oliver's horse away and Alexandra went back into the house.

A short time later, Zachary led horses up to the house and Oliver finished his repast. Alexandra saw them off, standing in front of the house and watching as they moved down the track at a slow canter, and she pondered what Oliver had said about Stephen Brendell. There seemed to be an auspicious interlocking of destinies, with Stephanie Brendell having delivered Jeremy, then her son being the one who might save Jeremy's son. Alexandra knew, however, that fate could be cruel and deceptive, often shrouding a path to disaster in circumstances that appeared reassuring.

She went back into the house and paced to and fro in the parlor once again, acutely apprehensive about Jeremy's heedless, precipitant haste when he had left. While her grandson was a man of the outback, the vast, arid region his natural environment, he was a mortal human being. The outback was an eerily strange, alien place for many, and lethally dangerous for everyone. It watched and waited, and in a moment of inattention, one of its innumerable perils could strike. Sheila Garrity had been a creature of the outback, born and raised on Wayamba Station, yet it had taken her life.

Moreover, all the risks of the journey might be for nothing. At best, it was no more than an attempt to grasp at a chance for help. Stephen Brendell might or might not be able to do anything to help Christopher, might or might not be willing to even try. And the boy's illness could reach a crisis stage before Jeremy crossed the Darling River at Wilcannia.

Feeling an urgent need for a physical outlet for her turmoil of anxiety, Alexandra decided to go for a ride. She stepped into the entry, put on a hat and cape from the closet, and left the house. When she walked down the hill and around to the station building and stock pens, retired employees stirred from a bench in the shade beside the barracks.

The men lifted their hats, exchanging greetings with Alexandra as she passed the barracks. Most of them were younger than she, but the ravages of time had been harder on them. Isaac Logan was thin and stooped, any but the most moderate exertion making him breathless. Eulie Bodenham was wrinkled, toothless, and almost blind, while Ruel Blake had become too stiff and feeble for the work of a stockman, as had others.

They seemed far older than her memories of them as young, strong men. The man who saddled a horse for her, Roger Corbett, was also a reminder of how decades had flown. It seemed only a few years since he had been a frail, sickly jackaroo. But he was a brawny, bearded man in his forties, the head stockman now, and married to one of Adolarious Bodenham's granddaughters. The maid Astrid was one of his children, and another was a stockman.

Alexandra rode across the valley from the house and reined up beside an ancient, gnarled gum tree as she gazed over the home paddock. The vast sheep station that stretched for hundreds of square miles in all directions was the realization of a dream, her life's work, but not for wealth or for herself. It was the heritage of her family, a point of reference for those with Kerrick blood in their veins. Wherever destiny might take each of them down through the generations, they would have a common origin known to all of them, a place that was the wellspring where the family had begun.

She dismounted and tethered the horse, then sat under the tree. Gathering a handful of soil, she savored the feel of it as it tricked through her fingers. The soil of Tibooburra Station, each handful was of greater value to her than gold. Only her family was more precious to her, and two members of her family were under a threat. One whose life had hardly begun could lapse into a slow, agonizing death at any time, and the one who had made her autumn years rich with joy could face mortal peril.

The sound of the corroboree carried across the valley from the Aborigine village down the creek from the house. Her anxiety swelling to an agonizing torment, tears of anguish filled Alexandra's eyes and overflowed. The tears streaming down her face, she prayed softly, pleading that her grandson be returned to her and the life of her great-grandson be spared.

Chapter Twenty-Two

"There's much ado about that rabbit plague," Morton remarked, plying his knife and fork vigorously with his usual hearty appetite. "Did you see the article about them in the newspaper today, Deirdre?"

"Yes, I did," she replied. "They're still spreading fairly slowly, it seems, and perhaps a means of dealing with them will be found soon."

"But they're such charming little creatures," Julia observed. "It does seem a shame that they're regarded as a pest and as a—"

She broke off, startled by a sudden loud, impatient hammering of the front door knocker, a fist also thumping the door. The housekeeper, supervising the maids serving the meal, frowned in disapproval and turned toward the door. Morton stopped her with a curt word, irately pushing his chair back and standing, and he stamped out of the dining room.

The commotion at the front door ceased, and Deirdre heard Morton exclaim in surprise and alarm. Then he returned, the smallish, portly man struggling to support his strapping son and help him to the table. Deirdre rushed to assist Morton, shocked by Jeremy's appearance. Haggard and unshaven, the tall, muscular man was on the point of collapsing from exhaustion.

"Brandy, please!" Morton snapped at the housekeeper. "Quickly, please!"

The housekeeper rushed out as Julia pulled a chair away from the table, and Deirdre helped Morton seat Jeremy on it. "What has happened, Jeremy?" she asked. "Has there been some disaster at the station?"

Her nephew started to mutter a reply, but the housekeeper ran in with a decanter and a glass. Morton grabbed them, splashing brandy into the glass, then Jeremy took it and gulped down the liquor. It revived him, and he sat up with an effort as Morton refilled the glass.

"It's Christopher," Jeremy explained hoarsely. "His illness is a very serious condition called perityphlitic abscess. Dr. Willis at Wilcannia said the only one who might be able to help is Dr. Stephen Brendell." He took another drink of brandy and looked up at Deirdre. "Grandmother said that he's a friend of yours. I must talk with him and ask him if he'll go to the station and try to help Christopher."

Deirdre exchanged a glance with Morton and Julia, who were appalled by the news about their grandson. She was as well, and she also dreaded having to disappoint Jeremy. "Stephen isn't in Sydney," she said regretfully. "He went to Bourke to help with the epidemic of typhoid there."

"No!" Jeremy groaned in despair. He slumped for a moment, then slowly pulled himself to his feet. "Father, I need a fresh horse," he said grimly.

An argument erupted, Morton and Julia insisting that Jeremy needed food and rest, while he was determined to immediately set out. "Stephen might not be at Bourke now," Deirdre told them, breaking in on the debate. "There are reports that the epidemic has been curtailed. His parents live in Wallaby Track, and I'll go ask his mother if she knows his whereabouts. Jeremy, what is the precise nature of Christopher's illness?"

"It's an abscess in his stomach," Jeremy replied. "Dr. Willis didn't know if Stephen Brendell would even try to treat it, because that would involve surgery to remove the abscess."

The explanation brought gasps of dismay from Morton and Julia. Deirdre continued: "I'll ask his mother about that as well. She may have an informed opinion as to what Stephen would do. It'll take me until well into the forenoon tomorrow to get there and back in my buggy, which will give you time to rest."

"No, you must go in my carriage," Morton put in. "It'll be somewhat faster as well as safer, and I'll have the stableboy take your buggy to your house. Jeremy, sit down and have dinner, then you can go to bed."

Jeremy hesitated, then logic won out and he sat down. Julia and the maids began dishing up dinner for him as Deirdre followed Morton out of the dining room. Morton went down the hall toward the back door to have the carriage prepared, and she went to the entry to get her coat and hat. Donning them, she hurried down the hall and out the back door.

In the stable courtyard, the coachman, groom, and stableboy harnessed horses to the large, gleaming carriage by the light of lanterns, Morton trying to help and mostly getting in the way. Deirdre told the coachman what Stephen had once said to her about the location of the Brendell home in Wallaby Track, then she stepped into the carriage. Moments later, it rumbled down the drive beside the house and turned onto the street.

The carriage moved through scattered evening traffic in the city, then the horses settled into a steady canter up Parramatta Road. Deirdre gazed out at the passing lights and dark buildings, pondering her grandnephew's illness. Along with her intense concern for Christopher, she hoped her mother was bearing up well under the stress of anxiety over the boy.

Its effect on herself, she reflected, had been to shatter her emotional doldrums of the past weeks. When she had ended her relationship with Stephen, she had thought that she could eventually overcome the pain. Unconsciously, she had related it to ending an affair with a man, which had always brought regrets for a time. There was no comparison, the two being entirely different, and her anguish was still just as much of a torment as at first.

Her work had been a refuge from other sorrows, but not this one. She had never confided her feelings about Stephen to others, but Morton and Julia, the Tavishes, and close friends had obviously suspected that it had been more than friendship. Their frequent invitations had filled her hours, but their companionship had been no substitute for that of the one she loved.

The carriage turned onto the road leading north from Parramatta, swaying and bouncing over ruts. As the hours passed, Deirdre contemplated an aspect of her late-night journey aside from its purpose. During the past weeks, she had grimly accepted her sorrow and remained characteristically steadfast in her decision, determined to put Stephen out of her life. Fate had decreed otherwise, drawing her back into the orbit of his life.

The Southern Cross had rotated in the sky in the quiet hours past midnight when the carriage turned onto a side road. A moment later, following the directions that Deirdre had given him, the coachman turned in and stopped at a large house. As she stepped out of the carriage and went to the house, Deirdre wondered how she would be received, given the circumstances of her relationship with Stephen and the late hour for making calls.

It was different from anything she expected. A moment after tapping the door knocker, Deirdre saw the glow of a lamp through the fanlight, then the door opened. In her nightgown and with her graying hair tousled from bed,

Stephanie Brendell was gracefully lovely. Most of all, she was strikingly similar to Stephen, an older, feminine version of her son.

Her smile was the same, a radiance with the emotional effect of a caress. "Deirdre Kerrick!" she exclaimed happily. "What a delight this is!"

Deirdre found herself exchanging a spontaneous hug and kiss with Stephanie, just as though they had long been close friends, and they both laughed in pleasure as well as surprise at their sudden warm response to each other. "I'm sorry for calling at this unconscionable hour," Deirdre apologized, collecting her thoughts. "It's most inconsiderate, but I—"

"Nonsense," Stephanie interrupted affectionately. "I'm often awakened at night, and I only wish it was always for such an extraordinary pleasure. I'll prepare refreshments for you and your coachman."

"That's very kind of you, but I must decline," Deirdre told her. "I must return to Sydney just as soon as possible."

"Then let's at least sit in the parlor while we talk," Stephanie said, gathering up the lamp from the entry table and taking Deirdre's hand. "I intend to make the most of the occasion, Deirdre."

They stepped into the parlor and seated themselves on a couch, and Deirdre explained the purpose of her visit, relating what Jeremy had said. Stephanie's smile was replaced by a somber expression as she listened, then she said, "I'm sure Stephen is still in Bourke. Typhoid patients remain infectious even after they begin recovering, and he'll stay with them for a time. As to whether or not he would attempt to treat Jeremy's son. . . ." Her voice fading, she hesitated, then continued: "Ever since I met your mother years ago, I've felt certain that our destinies are connected in some way. Does that sound like a tale of ghosts and goblins to you?"

Deirdre shook her head, readily believing that Stephanie

was exceptionally intuitive. The woman had an air about her of insights far more profound than those from rational thought, which was one of the reasons she was so intriguing. "No, certainly not," Deirdre responded. "Those who think their lives are governed only by what they can detect with their physical senses lack a belief in God and have never traveled in the outback."

"That is why I can't offer an opinion on what Stephen would do," Stephanie summed up. "Ordinarily, I don't believe he would attempt to treat perityphlitic abscess. In this instance, however, I don't know."

"But the primary question has been answered," Deirdre observed, standing. "Stephen is in Bourke, so Jeremy can go there and talk with him."

Stephanie stood, picking up the lamp. "To say that I've enjoyed meeting you hardly touches upon the matter," she remarked as they stepped back to the entry. "I hope that you and I will see each other often in the future."

"And I," Deirdre assured her emphatically. "Our meeting has been most unusual, but more enjoyable by far. I regret that I'm so rushed now, but you can be certain that I'll visit again soon and then very often."

The smile that was poignantly reminiscent of Stephen wreathed his mother's features. Deirdre exchanged a hug and kiss with her, then went out to the carriage and stepped into it. As it turned toward the road, a glow of contentment suffused her in the aftermath of talking with Stephanie.

Then, her pleasure fading, she contemplated a fact that had occurred to her during the conversation: Stephen would obviously do more for her than for Jeremy. At the very least, if she asked him he would agree to travel to Tibooburra Station and examine Christopher himself.

Weighing whether or not to accompany Jeremy, Deirdre searched within herself to determine if her yearning to see Stephen again was a factor in her feelings. All the evidence was to the contrary. She was keenly aware that it would only increase her torment once she was separated from him again.

She realized that a disadvantage in her going to Bourke lay in the fact that time was crucial, and Jeremy could travel faster alone. Moreover, her personal inclination was to avoid an active role in what threatened to be a tragedy. But set firmly against that impulse of weakness were her responsibilities toward Christopher and the rest of the family.

In the end, the determining factor was her personality, her predisposition to do anything rather than nothing. It had brought on worse problems at times, but she had always preferred that to being controlled by events. She decided to go to Bourke, and now that she had chosen a course of action, her doubts faded into unwavering resolve to fulfill her decision.

The sun was well above the horizon by the time Deirdre finished her arrangements to be absent from Sydney and arrived at Morton's house. Jeremy, at breakfast with Morton and Julia, was himself again—neat, shaven, and rested. He was also as alert as usual, and though she had left her baggage outside at the stables, Deirdre saw his pale blue eyes take due notice of her workaday dungaree dress the moment she stepped into the dining room.

As she related her conversation with Stephanie, Deirdre filled a plate at the buffet and then sat down at the table. "Very well," Jeremy said when she finished, "I'll go to Bourke and talk with Stephen." Then he pointed a finger at Deirdre: "And you're not going with me."

The argument that Deirdre had expected began, and it continued for several minutes. The dispute ranged over the variety of reasons that she had anticipated, but Jeremy kept returning to the fact that time was critically important, which she countered by explaining that she could be more persuasive with Stephen. "Do you take me for a poddy?" Jeremy finally scoffed. "I can be as persuasive as needs must. If it appears to me that he can help my son, he'll go to Tibooburra Station whether he wants to or not."

"Then you're taking Stephen Brendell for a poddy," she shot back, "and you'll come up a shilling short on a six-penny wager."

"Deirdre is quite right, Jeremy," Morton chimed in. "Going athwart of Stephen Brendell would be a mistake. Any amount of haste is useless if you fail your purpose when you get there, isn't it?"

Jeremy pondered for a moment, then gave up with a resigned shrug. "I'll take you with me, then," he relented grudgingly, "but I don't intend to tarry along the way. You'd best have as much sand in your craw and be able to travel as well as your mother, Deirdre."

"As the boss cockie, you'd best be able to stay in the lead," she retorted. "I'm my mother's daughter, and as much a Kerrick as you."

Jeremy grumbled that she was as stubborn as any of the family, Morton and Julia laughing in agreement. Through with breakfast, Jeremy and Morton left to see to the horses. Deirdre finished hers, talking with Julia, then they went out to the stables.

Morton tried to be of assistance while the groom and stableboy helped Jeremy saddle two horses and load a pack on a third, Deirdre's baggage among the supplies and camping equipment. When they finished, she exchanged hugs and kisses with Morton and Julia, then grabbed the halter rope on the packhorse and climbed up on her saddle. Jeremy made his farewells and stepped into his saddle, leading the way down the drive.

Instead of crossing the city toward Parramatta Road, Jeremy took a route through the western outskirts of the city to avoid the traffic on the main road. Deirdre followed him through the streets, knowing the journey would be difficult for her at first. Already tired from lack of sleep the night before, she was also unaccustomed to riding horseback.

When they reached the lightly traveled back roads west of the city, Jeremy increased the pace to a fast canter, and

Deirdre's misery began. Her weariness from the sleepless night turned into grinding fatigue, while the hard, steady pace made her legs and back ache. Shortly after midday, they reached a narrow road leading up the Nepean River toward Penrith. After what seemed a very long time to her, she gazed ahead and saw the main road that stretched between Parramatta and Bathurst.

At its intersection with the river road was the thick forest where she had spent happy hours with Stephen. Jeremy slowed to a walk when they passed the forest, and Deirdre sighed in relief as she tried to find a position on her sidesaddle to ease the pain in her back and legs. The horses panted heavily from the fast pace, crossing the main road through afternoon traffic, then they plodded down the short road leading into Penrith.

A groom sitting in front of the stables at the Nepean Inn leaped to his feet as Jeremy and Deirdre turned in off the street. "Jeremy Kerrick!" he shouted exuberantly. "G'day, Jeremy!" He turned to a stableboy. "Go tell the innkeeper that Jeremy Kerrick is here."

The boy raced away, other grooms came out, and then the innkeeper ran from the inn, all of them greeting Jeremy with hearty, admiring warmth. They spoke to Deirdre as well, but her nephew was known and highly respected as a man of the outback. Deirdre was thankful that their attention was diverted as she climbed down from her saddle with care to keep from falling and making a fool of herself. Then she sat down on a bench.

Cook's helpers rushed from the inn with trays laid out with roast pork and vegetables, bread, and pannikins of tea. Jeremy talked with the innkeeper about his journey while he and Deirdre ate, and the grooms transferred the saddles and pack to fresh horses. The respite for Deirdre was very brief, the innkeeper shrugging off Jeremy's thanks as he mounted up and she wearily climbed up to her saddle. Then they rode away.

The horses pounded across the bridge over the river, then up the road through the Emu Plains. By the time Deirdre and Jeremy reached the foothills, sunset had shrouded the mountains in deep shadows. The horses climbed the slopes at a walk and then galloped downhill and on level stretches, the broken pace even more uncomfortable for Deirdre than a steady fast gait.

After dusk, the road wound up one steep slope after another in the moonlight, the horses finally settling down to a plodding stride. Deirdre slumped on her saddle, numb with fatigue, and she slept for a few minutes at a time. She woke when rocks clattered or her horse took a faltering step on the rutted road, then she fell asleep again.

When she woke after a longer nap, the darkness was thickened by clouds at the high altitude, the mist clammy against her face. Jeremy was a dark form in the gloom, taking her reins to lead her horse. "There are sheer drops at the edge of the road ahead," he explained, turning off the road into trees. "Between the darkness and these clouds, it would be easy to stumble over one of those drops, so we'll camp until daybreak."

A short distance from the road, he dismounted and kindled a fire. Deirdre climbed down from her saddle, the firelight illuminating a glade among the trees, and a brook splashed over rocks a few yards away. She wondered if Jeremy had stopped so she could rest, but she was too weary to raise the question with him. After helping him unsaddle the horses, she snuggled in her blanket beside the fire and immediately fell asleep.

A clatter of cooking utensils woke Deirdre, and she opened her eyes to dawn light that was thin and milky through the clouds. Jeremy knelt on the other side of the fire, placing a pan and billys on the coals. Sharp pain stabbed in Deirdre's sore, stiff legs and back when she sat up, but she endured it, forcing herself to move normally. Jeremy spoke to her cheerfully, and she replied in the same tone as she stepped toward the brook.

After washing her hands and face, Deirdre returned to the fire and set about helping prepare the porridge and tea. "You found this place to camp last night," she pointed out, "so you could have avoided dangerous places on the road. You don't have to stop so I can rest, Jeremy."

"It was for that, but also another reason," he told her. "Coming in from the station one day, I was in too much of a rush and wasn't watching what I was doing, and I was almost bitten by a death adder."

Deirdre paused in stirring the porridge, shaking her head in disapproval. "That was too much of a rush by far," she commented.

"Yes, it was," he agreed, "so we'll travel at a fast but sensible pace. In any event, Jarboe Charlie once told me that a hunter can be in such a hurry after a possum that he'll miss seeing a 'roo."

Deirdre smiled, familiar with his fondness for quoting his Aborigine companion during his years in the far outback. She divided the porridge between their tin plates, and Jeremy moved the billys off the fire and sprinkled tea into them. They ate breakfast quickly, then Deirdre washed the dishes in the brook while Jeremy took the hobbles off the horses and saddled them.

The sun was a bright disc in the clouds when they set out, passing drays and wagons, other riders, and prospectors on foot. They crossed the crest of the mountain range and rode down the western slopes, leaving the clouds behind, and Deirdre's discomfort reached a new intensity. Her horse's gait was stiff and awkward with the road falling steeply away in front of it, making each pace the horse took a jarring impact.

Gritting her teeth, Deirdre endured the ordeal and told herself that eventually it had to end. That prospect seemed very distant while they were in the foothills and the pace was broken again, with the horses plodding up the rises and then galloping down slopes and on level stretches. At last they reached the straight, level road leading into Bathurst, and Jeremy slowed to a walk in the congested traffic at the outskirts of the town.

The hard, driving pace since early morning had covered the miles swiftly, the sun barely at its zenith. It beamed down with torrid intensity on the late summer day in February, and the street through the town teemed with midday activity. Then the business district was left behind and the traffic thinned out in the western outskirts of the town, where Deirdre and Jeremy turned in off the street at the Bellwether Inn.

Their reception was even more boisterous than at Penrith, for several travelers were at the stables and were delighted to see Jeremy. They and the grooms greeted him in a chorus of happy shouts, a stableboy running to fetch the innkeeper. In the midst of the hubbub, Deirdre painfully dismounted and sat down on a bale of hay at the door of the stables.

The innkeeper came out, followed by cook's helpers bringing mutton stew, damper, and tea. The thick, meaty stew restored Deirdre's energy to an extent, and she listened to the conversation around Jeremy while she ate. A groom had told the innkeeper that Jeremy had stopped in three nights before, pausing only long enough to hastily saddle a fresh horse. The innkeeper had been waiting to ask Jeremy the purpose of his journey, and Jeremy explained about his son's illness that only Dr. Brendell could possibly treat.

"Stephen Brendell?" the innkeeper exclaimed when Jeremy finished. "He spent the night here on his way north, Jeremy. In my best room and at no harm to his purse, what's more. The groom could have told you that, and you bagged your head when you didn't tell him what you were about."

"I certainly did, and I've wasted days," Jeremy agreed ruefully, then he glanced over at Deirdre: "I was in such a hurry while chasing after a possum that I missed seeing a 'roo."

Deirdre smiled sympathetically, knowing that the self-recrimination he felt was far greater than he revealed. The conversation continued, Jeremy talking with the men about the northward journey. Home paddocks were so far apart that obtaining fresh horses daily would be difficult, necessitating a slower pace than he liked, but he and the men agreed that weather and other factors would be just as important in how long the journey would take.

By the time the grooms transferred the saddles and pack to fresh horses, Deirdre and Jeremy had finished their hasty tiffin. Clenching her teeth, she forced herself to move normally and climbed up on her saddle. As she and Jeremy rode away amid shouts of well wishes from the men, she pondered the conversation about Stephen's stay at the inn, the implications of how events had unfolded seeming significant to her.

During his journey to Sydney, she reflected, circumstances had set the time when Jeremy reached the inn. His intent had been to travel as rapidly as possible, but chance had been important in how fast he actually traveled. Horses stronger or weaker than average, incidents that had made him lose or gain minutes here and there, and innumerable other conditions beyond his control had determined when he arrived at Bathurst.

If chance had so dictated, he would have arrived during daytime, when many people were about. He would have learned that Stephen was in Bourke, then gone there himself. Instead, he had arrived at night and rode on to Sydney, setting in motion events that had involved her. Deirdre wondered if going to Bourke had actually been her own decision, or if she had been guided by fate into going there and meeting with Stephen.

A steady canter on the track leading north from Bathurst was less strenuous for Deirdre than the faster pace of before, allowing her to relax on her saddle. Traveling across the rolling terrain was also much easier than the trip through the rugged mountains, but most of all, her reaction to the setting made the journey less of an ordeal for her.

Though she had lived in Sydney most of her life, she had been born in the outback. Consciously as well as at a deep emotional level, she had a sense of belonging and an all-embracing knowledge that it was her place of origin. When the vast, majestic sweep of landscape opened out around her, her attitude to her surroundings changed. In place of her expectation of comfort and security of the city, she accepted the harsh, austere nature of life in the outback. As part of the hardships that the land imposed, her discomfort was no less acute, but it was easier to endure.

Her robustly healthy constitution also asserted itself, along with her impatience toward any weakness within herself. When she and Jeremy stopped for the night at dusk, she ignored the protests of pain from her aching muscles and bustled about, doing more than her share of camp chores. After a large dinner and hours of sound sleep, she was less stiff and sore the next morning, beginning to adjust to the rigors of the journey.

Shortly after they set out, they passed a track leading back to a home paddock. The horses were still relatively fresh, and exchanging them would be a waste of time that could be better used for traveling, but Jeremy speculated that the animals would probably be very weary before the next opportunity came to obtain fresh ones. His prediction proved to be true, the hours passing and the horses' energy flagging from the steady canter in the intense heat, and the next track to a home paddock was still somewhere ahead.

With fatigue and discomfort no longer a distraction, the journey became a more meaningful experience for Deirdre. It was similar to her trips of years before to photograph scenery in the outback, but there was a distinct difference. On those occasions, her mother had insisted that she be escorted by stockmen and jackaroos from the station, and the bustle and conversation of others had been constantly around her. Accompanied only by Jeremy, she had a much closer contact with her surroundings.

Her impressions were similar to before, but incomparably more intense. The sheer size of the outback defied understanding, its elastic horizons always stretching farther ahead. The rolling terrain appeared to go on endlessly, the immense, parched landscape on a scale too vast to comprehend. Its eerily strange character was also more evident now, conveying a sense of primal wisdom.

Deirdre felt diminished by the landscape, dwarfed to insignificance, while her entire lifespan was less than an instant on its timeless calendar. From that perspective, Deirdre knew that somehow she should have stopped her sister-in-law from wandering aimlessly between Sydney and Tibooburra Station. To minds far more rational than Catherine's had been, it would be logical to choose suicide over a life that was only emotional torment and no more meaningful than a mote glinting momentarily in the sunlight.

The horses were barely able to maintain a canter at sunset, when Deirdre and Jeremy stopped for the night. They unsaddled and hobbled the horses, speculating hopefully that they would be able to obtain fresh ones early the next day. After the other camp chores were done, Deirdre made tea in the billys and put dried beef and vegetables in a pot to boil while Jeremy mixed flour, salt, and water in a pan to make damper.

Darkness closed in around the campfire, Deirdre chatting with Jeremy as they prepared and then ate dinner. The subject of his walkabout of several years before came up, and the discussion gave her a different view of it. She had always believed that a walkabout was a journey that ended at a destination, but she learned that it was much more complex.

"A walkabout can be many things physically," he explained. "It needn't necessarily involve a journey. It's a search for something to make oneself complete, and it ends with a state of mind rather than at a place."

"Can anyone go on a walkabout, then?" Deirdre asked.

"Yes, anyone at all," he replied. "Aborigines have made it a customary practice, and we'd do well to be as concerned as they are with things of the spirit. A carpenter who was meant to be a sailor, or a housewife whose destiny was to be a business owner, will be unhappy until they search for and find their right places in life. That would be their walkabout, which is different for everyone and yet the same in some ways."

The subject intriguing her, Deirdre continued exploring it with Jeremy for a time. It was only after she was lying beside the fire in her blanket and awaiting sleep that she thought about applying what Jeremy had said concerning walkabouts to herself. She was unhappy without Stephen, and events involving them could be construed as indications that they were destined to be together. Then she dismissed the train of thought, reflecting that wishful thinking could readily arrange random circumstances into seemingly significant patterns.

The next morning, the sun was still inching up the eastern quadrant of the sky when Deirdre and Jeremy came to a track leading to a home paddock and turned onto it. A short time later, the excitement created by their arrival at the home paddock changed into disappointment when Jeremy explained the purpose of their journey. The owners, a middle-aged couple named Ben and Amy Givens, nodded in resigned understanding.

"Aye, you must get to that doctor as soon as you can," Ben agreed. "You have our heartfelt hopes that he will speedily put your son on the improve, which I'm sure he will. You're welcome to fresh horses, and I only wish we could do more for you." He turned to the employees who were crowding about and pointed: "You and you, fetch three of the best horses."

Two stockmen ran to get the horses and hurry back with them, wanting to hear all of the conversation. Meanwhile, Ben and Amy made the most of their limited opportunity to gather information for discussions to while away the evening hours. They plied Jeremy and Deirdre with questions about the family and station, and about the Garrity family and Wayamba Station.

After the saddles and pack were transferred to fresh horses, Deirdre and Jeremy made their farewells and rode back to the track. They resumed the steady canter up the track, the temperature rising higher than usual during early afternoon. The torrid air was perfectly still, with no hint of a breeze to stir the drooping eucalypt leaves, or to drive away the flies.

Deirdre fanned the flies away, the arid landscape baking under the searing glare of the sun. The sweltering heat of midafternoon was like a stifling blanket, and the horses sweated heavily as they maintained their pace. Deirdre looked forward to a late afternoon breeze to bring relief from the heat, but late afternoon came without a stir in the air.

The air remained still and sultry at sunset, when they stopped for the night. Jeremy commented that if the heat failed to subside, it could bring weather that would delay them. It gave no indication of easing as the evening wore on, and Deirdre used her blanket as a pallet instead of pulling it around herself when she lay down beside the fire to sleep.

The heat wave continued the next day, the temperature rising with the sun. A steely quiet settled by midday, animals and birds sheltering in the shade, and the horses were tiring rapidly. The occasional swagmen on the track were remaining at creeks and billabongs, and they called out and waved as Deirdre and Jeremy passed. At midafternoon, they came to a track leading to a home paddock and turned onto it to obtain fresh horses.

The track wound through hills that had been scabbed by grassfires, an odor of smoke still lingering in the breathlessly hot air. The home paddock was several miles back from the main track, but when it came into view, it was an island of greenery in its parched surroundings. The buildings were modest, but they were in a valley where two creeks watered flourishing vegetable gardens, orchards, and acres of lush grass.

The welcome that Deirdre and Jeremy met with was equal to the inviting atmosphere of the place, stockmen and jackaroos greeting them exuberantly. A woman came out of the house and a man out of a storage building, and they beamed with delight as they introduced themselves as the owners. A handsome couple in their forties, they were Thomas and Abigail Haynes.

Thomas had been injured and was getting about on crutches made from tree forks. "I had a barney with a wild boar," he explained, laughing. "He lost, but I'm still not sure whether I won."

"You're alive," Jeremy pointed out. "That's winning by my lights, and it was the other way about for my grandfather and uncle."

"Aye, we know about that," Thomas said, "and much else about your family and Tibooburra Station that we'd enjoy discussing with you. We're back to taws for some necessities, but we're overrun with horses and we've enough tucker to field an army. We'll provide fresh horses and a purler of a dinner, and we'd be most grateful if you'd stop for the night."

The remaining daylight was barely more than enough to return to the track, and Jeremy nodded, agreeing to stay. The employees raised a cheer, gathering around the horses to unsaddle them and take the pack into the house. Deirdre had noted the evidence of what Thomas had said about the lack of some necessities, his and the others' clothes the worse for wear. When she went inside and Abigail showed her to a room that children were vacating, Deirdre saw that the house was spotless but spartan.

Thomas's remark about dinner was also true, for it was a feast. Abigail had prepared dinner for her family in such a lavish quantity that was ample for guests, with food left over. A welcome change from the hasty meals on the track, it was delicious, the roasted leg of lamb tender and juicy, and the fresh garden vegetables seasoned to perfection.

After the meal, Deirdre and the others went out to the veranda where the stockmen and jackaroos had gathered. While much of the talk was about Tibooburra Station and the family, Thomas and Abigail related events at their station, revealing the reasons for their financial difficulties.

The damage to the paddocks from grassfires had been evident, and the attack by the wild boar had disabled Thomas for several months. There had been other misfortunes as well, including floods, drought, and invasion of dingoes, and disease among the sheep. Despite all that, Thomas and Abigail were optimistically looking forward to rebuilding their flocks.

"Abby and I take things as they come," Thomas said, "since things persist in coming so often, whether or not they are wanted."

The jocular remark brought laughter from everyone, Deirdre joining in, but it impressed her as far more than merely an amusing comment. It was an apt description of the unending struggle that was the way of life in the outback. In addition, it reflected the resilient, tenacious nature of those who lived at remote, isolated sheep stations, the outback breed.

It also denoted their courage, their acceptance of risks in order to have the life they wanted for themselves, for they could seek safety in the cities if they chose. That thought led to a question which kept Deirdre awake long after the conversation ended and she went to bed: In deciding not to marry Stephen, she wondered if she had simply chosen the safety of her solitary life over the risks involved in a blissfully happy life with him.

The question remained at the forefront of her thoughts when she and Jeremy returned to the track the next morning.

It was another sweltering day, the temperature soaring during the forenoon, but there was something more. The torridly hot, still day had an oppressive atmosphere, a sense of powerful forces gathering strength in preparation to unleash themselves.

Deirdre took only passing notice when Jeremy mentioned the likelihood of a change for the worse in the weather. She was completely absorbed in her thoughts, her own storm brewing within her. Judgment and principles had guided her life, and she had never allowed herself to be ruled by fear. But it seemed possible that without realizing it, she may have arrived at her decision not to marry Stephen through cowardice, not judgment.

During early afternoon, Deirdre's attention was forcibly drawn to her surroundings while she and Jeremy were riding up a hill. An abrupt burst of wind shattered the stillness, stirring up leaves and dust, and she looked around in surprise. "You were right about a change in the weather, Jeremy," she called. "If this persists, we'll have a dust storm."

"We're going to have one, and it'll last for hours," he replied over his shoulder. "Hours that would take us miles up the track."

Having experienced dust storms and learned the first defense against them, Deirdre took out her handkerchief and dampened it with water from her canteen. She tied it over her mouth and nose, ducking her head in the swirling dust as she and Jeremy reached the crest of the hill in the teeth of another gust. When the wind passed, she looked ahead.

Puffs of wind sweeping from the north stirred up dust, but she could see the approaching dust storm at a distance through the haze. It looked like a massive tidal wave rushing toward a shore, seeming more solid than dust, and its lower edge boiled with the violent force of the wind that was driving it across the terrain. It towered high into the air, obscuring the sky, and reached from the eastern to the western horizon.

Jeremy dismounted, tying his dampened handkerchief over his mouth and nose, then took a rope from his saddle and stepped back to Deirdre's horse. "I don't see anyplace near here that would do for a shelter," he said, fastening the rope to her horse's bridle. "We'll go on up the track until we find one. Hopefully, the storm will pass within a few hours."

He returned to his horse, and they rode down the hill and on up the track through the dust from increasingly strong gusts. The leading edge of the dust storm approached swiftly, darkening the day to twilight.

It struck in a blinding swirl of dust and buffeting wind that thrashed the trees wildly, ripping leaves and branches from them. The horses slowed to a walk, and Deirdre huddled down on her saddle as she shielded her eyes with a hand and peered around. Everything farther away than her horse's head blended into formless, murky shadows in the thick cloud of dust, but somehow Jeremy was able to see well enough to stay on the track.

Typical of natural forces in the outback, the dust storm seemed something more than an atmospheric event, hurling itself at the landscape with vindictive fury. The howling wind continued with unabated force, whipping leaves and branches past Deirdre. Every few minutes, her handkerchief began drying, and a powdery smell of dust seeped through it. She opened her canteen, poured water into her hand, and dashed it onto the handkerchief.

When she glimpsed a tree a few feet away, Deirdre realized that they had turned off the track. Her horse pushed through brush, following the rope attached to its bridle, then went down a steep slope. Deirdre saw that Jeremy had found his way to a donga, a deep gully, and it was lined with large trees that further broke the force of the wind.

The donga was like a quiet backwater at the edge of a violent riptide, but thick dust and eddies from the gale that was tearing at the tops of the trees found their way down into it. Deirdre helped unsaddle the horses, still barely able to see in the gloom, and hobbled the animals while Jeremy constructed a hut from fallen limbs and slabs of bark the trees had shed. He found a large slab to use as a door, then pulled it over the opening at the front of the hut after he and Deirdre crawled inside it.

The hut was in total darkness and crowded with the saddles and pack, but it was a secure haven from the storm. Deirdre searched around and found her canteen, and poured water onto her handkerchief. She washed the dust off her face, commenting in relief on being out of the storm. Jeremy agreed absently, his voice conveying his intense regret over the delay.

"Being stopped like this is troublesome," Deirdre acknowledged, "but no other man could equal what you've done so far for your son."

"That means nothing if I fail," Jeremy replied tersely.

Deirdre responded by telling him that he was human, with limits on what he could do, and he made another brief, dismissive remark. The basis for her decision about marrying Stephen still tugged strongly at Deirdre's thoughts, but she put it aside. She continued talking with Jeremy, trying to lift his spirits and assure him that he was doing everything possible. He remained moody and remorseful, but he discussed the subject with her.

"Much of the time, I worry about Fiona," he explained. "I worry about not succeeding in doing everything possible for our son."

The statements confused Deirdre as to the specific reason for his troubled feelings, and he seemed reluctant to be candid on the issue. She searched for a response to draw him out, then offered, "Your concern for Fiona is a reflection of your love for her."

"It's more than love," Jeremy told her. "Fiona is more precious to me than life itself. Grandmother has never said it openly, but she feels that Fiona and I are too completely involved with each other."

"Mother is totally devoted to the family, without reserve

or restraint, but only to the family as a whole," Deirdre observed. "Her feelings for each of us as individuals are less extreme. She would be grief-stricken if one of us died, as she was when Father and Jonathan were killed, but her life would go on. Catherine's did not. But whatever Mother's concerns about you and Fiona may be, you can be certain they arise through love."

"That's true," Jeremy agreed. "The family is her purpose in life, and none of us can ever doubt her love. For myself, I don't know if it's possible to love someone too much, but I can't imagine life without Fiona. From the first moment we met, we've known that we were meant for each other."

Pondering what had been said, Deirdre drew a conclusion as to the key issue that was troubling Jeremy, and she found comments to nudge the conversation closer to it. He continued talking in a soft, reflective voice that was barely a whisper over the sounds of the storm, and at length the discussion reached the central point that bothered him. It was what Deirdre had suspected: His concern for Fiona's emotional state was at least comparable with that for his son's life, and he felt guilty about it.

Deirdre considered it ample reason for guilt, and she shared her mother's opinion about Jeremy and Fiona. Their love seemed obsessive, but at the same time, she knew that their relationship was entirely their affair, and she had no right to meddle in it. Her only involvement, arising from her deep affection for Jeremy, was to ease his guilt if possible. She began talking with him about it, taking the approach that his feelings resulted from his adoring love for Fiona, not from any lack of love for his son.

During the conversation, with the storm continuing, the dim, gray daylight that found its way through cracks in the bark on the hut faded. Deirdre opened the pack, and she and Jeremy made their dinner on cheese and ship biscuit while they talked. When the discussion ended, she was unsure if she had relieved his guilt or if he had simply needed to talk with her about his feelings, but in either case he was evidently content.

They unrolled their blankets and lay down, and Jeremy fell asleep moments later, his breathing slow and deep. Deirdre gazed up into the darkness, listening to the dust storm outside while an emotional storm raged furiously within her. Her decisions had always been articles of faith with herself, mileposts in the path of life that had been behind her and never revisited. However, it had become obvious to her that events of the past days compelled her to reconsider her decision not to marry Stephen.

One event was a change in her surroundings, being in the outback. Fundamental truths were more apparent in the elemental outback, and a fallacy in her reasoning of before was glaringly evident. How matters would stand between her and Stephen in the future had been the major consideration, but now it was of little importance. In the harsh, unforgiving outback, the uncertainty of life itself was graphically evident, and it was too much to assume that she would even be alive ten or twenty years hence.

Her thoughts ranged over her unusual, immediate friendship with Stephanie, then the chance circumstances that had led Jeremy to Sydney instead of taking him to Bourke. Stephanie believed that the Brendell and Kerrick families were linked by fate, and Deirdre found it plausible. It also seemed entirely believable that events of the past days which had guided her toward Bourke had been more than coincidental.

The point as to whether her decision about Stephen had been motivated by cowardice was no longer a question in her mind, but an inescapable fact. It had been a denial of her bloodlines, the antithesis of her parents' courage in risking everything to establish Tibooburra Station years before in an untracked wilderness. It had been a surrender to fear, a choice of the security of a lonely, colorless, but safe life over the risks involved in striving to keep intact a life of happiness beyond her wildest dreams.

While she gazed up into the darkness and pondered, the analysis of her decision awakened the hopeful voice of her love. A yearning wail across the chasm between heart and mind, the voice became more gleeful as the hours passed and her thoughts led to conclusions that narrowed the rift between her emotions and logic. Then, late in the night, Deirdre realized that the wind had died. She was no longer gazing up into darkness, but at moonbeams gleaming through cracks in the bark on the hut. The storm had ended.

Moving quietly to avoid waking Jeremy, Deirdre lifted the bark away from the opening at the front of the hut and crawled outside. The air was refreshingly cool, the temperature normal for nighttime once again, and the horses were grazing peacefully a few yards away. The only lingering effects of the storm that she could see in the moonlight were broken tree limbs that would slough away and fall to the ground to nourish new growth.

She climbed out of the donga, then up a hill overlooking it. The mournful wailing of dingoes in the distance, chirping of insects, and soft hooting of owls gave the night a velvet texture. The sounds and atmosphere brought back her childhood at Tibooburra Station in a flood of memories.

The top of the hill was covered with low brush, nothing obstructing her vision. When she reached the crest, the landscape opened out around her under the pale light of the moon, its vast canopy of stars sparkling with incredible brilliance. It seemed as large as all eternity, then beyond.

Deirdre looked out at the moonlit scene and reflected that for her, this journey matched Jeremy's definition of a walkabout. When she left Sydney, her life had been incomplete and burdened with sorrow. Events had turned the journey into an odyssey within herself, guiding her toward her destiny. Now she intended to join the one whom she belonged with and marry him, making her life complete. She was deliriously happy.

*   *   *

Stephen woke with his hands clutching at the air above his cot. An instant after waking, his exultant joy was crushed by disappointment and sorrow. He realized that he had been only dreaming once again.

This time, however, the dream had been different. Each time before, Deirdre had raced away and reached back entreatingly while he vainly tried to run fast enough to catch her. This time he had grasped her hands.

Knowing he would be unable to fall asleep again, Stephen threw his blanket aside and rose from the cot. He dressed, then left the small room and made his way between the cots in the warehouse in the dim light of lanterns in the corners, going out to the porch.

Stephen stood on the porch and gazed out at the silvery sheen of the river in the moonlight, thinking about the dream. The fact that he had grasped her soft, warm hands created a fervent hope within him. He tried to dismiss it, but it remained vibrantly alive.

Even though it was illogical, he felt that the dream was meaningful. When he left Bourke within the next few days, he had intended to go to Brisbane and work at the hospital there for a time. But now a yearning urge deep within him tugged him toward the south, the direction of Sydney, and it was another feeling that he was unable to dismiss as wishful thinking.

Chapter Twenty-Three

"They're the only dunnocks we've ever had here," one of the men observed. "It takes a man of the outback to mob dunnocks and fetch them in out of the never-never. No one else could do it."

"No one else could stay alive out there," the other man added. "But the dunnocks looked like ordinary cattle aside from being a bit shaggy."

"We let them graze their fill," Jeremy explained. "All cattle will be spindling if they're driven too fast and not grazed enough."

The men agreed and continued reminiscing about herds of wild cattle they had bought from Jeremy several years before, happy to see him again. Livestock dealers, they had been dickering with the owner of a small herd of some twenty cattle when Deirdre and Jeremy had arrived at a broad, dusty mustering grounds for livestock on the outskirts of Bourke. The owner of the cattle stood at one side, silently gazing at Jeremy in awe.

Having observed the courtesy of chatting for a few minutes, Jeremy began drawing the conversation to a close. "As I mentioned," he said, "we've come from Sydney to see Dr. Stephen Brendell. He's still in town, then?"

"Aye, he is," one of the stock dealers replied. "You'll find him at the waterfront, in a warehouse being used as a hospital. He was a godsend, because he saved scores of lives here."

"And everyone's livelihood as well," the other man put in. "He ended the epidemic in time for the shipping season. If he hadn't, everyone in town would have been without work and wages."

"I'm very pleased for you," Jeremy said, gathering his reins and turning his horse. "I enjoyed seeing you again and talking with you."

The stock dealers replied in farewell, then turned back to the owner of the herd as Jeremy and Deirdre rode away. At the edge of the mustering grounds, Jeremy turned onto a street leading into the town. Deirdre followed him, seething with excited anticipation of seeing Stephen again.

More than ever, it seemed that fate had guided her, for events had transpired to put her at best advantage to meet Stephen. The previous evening, when Jeremy had been looking for a place to camp, they had come to a track leading to a home paddock. She had been able to scrub away the dust from the journey in the station bathhouse, then take out an attractive dress in blue dimity from her baggage. The last of the journey had been a comfortable ride, the day still only moderately warm in midafternoon.

The street led into a frontage street at the river, piers on one side of it and warehouses on the other. Deirdre saw Stephen on a warehouse porch down the street, talking with another man in a hospital smock. His back was turned and he was some two hundred yards away, but she knew she would have recognized him immediately at even a far greater distance.

Her heart pounded furiously as she and Jeremy rode

down the street, passing a single large riverboat at the
piers. Stephen turned, logically because he heard the horses,
but Deirdre preferred to think it was through some inner
awareness of her. He froze for an instant, then rushed
down the porch steps and walked up the street with long,
quick strides.

When the distance closed to a few yards, Jeremy leaped
down from his saddle. "Dr. Brendell?" he said, stepping to
Stephen. "I'm Jeremy Kerrick, and I've come a long way
to find you."

Stephen was reluctant to take his eyes from Deirdre, his
gaze lingering on her a moment longer, then he turned to
Jeremy. "Please call me Stephen, and I'm delighted to
meet you, Jeremy," he responded. "I might also say at
last, because I've heard about you all of my life."

Deirdre dismounted and stepped toward them, struggling
to contain her feelings, and she saw another reason for joy.
She had earnestly hoped that Stephen and Jeremy would be
friends, and it was evident that they immediately liked each
other. Stephen turned to her, that special, captivating smile
he shared with his mother on his features. Animated with
radiant happiness, his smile reached within Deirdre and
unlocked a glowing warmth.

"Nothing else on earth could have given me as much
pleasure as seeing you again, Deirdre," he told her. "From
your appearance, it strains belief that you've just finished
traveling up the track."

"Had you but seen me yesterday it wouldn't," she replied,
striving for a light tone. "I'm more than pleased to see you
again, Stephen."

Silence fell, Stephen gazing at her and his eyes searching her face, feeding a hunger within himself. Deirdre
noticed that Jeremy glanced back and forth between them,
suddenly understanding that far more than friendship was
involved. Stephen then turned back to Jeremy, who began
talking about his son's illness, but he was interrupted a
moment later.

The man who had been on the warehouse porch with Stephen, an older, bearded doctor, had followed him. Stephen introduced him as Dr. William Brodie, and he exchanged greetings with Deirdre and Jeremy, amiably telling them that everyone called him Doctor Bill. Jeremy finished explaining about his son's illness, Stephen and Doctor Bill listening gravely.

Their reaction was disheartening, Stephen frowning in deep thought and Doctor Bill shaking his head sadly and muttering in sympathy. Deirdre felt that it was time for her to speak up. "I understand that the epidemic here is at an end, Stephen," she said. "Will you go to Tibooburra Station with us and examine Christopher yourself?"

"Yes, of course," he replied. "In fact, I was going to suggest that, because it's never amiss to have a second opinion on serious cases. Jeremy, when Oliver came to the station to see your son, did he take a drop of blood from your son's finger and examine it with a microscope?"

"No, he didn't," Jeremy replied. "He didn't bring his microscope with him. He could have made a mistake, then, couldn't he?"

"It's possible," Stephen acknowledged cautiously. "He's a fine doctor, but the only absolutely positive test for perityphlitic abscess is to examine a blood sample. Failing that, there are other and less serious conditions that will sometimes appear to be that one."

"Yes, that's true," Doctor Bill agreed, his attitude less somber. "Particularly with children. I've had a couple of young patients who had severe colic, and at first I was sure it was perityphlitic abscess."

"Christopher is only five years old, and he could very well be the same," Jeremy pointed out eagerly. "When can you leave, Stephen?"

"At once, more or less," Stephen told him, then he turned to Doctor Bill: "I believe a few hours of work should finish me up here."

Doctor Bill nodded in confirmation, smiling wistfully.

"Yes, but I regret that you must leave, Stephen. Work-ing with you has been most rewarding in many ways." He pointed to the riverboat at the piers. "You could go downriver to Wilcannia on the *Taroona*. The engineer is the only patient among the crew now, and he's past the contagious stage and could leave."

"Yes, and it's a certainty that the captain has been ready to leave ever since that smaller riverboat left," Stephen added. "Let's walk down to the riverboat and discuss it with him."

They turned toward the riverboat, Jeremy smiling happily as he quickly stepped to the horses and grabbed the reins to lead them. Stephen talked with Doctor Bill about patients as they walked up the street. Deirdre gathered from the discussion that Stephen had kept busy, performing hernia and other operations when the number of typhoid patients had diminished. At potholes in the street, he put a hand under her arm in a gesture of assistance, and the warmth of his fascinatingly strong, sensitive fingers through her sleeve seemed to reach into every fiber of her body.

Leaving the horses tethered at the end of the pier, they walked out on it to the riverboat. Wide in the beam and over a hundred feet long, the huge vessel was well appointed. Benches stood against the wall on the long decks at each side of the large deckhouse that contained passenger accommodations, and the deck overhang was decorated with gingerbread trim. On the broad, open expanses of deck at the bow and stern, men who were obviously still recovering their strength after having had typhoid were sorting out equipment.

The captain, a tall, muscular man, came out of the wheel-house atop the deckhouse. Also pale and weak, he made his way down a ladder to the stern deck, then around to the side where Deirdre and the others were waiting at the gangplank. Stephen introduced him to Deirdre and Jeremy as Tom Babbitt, and he perked up at the mention of being able to leave.

"I can fire up my boilers and have a full head of steam by sunrise tomorrow," he told Stephen happily, "and I'll be glad to finally deliver this cargo of hides and tallow. Like you suggested, I found a cook who didn't catch typhoid. Her name is Maud Ruddle, and her husband died from it. She's taking her children and rejoining her family in Adelaide."

"Having her is a wise precaution," Stephen assured him. "Everyone on your crew should be past the contagious stage, but the danger warrants taking no risks at all. We'll need cabins for the three of us."

Tom nodded, pointing to the deckhouse. "Maud is using one, and the rest are empty. You can take your pick, and there'll be no charge for anything." He shook his head as Stephen started to thank him. "At the very most, that's farthings on the guineas against what you did for me. You can put your horses on the stern deck, where you'll find boards to make a pen for them."

"How long will it take to reach Wilcannia?" Jeremy asked. "It usually takes no more than a day or so from here, doesn't it?"

"Aye, but not this time," Tom replied. "Sandbars shift from hither to yon in this river, and logs wash down creeks into the river. Captains tell each other about hazards, but there's been no boats upriver for weeks, and I don't know what to expect. It'll be a dicey trip even with tying up at nightfall, and I can't say when we'll reach Wilcannia."

Jeremy nodded, Deirdre noting that he was unfazed by the warning, and for good reason. She knew that the only alternative to going by riverboat was an arduous overland journey that would take weeks. In addition, his high spirits were unshakable now that he had achieved his objective of ·finding Stephen, who had agreed to go to the station.

The conversation ended and Tom hurried away, shouting and gathering his crew. While walking back to the end of the pier, Jeremy talked with Stephen about preparations to leave. "You said your horses are at the livery stable, didn't you?" Jeremy said. "I'll fetch them, along with a supply of fodder."

"Thank you, that'll simplify my preparations to leave," Stephen replied. "I'll finish up my remaining work with surgery patients by the end of the day, and I'll bring my belongings to the boat tomorrow morning. I should be free for a time after dinner, and I'll see you again then."

On the final remark, his gaze met Deirdre's, and she smiled and nodded. She yearned to be alone with him now, but the situation was awkward. The discussion about patients and Christopher's illness, matters of life and death, created an atmosphere in which preoccupation with romantic feelings seemed trivial and selfish. Stephen and Doctor Bill walked back down the street, and Deirdre helped Jeremy lead their horses aboard the riverboat.

Leaving the saddles and pack on the side deck at two of the cabin doors, they led the horses to the stern deck. "He's a good man, and I'm very pleased for you," Jeremy said affectionately, commenting on her relationship with Stephen. "And to have you regard him favorably, he's the most fortunate of men." His smile widening to a grin, he added, "Next to me, I'd say he's the luckiest man in the world."

Deirdre laughed and nodded, walking back toward the cabins. She found them functional, but with decorative touches and furnishings that made them comfortable rather than spartan. After pulling the saddles and pack into Jeremy's cabin, she gathered up her baggage and lugged it to her cabin. She put it away in cupboards and drawers, then followed the scent of cooking food to the dining saloon on the other side of the deckhouse.

The saloon was well furnished, its long table and sideboards gleaming, and the cook was bustling between it and the adjacent galley. About fifty, the heavyset Maud Ruddle had a sunnily amiable, talkative nature matching her round, rosy face. Her two children, daughters of about eight and nine, were helping her set the table in preparation for dinner.

After introducing herself, Deirdre offered condolences over the death of Maud's husband, but the woman was cheerfully indifferent about it. "Aye, well, it was no great loss to me or to the world, m'dear," Maud remarked breezily. "Those who wish to be mourned in death should give it some thought in life, and I'll soon find a better one in Adelaide."

Deirdre agreed with the woman's sentiments and chatted a moment longer, then left the saloon. Jeremy had returned from the livery stable with Stephen's three horses and a load of fodder, and she walked back to the pen he had assembled on the aft deck to help him feed the horses. Sunset was turning the river into a shimmering swath of crimson when they finished, and a bell clanged in the dining saloon. They went to the saloon and found places at the table, along with the captain and his crew. Maud and her daughters carried in the food from the galley, then took seats.

The meal was delicious, a juicy pork roast with well-seasoned vegetables, accompanied by bread still hot from the oven and mugs of foaming beer. None of the crew did it justice, their appetites still poor from their sickness, but Deirdre ate with more than her usual robust appetite. Having seen but been deprived of even talking with Stephen, she had an inner hunger that fueled a craving for tastes, scents, and other sensations.

After the meal, Deirdre went out to the benches on the deck beside the pier with Jeremy and the crew. Dusk had fallen, and the captain lit lanterns set in brackets on the stanchions supporting the deck overhang. Then he sat down, joining the conversation among the men, and Deirdre watched the lighted doorway of the hospital down the street.

Moths fluttered around the lanterns as the minutes passed, and crewmen left one by one to retire for the night. Deirdre listened to them and watched the doorway in growing anticipation, knowing that after Stephen arrived, they would eventually be alone. Jeremy, Tom Babbitt, and two crewmen remained on the benches when Stephen stepped out of the warehouse.

Her heart leaping with joy, Deirdre immediately recognized his tall, slim form silhouetted against the light. He was visible only briefly, walking rapidly out the doorway, then he disappeared into the darkness of the street. It seemed an eternity until she heard his footsteps on the pier, then he came up the gangplank and into the glow of the lanterns.

"Come on and sit down, Stephen," Jeremy said happily, Tom seconding the invitation. "Have you attended to all your patients, then?"

"Yes, I've finished up here," Stephen replied, stepping onto the deck and smiling at Deirdre in silent, loving greeting. "The most recent surgery patients were my only concern, but now they're all . . ." He broke off and turned, a man calling to him from the street.

"Dr. Brendell!" the man shouted. "The hernia patient with chest congestion is coughing again. It's very painful, and the hepatica won't stop it. Also, Mr. Hawthorne has chundered his medicine along with some blood, and Doctor Bill won't be back for another hour or two!"

"Very well, I'll be there in a moment!" Stephen called, then turned back. "That's one of the apprentices," he explained, "and I evidently spoke too soon. It'll probably be late by the time matters are in hand, so I'll see you in the morning, when I bring my belongings aboard."

Jeremy and Tom replied, voicing resignation. Deirdre forced a smile in response to Stephen's wry smile as he glanced at her, then he disappeared back down the gangplank. The men resumed talking, and she watched the warehouse doorway again, crushed by disappointment. When she saw Stephen go through the doorway, she stood up and went to her cabin.

Lying in bed, Deirdre listened to the murmur of Jeremy and Tom continuing their conversation for a time. She heard them stir about and leave the deck, then the only sound was the groaning of timbers as the riverboat shifted in the currents around the pier. It seemed to her that fate was tantalizing her, bringing her close to Stephen, yet keeping him away.

Sleep evaded her, time passing slowly, and she thought about Stephen. In physical appearance and somewhat in personality, he was a young, masculine image of his mother. The resemblance between them intrigued Deirdre, making both more appealing in a unique way. Her love for Stephen was enriched by her affection for Stephanie, and the opposite was also true.

Her thoughts moved on to Stephen's strong, well-formed hands and his long, sensitive fingers. She recalled her reaction when his hands touched her, and then it was suddenly more vivid than a memory, the same glowing flush of sensation swelling within her. The cabin suddenly seemed stifling. Getting out of bed, she slipped on her robe. She quietly left the cabin and walked up the side deck to the broad expanse of deck at the bow.

Standing in the cool breeze at the rail, she told herself that she and Stephen would have many opportunities for private moments during the trip downriver. But even the next day seemed a very long time away.

Stephen was also wakeful, in a turmoil of mixed feelings. On the one hand, his spirits had soared with blissful delight ever since he and Deirdre had met on the street during the afternoon. Each time he had looked into her eyes, she had drawn aside the screen of reserve concealing her feelings and allowed her love to shine forth like a beacon.

At the same time, he feared that he was trapped in a hopeless situation. It was possible that Oliver Willis had been mistaken and the Kerrick boy had a treatable colic condition. However, Oliver was a skilled, experienced physician, and the diagnosis was probably correct.

Relatives of patients sometimes expected favorable results

even when it was obvious that nothing could be done, and Stephen was accustomed to that. This situation was different, however, far more intense and complex. He was actually part of it. In addition to his love for Deirdre, he felt a profound emotional attraction to her family. When he had met Jeremy, he had more than liked the man.

Stephen tossed and turned on his cot, torn between joy and apprehension over what he might find when he examined Jeremy's son. Finally realizing that he had too much on his mind at present to sleep, he decided that a few minutes in the fresh air outside might settle his thoughts so that he could sleep. He rose from his cot and dressed, then stepped out of his room and made his way across the warehouse to the door.

Walking out onto the porch, he looked at the riverboat. In the bright moonlight, its huge mass was a mottle of shadows against the gleam of the moon on the water, wisps of smoke from its tall stacks shredding in the breeze. Gazing at it reflectively, he thought about his dream of three nights before, a dream that had been an omen and had come true.

Stephen peered at the riverboat more closely, something on the bow deck catching his eye. It had appeared to be a movement, but he wondered if it had been only his imagination. Then he saw it again, looking like someone's clothes moving in the breeze. He knew it was unlikely that any of the crew, all of them still weak, would be up and about late at night.

Keeping his eyes riveted to the riverboat, Stephen stumbled and almost fell as he ran down the steps to the street. He impatiently recovered his balance and then hurried up the street. By the time he was halfway to the riverboat, he was certain that someone was on the deck.

He was equally certain that it was Deirdre. Although she was only a shadowy figure in the moonlight, something told him that it was she. She turned away from the rail and stepped toward the side deck, and he started to call out, thinking she was going to her cabin. But then she went toward the gangplank, and he realized that she had seen him.

Stephen walked out on the pier, Deirdre stepping down the gangplank to meet him. Numb with exultant joy, he wanted to run to her, but once he could see her clearly, for some reason his footsteps slowed of their own accord. Hers did as well, seconds passing while they gazed at each other and took paces that gradually closed the last few yards separating them.

Wearing a flowing robe and with her long, thick hair tousled about her head and shoulders, she was so exquisitely beautiful in the moonlight that a gentle agony throbbed within him. When they were within arm's reach, they stopped. Stephen searched for some remark, but no words could even hint at his feelings. Her lips opened as she started to speak, but she too remained silent. But she communicated more than words, freely exposing her very soul in her lovely face and in her eyes, revealing her love for him.

Deirdre raised her arms and reached out to him, and he took her warm, soft hands in his, strangely like his dream. The clasping of their hands broke intangible shackles and they rushed together, melding. She crushed herself to him, her open lips matching the demanding hunger of his. Their deep, searching kisses were driven by unleashed passion that had been suppressed for months, and they kissed until they were breathless.

Stephen held her slender body close and moved his lips over her face in kisses, the tips of her fingers caressing his face. "I've loved you since the first moment I saw you, Deirdre," he whispered. "I love you with every breath I take and every beat of my heart."

"And I love you just as much, Stephen," she replied softly. "You are my first and my only love."

"Will you marry me, then?"

"Yes . . . Yes! Yes!"

At her eager reply, his mental certainty that she would be his also became an emotional reality in his heart, creating an explosion of joy. His lips found hers again in long, lingering kisses until they were both gasping for breath once more. "I knew you had changed your mind," he said, moving his lips down to her throat in kisses. "When we met this afternoon, I could see it in your eyes. I had to hear it from you before I could really believe it, but everything kept us from talking."

"Yes, everything," she agreed. "I thought fate was keeping us apart, but as it happened, circumstances developed to our advantage. It's best that we met here and now rather than during the day."

He looked into her eyes, puzzled. "What do you mean?" he asked.

Deirdre smiled, taking his hand and drawing him toward the gangplank in a silent explanation that overjoyed him. He followed her quietly up the gangplank and along the deck to her cabin. When the door closed behind them, they held each other and kissed in the thick darkness.

In the privacy of her cabin, their kisses and caresses quickly became more ardent. Deirdre moved away from him and opened the cover on the porthole, and dim, indirect light from the moon filled the cabin. She shrugged out of her robe and tossed it aside, then her nightgown rustled as she took it off. Stephen tugged at his clothes and gazed at her stepping to the bed, an alluring vision of perfect beauty in the moonlight.

His clothes scattered on the floor, Stephen stepped to the bed. Deirdre reached up for him and then pulled him down into her arms. Their quickening heartbeats merged in their clinging embraces and kisses, their desire swelling into a fiery need for intimate contact, and she moved to meet him as he lifted himself over her. They joined and moved in a pulsing rhythm of blissful sensations, her body arching strongly to meet him.

A mounting tide of ecstasy gripped them, drawing them together in surging spasms, and she smothered her cry of pleasure against his throat. The quiescence it brought was fleeting, fading into passion renewed by the wellspring of their love and the wonder they had found in each other. She sighed in satisfaction and responded eagerly to his movements, the ebb and flow increasing in intensity once more to further peaks of rapture.

When the fiery edge of their desire was quenched, their lovemaking was an exploration and quest through its dimensions. They discovered a convergence of total empathy and became as one, sharing each other's pleasure. It was a communication at a range of levels, their bodies joined and their lips touching in kisses while they gazed into each other's eyes.

During pauses in their lovemaking, they slept briefly and then woke to keen, euphoric awareness of each other that was a path to returning desire. They talked at times. Deirdre told him about her visit with his mother, and Stephen described his dream and how it had been different three nights before. She expressed astonishment, explaining that it had been on the same night that she had changed her mind and decided to marry him.

"Your mother would probably regard it as more than coincidence," she added, speaking softly against his lips as they kissed. "She told me that she believes our families are linked by fate."

"Perhaps they are," he said. "Mother has always been very interested in your family, and she is inclined to be a mystic."

Deirdre agreed, commenting that it was one of the many characteristics which made his mother so fascinating. She started to say more, but the conversation was overcome by another upswell of sensual impulses. Her breath caught in her throat in a sigh from the touch of his hand on her breasts, and Stephen responded, partaking in her pleasure. Their caresses became purposeful and intense, leading to lovemaking once more.

Afterward, while they resumed talking quietly, Stephen pressed his lips into her long, thick hair, breathing its alluring fragrance. Deirdre's lips and fingers moved over his chest, then she stopped to listen closely when he told her more about his mother. He related what little he knew concerning her decades of peculiar, enigmatic sorrow associated with her father's death and the abandoned ruins of the old prison in the village.

"How terribly, terribly sad," Deirdre murmured despondently when he finished. "It's dreadfully sad that she's endured such cruel torment for so many years. Something must be done about it."

"I don't know what that would be," he replied. "As I said, Mother won't discuss it, and no one can even mention it to her. When the cause of a problem is unknown, finding a solution is a search in darkness."

"The cause isn't entirely unknown," Deirdre pointed out. "There also may be things you haven't thought to mention just now, facts that may unlock secrets when freshly examined. Let's think on it and discuss it again during coming days, and perhaps together we can find a solution."

Stephen assured her that was his heartfelt wish. Then he mentioned his misgivings about whether Oliver Willis's diagnosis had been incorrect, and expressed hopes that Jeremy and the rest of the family would not be overly optimistic. He remarked upon Jeremy's cheerful attitude, and Deirdre explained that it was a result of his having succeeded in what he had set out to do.

"Jeremy thought he would be failing Fiona if he didn't find you," she went on. "He loves his children deeply, but the feelings between he and Fiona go beyond love. It appears that Mother thinks they go too far, and perhaps they do. But on the issue of whether or not you can help Christopher, no one in the family will expect the impossible of you."

Stephen wondered if he would be able to satisfy his expectations of himself.

During the dark, early hours of the morning, they woke to the wonder they had found in each other. Tender kisses and

caresses rekindled desire, and they joined, moving together
in giving and receiving. Their lovemaking of before had
leveled the near heights of rapture, and their rhythm became
more and more intense in their striving for a more lofty,
more distant peak. Time warped out of its framework and
minutes became eternities for them in their straining effort,
their bodies touching damply with perspiration.

With a soft, exultant cry and tensing surge, Deirdre seized
a subtle flow of sensation that lifted her toward euphoria.
Stephen shared the momentum in harmony with her, his
quickening pace matching hers. They pulsed together and
soared to the heights of an ultimate summit, a vortex of
wrenching ecstasy draining their passion away. In the weak,
breathless aftermath, they laughed and kissed in triumph and
mutual gratitude.

When the first glimmer of dawn thinned the darkness
outside the porthole, Deirdre helped Stephen dress, then he
quietly left the boat and walked down the street toward the
warehouse. In his buoyant happiness, the dawn spreading
across the sky seemed to be bringing the first day in a new
life of joy. The day lacked absolute perfection, however,
marred by a nagging worry about what he might find when
he examined the Kerrick boy at Tibooburra Station.

The first curve in the river was less than a mile below
Bourke, but once the riverboat rounded it shortly after
sunrise, Stephen felt as though the town and the rest of
civilization were at a far distance. He was reminded of his
voyages to and from Britain, when the ships had been their
own small worlds set apart from other places. The riverboat
seemed even more isolated than a ship surrounded by the
sea, the outback reaching back from the riverbanks with
an impression of far vaster space than the ocean.

The cares of the wider world were set at a distance for
Stephen, his worry about the Kerrick boy's illness fading
in his enjoyment of the trip. He sat and talked with Deirdre
and Jeremy on a bench beside the deckhouse, and each time

his gaze met Deirdre's, her eyes conveyed a silent message of love and of their secret, private knowledge of each other. Jeremy's companionship was a keen pleasure, and Stephen had a warm sense of being welcomed into the inner circle of the fascinating Kerrick family.

The boat moved down the river slowly, Tom Babbitt watching for hazards as well as making allowances for the fact that his crew was unable to react as quickly as usual. In places where the river was wide and shallow, the boat probed for the main channel, its keel occasionally brushing submerged sandbars. When the river was more narrow, the engine telegraph in the wheelhouse clanged and the paddle wheel began turning backward to prevent the boat from gaining too much speed in the swift current.

Tiffin was a lavish spread of sausages, cheeses, various sorts of pickles, fresh fruit, and foaming mugs of beer. Crewmen took turns coming to the dining saloon except for the captain, and Maud Ruddle's daughters carried his meal up to the wheelhouse. After they finished eating, Stephen returned to the bench beside the wheelhouse with Deirdre and Jeremy.

The conversation was wide-ranging and occasionally touched upon affairs at Tibooburra Station. The subject of the rabbit plague came up, Jeremy explaining that some months before, a stockman named Zachary Cooper had spent several weeks in the vicinity of Geelong to survey the situation, and had reported that many farms and grazing runs had been devastated. Deirdre knew about the stockman's trip, and she wondered aloud why Jeremy had not gone to Geelong himself.

"Fiona had taken a fall on a horse," he replied. "She said she wasn't hurt, but I wasn't about to go just then. Grandmother sent Zack instead, and she was a bit narked at me because I wouldn't go."

His tone was defensive, creating a discomfiting silence. Smoothing over the uneasy pause, Stephen told them that he had an uncle in Adelaide named John Thorpe. He related what John had said about the damage that rabbits had done; then the conversation continued, the awkward moment passing.

At sunset, the captain steered the riverboat toward a bank to tie up for the night. The deckhands laid out ropes in preparation to jump ashore with them, but the jump would obviously be difficult for the men in their weakened condition. Stephen took the rope at the stern while Jeremy went to the bow, and when the keel of the riverboat began grounding in the shallow water, they leaped to the bank with the ropes and tied them to trees.

Dinner was another delicious feast, a succulent beef roast with potatoes baked in the pan. The boiler fire had been banked for the night, and the entire crew was at the table for the meal. Tom was pleased, the riverboat having gone well over a hundred miles during the day, and he was cautiously optimistic that they would reach Wilcannia during the forenoon of the following day.

After the meal, everyone went out to the benches, but for only a short time. The crew was weary, going to their bunks when darkness fell, and Jeremy tactfully went to his cabin to leave Stephen and Deirdre in privacy. The moon beamed down on the river, the night sounds of the outback an undertone to their words of love as they kissed. Then they went to her cabin for another night of discoveries in ecstasy, conversation, and brief naps that were somehow as restful as hours of sleep.

Stephen had just gone to his own cabin in the thick darkness before dawn when the riverboat began bustling with activity, Tom shouting orders. The crew bolted down breakfast between tasks, the stokers firing up the furnace and thick smoke billowing from the stacks against the first light of dawn. Stephen and Jeremy untied the ropes from the trees on the bank and leaped back aboard, then went to breakfast with Deirdre in the brightening dawn as the riverboat moved out into the current.

An hour after sunrise, tall hills rose on each side, the

river following a twisting path it had carved through them over the centuries. Creeks and occasional streams the size of small rivers wound through the hills and fed into the river, many of them dry channels that filled only during heavy rains. The river was relatively narrow, and the paddle wheel turned backward in the fast current to slow the boat as it went around the abrupt curves, giving a wide berth to clusters of driftwood that had washed out of tributaries and lodged against sandbars jutting out from the banks.

The boat rounded yet another sharp curve, and Stephen sat up on the bench in surprise, seeing the *Cobdogla* moored at the bank. The small boat had left Bourke days before, ample time to have long since reached Adelaide. The three former patients who were the captain and crew were lounging on the deck, and their surprise matched Stephen's as they gazed at the *Taroona*.

Then, after the hours of placidly steaming down the river, things began happening with blinding speed. The captain and owner of the *Cobdogla,* a short, skinny man named Jake Higgins, bounded up and ran to the deckhouse. A plume of steam joined the smoke trickling from its small stack, its whistle blasting shrilly in warning. The engine telegraph on the *Taroona* clanged furiously, and the paddle wheel began churning backward.

Jeremy pointed downriver, exclaiming in alarm. Some two hundred yards ahead was a wide streambed containing only a trickle of water, but evidently it had channeled a flash flood out of the hills during the past weeks. The flood had washed into the river a huge mass of driftwood that had formed into a logjam, completely blocking the river just below the streambed.

Even with the paddle wheel spinning backward at full speed, the swift current still carried the *Taroona* toward certain destruction against the tangled logs that would crush its hull. Tom bellowed at the deckhands to throw out anchors, and Stephen and Jeremy ran to the stern, Deirdre racing after them. At the rear of the deckhouse was a large locker, and the deckhands tugged at two anchors among the equipment inside it.

Shoving the deckhands aside, Stephen and Jeremy dragged the heavy anchors out of the locker, and Deirdre grabbed coils of rope. The deckhands followed them to each side of the stern deck, helping tie the ropes to the anchors, then looping the ropes around cleats on the rail. Stephen and Jeremy flung the anchors overboard, the ropes whipping around the cleats, then they tightened the ropes when the anchors bottomed.

The anchors held, but only momentarily. The swift current against the *Taroona* forced the anchors to break ground, and the riverboat continued moving jerkily downstream a few feet at a time. Tom stepped out of the wheelhouse, lifting a megaphone toward the *Cobdogla*. "Jake, can you bring me a line from the bank?" his voice boomed across the water.

Jake dived into his deckhouse and then ran back out, lifting a megaphone. "It'll take me a while to get up a head of steam," his voice roared tinnily in reply. "We've just been waiting here for a boat to come upriver and then go get some blasting powder to break up that logjam."

The captains continued shouting, discussing options. Jake suggested that Tom turn in toward the bank, as he himself had, but Tom rejected that except as a last resort. He explained that in the swift current, he was certain that his larger, heavier riverboat would ground with such force that its hull would be crushed. Stephen listened to them, knowing that something would have to be done soon. Sparks flew from the stack on the *Cobdogla* as the two crewmen hastily stoked the firebox to heat the boiler to full pressure, but the *Taroona* was gradually edging closer to the logjam.

Stephen looked at the logjam again, noticing that Jeremy was studying it, and he saw what had drawn Jeremy's interest. At the center and base of the tangled wood was a huge tree some sixty feet long and five or six feet thick. It had been uprooted, a large cluster of roots at one end and thick branches at the other. The massive tree was anchoring the entire logjam in place, the water foaming and swirling around it in violent eddies.

His pale blue eyes dancing with excitement, Jeremy turned to Stephen. A silent question contained in the wide grin on Jeremy's face allowed Stephen to decline gracefully if he wished, for what the man was obviously contemplating would be extremely dangerous. Stephen laughed, running to a rowboat lashed to the deck. He jerked at the ropes to untie them, and Jeremy ran to the equipment locker and grabbed two broadaxes.

"What are you doing?" Deirdre demanded, puzzled and alarmed. She followed Jeremy as he ran to Stephen and helped untie the rowboat. "Answer me, Stephen! . . . Then you, Jeremy! What are you doing?"

Making no reply, Stephen and Jeremy lifted an end of the boat and rushed to the side of the deck, dragging it. Deirdre ran after them and continued shouting, becoming angry and more apprehensive. They dumped the boat over the rail and flung the axes into it, then jumped down to it. The captains, noticing what they were doing, fell silent in perplexity.

When the rowboat moved away, Tom understood their intentions, and he shouted through his megaphone: "Belay that!" he roared. "If you go near that logjam, it's at sixes or sevens as to whether you'll be drowned or crushed, but you can be certain that one or the other will happen!"

His voice and Deirdre's frightened shouts fell behind, the rapid current sweeping the rowboat away. Jeremy hastily put the oars in the locks, then rowed backward to slow the boat. His shirt stretched tightly over the bulging muscles in his arms and broad shoulders as he rowed furiously, and the boat gradually slowed. It still sped down the river too rapidly, however, quickly bearing down on the towering tangle of logs and splintered limbs.

The water gushed around the logjam with a roar like that of a huge waterfall, the current breaking up into a churning turbulence of eddies several yards from it. They caught the rowboat, spinning it first one way and then the other as

Jeremy fought to keep it under control. The boat whipped sideward to the logjam, Jeremy shipping an oar just in time to keep it from being shattered when the boat slammed into the mass of wood.

The impact almost threw Stephen out of the boat, his full attention on dodging sharp, jutting limbs that threatened to gouge him. He recovered his balance, grabbing up an axe and climbing out of the boat, then almost fell. A tangle of slippery limbs and smaller trees covered the large one, some breaking under his boots and making the footing treacherous.

Jeremy climbed out of the boat with his axe, stamping his boots through smaller limbs to make a footing for himself. He picked out a spot on the large tree and cleared smaller debris away with a few strokes of his axe, and Stephen moved up beside him. Stephen lifted his axe and slammed it into the tree, then Jeremy drove his into it at an angle and a few inches from the cut that Stephen had made, cleaving a chip from the wood.

They swung their axes in alternating blows, gradually chopping a wide notch in the tree. When he began tiring, Stephen clenched his teeth and summoned his strength, trying to match the force that the brawny Jeremy put into his powerful blows with his axe. Stephen also fought off a sense of defeat, as what they were attempting began to appear impossible. The tree was a tough, ancient eucalypt over five feet thick, and the notch was barely a foot deep after several minutes of chopping.

The minutes that remained were limited, and fleeing rapidly. The horn on the *Taroona* droned sonorously in warning, and from the corner of his eyes, Stephen saw the riverboat edging closer. An icy chill of fear raced though him, which he used to fuel more force with his axe. Jeremy's strong, sun-browned face reflected only determination, and Stephen resolved not to be the first to suggest that they try to save themselves.

The warning from the riverboat's horn became a deep,

steady blast over the roar of the water. The approaching vessel loomed immensely, like a dark, massive cliff on the edge of Stephen's vision and less than a hundred feet away. The horn on the *Cobdogla* joined in, shrieking a shrill warning of dire peril, and over the bedlam, Stephen heard Deirdre screaming frantically at him and Jeremy to flee.

Worst of all, Stephen had a desperate, sickening feeling that their effort was for nothing, the notch in the thick tree still less than two feet deep. Then he felt the tree move, and his spirits suddenly soared with hope. The current was exerting tremendous pressure against the tree, which had been weakened, and it was beginning to break apart at the notch.

The tree moved again, bending slightly as the wood at the base of the notch began splintering. Jeremy whooped in glee, swinging his axe into the fracturing wood with slashing blows. Stephen slammed his axe into it, the chance for success renewing his strength.

The moments of greatest danger now came as the tree bent more deeply and moved violently. The entire logjam shifted, and limbs shoved against Stephen's legs and made him stagger as he swung his axe. The riverboat was scant yards away, its horn thundering in deafening blasts. The notch finally began spreading all the way through the tree, the wood cracking and snapping.

"It's breaking!" Jeremy shouted. "Let's get out of here!"

Stephen flung his axe into the boat and scrambled toward it, the shifting limbs catching at his legs. Diving the last few feet, he landed in the boat on his stomach. An eddy moved the boat just as Jeremy jumped, and he fell into the water, his fingers catching the gunwale. Stephen gripped Jeremy's arms and helped him aboard, the boat tilting and swerving wildly.

The bow wave from the riverboat lifted the rowboat and then washed into the logjam, the large tree breaking with a rending crash. The logjam began dissolving into a mass of flailing logs and limbs, the current and bow wave from the riverboat shoving the rowboat into the midst of it. Stephen dodged jagged limbs whipping around him, he and Jeremy grabbed up the oars, and they struggled to fend the larger logs away from the boat.

Logs still slammed into the boat, and it spun and careened violently in the turbulent water. A large log surfaced under the stern, lifting the boat sharply and almost spilling Stephen and Jeremy into the river. Then the log rolled away and the boat plunged back down into the water. The riverboat fell behind, its anchors still dragging, and the mass of driftwood from the logjam finally separated and began floating away in the current.

Jeremy took Stephen's oar and put both oars in the locks, then turned the boat upstream toward the riverboat. Caulking in the boat had dislodged, and it was leaking in several places. "After all that," Jeremy remarked jokingly, "now our boat is trying to sink under us. We're on beams' ends in keeping from being stonkered in one way or another, Stephen."

The comments vastly amused Stephen in the aftermath of the danger, he and Jeremy bursting into laughter, and their exuberance was shared by those on the riverboats. The *Cobdogla* had built up a head of steam and was chugging down the river to join the larger boat, the two crewmen waving and shouting while Jake Higgins bellowed happily through his megaphone. On the *Taroona,* Deirdre, Maud Ruddle and her children, and the crewmen cheered and waved. Tom roared through his megaphone in relief and gratitude, thanking Stephen and Jeremy for saving his boat from certain destruction.

At the side of the riverboat, Stephen threw a rope from the rowboat to the crewmen as Jeremy climbed up to the deck. Deirdre's high spirits were mixed with annoyance and lingering fear, and she shoved Jeremy back against the rail. "You're mad!" she exclaimed, both frowning and laughing. "You and Stephen as well! You're as mad as kookaburras, the two of you!"

Jeremy leaned against the rail in gales of laughter, Deirdre turning from him in exasperation and scolding Stephen as he climbed up to the deck. With her large blue eyes sparkling and her lovely features animated by a flux of elation, aggravation, and other emotions, her vibrant personality was like a physical force emanating from her. She had never been more beautiful and appealing, and Stephen grabbed her and kissed her.

More than responding, she vented her feelings, her lips avidly demanding on his. Maud and the crewmen hooted with knowing laughter, and Deirdre pulled away, flushing and laughing in confusion. Then the gathering broke up as Tom shouted from the wheelhouse and ordered the crew to haul in the rowboat and anchors. Stephen followed the crew to help them, and Jeremy went to his cabin to change into dry clothes after his dunking in the river.

When the rowboat and anchors were aboard, the riverboat continued on down the curving river at the same cautious speed as before, the *Cobdogla* trailing a hundred feet astern. Shortly after Stephen joined Deirdre on a bench, Jeremy returned from his cabin. "You may be a university man, Stephen," he observed as he sat down, "but you're anything but a bookish poddy. You'd be as bonzer a mate in the outback as anyone could want." He turned to Deirdre: "Stephen was rooted to that big tree, giving it his best with his axe."

The remark pleased Stephen intensely, and he was just as gratified by Deirdre's warm smile. "I was too petrified to move," he said, laughing. "For a moment, I thought our time had come."

"I was sterky myself," Jeremy admitted frankly. "Jarboe Charlie often said that courage is control over fear, and anyone who doesn't feel fear at times of danger is short a sheet of bark on his roof. I'm glad we cleared that logjam, but I won't be disappointed if we don't find others."

"We probably won't," Deirdre speculated, pointing ahead.

"We're almost out of this narrows, where the river is more easily blocked."

Stephen looked downstream, the riverboat rounding a last sharp curve, and he saw that the river became wider and followed a much straighter course ahead. A few minutes later, the tall hills were left behind and the more typical rolling terrain of the outback stretched away from the riverbanks to the horizons. The *Cobdogla* drew up abreast of the *Taroona* in the wider channel, pacing the larger riverboat at a distance of fifty feet.

Jake and Tom exchanged shouts with their megaphones, agreeing that the rest of the trip to Wilcannia would be without difficulty. Jeremy and Deirdre expressed satisfaction, but Stephen had conflicting feelings. He wanted to reach Tibooburra Station without delay, for avoiding situations was against his nature, but he was worried about what might confront him there.

If Oliver Willis's diagnosis had been correct, Stephen knew he would face the most formidable decision of his life. Through a careful diet and avoiding physical exertion, some people lived with perityphlitic abscess for years, if that could be called living. The end result, an agonizing death, was always the same. But deep abdominal surgery was considered beyond the boundaries of medical science, with a formidable mortality rate.

Chapter Twenty-Four

"Yes, without a blood test, I could have been wrong," Oliver Willis acknowledged. "Needless to say, I hope that I was."

"It's a mistake anyone could make," Stephen assured him. "I don't have a microscope with me to make a blood test, and I'd like to borrow yours."

"Of course," Oliver agreed readily, "but may I go with you? My practice is in sufficient order so that I can leave for two or three days."

Jeremy was standing with Deirdre at one side of the surgery in the doctor's modest house in Wilcannia, and he quickly spoke up: "We intend to travel posthaste, with no stops to rest," he advised Oliver. "After being absent for weeks, I'm most anxious to see my wife and son."

"That's more than understandable, but I wouldn't delay you," Oliver told him. "I've become far more accustomed to getting about on horseback than I was when I went to the station with you before."

Jeremy still had reservations, and turned to Stephen for

a decision. Stephen thought about it, reflecting that he
should be prepared as far as possible for all eventualities.
"Very well, Oliver," he said. "Please hurry in making ready
to leave."

"Yes, I will," Oliver replied, opening a cabinet. He took
out a wooden microscope case and a box containing slides
and stains, and handed them to Stephen. "I'll have a word
with my housekeeper and gather up a few things, then
saddle my horse. I'll be with you in a moment."

Stephen nodded, going back outside with Deirdre and
Jeremy. Their six horses were tethered in front of the house,
Stephen's belongings and medical supplies he had brought
from Bourke divided into loads between his two packhorses.
He opened one of the packs and put the microscope case and
box into it, then closed it and secured the ropes around it.
Oliver joined them as they mounted up, and they rode away
from the house and down the street.

The wide, dusty street was lined with shops, farriers,
wainwrights, and other businesses, the town of Wilcannia
serving as a commercial center for farms and stations in
the region. With the sleepy atmosphere of a far outpost, the
town also provided a point of contact between overland and
riverboat transport. The street ended at the waterfront and
its line of piers, where the *Cobdogla* had stopped briefly
to deliver long-delayed mail from Bourke while Stephen,
Deirdre, and Jeremy had disembarked from the *Taroona*.

A few yards downstream from the piers, a large, raftlike
ferry was moored at its slip. The portly, grizzled ferry
operator had just finished turning a winch and hauling
his cable back up into position after lowering it for the
Taroona and *Cobdogla* to pass, and he opened the gate at
the end of the ferry for the horses to be led aboard. While
Stephen and Jeremy engaged in a good-natured argument to
pay the ferry fee, Deirdre took the money out of her reticule
and handed it to the operator.

The man put a large rudder into place at the end of the
ferry, then cast off. The ferry moved out into the river,

the pressure of the current against its side and the rudder pushing it along the cable, which passed through large pulleys on the upstream side of the ferry. It picked up speed to the center of the river and then slowed, the operator adjusting the angle of the rudder to ease up to the bank on the west side of the river.

Stephen tied a rope to a post at the edge of the water as Jeremy led the horses off the ferry, the operator carrying the rudder to the other end to return to the slip. As the ferry moved away, they led the horses up the steep bank. At the top of it, a track stretched away straight to the west, and they mounted up and set out down the track at a steady canter.

Stephen knew that Wayamba Station lay south of the track and Tibooburra Station to the north, for Deirdre had told him about the area. Even more than on the track to Bourke, he had a sense of the distinctive, eerie atmosphere of the outback around him. He had often heard that the two sheep stations were at the most remote reach of civilization, at the edge of the far outback. Now that he was actually here, he experienced a sense of having passed some invisible milestone beyond which few ventured.

Similarly, he had heard that the two stations were huge, but personal experience raised his grasp of that fact to a different scale. They covered the distance between Sydney and Wallaby Track during the first few hours, but that was only a short span. The distances here reduced their fast canter to an inchworm's pace, for they were only gradually traversing the eastern portion of the border between the two immense stations.

Stephen occasionally glanced at Oliver, watching how he bore up under the strain of the fast pace. What the older man had said about himself seemed true enough, for he appeared little more weary than Stephen felt as the hours passed. The sun was just above the horizon in the west when they finally reached Barren Mountain, at the center of the border between the stations. A long, narrow landform that stretched east and west, it was entirely devoid of vegetation and rose abruptly as the highest point in the surrounding miles of terrain. Halfway along the mountain, a track branched off to the north, leading across the mountain and into Tibooburra Station.

The horses slowed to a walk, laboring up the mountain. From its crest, Stephen had his most extensive view yet of the outback, and it was breathtaking. On all sides, the enormous landscape of brushy hills, grasslands, and scattered stands of trees soared away in unbroken expanses that defied any attempt to estimate the distances. The land seemed a companion to the vast canopy of the sky, an equal in its limitless span.

Stephen knew that the station was bordered on the west and south by the river and track, and wondering about other boundaries, he asked Jeremy how far north it extended. Jeremy pointed to clouds lying to the north, replying that they were over Dingo Paddock, which was a few hours' ride short of being halfway to the northern border at Steeple Hills. His tone was offhand, conveying information he considered unremarkable, yet the clouds to which he referred were a smudge on the horizon, many miles away.

Just before darkness fell, they stopped at a billabong beside the track and shared the camp chores. A short time later, the billys were heating on the fire to make tea, and a pot of stew simmered beside a pan of browning damper. During the conversation, Oliver asked Stephen what he intended to do if the Kerrick boy's illness was perityphlitic abscess.

The question drew Jeremy and Deirdre's undivided attention, but it was a point that Stephen had deferred pondering, and he had no wish to discuss it. "I'll decide that if and when I'm faced with it," Stephen replied. "Until then, I'll hope for a far more favorable finding."

Oliver expressed the same hope, then began talking about recent developments he had read about in newspapers. Plans had been made for a telegraph line from Wilcannia to

Sydney, but that project was small compared to one already in progress. Work had begun on a telegraph line that would link Sydney and other cities in the east and south with Darwin on the north coast. When completed, it would be connected by submarine cable with Java, providing rapid communications with Britain and other countries.

"That will be a great convenience in the conduct of business," Oliver added. "Jeremy, you'll be able to find out very quickly how much money your wool shipments are sold for in London."

"We've no need for that," Jeremy replied, "and I've no liking for much of what people are pleased to call progress. Elizabeth Garrity said once that she feels as though she'll wake up one morning and find a railroad track through her home paddock, and sometimes I feel the same."

"But just think if there had been a telegraph in Wilcannia and Bourke," Oliver insisted. "It would have been of great help in dealing with your son's illness. You'll admit that's true, won't you?"

"Yes," Jeremy replied, laughing, "if you'll first tell me how Stephen could have got here through that telegraph wire."

Stephen and Deirdre laughed, Oliver chuckling and conceding the issue. Jeremy stirred the stew of dried beef and vegetables, making certain it had cooked through, and then filled the tin plates. They tore off pieces of damper and continued talking while eating and drinking their tea, then they lay down around the fire in their blankets. Stephen looked at Deirdre in the firelight, her smile a reference to their lovemaking of previous and of future nights, then he settled himself and fell asleep.

Jeremy stirred at the first light of dawn, breaking up wood and stoking the fire. Deirdre heated the leftovers for breakfast, and Stephen went with Jeremy to unhobble and saddle the horses. After a hasty breakfast, they mounted up and set out up the track as the sun rose.

During the forenoon, they rode through Gidgee Paddock

and into the next one. Jeremy watched for sheep, wanting to ask stockmen if they had recent word of his son's condition, and he saw a flock at a distance to one side in Boar Paddock. Stephen and the others slowed while Jeremy rode to the flock, and presently he returned, the stockman with the flock having had no contact with the home paddock for over a fortnight.

Near midday, in Bingara Paddock, Jeremy rode to another flock, but the stockman knew no more than the first. Jeremy tried again during midafternoon, still without success. They reached Dingo Paddock an hour later, the last one before the home paddock, but Jeremy commented that it was too far away and the horses were too tired to finish the journey by nightfall.

When they stopped at sunset to camp, Stephen saw fire-blackened circles of stones beside the track, others having camped there before. West of the track was a long valley with a knoll in the center of it, and a flock was in a fold on the knoll. Jeremy started to ride to the flock, but the stockman had seen them and was running toward the track on foot.

The camp chores were finished, the billys were heating, and a meal was cooking on the fire by the time the stockman reached the track, puffing from running. He was a muscular man in his early twenties, his features reflecting traces of Aborigine bloodlines. He lifted his hat to Deirdre and exchanged nods with Stephen and Oliver, Jeremy introducing him as Jacob Corbett.

Jeremy added that Jacob's father was Roger Corbett, the head stockman, then asked, "What are you doing on shank's mare, Jacob?"

"One of my horses cast a shoe, and the other got a thorn in a hoof," Jacob explained. "My jackaroo went on foot to lead them to the home paddock and get others, and he's either there or nigh onto it by now. I opined that you might not have heard anything recent of Master

Christopher. I had word of him four days past, and he was
tolerably well then."

"That's good to hear," Jeremy said, pleased. "I'm most
grateful that you came and told me. How did you get word
of him?"

"My pa came to wish me the best on my birthday,"
Jacob replied. "He said that Mistress Fiona was keeping
Master Christopher in the house and being choosy about
his tucker, but he was tolerably well." He lifted his hat to
Deirdre once more, turning away. "I'd best get back to my
sheep, because I don't like to leave them overlong with just
my dogs watching them."

Jeremy thanked Jacob again, and the stockman strode off
into the dusk. The news about his son raised Jeremy's spirits
as they sat down to eat dinner, but Stephen considered it
less than favorable. A careful diet and limiting the boy's
physical activity indicated that he was experiencing an onset
of his recurring illness.

When they lay down around the fire in their blankets
after dinner, Stephen exchanged a smile with Deirdre, like
the night before. Unlike the night before, however, sleep
evaded him. Hours passed while he lay and looked up at
the stars, wondering what the next day would bring.

An hour after they set out the next morning, Stephen
heard a sound that he thought might be a voice calling
out from the side of the track, but he was uncertain. The
pounding of the horses' hoofs at their cantering pace was
loud, drowning out even much of the noisy chatter of birds.
Jeremy and Deirdre also turned and looked, unsure of what
they had heard. She started to gather in her reins, then let
them go slack again when Jeremy shrugged and turned back
to the front, impatient to reach the home paddock.

Near midmorning, the trees and brush flanking the track
thinned out and then fell behind at the foot of a long,
gradual slope covered with deep grass. When they reached
the crest of the rise, the home paddock came into view, and

Stephen was stunned with surprise and awe. While he had
anticipated that it would be more impressive than home
paddocks at other stations, it was entirely different from
them and far exceeded anything he had expected.

It was in a broad, grassy valley with a tree-lined creek
flowing down the center, a setting of striking natural beauty.
After the long journey through the wilderness, the numerous
large, well-constructed buildings gave an impression of
having abruptly come upon a thriving town beyond the
farthest outposts of civilization. A knoll rose in front of the
creek, and east of it were cottages for married stockmen and
a small schoolhouse. An Aborigine village was on down
the creek, along with vegetable gardens and orchards. West
of the knoll were stock pens and a sprawling complex of
warehouses, the shearing shed, a large barracks, and the
cookhouse.

The station house, set on the knoll amid lawns and shade
trees, was a stately three-story stone mansion. It rivaled the
most expensive houses in Sydney, but it was so singularly
distinctive that, by comparison, the homes of the wealthy
in the city blended together into gray anonymity. Scorning
fashion, the house had austerely straight, simple lines, with
an architectural style reaching back through centuries to
feudal manors that had been symbols of power and dominating authority over their surroundings.

Built of native granite, it was a part of the landscape and
seemed to share the qualities of the outback. It had the
same majestic grandeur and ageless, enduring character,
appearing as though it would be unchanged when time had
reduced the most opulent mansions in Sydney to decayed
rubble. More than a house, it was the ancestral home of the
Kerrick family, the focus of the family domain that spread
for miles in all directions.

A bell began tolling at the station buildings, stirring
echoes in the valley that blended with its melodious chiming. Two women came out of the house, and Stephen
recognized them at a distance as Alexandra and Fiona

Kerrick, one with bright red hair and the taller woman
with white hair. Maids followed them out and stood under
the portico behind them.

Stockmen gathered in front of the barracks, and women
stepped out of the cottages. A woman came out of the
schoolhouse, some fifteen children of various ages following her. The people had the usual keen interest that the
arrival of travelers at a remote station created, but none
of the excitement. In its place was a somber quiet, and
Stephen saw that the people knew who he was, the Kerrick
boy's fate in his hands.

The track ended at the foot of the knoll, and stockmen
came up from the barracks as Stephen and the others rode
up to where Alexandra and Fiona were waiting. The
maids helped the stockmen unload the packhorses amid
the greetings, and Deirdre introduced Stephen to her mother
and to Fiona. The younger woman seemed to Stephen a
perfect match for Jeremy, her green eyes and lovely features
revealing a charming, self-confident disposition, but it was
Alexandra who drew and held his full attention. She was
fascinating, unlike anyone he had ever met.

Though he knew she was about seventy, she appeared
decades younger. Still strikingly beautiful, she had the bearing and the sparkling, clear blue eyes of a young woman.
Deirdre had inherited her mother's height and classically
attractive features, but had a more demonstrative, forceful
nature. Alexandra was soft-spoken and placidly composed,
but she had a powerful, magnetic personality that dominated
the gathering.

When they were introduced, Stephen started to greet her
with customary formality. But she gazed at him for an
instant, her gracious smile reaching her eyes, but they also
had a searching quality, as though probing into his thoughts.
Then she stepped forward and put her arms around him,
kissing him. "Welcome to Tibooburra Station, Stephen,"
she said. "Now and henceforth, do consider yourself at
home when you are here."

Her tone was sincere, the words meant literally instead of as a form of greeting, and Stephen was intensely pleased. "I shall, and I'm very grateful, Mistress Kerrick," he responded. "It's easy to understand why my mother's meeting with you years ago made such a strongly favorable impression on her, and she has spoken of you very often."

"No more often than I've thought of her," Alexandra assured him. "The pleasure of your mother's company is one of my most treasured memories, and I'm more than eager to hear about how she fares and what she is doing now. First, though, do you wish to examine Christopher immediately?"

"Yes, at once, please," he replied. "I'd like one member of the family present to keep him pacified, then I'll discuss my findings with the family. I'll need my medical bag and other things out of the packs."

Alexandra nodded, turning to the others: "Fiona, I'm sure you wish to be the one with Christopher, and it's only appropriate that you should be. Astrid, you and the other maids take the packs from Dr. Brendell's horses to a guest room." She turned back to Stephen, linking her arm through his. "The rest of us will wait in the parlor, Stephen."

They filed inside, and Stephen and Oliver went upstairs with Fiona, following the maids with the packs. The maids took the packs into a room, where Oliver helped Stephen gather up his bag, the microscope, and the box of slides and stains, then Fiona led them to a room at the end of the hall.

A maid was placing a basin of water, soap, and a towel on the table in the room, and another one sat on a chair beside the bed. They left, Fiona stepping to the side of the bed, and Oliver set up the microscope on the table. Stephen washed his hands and turned to the bed, keenly worried about what he might find as the boy looked up at him with a winsome smile.

Christopher had his mother's red hair and his father's strangely pale blue eyes, along with a resolute disposition from both. He was in some pain but endured it stoically, and there was no real need for anyone to keep him calm. Immediately fond of the small, brave boy, Stephen forced his feelings aside as he took out his stethoscope and began examining him.

The boy's heartbeat and pulse were rapid but strong, and he had moderate fever and abdominal pain. A range of illnesses was possible at that point, but the following symptoms rapidly narrowed them. The pain was centered in the lower right abdomen and the lymph glands were swollen, and Stephen's heart sank as he became reasonably sure that Oliver's diagnosis had been correct. He took a drop of blood from the boy's finger on a microscope slide, then stained the slide and put it on the microscope stage.

The boy's bloodstream was alive with leucocytes, the white blood corpuscles battling an infection. He had perityphlitic abscess that was presently neither dormant nor causing severe discomfort, a perilous ferment that could explode into the crisis stage at any time. Stephen glanced remorsefully at Fiona, stepping back for Oliver to take a look at the slide.

Fiona's features reflected despair for an instant, then she composed herself and leaned over her son, smiling and kissing him. Oliver's aged, bearded face was somber as he turned away from the microscope. He and Stephen crossed the room to the door with Fiona and went back out, and the maid waiting in the hall stepped back into the room to sit with the boy.

Stephen and Oliver followed Fiona down the staircase, and their footsteps brought the others out of the parlor off the wide entry. Jeremy hurried out first, the eager hope on his face changing to disappointment and shared sorrow with Fiona as he gazed at her. Deirdre sighed despondently, but Alexandra appeared to have been certain all along of what the finding would be.

"It's definitely perityphlitic abscess," Stephen confirmed. "Oliver's diagnosis was absolutely correct."

"To my great distress," Oliver commented sadly. "Now it comes down to an extremely difficult decision, one that I'm glad I don't have to make."

Fiona turned from Jeremy to Stephen. "We'll abide by your decision," she told him. "Whatever you decide to do, we'll know it will be the course of action that provides Christopher with his best chance. Whatever the outcome may be, we'll know that he had his best chance."

"That's well said, Fiona," Alexandra put in approvingly, "but any decision needn't be made at this very moment. Stephen, Deirdre and I agreed that you might want to freshen up and have an opportunity to sort out your thoughts after your journey. I took the liberty of having a maid collect a change of clothes and your razor and other things from your baggage. They're in the bathhouse, and I'll show you to it, if you wish."

It was precisely what Stephen wanted, for events were occurring too rapidly for adequate reflection. Even though the day was little more than halfway through the forenoon, many hours seemed to have passed since sunrise. He gratefully accepted the offer, and Alexandra led him down the hall and out a rear door to a large bathhouse behind the house.

Like the large house, the bathhouse was more than comfortable and just short of luxurious in that its furnishings were functional rather than fashionable. It had every convenience, including hot water piped in from the scullery. After shaving, bathing, and donning the clean clothes, Stephen felt refreshed and more ready to consider his options.

When he stepped out of the bathhouse, Alexandra was waiting a few yards away, smiling affectionately and watching a nurse and a small, redheaded girl in a play area set back from the house. Among the teeter-totter and other amusements, the nurse was pushing the girl on a swing. "That's Sheila, my great-granddaughter," Alexandra explained proudly.

"She's very bonny," Stephen remarked, smiling.

"Indeed she is," Alexandra agreed, "and she's a constant source of joy for me. Come, let's go into the gardens at the side of the house and talk, Stephen. I've learned that I owe you an apology."

"Apology?" he echoed in perplexity, walking up the path with her.

Alexandra nodded, explaining that weeks before, she had received a letter from Deirdre concerning marriage with him. "Christopher was ill at the time," she continued, "and while talking with Deirdre, I learned that I must have allowed my worry about him to influence my reply. I regret that, and I'm delighted beyond measure that you and she are to be married."

"I'm equally pleased that you approve, Mistress Kerrick," he told her. "Whatever may have gone before is of no consequence now, and I assure you that I'll spare no effort to make Deirdre happy."

"I'm sure you won't, and also that Deirdre will have the same concern for your happiness," Alexandra responded. "She tells me that you intend to devote time to going to hospitals here to give other doctors the benefit of the latest developments at Edinburgh University. Wouldn't it be more practical for the doctors to come to you instead?"

"No, because none of the hospitals would be suitable," he explained. "As you know, they're mostly for the poor, and none would be large enough to accommodate enough doctors to make it worthwhile. In time, I hope hospitals become places where anyone would be willing to go for treatment."

Alexandra agreed with him and then fell silent, but she still seemed to be pondering the issue as they walked up the path through the gardens. It led to a small cemetery with a bench at one side. As they sat down on the bench, Alexandra ended her silence, inquiring after his mother and the rest of his family.

The conversation was a respite for Stephen, placing the

events of the morning at a distance. Alexandra's companionship was enjoyable, her serene composure pleasant and relaxing. The discussion was on light topics, and as they chatted, he weighed what to do about the boy's illness.

He knew that his hindrance in making a decision was the same as that which Hamish Mcfee had once mentioned. The doctor's wife had been stricken with infantile paralysis years before, and he had talked about the difficulty of making decisions when the emotions were involved. Stephen struggled to put his love for Deirdre and his feelings for the rest of the family aside, and think of the boy's illness only in a medical context.

Once that was done, he quickly defined his options as a choice between an unacceptable situation and an uncertain, dangerous alternative. It was a choice he had faced on other occasions, as with Danny Hawkins. The safe medical procedure of amputation had been unacceptable. He had saved the boy's legs, but only through some risk to the boy's life.

This case was different in that he would be venturing completely beyond the limits of medical science. Similar attempts had resulted in the death of most patients, but he was unsure of all the circumstances in those instances that might have contributed to the high mortality rate. However, he was sure that at some time, and probably soon, the Kerrick boy would suffer a slow, agonizing death. And that was an unacceptable situation.

Abruptly changing the subject, Stephen told Alexandra that he had decided to perform the surgery. "I thought you would," she said, smiling. "You're a man who takes control of a situation instead of waiting to see what happens. When do you want to do it, Stephen?"

"As soon as we can make ready," he replied. "I brought phenol with me, and the room where the surgery is performed must be completely drenched with a solution of it in water. The room should be one that isn't often frequented by people, which will make it relatively free of germs."

Alexandra pondered for a moment as they left the bench and walked back down the path toward the house, then said, "One of the cottages for married stockmen has been vacant for several weeks. The parlor in it should be suitable. The stockmen's wives will be pleased to help, and Deirdre and I can see to preparing it for the surgery."

Stephen nodded in satisfaction and discussed other arrangements with Alexandra as they went into the house. Oliver and Deirdre were in the parlor, Fiona and Jeremy with their son in his room. A quiet atmosphere in the house changed into activity, Deirdre running upstairs to summon Fiona and Jeremy while Stephen brought the demijohn of phenol down to the parlor.

During the conversation in the parlor, Stephen detected an unspoken question that Fiona at length voiced, asking when they would know if the surgery had been successful. "Within twenty-four hours," he replied. "The number of leucocytes in the boy's bloodstream should decline by then. If it hasn't, that will be evidence of internal infection from the surgery."

"And then?" Fiona persisted.

"Then worse will have come to worst," he told her candidly.

A somber stillness fell, Fiona nodding in fearful resignation. Alexandra ended the quiet, touching Deirdre's arm and turning to the phenol. They hoisted the demijohn by the handles on its wicker basket and lugged it toward the front door to go down and organize the preparations at the cottage, Stephen and the others following them out of the parlor.

Stephen went up to his room and carefully selected the instruments he would need, then gave them and an atomizer for phenol to a maid to take down to the cottage. Presently, Deirdre and Alexandra returned to the house and told him that the preparations at the cottage had been completed. Oliver was waiting with a thick bandage and a bottle of chloroform, and he went down the hall with Stephen to the boy's room.

Fiona stood back from the bed, biting her lip and restraining tears. Stephen placed the bandage over the boy's mouth and nose, then dripped chloroform onto it. At the first strong whiff of the anesthetic, the boy started to resist and involuntarily drew in a deep breath. He went limp, his eyes closing, and he was completely unconscious a moment later.

Jeremy brought in a stretcher he had made, and he and Oliver placed the boy on it. They carried the stretcher out, Stephen and Fiona following them. As they filed down the hall toward the staircase, Stephen heard the distant sound of a corroboree beginning at the Aborigine village.

Deirdre and Alexandra were waiting in the entry, and they joined Stephen and Fiona, following the stretcher out the door. The corroboree was loud outside, and the late summer day seemed to pulse in cadence with the deep, monotone dirge of didgeridoos, clattering rhythm sticks, and voices chanting in harmony. It was the only sound at the home paddock, all activity at a standstill and the people gathered at the cottages.

The household staff, stockmen, and others were in clusters at one side of the path in front of the cottages. Women stood in cottage doorways, holding babies and small children. The schoolteacher, an older half-Aborigine woman, was in front of the schoolhouse with her students, boys and girls of European, Aborigine, and mixed ancestry. The only movement in the scene was smoke rising from the corroboree fire in the Aborigine village, the people gazing somberly at the boy on the stretcher as it passed them.

The fresh, pungent smell of phenol wafted from the last cottage, where Jeremy and Oliver turned off the path. Deirdre and Fiona remained outside, Alexandra accompanying Stephen into the cottage. The front room was empty except for two heavy tables, they and the entire room damp with phenol. The surgical paraphernalia was on one table,

along with cloths, basins, and an atomizer. Jeremy and
Oliver lifted the boy onto the other table, then Jeremy went
back outside to join Deirdre and Fiona.

Stephen washed his hands with soap and water, then
dipped them in phenol. Oliver lifted the boy's nightshirt
and swabbed his stomach with phenol, Alexandra standing
beside the table with the atomizer. She squeezed the bulb,
and a mist of the antiseptic drifted across the table as
Stephen took a scalpel from a basin of phenol and turned
to the boy.

He lowered the scalpel to the area directly over the
veriform appendix, then drew the blade across it in a three-
inch incision. The only time he had ever done such a thing
was during his study of morbid anatomy at the university,
but this was entirely different. The body was that of a living
child, not an aged, withered cadaver. Instead of the scalpel
sinking into flesh as inert as wood, a thick flow of capillary
blood exploded behind the blade.

Oliver wiped the blood away with a cloth, Stephen
stroking the scalpel through the layers of skin. The loud,
droning beat of the corroboree resounded through the room,
seeming to make the very walls vibrate. For a few minutes, it
was an annoying distraction for Stephen, an insistent pulsing
that pounded in his ears. Then, when his movements with the
scalpel fell into rhythm with it, it faded into a background
of noise.

The skin opened, the glistening white sheath of the apo-
neurosis beneath it. Stephen sliced through the membrane,
exposing the muscles of the abdominal wall. The scalpel
began losing its keen edge, starting to tug, and he set
it aside and took another one out of the basin. As he
began incising the muscle tissues, blood spurted from veins.
Oliver grabbed clamps from the basin and fastened them on
the severed ends of the veins.

Stephen took a retractor from the basin, placed the blades
in the incision, and applied pressure to spread the incision
open. He was acutely aware that he had passed beyond

proscribed limits and was peering into a forbidden region, the abdomen of a living human being. Bacteria that could devour the vulnerable, delicate tissues with raging infections were rushing through the incision, at least some undoubtedly escaping annihilation in the mist of phenol drifting across the table from the atomizer.

Inside the incision, the peritoneum was a shining blanket over the viscera. Stephen cautiously lowered the scalpel into the incision, knowing that a touch of the keen blade on an intestine would flood the abdominal cavity with its contents. He estimated the location of the caecum, the large intestine, and gingerly nicked the peritoneum. Inserting a finger into the slit, he lifted it and stroked with the scalpel.

The taut, shiny tissue separated over the deep bend in the caecum where the veriform appendix was located, then Stephen saw it. In the veil of its mesentery, the fan-shaped web of membrane that enfolded and supported it, the organ should have been a small, wormlike extension on the caecum. Instead, it was puffily fat and discolored, bloated with putrescence.

The mesentery, laced with blood vessels, concealed the point on the caecum where the veriform appendix was attached. Stephen took a speculum from the basin and avoided the blood vessels as he made a path through the web with the spoon-shaped instrument. When he could see the base of the veriform appendix, Oliver handed him a ligature.

Guiding the ligature around the veriform appendix with a finger, Stephen was careful not to move the swollen organ for fear that it would burst. He looped the ends of the ligature into a knot, then slowly pulled the knot down the length of the thread. It closed around the base of the organ and then tightened. He tied another knot and pulled it down tightly, then used the scalpel to trim the excess ligature away from the knot.

Stephen cautiously worked the fingers of his left hand down into the incision, then under the veriform appendix.

Cradling it in his fingers, he pinched it adjacent to the knot with his thumb and forefinger. A touch with the scalpel severed it. He lifted it out and dropped it on a cloth on the other table, Oliver gazing in wonder as putrescence gushed from it.

Peering into the incision, Stephen made certain the ligature was holding firmly. He removed the retractor, and Oliver threaded lengths of suture through needles and placed them on a cloth. Stephen sutured the incision with tight, closely spaced stitches, Oliver removing the clamps. Blood seeped from each of the severed veins when the clamp on it was removed, then stopped as soon as Stephen knotted a suture tightly over it.

Alexandra replaced the atomizer on the table and helped Oliver swab the blood off the boy's stomach, and Stephen dampened a bandage in phenol. He placed the bandage over the incision, then pulled the boy's nightgown down. Oliver gathered up the instruments, Alexandra stepping to the door to summon Jeremy, and Stephen washed his hands in a basin.

Just then, the corroboree ceased. Stephen wondered what that meant, if anything. And he wondered if he had saved the boy's life or ended it.

When the boy woke during early afternoon, Stephen examined him and found his condition satisfactory. He was dazed after being anesthetized as well as in pain from the incision, which was normal. Stephen left Fiona and Jeremy coaxing the boy to take sips of water and broth, and went downstairs to join the others in the dining room.

The late tiffin was a delicious assortment of food, but Oliver was the only one with an appetite. Though he shared the concern about the boy, he was also enthused over having participated in what was potentially a new breakthrough in medicine. After the meal, he made his way to the parlor to doze over a newspaper, and Deirdre went upstairs to sit with Jeremy and Fiona in their son's room. Stephen,

feeling restless, quickly accepted when Alexandra offered
to show him around the home paddock.

An atmosphere of tension in the house was mirrored
throughout the home paddock, with activity remaining at an
ebb. People stood about in conversational groups, counting
the hours until the boy's fate would be known the following
afternoon. A tall, muscular man at the horse pen stepped
over to meet Stephen and Alexandra as they walked toward
the station buildings.

The man lifted his hat to Alexandra, then put out his
hand to Stephen. "I'm Roger Corbett, Dr. Brendell," he
introduced himself. "When you see your mother again,
please give her my best regards."

Stephen shook hands with the man, recalling only a
mention of him as the head stockman. "Yes, I will," he
replied. "You knew her, then?"

"Aye, but it was before your time," Roger explained.
"I'm from Wallaby Track, and I had consumption as a boy.
Your granddad and mother advised my ma and pa to send
me here, and that's what they did."

"And provided this station with an excellent head stockman," Alexandra added. "Jeremy told me that Jacob's horses
went lame and he's afoot down in Dingo Paddock. When
will he have other horses?"

"Very shortly, mo'm," Roger told her. "Jacob's jackaroo
got here last night, leading the lame ones. He left this
morning with the replacement horses just after Dr. Brendell
and the others arrived."

Alexandra nodded and then returned the greetings of a
couple of other men who walked over. She introduced them
to Stephen, both of them stockmen, then several older men
sitting on a bench beside the barracks came to join the
conversation. They were retired stockmen, their status the
same as that of a few older women whom Stephen had
noticed at the house.

Most of the conversation was about Christopher, but
enough was said on other things to give Stephen an insight

into the reasons for the intense loyalty and warm regard for the Kerrick family among the employees. Along with being treated generously and with respect, there was a sense of belonging, some employees being the second and third generation of their families at the station. In addition, the employees placed a high value on their association with a station and a family that were legendary in the outback.

After talking with the men, Stephen and Alexandra walked around the knoll below the house and down the creek to the Aborigine village. It consisted of a score of bark huts where some fifty people lived, ranging from oldsters to boys and girls whose hair was the bright blond that was characteristic of young Aborigine children. They were going about their affairs and working over baskets, animal skins, and traditional tools and weapons.

Few spoke English, and Stephen and Alexandra exchanged smiles and waves with them. Turning back up the creek, Stephen asked Alexandra what the Aborigines did at the station. "Whatever they wish," she replied. "They were on this land first. On occasion, they deal with dingo infestations and things of that nature. We provide them with rations and other necessities, and those who wish send their children to the school."

Stephen had asked her about the corroboree earlier and learned that she was unaware of its specific purpose, but she had intended to ask others about it. "Did you determine the purpose of the corroboree?" he asked.

"No, I talked with Emma Bodenham, and she either didn't know or didn't want to say," Alexandra told him. "Jeremy grew up with the Arandas, but this tribe has a different language and customs, so he doesn't know. However, I'm sure it was meant to aid Christopher in some fashion."

Stephen nodded, thinking about the cessation of the corroboree at the end of the surgery. That could be interpreted as very promising or equally discouraging, but nothing in between. It had been as though the Aborigines had considered the ceremony either no longer needed, or entirely futile.

At the orchards, most of the fruit had been gathered, but some apples, pears, and peaches remained to ripen into the mellow richness of late summer fruit. Spoiled fruit had been left on the ground for bees in hives along the creek, and they were swarming over it and drawing nectar that would make a honey of luscious sweetness and piquant flavor. Stephen found that Alexandra was skilled in horticulture, pausing with her at the orchards and then vegetable gardens while she explained how they were cultivated.

Alexandra also had a practical knowledge of medicine, discussing the subject with Stephen as they walked on up the path. She told him that there had been instances when she would have liked a doctor to be immediately available, however, and she would provide a house, rations, and salary for any young doctor who would like a position at the station. He promised to keep it in mind in the event that he met a young doctor in need of a position.

The sun was touching the horizon as they walked past the cottages, smoke from dinner fires rising from the chimneys. The last glow of sunset was fading into dusk by the time they reached the house, and Stephen went upstairs for his bag, then to the boy's room.

Jeremy and Fiona stepped back from their chairs beside the bed while Stephen examined the boy, finding his condition still as favorable as could be expected. The effects of the anesthetic had passed, his pain increasing, and Stephen gave him a small amount of antipyrene. He told Fiona and Jeremy to continue giving the boy as much water and broth as he would take, then he returned his bag to his room and went back downstairs.

A funereal quiet at dinner was averted by Alexandra's having brought little Sheila to the dining room, her cheerful, childish talk providing a pleasant distraction. After the meal, the nurse came for Sheila and took her to her room, and Stephen went to the parlor with the others. The conversation was desultory, the solemn ticking of the clock seeming very loud as it counted off the minutes. At bedtime, while the others filed upstairs to their rooms, Stephen got his bag and went to the boy's room again.

The wan smile on Christopher's small, handsome face went straight to Stephen's heart, as it did each time he examined the child. The boy was starting to recover from the shock and blood loss of the surgery, his general condition improving, but Stephen knew that a lethal onslaught of infection could by now be in the first, undetectable stage within him. After sedating the boy with antipyrene so he would sleep through the night, Stephen told Jeremy and Fiona to wake him if there was any change, then he went to his room.

Hours passed before Stephen finally fell asleep. He was awakened during the dark hours of early morning by a loud, insistent pounding of the front door knocker. A moment later, he heard footsteps in the hall that could only be Jeremy's, the rapid, heavy pace conveying anger. The noise stopped, and Stephen went back to sleep a few minutes later.

At the first glimmer of dawn, he woke to gnawing anxiety about the boy. After dressing, he went downstairs to the bathhouse, the house quiet and dark in the twilight of early dawn. By the time he finished washing and shaving, the household staff was at work and the cook had made coffee. Stephen filled a cup and stepped back outside with it.

Drinking the coffee, he watched the sunrise of one of the most important days of his life. His personal involvement made the boy far more than a patient to him, and the case was vital in another way. It could be a guiding light, or it could be a warning to retreat for further years of study, during which others would die in agony with perityphlitic abscess. He stepped inside and left the cup in the kitchen, then went upstairs.

Jeremy was gone from the boy's room, Fiona sitting

beside the bed by herself, and Christopher was still sleeping soundly. Deciding not to disturb the boy, Stephen turned his attention to Fiona. Strain and fatigue had taken a toll on her, her face pale and drawn. Moving quietly to avoid waking the boy, Stephen mixed a bromide in the glass on the nightstand.

When she tried to decline it, he insisted that she take it. "Drink it, Fiona," he ordered firmly in a soft voice. "Do you know what all the commotion was about before daylight this morning?"

Fiona drained the glass, wincing at the taste, and replaced it on the nightstand. "Yes, it was some lad who arrived here last night with a swagman," she whispered in reply. "I'm not sure what he wanted, because Jeremy said no more about it."

Stephen nodded and turned to the door, telling Fiona that he would return when Christopher was awake. He stepped down the hall and left his bag in his room, then went downstairs and joined Deirdre, Alexandra, and Oliver in the dining room. They expressed satisfaction when he told them that Christopher had spent a restful night, then the conversation turned to the disturbance in the night. Stephen related what Fiona had told him, then he and the others speculated about what the boy may have wanted.

The speculation ended when Jeremy stepped in, an annoyed frown making his pale blue eyes icily cold. He explained that the swagman was ill, and the boy had demanded that the two doctors at the house immediately come and see to his mate. "The boy's name is Lesley Holleck," Jeremy went on, "and he's a saucy little birkie. I went down to the barracks and had a look at the swagman, and he was most regretful that his mate had caused such a barney at that hour. His name is Alfie Gunch, and he's an agreeable old loppy. He said that he'd rather await the doctor's convenience."

"When we rode through Dingo Paddock yesterday,"

Deirdre recalled, "I thought I heard someone shout. It may have been them."

"It was that little spoonbill," Jeremy confirmed. "He kept on about it last night until I was ready to choke him. I've just been down to check on Alfie again, and it would be good if you'd have a look at him, Stephen."

"What seems to be wrong with him?" Stephen asked.

"I'd say it's mostly age," Jeremy replied. "He gets winded easily, his chest aches, and his feet swell if he's on them for too long."

Stephen exchanged a meaningful glance with Oliver, the old doctor shaking his head somberly as he continued eating his breakfast. The symptoms were those of cardiac insufficiency, a serious, eventually fatal condition for which there was no corrective treatment. Stephen had finished as much breakfast as he could eat, and he followed Jeremy out.

Jeremy went to look in on Fiona and his son, and Stephen got his bag from his room and stepped on down the hall to Christopher's room. Fiona was spooning up the boy's breakfast of thin porridge, and he was alert and in good spirits despite the pain from his incision. Stephen gave him another small dosage of antipyrene to depress the pain, then accompanied Jeremy downstirs and out the front door, going down to the barracks.

It was a long, narrow building, airy and well lighted, and with a fireplace at both ends for winter months. Bunks were under the windows along each side, and the swagman was lying on an end bunk, the boy sitting on a stool beside him. Stephen introduced himself, taking out his stethoscope. Alfie was a portly man in his late sixties, and his heart was laboring with a faltering rhythm. Under the dark tan on his wrinkled features, the man's skin had a cyanotic tinge, a symptom of advanced cardiac insufficiency.

The condition severe, Stephen knew the man's chest pains had been intense when he had arrived on foot the night before. However, the man's reason for preferring to wait until the next day for a doctor to see him became evident to Stephen while examining and talking with him. Alfie was a modest, self-effacing old man, not wanting to be any trouble to anyone.

His meek nature was a sharp contrast to that of Lesley Holleck, whose hazel eyes peered aggressively from under an oversize stockman's hat. Jeremy had said that the boy was about thirteen, but Stephen thought he was older and simply maturing more slowly than average. Although he was well over five feet tall, his well-modeled features were still delicate, lacking a masculine cast and any trace of facial hair. He was threadbare but conspicuously cleaner than others who lived on the tracks, his faded, patched shirt tucked neatly into ragged trousers belted with a rope.

Stephen returned his stethoscope to his bag and selected a bottle of digitalis tincture from among its contents. "Take a sip of this three times daily, Alfie," he told the swagman. "You'll probably want to follow it with water, because it has a bitter taste."

"I'm much obliged, Dr. Brendell, indeed I am," the man said gratefully. He drew the cork from the bottle and sniffed it, his snowy mustache and beard opening in a wry grin. "Bedad if you're not right that it's bitter. Lesley, fetch me a drop of water, if you would."

Keenly eager to help the aged man, the boy hastily rummaged in the swag under the bunk. He grabbed a fire-blackened billy, then ran toward the door. As soon as his young mate was out of earshot, Alfie gazed up at Stephen solemnly. "How bad am I in holts with it, Dr. Brendell?" he asked. "I opine that I'm nigh onto doing a perisher."

"Yes, you are," Stephen agreed candidly. "The medicine will ease your discomfort and help you somewhat, but the end will come soon. Your days on the tracks are finished, because you can't travel."

Alfie nodded, turning his gaze to Jeremy. "I'm sorry for coming here to die, Mr. Kerrick," he said, "but there's a furthersome I must ask of you. I'd like to know that Lesley can stay here. You'll never find a harder worker or a better one at dealing with sheep and other animals."

"You've no need to be sorry, Alfie," Jeremy assured the aged man. "You are more than welcome to spend your last days here, and I only hope that they'll be happy ones. And you can set your mind at rest about your mate. Saucy poddy that he is, he can have a job as a jackaroo."

Tears filled the swagman's faded eyes, and he struggled to find words to express his gratitude. The attempt was cut short, Lesley's footsteps ending the conversation, for the aged man obviously wanted to conceal the seriousness of his condition from the boy. Stephen and Jeremy stepped toward the door, the boy bustling past them with the dripping billy.

Leaving the barracks, Jeremy hurried ahead to return to his wife and son. Stephen walked toward the house at a more measured pace, thinking about the events involving Alfie and Lesley. The outcome was an illustration of the reputation of Tibooburra Station, its unstinting generosity to one and all who came up the track as legendary as the vast station itself.

As they pertained to himself, however, Stephen found an interpretation for those same events that was disquieting. Alfie's incurable condition had been a stern reminder of the limits on what medical science could do. With his surgery on the Kerrick boy, Stephen wondered if he had moved those limits farther out, or if meeting the aged swagman had been a warning that he had overstepped those limits into failure and the death of the child.

Shortly after returning from the barracks, Stephen examined Christopher and found his general condition continuing to improve. Stephen was tempted to examine a blood sample, but he resisted it. What it revealed could be misleading; a few more hours were needed for the leucocytes from the abscessed veriform appendix to diminish. That same time was also needed for them to become numerous in a foredoomed battle against internal infection.

The remainder of the hours until early afternoon seemed to Stephen the longest of his life, and he felt inundated with reminders of death. For a time he sat in the parlor, where Alexandra and Oliver discussed people they had known over the years, and virtually everyone they mentioned was now dead. Later, he walked with Deirdre in the gardens beside the house, and the station cemetery kept drawing his gaze. Down at the barracks, Alfie had joined the aged men on the bench beside the building, grasping at the enjoyment of companionship and conversation in his last days.

Near midday, Stephen and Deirdre rejoined Alexandra and Oliver in the parlor. They discussed tiffin and then agreed to defer the meal until later, even the old doctor having no appetite for once. The general conversation was a veneer of sociability over suspenseful waiting, and Stephen tried to keep up his side of it.

The grandfather clock chimed twelve times, twenty-three hours having elapsed since the surgery. An hour either way would make no substantial difference, but when setting a time for the waiting to end, Stephen had decided upon precisely twenty-four hours. A few minutes later, Jeremy came down from his son's room and took a seat in the parlor. Everyone glanced frequently at the clock, its measured ticking a background to the conversation.

Alexandra brought up the subject of the clock, explaining how she had set the time on it. "At first I kept it on the time in Sydney," she said, "then I moved it ahead. The time there is too early for here."

"Yes, it is indeed," Oliver agreed. "The time at Adelaide is used in Wilcannia, but that might also be too early. Even though the shops there open and the workday begins at a later hour during winter, like in many places, my housekeeper tells me that it's well before cockcrow."

Jeremy remarked that activities at the station were governed by daylight hours rather than a clock, Alexandra agreeing with him. The conversation was symbolic to Stephen of everything about Tibooburra Station. It was at a distance from other places in so many ways not measurable in miles, and having its own framework of time seemed logical to him.

The conversation became desultory, then it was gradually smothered by increasing tension. While the final few minutes passed, seeming an eternity to Stephen, the only sound was the slow, grave ticking of the clock. Then it struck the hour, a single chime that shattered the quiet. Stephen stood up and stepped toward the door, Oliver following him out.

A maid was watching from down the hall, and she stepped to the kitchen. She spoke with the rest of the staff, someone relaying the comments to stockmen outside the back door. It was a stir of anxious whispers more felt than audible as Stephen went up the stairs, and he heard Deirdre, Alexandra, and Jeremy file out of the parlor to wait outside the boy's room.

Fiona stood up from her chair, torn between satisfaction at the end of the suspense and an agony of dread for what it might bring. The boy was asleep, and Stephen gently woke him. A poignant upswell of fondness within Stephen answered to the drowsy smile that wreathed the boy's small, handsome face, Oliver handing over a needle and microscope slide.

The boy flinched involuntarily, a bead of blood forming on his finger. Stephen smeared it onto the slide, then stepped to the table. His hands trembling with nervousness, he stained the slide and placed it on the microscope stage. The lens was out of focus, and he was suddenly and irrationally enraged, twisting the focusing knob furiously.

The view through the lens swam into focus, but the hours of grueling tension had instilled in him something more than caution. At the crucial juncture of events, so much depended upon the outcome that he mistrusted what he saw. He moved the slide on the stage and examined a different area of the blood. Still unable to believe, he moved the slide again.

Oliver became impatient, plucking at Stephen's sleeve. "What's taking you so long, Stephen?" he asked plaintively. "Let me have a look."

The old doctor eagerly leaned over the microscope as Stephen moved away from it. At last believing what he had seen, Stephen turned to Fiona with a triumphant smile. Her searching, fearful gaze changed to an expression of joy, and she started to ask a question just as he began speaking. Their voices ran together, both of them drowned by Oliver's excited shout. "You did it, Stephen!" he whooped. "You did it! The lad would have this many white blood cells from an infected scratch on his hand!"

The door flew open, Deirdre and Jeremy rushing in, and the room was suddenly a pandemonium. Jeremy shouted his delight, Fiona bursting into tears of joy and throwing herself into his arms. Oliver grabbed Stephen's hand and shook it vigorously, loudly congratulating him, and Deirdre hugged and kissed him. The nurse was in the hall with Sheila, and they followed Alexandra into the room. The small, redheaded girl had no idea of the reason for excitement, but she happily joined in with shrieks of enjoyment.

Maids in the hall ran toward the staircase, shouting the news, and those downstairs responded in a chorus of cheering voices. The joyful bedlam spread outside the house, where stockmen yelled elatedly and informed the rest of the home paddock. In the midst of the uproar, Alexandra stood quietly on the other side of the room from Stephen.

He knew that she only appeared impassive, and like his own happiness, hers went far beyond expressions of joy. The ageless, beautiful woman was ever more fascinating to him. Her eyes met his gaze across the confusion in the room, and she smiled warmly while silently forming words with her lips: Thank you. He smiled and nodded in reply.

Then he took control of the situation, quieting the room. "Let's let Christopher rest now," he announced over the noise. "The more rest he has, the sooner he'll be up and about."

"Yes, Christopher must rest," Alexandra seconded firmly. "Beryl, please take Sheila to her room. Jeremy, I believe it would be appropriate to have a shivoo so everyone at the home paddock can celebrate."

Jeremy agreed emphatically, he and Alexandra following the nurse as she carried little Sheila out of the room. Oliver put the microscope into its case and carried it out, and Deirdre stepped to Stephen. A glow of buoyantly high spirits animating her lovely features, she gave him a quick, fierce kiss that was a promise of passionate lovemaking, and then she left. Fiona sat beside the bed and held her son's hand, tearful with gratitude and happiness. Stephen examined the boy and made certain he was comfortable after all the excitement, then he went downstairs.

The house had been transformed, the somber tension replaced by a cheery, lighthearted atmosphere. The breeze wafting through open windows carried a distant hubbub of happy voices from the station buildings, where Jeremy was organizing preparations for the celebration. Deirdre, Alexandra, and Oliver were in the dining room, and Stephen joined them.

The cook had rustled up a hasty but lavish and delicious tiffin that included cold chicken, smoked fish, fresh salad and fruit, an assortment of pickles, and a dish of hot, crisp scones soaked with butter. After the past two days with little appetite, Stephen was ravenous, and he heaped his plate with food. During the lively conversation around the table, Oliver stoutly maintained that Stephen had made medical history, and he should submit an article on the surgical procedure to the medical journals.

Stephen was more cautious, intending to repeat the procedure several times before announcing it to others through the journals. "I must make certain of how internal infection was avoided," he explained. "The results here were the precise opposite of those at Edinburgh and elsewhere."

"You must have some idea of the reasons now," Alexandra pointed out. "Otherwise, you wouldn't attempt the surgery again, would you?"

"One is speed," Oliver put in firmly. "Stephen is faster and yet still more skillful with a scalpel than anyone I've ever seen. That reduces the shock and blood loss that a patient will suffer from surgery, and it also cuts down on the chances of infection getting into an incision."

"Not loitering certainly helps," Stephen acknowledged, "but also, that cottage was relatively free of germs. Hospitals are anything but that, and before I attempt the surgery again, I'll have orderlies put special effort into cleaning a treatment room. The best solution, if it could be done, would be to have a room where only abdominal surgery is performed."

Alexandra pursed her lips and nodded thoughtfully, pondering what he had said. Deirdre asked when Christopher would be able to leave his room, leading to a discussion of the subject. Stephen concluded it by deciding that if the boy continued improving, he could start moving about the next day.

After the meal was finished, Oliver went to the parlor and Stephen walked out into the gardens beside the house with Deirdre and Alexandra. At the station buildings, the stockmen had been joined by women from the cottages as well as the schoolteacher and her pupils in making arrangements for the celebration. Some were hanging strings of lanterns, while others set up long tables and dug a pit in preparation to roast a whole bullock. The mild sunshine of late summer cast a soft, golden glow over the scene as the people scurried about happily, their cheery voices carrying up to the gardens.

In his own triumphant joy, the day seemed the most wondrous of his entire life to Stephen. Upon his return to Australia, he had looked forward to personal and professional satisfaction, but his expectations had been immeasurably exceeded. Having found the only woman he could ever

love, he had won her over. Through her, he had been drawn
into the fascinating Kerrick family, the owners of this vast
domain at the remote edge of civilization. He had saved the
Kerrick boy's life, and through doing so, he had discovered
a means to thwart a deadly killer, a way that would rescue
many from an agonizing death in years to come. Glowing
with bliss, he was certain that nothing more could happen
to make the day more perfect for him.

But something did. Alexandra brought up a subject they
had touched upon the day before, making an intriguing
offer. While it would benefit him professionally, it also triggered an exciting train of thought about another possibility,
one that made his spirits soar to supreme happiness.

Chapter Twenty-Five

"How long has Betsy been troubled with this?" Stephanie asked.

"About a year, off and on," Enid Carrigan replied. "Every time it has healed up, it went away on its own. Dr. Mcfee has tried any number of remedies, but not one has been of any avail whatsoever."

"Yes, as I mentioned, he asked me to look at it," Stephanie reminded the woman, "the same way that I ask his opinion with some patients." Seated at the table in the farmhouse kitchen, she peered at the girl's ears. A pretty, sweet-natured child of twelve, Betsy Carrigan had a rash on her earlobes that extended halfway up her ears, and she was wearing earrings. "Are you certain that Betsy's earrings are made of gold?" Stephanie asked.

"I'm positive," Enid stated firmly. "Betsy was wearing those earrings for more than two years before she started having those sores."

The explanation appeared to eliminate sensitivity to base metal as the cause of the rash, but Stephanie was still suspicious about the earrings, which had been the cause of virtually every rash she had seen on a girl's or woman's ears. She pulled the girl closer, studying the earrings in the late afternoon sunlight streaming through the kitchen window.

"Your son and his wife bought a house in Parramatta, didn't they?" Enid offered conversationally. "I had it in mind that he was going to visit other cities to teach doctors things he had learned."

"Stephen has had patients with perityphlitic abscess and other illnesses coming to him from all parts of Australia," Stephanie explained. "He's using the facilities at the Sydney hospital, and it appears that he'll be there for a considerable time, because the patients continue arriving."

"I'm sure that you're happy that he and his wife are living close enough to visit often," Enid observed. "Have you seen their house?"

"Yes. Eric, Yulina, and I visited them a fortnight ago last Sunday," Stephanie replied. "It's very comfortable, and in surroundings much more congenial than the noise and smoke of the city. Now that Parramatta Road has been improved, Stephen and Deirdre can travel between their home and their work in the city within a very short time."

Enid agreed that it was an excellent arrangement, and Stephanie turned her full attention to the earrings again, questioning the woman about them and the rash. At times the rash had been on only one ear, which made Stephanie suspect even more that the earrings were the cause. Then she became deeply suspicious when she learned who had sold them to Enid.

"So you bought them from a pedlar," Stephanie mused. "They appear to be gold, but I'd be much more confident about that if you had bought them from a goldsmith instead of a pedlar. It would be wise to remove them for a few weeks to see if the rash recurs without them."

"That's what Dr. Mcfee said, but if I did that, the holes in Betsy's earlobes would close," Enid objected. "Regardless of who sold them to me, I'm positive that they're pure gold. I'll take one of them off so you can look at it better and see for yourself. Come here, Betsy."

The girl stepped to her mother, who removed one of the earrings and handed it across the table to Stephanie. Thin and small in circumference, it was too light for her to judge if it was gold from its weight in her hand. It was the color of gold, but when she held it close to her eyes and studied it, she saw streaks of a slightly different shade.

Stephanie nodded in satisfaction, the streaks revealing the cause of the rash. Years before, a London metalsmith named Forney had developed an alloy of brass and copper for inexpensive jewelry that closely resembled gold. It had been called forney originally, but the word had become altered over the years. "Betsy's earrings are phoney," she said, "and only plated with gold. The gold gradually wore off in places, and that's when the rash began. Now, whenever the earrings turn in Betsy's ears so that the spots of base metal come into contact with her ears, they cause the rash."

Enid frowned as she grabbed the earring and held it near her eyes, peering at it. "Aye, you're right," she agreed angrily. "They're phoney, plated with gold. That pedlar had better never show his face at my door again." She sighed and shrugged in resignation. "Well, at least you'll be able to put a quick end to those sores, won't you?"

"Yes, this will heal it up quickly," Stephanie replied, taking a small tin of zinc oxide in Seneca oil out of her bag. "Put this on her ears twice each day until the rash is completely gone."

Enid took the tin, thanking Stephanie, and saw her to the front door. After donning her coat and hat, Stephanie went out into the balmy, mellow sunshine of the autumn afternoon in late April. Stepping into her buggy, she drove away from the house and toward the main road.

The success of the call seemed an appropriate ending to the day, which had been notable. She had attended a birthing from early morning, and during midafternoon, a baby girl had been born to Martha and Joshua Kenney. While the event in itself had been a repetition of many others, this one had been special. Twenty years before, almost to the day, she had delivered Martha. Just over two years before that, she had delivered Joshua.

Turning onto the main road, Stephanie thought about her conversation with Enid about Stephen and Deirdre's living a relatively short distance away. Despite that, she had seen far too little of them, over a fortnight having passed since the last time. While she yearned for their companionship, her love and pride in her son matched only by her close, warm relationship with her captivating daughter-in-law, it was without impatience. She accepted that they had urgent affairs at present, knowing that the occasional times they could spend with her would enrich the years ahead.

Their return from the outback as a married couple had occurred in autumn, which had always been her favorite time of year. With crisp mornings and the smell of smoke from stubble burning in the fields, autumn was the time of reaping the results of a chapter in life. The people gathering in crops at the farms beside the road were laughing and singing while they worked, the harvest a particularly good one this year. Stephanie's mood matched theirs, for the harvest of her life was also abundant. A marriage that remained loving, successful children, Deirdre as her daughter-in-law, and innumerable devoted, loyal friends were a richly bountiful harvest. And now she was delivering babies who were in a sense her grandchildren.

Autumn was also tinged with melancholy for her, with nostalgic longing to grasp at an indefinable something that was slipping away. She knew that the feeling arose from the mortal condition, from being rudderless in the tides of fate and time. But the most exquisite pleasure was always found at the threshold of pain, and that bittersweet aspect made the season even more poignantly enjoyable. It made the soft, hazy days more precious, a time to savor and then to hold in memory against the icy gales of winter.

Similarly, the great sorrow in her life had in a way become a contrast against which to measure her happiness. The desolate, ruined hulk of the prison remained a source of harrowing grief for her, her father's vital spirit trapped within its dark, dismal stone walls for eternity. The agonizing wound would never heal, but over the years she had struggled and succeeded to some extent in placing it in proportion with the joys of her life.

The dark, somber prison roof came into view above trees on the hill where the village sat, and as always, it immediately drew Stephanie's gaze. But moments later, she turned onto the village road and her view of the prison roof was overcome by that of her house, with its promise of homey comforts and loving companionship. Glancing at her watch, she saw that the district clerk's office would still be open, and she drove past the house and on up the road to register the birth of the Kenney child.

When she passed the road leading to the sawmill, Stephanie noted with satisfaction that work had ended for the day. Recently, Eric had worked late each day to fill orders from farmers making repairs to buildings in preparation for winter. She was pleased that that evidently had been finished, for her hours with him were priceless. She drove on up the road, and at the top of the hill, it led into the cobblestone main street of the village, which had changed very little over the past decades.

Now something was different, however, and the realization that a change had occurred broke into Stephanie's pleasant reverie. She sat up in her buggy and looked around. Then her contented mood withered, annihilated by a blast of raw, ghastly horror that struck her like a juggernaut.

The overgrown lane leading back to the abandoned prison at the edge of the village had been cleared of growth. The tangled brambles and rank weeds in the prison yard and around the grim, hulking structure had also been chopped down, and it was no longer deserted. Workmen were dragging out charred, rotted timbers and throwing them into a large dray parked in front, and two men in suits were supervising the work.

Thomas Miles, a middle-aged farmer, drove a wagon up the lane from the prison, a dour expression on his bearded face. Turning onto the street, he stopped his wagon. "G'day, Mistress Brendell," he muttered, touching his hat. "I'd far sooner have the plague of rabbits that will ruin us when it gets here, but we're to have convicts again."

"Is that what the men in charge said?" Stephanie asked numbly.

"No, they're silvertails, fancying themselves too good to talk with the likes of me," Thomas grumbled. "But that's the only use that could be made of that place, and they're probably keeping a still tongue about it so as not to have a ruction with the people here on their hands." He touched his hat again, snapping his reins. "G'day to you, Mistress Brendell."

The wagon moved away, Stephanie gazing in despair at the men moving about the dark, towering building. The peace and quiet of a revered presence was being rudely disturbed. It was as though gravestones were being cast aside like debris and hallowed ground was being tilled for crops. She turned away, driving through the village toward the district clerk's office.

Tipton Bellamy was aged and hard of hearing, and at first he failed to understand Stephanie's question. When she repeated it loudly, he finally grasped it. "Yes, I received a message from the Land Commissioner," he said. "The prison is being restored so it can be used again."

"As a prison?" Stephanie specified.

Tipton blinked in surprise at the question, then nodded. "Why, certainly," he told her. "It couldn't be used for anything else, could it?"

The reply confirmed Stephanie's fears, creating sorrow more intense than any physical pain. Now she knew that the peace and quiet which had reigned within the stone walls for decades would be replaced by the clanking of chains and an atmosphere seething with rage, agony, and grief. In her distraction, she almost wrote in the ledger that Tipton had placed on his desk before she noticed that it was the death registry. She called it to his attention, and he apologized, going to the shelf for the birth registry.

Leaving the office, Stephanie dreaded going home. Eric and Yulina would know about the work at the prison and want to comfort her, and while she was always grateful for their concern when troubled, she greatly preferred simply to be left alone. She knew it was something she would have to endure, however, and she drove back through the village. Work at the prison had ended for the day, but she knew the men would return.

The atmosphere at her house was just as she had anticipated. Eric came out to attend to her horse and buggy, giving her a sympathetic greeting, then she went into the kitchen and met with the same attitude from Yulina. When Eric came in and Yulina served up dinner, they began a lively conversation between themselves. Stephanie knew it was meant to raise her spirits, but it was nerve-racking and made her even more depressed.

Stephanie picked at her food without appetite during the meal, then sought the solitude of her surgery. She puttered about in it, whiling away the hours until bedtime. Dusk fell quickly, and after lighting the lamp, she stepped to the window and looked out. In the thin, fading daylight, she saw that thick clouds were moving in from the east.

A short time later, she realized that the weather was matching her abrupt change of mood upon going to the village. The wind rose in a sudden blast that thrashed the trees outside and howled around the house. It found its way into the room, making the flame in the lamp flicker and bringing an icy, penetrating chill from the far reaches of the sea. An unseasonable winter storm had rushed down upon the coast and was making landfall.

The wind increased to a gale that battered at the house and the trees outside with its surging gusts, then the rain came. Scattered heavy drops thudding against the house were followed by drenching waves, and by the time that Stephanie went to bed, the storm was raging in its full fury. It continued through the night, subduing dawn the next morning to feeble gray light that seeped through the thick clouds and driving rain.

When she set out to make her calls, Stephanie was torn between desire to avoid the prison and a compulsive need to know if the work was proceeding during the storm. The compulsion won out, and she drove to the village. From the street, the towering, dismal hulk was a somber backdrop for shadowy forms scurrying about it in the dim light and pouring rain. The work seemed to be some evil undertaking driven by a remorseless, powerful force that was immune to unseasonable weather or any other hindrance.

As well as replacing balmy autumn weather with winter cold and damp, the storm had shattered the leisurely pace in the valley. The last of the crops were being frantically gathered before they spoiled, and people and horses struggled with wagons bogged down in muddy fields. Farmers were hastily moving stock from low-lying pastures that could flood, and contemplation of repairs in preparation for winter had changed into a frenzy of work.

The prison had always been a blight upon Wallaby Track to Stephanie, the one blemish that marred the otherwise perfect scenic beauty and idyllic pattern of life in the valley. It seemed to her that during the decades when the prison had been a forgotten, abandoned hulk, some baneful influence had been quiescent. But on the same day that work had begun to restore the prison, an untimely storm had swept down on the valley, bringing disruption and misery. She found it very compelling to view the work and the storm as something more than completely unrelated.

The storm raged with undiminished force through the night and into the next day. At farms where Stephanie made calls that day, most of what could be done to save crops had been accomplished, but the ordeal from the storm continued. Shingle roofs leaked, chimneys constructed with less than expert skill filled houses with smoke, icy drafts found cracks around windows and doors, and the people were cold, wet, and miserable.

In their discontent, they grumbled about the work being done at the prison. There was some talk about preparing a petition to protest the presence of convicts again, but Stephanie knew it would be futile. Once funds had been committed to restoring the prison, nothing would stop it.

At a house where she made a call during the afternoon, Stephanie had a conversation that took her thoughts entirely away from the prison and storm for a time. An adult son at the farm had just returned from a stock auction at Bathurst, and he told her about having traveled through snow in the Blue Mountains. She realized that the two gang gang cockatoos which for decades had lived in a tree beside her house during late autumn and winter should have arrived now that the storm had brought snow to the mountains.

During those decades, Stephanie had regarded the mated pair of birds as her pets and kept them supplied with their favorite food of barley during the months they had lived at her house. Moreover, their annual migrations had framed many events in her life. She had worried about them each year until they returned, and increasingly during recent years. Even though gang gang cockatoos were reputed to be long-lived, these were now very old.

Stephanie was even more uneasy after talking with the man, concerned that the birds may have been caught in the mountains by the sudden storm. The only time they sang was upon their arrival and departure, which were always during early morning. While she had not heard them, the noise of the storm would have drowned their singing the past two mornings. She anxiously hoped that they had set out from the mountains before the storm struck, then took shelter somewhere on their long flight to her house.

She tried to finish her calls in time to see if the birds had arrived, but nightfall came early on the stormy day, darkness closing in while she was hurrying home. Over dinner, Stephanie asked Eric and Yulina if they had happened to notice the birds, but he had seen nothing of them, and she had remained indoors the past two days. Eric and Yulina tried to assure her that the birds were safe, but only seeing them would ease her fears.

When the first glimmer of light penetrated the clouds and rain the next morning, Stephanie was at her bedroom window. Eric stood behind her, silently waiting. The light slowly brightened, the tree where the birds always perched emerging from the darkness. Moments later, through the rain streaming down the window, Stephanie could see the sheltered limb they chose each time. The cockatoos not on it, she sagged in bitter disappointment.

"Perhaps they're in a different tree this time, love," Eric suggested uneasily. "Or it could be that they—"

He broke off, Stephanie leaning closer to the window. At the base of the limb on which the birds always sat, she saw what could be loose bark on the tree trunk, or a small, rain-drenched bird. Stephanie threw the window open and leaned out, oblivious to the rain pouring down on her, and saw that it was the female cockatoo. Spinning away from the window, she grabbed up the hem of her skirt from her toes and raced toward the door.

Eric closed the window and his rapid footsteps followed Stephanie as she rushed out the door and toward the staircase. She went down the stairs two at a time, and ran down the hall and through the kitchen, Yulina jumping out of her path. Stephanie flung the back door open and raced around the house to the tree outside her window. Then she could clearly see the cockatoo at the base of the limb, some twenty feet above the ground.

The small, owl-like bird was pitiful, its feathers bedraggled and its pattern of pale red a dull, dark gray from the rain. Its eyes frequently closing for a few seconds at a time, it was leaning against the tree trunk for support. It appeared to be completely exhausted.

Eric caught up with Stephanie, shrugging into his oil-skins, and he helped her on with hers. "I could get a ladder and see if I can catch him," he offered. "Perhaps if we took him into the house—"

"Her," Stephanie interrupted, correcting him. "Trying to catch her might frighten her away, and the house would be unhealthily warm for her."

"Well, the storm could have separated it from the other one, love," Eric observed. "The other one might arrive here today."

It seemed at least a possibility to Stephanie, one she urgently wanted to believe, and she nodded hopefully. A moment later, Yulina came out in her oilskins, carrying a bag of barley. Stephanie took the bag and stepped to the tree, and Eric and Yulina went back into the house.

At the foot of the tree was a flat stone that she had used for years as a feeder for the birds. She brushed leaves off the stone, poured out the barley, and propped a slab of bark over it to protect it from the rain. Then she stepped back and watched the cockatoo. After several minutes, the bird making no move to fly down, Stephanie went into the house.

Yulina had prepared the usual large breakfast, but Stephanie could eat only a toasted round of bread with a cup of coffee, then she stepped back out to the tree. The barley was untouched, the small bird in the same position as before. She longed to stay and watch for the male cockatoo, but in addition to scheduled calls, she needed to check on the most recent newborns to make certain they were suffering no ill effects from the change in weather. She turned away, walking around the house toward her buggy.

The rain slackened during the forenoon, but the cold, gusty wind continued. The first calls were scattered in the south end of the valley, and driving up and down the muddy roads consumed as much time as the calls. By midday, when Stephanie drove toward farms at the north end of the valley, it was obvious to her that it would be well after dark when she returned home, but she knew that Yulina would watch for the other cockatoo.

The bleak, raw afternoon passed, then the thin daylight faded while Stephanie was making the last of her calls. She drove back down the valley, the coachlamps on her buggy gleaming in the darkness thickened by the drizzle and wisps of fog swirling in the wind. When she drove into the barnyard behind the house, Eric came out of the kitchen.

The lantern he carried illuminated the regretful expression on his face, answering the question on her lips even before he spoke. "The other cockatoo isn't here yet, love," he told her soberly. "Yulina kept an eye on the tree today, and I came home before dark to have a look. This weather must still be delaying it, and it'll probably be here tomorrow."

His hopeful prediction seemed unlikely to Stephanie, the circumstances now pointing to an infinity of tomorrows that would never arrive. But it offered the only defense, albeit a flimsy one, against a tide of bitter sorrow that surged at the back of her mind. She seized upon it, willing herself to accept it. Eric led her horse into the barn to unharness it, and she lit a lantern in the barn and followed its puddle of yellow light through the gloom and drizzle to the tree at the side of the house.

Trickles of rainwater had found their way around the edge of the bark to the flat stone, disturbing the barley and making it difficult to tell if the cockatoo had eaten any. Stephanie tried to convince herself that it had, and she returned the lantern to the barn and then went into the house with Eric. She forced herself to eat a few bites of dinner to satisfy her need for food, then found things to do in her surgery until bedtime.

It was a restless night for Stephanie, her shallow, broken sleep haunted by dreams that took form from her depressed thoughts during wakeful moments. She visualized the small male cockatoo battling the storm, struggling to reach his refuge. Against her will, she also had mental images of the bird with his last dregs of strength drained, plummeting to the ground somewhere across the distance between the mountains and her home.

Stephanie also thought about the female cockatoo, driven by instinct and ingrained habits to fly on alone. While leaning against the tree trunk, her large, velvety eyes closing, the bird had appeared exhausted. Stephanie wondered if instead, the bird had been bereft by loneliness, confusion, and advanced age, and willing her life to end.

The wind diminished and then ceased just before dawn, the drizzle a soft rustle on the roof. When Stephanie rose and dressed, the room had a damp chill from thick fog that was like a gray curtain outside the window. She started to rush out and see if the cockatoo had eaten any of the barley, but Eric stopped her, insisting that she put on her oilskins first.

Shrugging into her oilskins, Stephanie went out into the dense fog and cold, thin rain. In the dim light, the fog limited visibility to a few feet, and she stepped toward the tree slowly in the event the bird was feeding. The rock and bark propped over it came into view, the cockatoo not there. Stephanie looked at the barley, which appeared to be the same as the night before, then backed away from the tree and looked up at the limb.

The fog concealed the limb, but it billowed and thinned from a slow movement in the air. A moment later, Stephanie glimpsed the limb through a rent in the fog, and the cockatoo was gone. Apprehension gripping her, she rushed back to the tree as her eyes searched the ground. Then she saw the small, lifeless form on the grass and leaves under the limb.

Grief struck her with savage force. The birds had been her cherished pets, and more. Their migrations had been milestones in her life, marking the seasons and important events. Something ineffable but treasured had gone with them each time they had flown away and returned to her when they had come back. Now it was gone forever. Her tears welling up in a hot flood, she leaned against the tree, shaking with heartbroken sobs.

Eric's footsteps approached slowly and hesitantly. He put a hand on Stephanie's shoulder and started to say something, but she pulled away from him, wanting to be by herself. While she could share happiness with others, she had to bear her sorrows alone.

His footsteps moved away and then faded. He returned presently and placed a small, wooden nail box and a shovel beside the tree, then walked away again. Stephanie heard him and Yulina talking quietly as they went back around the house toward the kitchen door.

After a time, Stephanie controlled her tears, but her grief and devastating sense of loss were unrelieved, remaining a tightly contained, searing agony within her. She scooped the barley off the stone and put it in the box, then lifted the small, limp bird and placed it in the box. With the shovel she dug a hole and buried the cockatoo under the limb where the birds had spent their autumns and winters. Then she went into the house through the side door to get her bag and set out on her calls.

The scene around Stephanie answered to her sense of isolation in her sorrow, the fog a dense, swirling curtain that separated her from others. People working on fences beside the road and passing in vehicles were only dim forms through the mist. Her feeling of separation continued even at the houses she visited, where the people were involved in their concerns and she in her heartbreak. The only contact was through illness and other physical conditions, a communication of the body and not of the mind.

The nature of the fog also coincided with her inner feelings. It carried sound over long distances, and even from afar she could hear hammering and sawing at the prison among other noises in the valley. The constant reminder of the great sorrow in her life was similar to the way in which this new grief was a keen knife within her, gashing at that old wound.

Like a disease that had been in partial remission and had flared up again with virulent force, her anguish that flowed from the prison had a renewed, harrowing intensity. But as always, her work was a refuge from distress, a means to seal herself off from her emotions. She buried herself in it and filled the hours with extra calls on recent newborns and expectant mothers. The day and then the next one passed, with the weather gradually starting to change and become more normal for the season.

The rain ended on Saturday, and a warming trend thickened the fog into a dense blanket. The roads began drying and were busy early in the day with families going to Parramatta and Sydney, disembodied voices and vehicles passing Stephanie. The valley was quieter after many of the families left, the sound of the work at the prison carrying more clearly.

The work stopped on Sunday, and it seemed to Stephanie that some malevolent influence that the restoration was exerting also eased. In the absence of the hateful sound, the weather foreshadowed a return to the mild, fair days of autumn. While she drove to Broken Bay to make calls on patients at the coastal village north of Wallaby Track, a warm breeze rose, taking the last chill from the air and gradually starting to disperse the fog.

When she returned during late afternoon, the fog had broken up into banks of mist drifting in the breeze. The valley was quiet, dozing through a Sunday afternoon that was becoming brighter, with broken clouds occasionally in view overhead. Through a rent in the fog, Stephanie saw a buggy far down the road coming toward her, then it was hidden again.

The next time Stephanie glimpsed the buggy, it was much closer. And to her surprise and delight, she saw Stephen and Deirdre in it. More than a joy and source of keenest pleasure for her, they were the son of her heart and the sister of her soul. Her spirits soaring, she grabbed the whip out of its socket and cracked it above her horse.

The other buggy plunged into the fog and disappeared, Stephen cracking his whip and his horse running. Stephanie peered into the mist, her buggy speeding down the road, then pulled back on her reins when she saw a vague movement ahead. They met in a thick fog bank, Stephanie hurriedly stepping out of her buggy to greet them as their buggy slid to a stop.

Deirdre leaped out of her buggy just as eagerly, her lovely face wreathed in a smile of delight. Stephanie experienced the wondrous, poignantly enjoyable sense of harmony with the enchanting woman that she felt each time they were together, as though they had known and loved each other for years. That special feeling was followed by love and pride in her son as she exchanged lingering, deeply affectionate hugs and kisses with them.

Neither of them expressed regrets about the death of the cockatoos, which they would have learned about at the house, and Stephanie was thankful. Her meeting up with them was a bright moment, one she wanted to remain unspoiled. "I should have remained at home today," she commented. "Now it's late in the day, and I've missed the enjoyment of the greater part of your visit."

"No, we made a late start and arrived at your house only a short time ago," Deirdre explained. "We were determined to visit you today, because we meant to last Sunday." She glanced at Stephen, as though not wanting to say too much, then turned back to Stephanie. "We had to defer our plans last Sunday when one of Stephen's patients took a turn for the worse."

"That was certainly more than enough reason to defer plans," Stephanie assured her, somewhat puzzled by Deirdre's hesitancy. "I have no more calls today, so let's go to the house where we can be comfortable while we talk. Stephen, I assume that your patient has improved now."

"Yes, she's completely out of danger now," he replied. "I'll go with you in your buggy, if you don't mind, Mother."

Stephanie quickly agreed, having hoped one of them would ride with her, and he assisted her into her buggy. Deirdre stepped into the other one, turning it around. It disappeared into the fog as Stephen seated himself and took the reins, then they drove down the road through the fog.

Stephen explained about the patient who had been mentioned, a woman whom he had operated on for perityphlitic abscess. She had contracted a relatively minor abdominal infection, which was difficult to prevent at the hospital, and had recovered. He talked about the necessity of finding better ways to avoid infection, Stephanie agreeing, but she also considered the surgery itself as a virtual miracle. Over the years, her grim memory of watching young Billy Digby die had remained painfully clear and fresh.

The conversation continued, Stephanie's rapt interest in it enhanced by her keen pleasure in her son's companionship. The weather matched her mood, the late afternoon becoming ever brighter. The breeze freshened and scattered the fog into thinning banks of mist more rapidly, while the clouds overhead became more broken, with patches of blue sky between them.

The other buggy drew far ahead, Stephen driving at a slower pace as he and Stephanie talked. By the time they reached the village road, Deirdre had parked her buggy in front of the house and gone inside. "I'd like very much to drive up to the village before we join the others," Stephen said, turning onto the road. "Please indulge me, Mother."

"You wish to see Hamish Mcfee?" Stephanie concluded. "Very well, but let's do make it a brief visit, Stephen. I'm willing to share your company with Hamish for a time, but not a lengthy one."

Stephen silently smiled, driving past the house, then he changed the subject. He explained that while he had been at Tibooburra Station, Alexandra Kerrick had told him that she would like to have a doctor at the station. A staff

member at the Sydney hospital named Jerome Arnold, who
had been recently licensed to practice medicine, had wanted
the post, and the young doctor had left on the mail coach to
Wilcannia the week before.

Anything concerning Alexandra interested Stephanie, and
it also served to draw her attention away from the prison.
The slate was new in places on the roof towering above
the trees, a reminder that work on the grim building was
proceeding apace. The depressing fact tainted Stephanie's
pleasure in talking with her son, and she struggled to keep
it out of mind.

When they reached the top of the hill, the village was
quiet in the interval before evensong at the church. Then,
instead of driving through the village toward the Mcfee
home, Stephen turned off at the lane leading back to
the prison. "What are you doing, Stephen?" Stephanie
demanded, distressed. "You know full well that I abhor
this place!"

"Please bear with me, Mother," he begged her earnestly.
"Please bear with me, and I'll explain fully in a moment."

Stephanie ceased protesting, mostly through an inability
to find words in her disquiet. The lane and surroundings of
the prison were deserted, but the invasion of the workers
upon the peaceful quiet of decades was in evidence on
every side. Building materials were stacked about, along
with ladders and tools. Instead of abandoned, the gruesome
structure now looked much as it had many years before.
It was gloomy and menacing, its dark, thick stone walls
evoking images of brutality, torment, and despair.

Stephen stopped the buggy in the prison yard, stepping
out of it. "As Deirdre mentioned," he said, "we had planned
to visit you last Sunday. I wanted to talk with you before
this work began and try to set your mind at ease about
it. I was unable to get away during the week and had
some difficulty in doing so today, but I knew I must talk
with you."

"You're involved in this, Stephen?" Stephanie exclaimed

in astonishment and dismay. "How could you do something so deplorable?"

"Please let me explain, Mother," he urged her anxiously, lifting a hand to assist her out of the buggy. "I'm not sure that what I've done is best, but I believe it is. But do let me explain it to you."

Confused and distraught, Stephanie dismounted from the buggy, the huge, somber building looming over her. Stephen took a large, folded paper from his coat pocket and began opening it, telling her that Alexandra Kerrick had offered to endow a hospital where he would be the director, and it was to be named the David Kerrick Memorial Hospital. She had written letters for him to deliver to Morton and the Tavish family, and they had eagerly joined in on the project, committing substantial funds to it.

"When the subject first came up," Stephen went on, "I immediately thought of this building. It occurred to me that this might relieve the sorrow it has always caused you. Morton obtained official permission to convert it to a hospital, and he contacted an excellent architect who agreed to take charge of the conversion." He finished unfolding the paper and handed it over to Stephanie. "Here is how it will look, Mother."

The paper was an architectural drawing, at the top of which was a sketch of the building after completion of the work. Below that were diagrams of the floors, showing their layout. Stephen pointed to it, explaining that doctors could visit to learn the latest techniques at Edinburgh, eliminating his traveling to other hospitals. The standards of care would be such that anyone would be willing to come to it for treatment, and he would have a separate, completely sanitary room for abdominal surgeries.

"That should prevent infections in most instances," he added. "Also, this is one reason why Deirdre and I bought a house at Parramatta. It's close enough so that I can drive to work every day, as can she." He started to say more, then ended his explanation with an uneasy sigh, gazing at

Stephanie. "What do you think about it, Mother?"

Stephanie was unsure of what to think, totally incapable of relating the drawing to the building in front of her. The prison had been a focus of evil to her for decades, a scourge and a source of heartbreak, and she was unable to immediately view it as the diametric opposite. At the same time, she was deeply touched by what her son had done, knowing he had meant well. "I'm not displeased," she replied, which was true enough, but mostly meant to satisfy him. "This is very unexpected, and I'd like to think about it. Take the buggy and go to the house, and I'll be there presently, dear."

"I don't intend to put you afoot, Mother," he protested, smiling in relief and happiness over her reaction. "I'll walk down to the house and let everyone know that you'll join us directly."

They exchanged a kiss, then he walked away and disappeared down the lane. Once solitude in the quiet place closed in around her, Stephanie struggled to sort out her thoughts, for she had never been more confused and torn by opposed feelings. In one way she verged on exuberant delight over what her son had told her. But that uplift in spirits met with a bulwark of strong reservations from deep within, difficulty in accepting that the prison could ever be anything other than what it had always been to her.

The sketch seemed to overstate what a conversion could accomplish. It appeared to be of an entirely different building, one that was imposingly large, yet cheerful, inviting, and handsome. The huge, sinister prison had nothing in common with it, even a different outline. Stephanie glanced between the sketch and the building, looking at individual features and identifying how they were to be changed during the conversion.

Stone trim would be added to the roofline and corners, making them decorative instead of fortresslike. The tiny, glowering windows were to be made much larger, letting in fresh air and light. The small, massively thick front door, which was conspicuously meant to keep people in instead of out, would be eliminated. In its place would be a generously wide, welcoming entrance surmounted and fronted by an attractive portico.

Feature by feature, the hospital began emerging from the prison for Stephanie as she studied the sketch and building. Then the sun broke through the clouds, low in the west. Its rays had the warm tones of approaching sunset, and they washed away the somber darkness of the stone walls with a soft, golden glow. Instead of massively thick and forbidding, the walls became reassuringly solid, well-built, and enduring.

Her reservations fading, the building was transformed in Stephanie's eyes. Instead of being confined among dungeons, the revered presence would rest peacefully in a hospital, a place of special meaning and esteem to generations of her family. Her spirits soared, lifting away the grueling sorrow that had tormented her for decades. Tears of rapture filled her eyes, her happiness needing only to be shared in order to be perfect.

Stephanie walked to the side of the building, at the edge of the hill overlooking the valley. Wallaby Track had never been more compellingly beautiful, with the tranquil, enchanting ambience of autumn returning in the wake of the storm. The broad river gleamed in the sunset, the thin, lingering wisps of fog adding a shimmering sparkle to the air.

On the roads among the checkerboard of neat farms and stock runs, people were making their way toward the village for evening church services. Then the church bell began tolling the call to evensong, awakening echoes that rippled across the broad valley. The melodious chiming of the bell enhanced the serenely calm atmosphere, giving it richness and depth.

Stephanie turned to the stone wall, stepping closer. "Father," she whispered. "Father, I am here. . . ."

The tolling of the bell smothered her words, but they only

formed the thought that she cast into the void. A moment later, there was a stir about her more subtle but still more tangible than the breeze. She concentrated and searched into it, and an answering response came to her.

The being that had been familiar and cherished to her since her childhood was with her, surrounding her. A sense of gratification at her summons and of greeting touched her mind. But along with it was the pervading impression of weary, hopeless melancholy, the oppressive sadness that was always the overriding feeling communicated by the presence.

Stephanie lifted the drawing, displaying it. "Father, my son has arranged to have this place changed into a hospital," she whispered. "It is to be changed from a place of misery and death into one of healing and life. My son and your grandson has arranged this, Father. It will be a beautiful, magnificent hospital, and he will be the director. . . ."

Tears of bliss filled her eyes and overflowed, her voice breaking with sobs as she continued talking and explaining. Her buoyant happiness far exceeded what she had sought by sharing it, an ecstasy of elation swelling within her, for she detected a change in the touch on her mind. At long last, the dreary sadness that had always accompanied the beloved presence altered, turning into a different impression. It was joy.